ADAM

IN THE COMPANY OF SNIPERS

Book 11

IRISH WINTERS

COPYRIGHT

ADAM; In the Company of Snipers, 11

Cover design and author photo by Kelli Ann Morgan,
http://www.inspirecreativeservices.com

Interior book design by Bob Houston, eBook Formatting

Editor: Lauren McKellar, McStellar editing,
http://mcstellarediting.blogspot.com

Editor: Katie Johnson, katiestefan333@gmail.com

ISBN Paperback: 978-1-942895-22-0
ISBN eBook: 978-1-942895-21-3
Library of Congress Control Number: 2016935820

Irish Winter's author websites are: http://www.irishwinters.com
and irishwinters.blogspot.com

In the Company of Snipers

You can find Irish Winters on Facebook: https://www.facebook.com/author.irishwinters

On Twitter: https://twitter.com/irishwinters1

For news on upcoming releases, sign up for Irish Winters' Newsletter at IrishWinters.com.

For more information about all my books, visit IrishWinters.com.

IN THE COMPANY OF SNIPERS

This series revolves around ex-Marine scout sniper, Alex Stewart, and his covert surveillance company, The TEAM, home-based out of Alexandria, Virginia. An obsessive patriot and workaholic, he created the company to give ex-military snipers like him a chance at returning to civilian life with a decent job.

This is not a serial with each book ending at a cliffhanger. I wouldn't do that to you. *In the Company of Snipers* is a collection of passionate love stories involving women and men who are tough enough to take on the world alone. Each is a stand-alone read, where in the course of an active TEAM operation, one agent comes face to face with his or her demons. The men and women I write about are all patriots and warriors, dealing with what they've lived through or the mistakes they've made

Spoiler alert: Every novel contains adult scenes including sexual situations (some explicit), language, and violence. I don't write sweet romance, so be forewarned.

At the end of each story, it's my hope that you, along with my heroes, will come to realize...

Love changes everything

Prologue

Not again! Shannon woke with a start.

Once would've been enough, but she'd dreamed this exact same dream for three nights in a row. Three, mind you. And Brit's Grandpa Denver starred in every single showing.

Sweat trickled between her breasts under her nightgown, but she dared not look at her bedside digital clock. It couldn't be three in the morning, could it? She cracked one eyelid, the sheet still balled tight in her fists, but yes. Three a.m. Straight up. Again.

Sheesh. How utterly straight out of all the best horror classics could this get? Only a church bell tolling overhead would make this chapter in her life any creepier. For the past year, her dreams had gotten progressively more bizarre, but these exceeded the limits of weird by leaps and by bounds.

Yet, Grandpa Denver had come faithfully to her for three nights in a row, like Dickens' ghosts of old, and always with the same words. She squeezed her eyes shut, and there he was again. Silver haired. Grandfatherly. Kind but stern. And for the third time, childish embarrassment rose up in her when he declared, "It's time you left him, Shannon, and you know it. That boy never appreciated you. He's always taken you for granted."

Tears flooded her eyes. She, of all people, knew precisely who the boy was. His grandson. Her husband. Brit Paxton.

Her marriage to Brit had failed. Miserably. From the beginning, his steady absences weakened their marriage vows, and too soon his vows had turned into idle promises. For better or for worse became only worse. Then worst of all. Brit betrayed her at every turn. First with Lana. Then Cheryl. Now some cheap trick called Tia Mia, like that was a name for a real woman.

The harder Shannon tried to be the wife she thought he'd wanted, the moodier he'd gotten until…

Ugh. She cringed at the awful memory, her fingers to her fluttering heartbeat. He'd come home drunk and more crude that usual one night. Forceful. Mean. She'd had no choice but to submit, not after he'd slapped her to the floor and climbed up and over her like a rabid dog in heat. And yet, she'd stayed with him. Like a fool… *I stayed. Ugh. Just—ugh.*

Shannon gulped at her incredible weakness when it came to Brit. How odd that she ruled her small but successful boutique publishing business, *The Dewy Rose,* with business savvy and fortitude, but when it came to Brit, she held on with foolish, schoolgirl hope. She'd let him treat her so badly.

But Grandpa Denver's eyes twinkled as he'd continued with the most outlandish pronouncement. "You've done all you can. He is what he is. Think of the baby."

And in her dream, a flock of powder-blue baby pelicans fluttered away at that precise moment. Little children and baby animals of all sizes and colors scampered around Grandpa Denver. A rainbow of achingly vivid hues arched overhead while multi-colored baby turkeys stood in a row beneath it, singing the song that could stick in a person's head forever—"It's a Small World After All."

It was nothing but a dream—*after all.*

Shannon drew her knees up for a much needed hug. There was no baby. There couldn't be. She'd religiously protected herself against unwanted pregnancy when she'd realized how oblivious Brit was to her need for companionship. How vacant her marriage bed became too quickly after a less than fulfilling honeymoon.

At that point, the crazy dream had three times now, morphed into the same scene of a Navy ship, and oddly, her fears fled. How bizarre? Yet she'd found herself feeling brave for the first time in—forever, at the striking sight the Naval officer standing stiff and stern at the bow of his ship, the gray-blue sea beyond him.

Sandy haired. Impeccably dressed in his white uniform. He'd stood proud, his spine erect in the way of honorable men, facing the ocean beyond him as if he were a solid equal to its capricious power. Perhaps equal was too small a word. Despite the monstrous vessel beneath his feet, an unworldly authority emanated from the man. His fierce posture declared that he and he alone commanded this mighty craft. That he brought it to heel, and it dared not go but where he ordered it to go.

To say her heart stuttered was to say that he was a mere mortal when he looked to be so much more, possibly as mighty as Poseidon, the *God of the Sea,* himself. Indeed, this solitary soul seemed willing and able to take on the world if it dared challenge him. If it so much as hinted that it needed a good, sound thrashing.

Shannon swallowed a tiny gulp against the flutter in her chest at the memory. It was said that a true commander loved his ship above all women, but oh, to be this man's vessel, to be commanded by this all-male specimen of shocking virility. To have those masculine hands that had gripped the rail of the boat, grip her writhing body instead, and to ride the waves of passion with him, and…

Oh. My. God.

Without uttering a word, this stranger had evoked her most feminine responses, some she'd never felt before. She couldn't help but notice how her thighs clenched just remembering. How she couldn't cease licking her lips at this decadent, manly morsel. How her inner wellspring dripped with unrequited need and unfilled expectation. How she ached with desire for true commitment. For the love of an honest man. For the family she'd never had.

Her faithful ghost, Grandpa Denver had nudged her forward at that point. Three times he'd told her the same thing. "Now go. Be happy."

It seemed so easy, but… logic intervened. *Dreaming here. None of this is real. You'll wake up, and, poof, he'll be gone, and Brit will be back, and ugh!*

Yet, the scene shimmered and she found herself naked and under the covers with the handsome stranger. Like a faithful lover, he'd nestled her into the crook of his arm and pressed her to his muscular chest with exquisite gentleness. He'd placed a tender, chaste kiss in the middle of her forehead. The fragrance of Old Spice on his clean-shaven cheek still filled her nose. It still calmed her with an unfamiliar sensation of familiarity.

"Shannon baby," he'd crooned. "I've missed you so."

Ah! Those sweet words. Shannon baby. The words her mother had spoken so long ago. And with them came the fresh hint of wintergreen on his breath and a surge of hope in her heart.

I know this man. I know I do. Shannon lifted her face to him and offered herself, like a willow to the wind. Like the ocean to her captain. A lover to her mate.

He lowered his lips. He came so close to kissing her that her heart stopped, the deliciousness of his breath filled her nose, the masculine scent of him enveloped her like an old friend, and—

The dream vanished. Every darned time. Right there. Right then. It popped like a bubble on the wind just as their lips would have touched. Just as she would have finally tasted what her heart hungered for. Ironically, also just at the point of no return, when she would've betrayed her marriage vows. When she would've sunk as low as the deceitful man she'd married.

My God, what does this dream mean?

The big, empty, and too-quiet house around her offered no suggestions or comfort. There was a time it might've been a home, but now it ticked and creaked in the hollow way of all empty houses in the middle of the night, when boards and joists expanded and contracted, whispering their toils and troubles to weary souls who cannot sleep.

Shannon had been born, it seemed, to a life of perpetual loneliness. Motherless at an early age, her important and highly influential father had ensconced her in the lap of luxury, then all but left her. He'd assigned her to the oversight of a kindly nanny instead of concerning himself with her upbringing. True friends were few and far between. She'd grown up a solitary child with more books for companions than people. Well-travelled and well read, if not well loved.

With attendance in only the finest schools, Shannon's aptitude for all things literary developed early. She thirsted for the life and worlds beyond pretentious Reagan Manor, where mythic heroes like Odysseus struggled ten long years to return home to his sweet Penelope. Where Mr. Darcy overcame his pride and Elizabeth her prejudice. Where she, Shannon Olivia Reagan, could dream.

But now she knew. Grandpa Denver was right. It was time to leave.

Quietly, as if she needed to be stealthy in a house so empty, Shannon set her feet to the floor and left her marriage bed behind. After dressing quickly, she went to her office and stuffed her laptop with all its cords, thumb-drives, and chargers, into her briefcase. By the time she'd finished packing, Shannon had emptied her bathroom toiletries into her suitcase, her closet into a travel trunk, and their joint savings into her private account. The rest of her furniture and things could wait. She had a life to live, one that no longer included Brit Paxton, and she meant to live it. Who knew? Maybe she had a sailor to find as well.

Standing breathless in her bedroom with her old life behind her and the thrill of the unknown ahead, she took a tube of lipstick from her purse. In the lovely shade of *Hidden Rose*, the shade Brit Paxton would never taste again, Shannon wrote her final message on her dresser mirror to the man she'd once thought she would love forever.

Gone.

Chapter One

There comes a time when a man has to do what a man has to do. For Junior Agent Adam Torrey, that moment had come.

"Sir, we are currently at thirty-five thousand feet and holding."

Adam nodded one curt acknowledgment to the Air Force crew out of Ellsworth Air Force Base, stepped to the vibrating loading ramp of the powerful C-130, and, with a backward step and a cocky wave, he pitched his body forward into the midnight sky. The flight chief's acknowledgement, "Jumper away," faded in his earpiece.

Frigid air whipped Adam, making him instantly thankful for the polypropylene thermal undergarments beneath his TEAM flight suit. He leveled his six-foot, three-inch frame into a belly dive, his arms and legs extended like a giant bug descending to the planet below.

Man, I love my job.

HALOs, high-altitude low opening parachute jumps, were not uncommon in his line of work, at least for him. Known by everyone on The TEAM as the flying squirrel, the ex-Navy SEAL thrived in the weightless realm between earth and sky. All agents working for Alex Stewart had to be capable, physically fit, and qualified to jump. The day a man couldn't perform he was put to pasture, or worse, turned into something dead called a *senior agent*. Adam was an ex-Navy SEAL, a man of action and a lethal sniper. He never intended to graze clover. He loved the sensation of flight too much, the freedom of falling, the heady rush of air over, around, and seemingly through his body.

Specialized equipment allowed this miracle, and he relied on it. Every last piece of it. From the Special Forces HALO helmet with its oxygen mask strapped snuggly over his nose and mouth, to the goggles that allowed peripheral vision and much-needed facial protection, to the backlit altimeter on his wrist that registered nothing at the moment, its altitude range less than his. The lightweight auxiliary pack strapped to his belly provided a measure of assurance if his main parachute failed. His gloves kept his ten digits warm enough.

God, what a ride.

The experimental GPS wrapped around his wrist matched its digital partner's lack of information. No matter. They'd both flash on soon enough—within seconds if the new technology behind them functioned as expected. The GPS was part of the reason for this extreme jump. This was its maiden flight, its beta-test, and he was just the man for the job.

Until it kicked in, supposedly at a higher altitude than others now on the market, he gloried in the adrenaline rush, free-falling to what very well could be his death. Therein lay the rub and the magic of a precision drop—all the risk of dying only to pull up at the last possible second and spit in the stone-cold eye of the Grim Reaper.

Nothing like it in the world.

The fact that another brave soul had recently made a twenty-four-mile high jump from the stratosphere only proved Adam's point. Some men were made to fly, and he was one of them. This ordinary jump of nearly seven miles straight down was enough for the adrenaline junkie he'd become. For now. Maybe someday he'd match that other guy's record. Maybe not. Adam truly didn't care about records. Just the fall. Just the flight.

He liked that initial *'What the hell have I done?'* sensation in his gut even more so because he understood the physics behind a HALO, the very real concept of terminal velocity when the downward force of gravity equaled the restraining force of drag. Law of gravity. Risk of splat. Gotta love it.

Every HALO jump involved unique dangers—the frigid cold, decompression sickness, and hypoxia. Death never lingered more than a heartbeat away. But the thrill. The view.

He could've pulled his body into a compact, cylindrical projectile, secured his arms to his sides and his legs together instead of splayed like they were, in order to increase his speed. Skydivers called it free flying, when a man's body became more bullet than flesh and blood. But as much as Adam loved the thrill of downward acceleration, he loved the journey more. Only HALO jumps brought him this close to Heaven. He truly loved the sea, but God, he loved the sky more. In the sky he was free, not so much bird as shooting star. On land he became a bulky beast of burden bound to the earth's core. A turtle. Why hurry a three-minute ride?

Suspended between earth and space, it seemed time stopped on a night like this one. No moon tonight, just the constellations and Ursa Major glittering in the sub-polar altitude, crisp and clear. Adam's buddy, Polaris, shone exactly where the pointer stars in the bowl of the Big Dipper indicated it should be. The North Star beckoned like the true friend it was, as constant and a thousand times squared more reliable than any woman he'd ever known. Always beckoning him home.

His failed relationship with his ex-girlfriend and ex-nightmare flashed to mind. The one he'd been damned glad he'd left behind. But none of that mattered now. He forced his very disciplined mind to the work at hand. Shirley was old news, the poison of her manipulative grasp at last diluted with enough good times mingled with plenty of scotch.

The experimental GPS digital readout flashed to life right on schedule, reminding him he had better things to do than dredge up the past, like finding that wayward drone.

Impact in less than two.

South Dakota lay below, now the site of a lost prototype, the multi-million dollar HH UAV, the Hummingbird Hawk Unmanned Aerial Vehicle. Named for its compact but predatory stealth design, it had gone down during its initial test flight out of Ellsworth Air Force Base, just a few miles away. Its advanced technology made it immeasurably valuable in the world of military intelligence. All of DoD held its breath when they'd heard it went missing. The CIA, too. This was their baby, their future, and now their worst nightmare. Too many foreign powers wanted the technology behind this particular drone. Russia. China. Terrorists. Allies.

Ellsworth had been alerted. They knew he was dropping in tonight, but were advised not to engage in the search, only to assist with the drop. For now, this operation was just him, a missing baby bird, and maybe a few barking rodents.

The peculiar nature of his mission still nagged, though. The very capable folks at Ellsworth would've been happy to retrieve the UAV. They could've, and they should've. The request for a HALO was one hundred percent unnecessary, but the CIA said, *'Hell, no,'* to the Air Force offer to assist. Hands off. Like the control freaks they were, the spooks demanded a non-defense-related contractor perform the retrieval.

Enter the man responsible for developing the prototype, Mr. Paul Reagan, inventor and billionaire CEO of the prestigious Reagan Industries out of northern Virginia. He'd made the CIA's paranoia look tame when he'd circumvented them and went straight to Alex Stewart, the owner of the covert surveillance company, The TEAM. Before the Air Force or CIA could shoot off their well-prepared rebuttal, the deal between Reagan and Alex was struck.

One agent and one only would handle retrieval. Given his aptitude for HALO drops, it was a no-brainer from the get go. Adam Torrey, ex-Navy SEAL was the best flying squirrel on The TEAM and in transit before his boss's signature had dried on the dotted line.

But why one agent only? Why a HALO? Why not Ellsworth's assist? Very odd indeed.

Checking altimeter and GPS coordinates again, Adam allowed a small smile of success. No meteorological events interfered with his flight tonight. Smooth descent. Right on target.

Earth approached fast.

Fifteen thousand.

His favorite country western song popped into his head, its heavy bass a heartbeat that matched his philosophy. What *was* life for if you didn't live it? And man, this was living at its most extreme.

Eight thousand.

His GPS flashed once. Then twice. His target might as well be already acquired and the mission over. Smoothest drop ever.

Six thousand.

Thicker atmosphere at the earth's surface brought warmer temperatures. Almost time. He stalled the inevitable, wishing he didn't have to land.

Four thousand.

Two.

Begrudgingly, Adam jerked the ripcord. *Whoosh.* The flat-black nylon, eight-celled, ram-air canopy released, stopping death in its tracks, and offering a few breathless seconds to view the LZ before his boots hit the dirt. Drifting toward touchdown, the sight below was all he expected. Prairie. Flat. Damned dark.

He activated another specialized tracking device set to pick up the HH locator signal only. Just in time. South Dakota rushed up to meet him. To be safe, he removed the night-vision goggles from the zippered pouch on his belt and strapped them around his neck. It never hurt to be prepared. Freedom lived in the heavens. Not on the earth.

He braced for impact, his knees bent and his senses sharp, primed for any and all possibilities.

Oomph. Touchdown.

Adam rolled as he landed, expelling nothing more than a soft grunt that none heard, unless the few curious prairie dogs scampering out of his path mattered. Gathering big handfuls of the black nylon, he stuffed it into the empty nylon bag he'd brought with him, using those same few minutes to survey the wide-open space around him. The pure sounds of the dark Dakota night met his ears...

Smoothest landing ever.

Once he'd stowed his gear, he let the rucksack drop from his back. It carried what-if supplies like water, MREs, medical supplies, and his all-important EPIRB, his emergency position-indicating radio beacon.

The feeling that this was some bizarre game persisted, mostly because a HALO drop into harmless South Dakota made no sense in the wary world of a black operator. HALOs were last-option only, the safest way into deadly terrain. Not prairie. Why, oh why old man Reagan, the billionaire eccentric behind this op, had demanded such a high-security measure in the middle of grassland seemed irrational and foolish.

But there was a job to be done, and until an adversary presented himself, Adam had no reason for alarm. The soft green glow from the screen displayed a map of his immediate area, a red dot pinging a heartbeat less than three clicks to the northeast and the exact position of the missing drone. Good enough.

Setting a steady pace, he jogged toward it, watching where he stepped. Landing in a prairie dog hole could snap a man's leg. He had no intention of being airlifted for such a stupid mistake, not after the exhilaration of this perfect drop.

The sweet Dakota air smelled good at 0245 hours. Cool. Pleasant. And a good run relaxed a man. It allowed the adrenaline overload from the falling out of the sky to burn away. He checked the tracker again. Less than a thousand meters straight ahead. Instantly, his very analytical brain provided mathematical equivalents. Three thousand, two hundred, and eighty-one feet. One thousand, ninety-four yards.

Man, I love my job.

A prairie dog barked off to his left. Then another. Adam grinned at the exhilaration of a night so rare. He wasn't even breaking a sweat. What's more, this very expensive, very top-secret UAV would be home in its cradle before the world knew it had gone missing.

The tracking device that indicated he was nearly on target sounded steady beeps. Slowing his gait, Adam glanced to his right and then left. Only grass and more grass. All good. How hard could it be to find a two-foot long baby bird, attach it to a miniature aerostat, punch the can of helium to inflate the balloon, and let it fly away home? Not hard at all. Once the prototype was airborne, a larger UAV would snag the line between baby bird and the aerostat with a specially designed pincer attached to its nose. By the time Adam's boss inhaled his first cup of coffee in far off Virginia, the baby bird would be back in its hanger at Reagan Research, and all would be well.

As big a fiasco as this loss might have been, the mechanics of baby bird's rescue would once again prove the undeniable need for drones in defense and industrial missions. A drone rescuing another drone. Technology upon technology. The world was an amazing place, and Adam reveled in it. It helped him fly.

Brushing his palms over the knee-high grass, Adam let it tickle his splayed fingers. Everything about the prairie was just plain magic. Buffalo used to roam here. The Lakota and Sioux Indian tribes, too.

The GPS pinged louder, leading him straight to his prize. A dark shadow carved into the tall grass revealed the landing skid, and ultimately, the smooth body of the tiny predator. He knelt one knee to the ground in awe, pulling the little guy gently out of the shallow depression of its crash-landing. The weight of the tiny drone surprised him. He'd expected more, but it felt less than twenty pounds. Coated in flat-black, radar-absorbent material, the overall smooth design contributed to its invisibility. It was the perfect predator. Small. Invisible. *Deadly.*

He cradled it tenderly, proud of his skill and his aptitude. *Best day ever.*

"Come on, little guy," he said fondly. "Let's get you home."

He pushed to his feet with a sigh of relief. In the moonlight, the drone didn't appear damaged, other than a few scrapes along one side of its sleek metallic skin—nothing a good buffing wouldn't solve. He committed the serial number from the metal plate at the edge of its polycarbonate nose to memory: UVZ172661. And hot damn. Operation baby bird was nearly over. *Way to go, Torrey!*

A soft whirring overhead, the telltale ruffling of silky nylon ballooned tight with air, interrupted his self-congratulations. Adam jerked his gaze heavenward. It couldn't be. Another jumper? Here?

Nothing revealed itself, but his ears hadn't lied. He crouched to one knee and hunkered low in the tall grass. With the infant UAV tucked tightly to his chest, he let nature provided the camouflage while he went into full alert.

Sliding his night vision goggles up over his face, the world turned lime green. His sixth sense screamed, *"You're not alone,"* but no other sound rent the silence. No boots on the ground. No motorized engine. No un-oiled squeak of a control lever to bring a parachute or a one-man glider to pinpoint landing. Nothing.

He held his breath, trusting his gut more than his ears or sight. But who was out there and why? Better question—how could anyone have known he was there? Or was he just that paranoid?

A rippling breeze parted the tall grass ahead of him for mere seconds. He'd switched to NV too late. From up high, somebody dropkicked the side of his head, hard, but not hard enough to make him release the baby in his arms.

Adam crouched to adjust his goggles, searching after his assailant. And there the bastard was. A lime-green tinted man sat beneath a triangular-shaped paraglide floating overhead, as silent as the night itself. An engine noise would've confirmed the visual, but there was none. Whoever this guy was, he'd banked and was coming around again, no doubt thinking he'd rendered his target unconscious.

Guess again. Adam growled low in his throat. The predator in him sprang to life. Two could play that game.

Rolling to his back with the baby still in his arms, he waited until his assailant was nearly on top of him again. But this time, automatic rounds strafed the ground alongside

Adam. Enough was enough! He flipped to his stomach, set the drone down, and charged the would-be assassin.

Surprised, the guy banked sharply. Too sharp. With a running leap, Adam grabbed his ankle and jerked. Either the idiot hadn't buckled up or the harness broke. *Umph.* Down he came, hitting the dirt hard. Adam followed through with a kick to the guy's midsection. His boot connected with body armor. The guy had anticipated trouble.

Good to know. Me too.

Reaching to his ankle holster, Adam pulled his knife up, and—

"Got it!" a woman shrieked behind him. He whirled as another black silhouette materialized against the midnight sky. Whoever she was, she now had the HH.

He cocked his arm back and hurtled his knife at the thief. *Bull's-eye!* She grunted, sagged, and collapsed limp in her harness. The paraglide continued into the night with the tiny drone tucked into the silvery netting beneath the woman's seat.

No way! Adam ran with long-legged strides, his lungs bursting and every muscle on fire to get that damned HH. The nearly silent engine offered the barest hum as he closed the distance, his heart pounding with adrenaline and rage. No one—and I mean *no one*—messed with Adam Torrey.

Six more yards. Maybe less. Almost there. *Almost got it.* He forced his last reserve of strength into a final lunge, stretching with all he had to secure that baby bird again when—

BLAM! A wicked blast of fire and pain caught his shoulder. It spun him around and turned him into a ragdoll, tumbling end over end through the grass. Forward momentum finally ceased when he came to a breathless stop, face up, blood streaming out of the hole in his chest. A universe of stars swirled overhead. He had no way to reach his gear bag. Thunder rumbled too close. Not thunder. Maybe boots on the ground. Running fast. Coming straight toward him.

A black shadow descended, cruel and cold.

The butt of a rifle.

The last thing he saw.

Chapter Two

"I'm questioning him?" Shannon asked in wide-eyed amazement. "Why me?"

"You're capable aren't you?" Paul Reagan looked up from his cluttered desk, snarky as always. "You're smart. You've got a degree."

She hated the mincing tone he'd used. Since her divorce, he'd gotten increasingly short-tempered with her. Yes, she had a degree, but it was in Fine Arts, not Chemical Engineering or Mechanical Engineering like his.

Point well made. You're smarter than me. Like you would ever let me forget.

"For one thing, I know nothing about this prototype of yours," she rebutted. "It's technical and the drone sounds dangerous. I've never done—"

"Nonsense." He waved his hand, dismissing her arguments as he usually did. "Find out if Stewart's interested in a second chance at fulfilling his end of the contract. That's all. He had better if he knows what's good for him. If not, we'll pursue further legal remedy."

She sighed quietly, not sure why she bothered to argue with her father. An alpha male with out-of-control ego issues and deteriorating health, he'd already stopped listening. She was going, no ifs, ands, or buts. Might as well make the best of it. "I'll need the back-up documentation for the missing drone then."

"Of course you will." There was that condescension again. He really knew how to target her insecurities. His desk phone rang. "Myrtle will get it for you. See her on your way out."

And that was that. Discussion closed. *Go. Do as you're told, and be done with it.*

Shannon rose from the chair across from her father and turned to leave. Surrounded by glass and a twenty-one-story view of the common people below him in Rosslyn, Virginia, he was engrossed in another technical debate before she hit the door. She'd already lost his attention—if she'd ever had it.

Her father's health failed more each day, yet like everything else in his life, she had no idea what was wrong with him or why. He kept his personal life and problems private, even from her. It never ceased to amaze her how distant a father/daughter relationship could be.

Myrtle Brant, his secretary, was also on her phone. At least she smiled, her hand extended with an unclassified version of the drone's schematics. She'd obviously anticipated the outcome of Shannon's conversation with her father.

Shannon pasted a smile on her face, offered her usual stiff upper lip, and accepted the folder. "Excuse me, but when is the meeting?"

Myrtle covered her receiver with her fingers, her brows furrowed at the interruption. "Two p.m. sharp, Miss Reagan."

"Today?" Shannon's stomach clenched, spewing acid nearly up her throat.

Ms. Brant nodded and resumed her telephone conversation.

An hour! Oh, my gosh! Shannon shot a baleful glance over her shoulder at her father's closed door. "Shit." The improper word slipped from her lips while her heart rate kicked into supersonic anxiety. Including travel time, that gave her less than an hour. How could he expect her to absorb enough technical information on the drive from Rosslyn to Alexandria and effectively confront the man responsible for the prototype's disappearance in South Dakota, and do it with class and dignity? That was what? Eight, maybe ten miles that on a bad traffic day might take a half-hour to get there?

She cringed, the reality of being her father's only heir a harder burden to bear than most days. There was no way she could be a proper ambassador of Reagan Industries at this rate. It seemed he'd sabotaged her yet again, his customary agenda. Still, she skimmed the first few pages of the unclassified document on the elevator ride to the first floor, then a few more once she was in the backseat of the limousine chauffeured by her friend and oftentimes only confidant, Raul Ortega.

A middle-aged Hispanic with short thinning hair, he might as well have been her girlfriend. He'd certainly heard it all. "You're late for this appointment?" His dark eyes worried for her in the rearview mirror.

Shannon dropping the technical schematics onto her lap, her palms sweaty. The more she read, the less she understood. Panic for what could very well be another epically disappointing failure didn't help. Once again, she'd look like a fool in front of her father's business associates. Did he do this on purpose?

"Not so much late as very unprepared," she admitted, meeting Raul's sympathetic gaze. Traffic on the GW flew by. With Arlington National Cemetery on her right and the Potomac River at her left, apprehension grew. She was meeting with the man, as in THE man who'd lost her father's Hummingbird Hawk on what was supposed to have been a simple recovery. According to her father, this Agent Adam Torrey guy had bungled the entire operation. He'd been lazy, ill-prepared, and inexperienced. An oaf.

"He's done it to you again, hasn't he?"

She nodded. Raul knew what she was going through. She saw it on his face. Her personal driver for the past four years, he'd accompanied her on more of these ill-fated meetings than she could count. She'd become her father's blood sacrifice to another bunch of angry gods.

"I would like to be there the day your father hears you say the word no," Raul muttered quietly, his eyes on the traffic.

Ha! Me too. All hell would break loose when or if that ever happened. She worried her bottom lip, biting it at the faith Raul had in her that her father didn't. Her problems with Paul Reagan stemmed from her lack of self-confidence as much as her chosen profession. He hated that she toiled over novels and best sellers. He had no use for the creative world or romance and fiction.

She'd long ago recognized the disparity between him and her; she just didn't know what to do about it. She'd never been able to stand up to him. That required personality traits she didn't come by naturally. He was the dynamo in the family, the *lead, follow-or-get-out-of-my-way* guy, the hard driver with over-the-top alpha traits that served him well. They just hadn't passed from father to daughter.

Shannon tried to understand, she really did. He yearned to pass his company on to his only living child. What man didn't? It made sense on the surface, but Shannon wasn't an engineer. Her field was writing, the recording of people's lives and feelings, their testament to the world. Her heroes were Walt Whitman, Emily Dickinson, and Henry Thoreau, not robber barons the likes of Dale Carnegie, John D. Rockefeller, or Donald Trump. The writings of authors as old as Shakespeare made more sense to her in this modern-day than the technical weapon systems her father had invented, created, then mass-produced for the federal government. He was the weapons dealer in the family. She the dreamer.

Self-assured and over-confident, he'd pushed her into the limelight with his unexpected press release the day he'd proclaimed she'd soon take over the reins of Reagan Industries. It would've been nice if he'd told her before he told the press and the world, though. Yes, he'd given her a corner office, but not once had he asked if she was interested in the prestigious title, much less the pressure.

She hadn't even worked for him until that dreadful day. But move out of her comfortable publishing office and into his lavish industrial complex she did. That's when her life fell apart. Literally. The unexpected announcement and the following unwelcome hurrah from the press and media confounded her husband, Brit. His first nasty affair followed shortly after. And then another...

"Do you want me to wait for you, Miss Reagan?"

Raul's question jolted Shannon from her depressing reverie. He'd already pulled up to the curb and parked.

"Yes, please," she answered, glancing up at the five-story plate-glass windows of her destination. "I shouldn't be long. Will that be okay? If you have something else to do, I can always call when I'm done."

His kind smile lit the rearview mirror again. "You know better than that. You're my number-one priority every single day of the week."

"Thanks."

He ran around the limo to open her door. "No need to call. I'll be waiting for you."

She gathered her courage along with the papers, drew in a deep breath, and accepted Raul's hand up from the limo. "You're too good to me."

"Oh, wait a minute." He reached to tuck a loose strand of her hair behind her ear, a smile of approval on his olive-toned face. Dark brown eyes sparkled with encouragement. His pencil-thin moustache lifted with approval. "There you go. Picture perfect, as always. Knock 'em dead."

"I wish." She rolled her eyes at that very gracious statement. Raul always had more confidence in her abilities than she did. "This won't take long."

Shannon hurried through the heavy-looking glass doors that surprisingly opened automatically at her approach. The empty lobby accommodated an elevator and a brightly-colored mosaic tile of the American flag opposite the entry. The words 'Never Forget' were emblazoned in gold beneath the flag. It was so artistically done that it took her breath, hardly what she'd expected from an ordinary defense contractor.

Beautiful. I like it.

Taking that as a positive omen, she pressed the only elevator button and prepared to walk into yet another lion's den. The elevator opened at floor two onto a red carpet that directed her toward the middle of a large room filled with cubicle-type offices. A quiet but steady hum of people at work met her ears. A pretty blonde woman with soft green eyes looked up from behind the customer service counter at the end of the red carpet. "Can I help you?"

"I'm here to speak with Junior Agent Torrey," Shannon replied in her most professional tone. No need to let this woman know she was scared out of her mind and way out of her comfort zone. She'd figure it out soon enough.

"You must be Shannon Paxton." The blonde must not have known what this meeting was about, or she wouldn't be so exuberant. "Hi! I've been expecting you."

"Shannon Reagan," she corrected, holding up her left hand with its naked ring finger. "Just Shannon."

"Okay, good enough. I'm Ember Dennison, one of Mr. Stewart's admin assistants. I think Adam's in the Sit Room. Follow me." She came around the corner of her desk, and Shannon had to look twice. This *secretary* could've passed for Marilyn Monroe's twin sister in that flowing white halter-top dress that accentuated her full figure. An elegant pair of tattooed angel wings graced her bare shoulder blades, but honestly. All Ember needed to step over an air vent, let the updraft toss that pretty dress, and she'd be on her way to fame and fortune instead of what Shannon hoped would be a boring meeting.

A few guys glanced up from their desks. One particularly handsome, dark-haired guy winked at Ember. She fluttered her fingers back at him, but kept walking. No one seemed impressed or star struck. Only Shannon.

"So, how bad is it?" Ember asked in a hushed whisper.

"I'm sorry?" Shannon had no idea what she meant.

"I mean how mad is your old man? On a scale of one to ten, is he like a fifty? Maybe a hundred?"

Shannon smiled. Ember was a breath of fresh air in the dog-eat-dog corporate world. "I think he's simmering somewhere around a solid ten... thousand."

"Wow. Not good, huh? My boss is boiling too, probably not for the same reasons." She reached for the polished steel handle of the door labeled Sit Room, glancing at Shannon's feet. "Are you sure you're ready for this? Maybe you'd rather go shopping instead. I know a place. It's kind of eclectic and a little bit crazy, but you could use some fun shoes, girlfriend."

When Shannon looked down at her very practical, low-heeled shoes, she caught sight of Ember's. Another surprise. White high-top Keds with bright pink laces graced her elegant summer ensemble. "I want a pair just like yours," she teased.

Ember's face lit up. "You'd look so cool in these puppies. They're way comfortable, too. We ought to do that one of these days. It'd be fun."

Maybe this day wouldn't end so badly after all. "I've got time after this meeting. Do you?"

"You betcha." Ember high-fived Shannon and swung the door open. "Alex Stewart. This very pretty lady is Miss Shannon Reagan, not Mrs. Paxton like we thought, because she's not married to that dirt-bag anymore, and..." Ember made a small flourish toward the table, "she's here to represent her father today concerning the missing Hummer."

A gentleman in a gray business suit, black shirt, and silver tie jumped to his feet, followed quickly by the other four men in the room. They'd very nearly snapped to attention as if she were someone important, perhaps her father.

Anxiety spiked quicker than a lightning bolt up her spine. This room full of men looked like a delegation waiting on her. Or an ambush. That easygoing, yeah-I-could-shop feeling fled. *I'm going to die in here.*

Mr. Stewart stepped forward, his hand extended. The appraising look in his icy blue eyes flashed up and down her profile in a quick second's time. She tried to swallow again, but failed miserably. He radiated authority. This was his ballgame. She was so out of her league. "Miss Reagan. I'm Alex. It's very nice to meet you. These are my Senior Agents Mark Houston, Harley Mortimer, and David Tao. They'll be joining us today."

"Certainly," she answered, trying hard to return his handshake with firmness "It's good to meet you, too. I've heard so much about you. Gentlemen."

Mr. Houston, Mr. Mortimer, and Mr. Tao came around the table to offer their hands in turn. She couldn't help but notice they were hunks, all trim, athletic, and dressed in business-casual: denim jeans and black polo shirts.

Mr. Houston smiled warmly. He was big in that muscular, *I-can-take-care-of-the-world* way, that made Lois Lane fall for Superman. Mr. Tao seemed more subdued, but he wasn't openly hostile, which she'd expected after her father's less than stellar opinion of The TEAM. When the first drone went missing, he'd made Alex's company out to be an illiterate group of mercenaries who operated out of a warehouse on the bad side of town. This place and the people she'd met so far were anything but.

Mr. Mortimer put her more at ease when he winked. He had a definite drawl to his, "Nice to meetcha, darlin'. We don't stand on formalities 'round here. I'm Harley. Mind if I call you Shannon?"

A small sigh escaped her lips. "That would be nice." She was nearly back to calm and rational when Alex nodded to the final man at the table, also standing in perfunctory politeness, his hands clasped behind his back like he was ready for a military inspection.

"And this is Junior Agent Adam Torrey."

Oh... shit...

Chapter Three

All five senses sprang to life. Maybe six.

Shannon had to look upward to meet his smoldering gaze, his closeness a tantalizing threat. Her heart skidded to a screeching stop. It was suddenly difficult to swallow. Or breathe. Her shaky façade of confidence tumbled to the floor at his feet.

This was him? The miscreant? The troll? No way. Agent Torrey couldn't be the man who'd lost the HH drone. He wouldn't do that. Hercules might have. Adonis. Perseus. Possibly Jane Eyre's Mr. Rochester. But Adam Torrey? She couldn't imagine such a thing.

Tall with sandy-brown hair combed in a closely trimmed cut she wanted to run her fingers through, he stood resolute at his chair, absolutely the handsomest male specimen in the room. Maybe the universe. All the runner-ups she'd just met couldn't compare. She heard them out there somewhere, she just couldn't see them any longer. They'd ceased to exist. She was caught in a vacuum, just her and—him.

Of their own traitorous volition, her nostrils flared to inhale more of whatever men's cologne or aftershave Agent Torrey had splashed on that rugged, muscular chin and neck. She caught herself from leaning toward him for another—

closer—sniff. No angry man should smell that tempting or look so good.

Broad-shouldered and more than six-feet tall, he made two of her. Easy. Muscled forearms bunched below the short sleeves of his black polo, itself pulled tightly over his pecs.

The sheer mass of this man brought a fiery heat to her breasts, making it difficult to draw in a deep breath. Or think. There was no way she'd be able to function sitting next to him. *Uh-uh.* She just met this guy, and he'd already melted her butter. The second he opened his mouth, the moment he parted those masculine lips and spoke, she'd be lucky if she remembered her name.

Boyish freckles sprinkled his tanned cheeks, but that's where the adolescent charm ended. The half-smile on his face didn't match the steely blues that stabbed her with nothing but distrust. Another emotion shifted across his face. Scorn?

"Ma'am," he said politely, taking her extended hand in a quick, albeit limp shake, as if he didn't want to hold it any longer than he had to. Those steely blues offered no hint of friendship or reprieve. Their message was crystal clear. *Back the hell off. You're the enemy. That's all.*

"Nice to meet you," she croaked, her tongue too dry to come up with something clever like, 'lovely weather we're having, isn't it?' When he didn't respond in kind, she retrieved her hand, clenching it to her side to stop her fingers from trembling.

"Do you need me to stay?" Ember asked at the doorway, giving Shannon a much-needed opportunity to break eye contact with Mr. Stewart's stoic junior agent. She almost answered, *yes!* Just in time, she remembered that question wasn't meant for her. She blew out several shallow breaths to stave off an attack of hyperventilation.

"By the way, it's the Hummingbird Hawk drone, Ember," Mr. Mortimer spoke up, an amused glint in his hazel eyes. "It's an unmanned aerial vehicle. A UAV. Not a Hummer. That's a road trip waiting to happen."

"I know. I just thought I'd see if you guys were paying attention. You all look so serious. Call if you need me."

"Thanks, Ember," Mr. Stewart said, and Shannon was left alone, the only cheerleader in the middle of a very intense football huddle. With her limited knowledge of the sport, it felt as if she were facing two halfbacks, a couple of quarterbacks, and a very intense point guard who might want to stomp over her with his cleats.

"Please." Mr. Stewart offered her the leather captain's chair at the end of the table, putting her between him and Junior Agent Torrey. "Shall we get down to business?"

Stoically, she took the seat and smoothed her fingers through her hair, fighting to regain a shred of her emotional footing. Just as fast, Agent Torrey folded his athletic self to the chair at her side and her silly heart leapt up her trachea.

Alex opened the meeting. "First, I'd like to hear your concerns, Miss Reagan. Excuse me, I mean Shannon."

She didn't have much in the way of concerns, other than *'What on earth happened out there in South Dakota?'* But she'd have to face the man at her right for that question. She took extra time removing the file folder from her leather attaché case, hoping to be able to breathe again. Laying the unclassified file squarely in front of her, her fingers trembled, but that wasn't the worst of it. Her knees knocked until she had to cross her ankles. She would've crossed them twice if it would have helped.

At last, she raised her head and faced the guilty junior agent. Hostility and outright defensiveness flowed from him. *No kidding. I'd be defensive if I'd lost a multi-million-dollar prototype. Focus on that. He lost it. This mess is his fault. He should be nervous. Not me.*

Her internal pep talk helped. "Thank you, Mr. Stewart. First of all, I'd like very much to hear your version of what happened, Junior Agent Tor—"

"Adam," he cut her off, his fingertips a sharp snap on the table. Raw male energy blew past her feminine façade, a gale force to her summer breeze. "Just Adam."

Oh. My. God. Deep baritone aggravation, along with a sultry hint of southern honey had just poured past her eardrums and into the cracks of her feminine soul. She licked her dry lips. *Say it again. Say anything. Maybe my name...*

But the lapse in protocol also rattled her. She should've known better. Mr. Stewart hadn't used formal titles. Swallowing hard, she started again, only meeting Junior Agent Tor... ah, Adam's stare proved more difficult. Dark blue icicles stabbed at her, not a hint of first-name friendliness in sight. Compound that with angry brows knitted together with three definite *V* stitches, and she was in over her head and sinking fast.

Her inner diva piped up. *Be Ulysses. Be George Washington. Hell, be Aretha Franklin! Just be someone strong for a change. He's not your father. Stand up to him.*

"So, Adam," she said as confidently as possible, her gaze on the safety of her fingernails. "Please explain precisely what happened in South Dakota that led to the loss of the prototype."

"It's in the final report," he said icily. "Don't you read?"

Please don't get mad at everything I say. I'm just asking.

"Yes, I do read and I realize it's in the report." Gathering her nerve, she faced him again and softened her tone even more, not understanding how he could perceive anything she'd said as confrontational. "But a written report is one-dimensional. There's a human side to this story, and I need to hear it. Please. Indulge me."

He glared across the table at Mr. Stewart, umm, Alex. "Boss, how many times do I—"

Alex nodded curtly toward Shannon. "Tell her."

Expelling an impatient snort through his nostrils, Adam stared at the wall behind his boss and explained with measured, monotone control how he'd boarded the C-130 out of Joint Base Andrews in Maryland, flew to the requested altitude and coordinates over South Dakota, and HALO-jumped into the wide open prairie for no seemingly good reason other than her father had demanded it.

Distracted by the fascinating way Agent Torrey's brows arched, she almost lost the thread of conversation. Darn. He had gloriously beautiful eyes, glinting with tiny flecks of turquoise thunder. Maybe cobalt lightning. Fringed in decadently thick lashes, his terse gaze reflected the magnificent tumult of the deepest ocean depths. *Wow. A girl could get lost in there.* She'd become the wreck of the Shannon and sinking fast.

"Wait, umm," she stuttered, her face suddenly too warm for comfort. Gorgeous eyes or not, he'd just said something she didn't understand. "What's a HALO?"

His nostrils flared. "High Altitude Low Opening, ma'am," he replied with a hint of sarcasm. "It's a risk-filled parachute jump normally reserved for more dangerous operations than South Dakota."

"Like?"

"Like going in behind enemy lines," he snapped. "Which is exactly what I was doing, wasn't it? Only that little detail was left out of the contract my boss signed. I was sent to South Dakota thinking this operation was a piece of cake when all along, Reagan Industries had set me up, didn't you?"

Her internal filter failed the second he made it personal with that 'didn't *you*.' "Maybe you shouldn't have assumed it was a piece of cake."

She wanted to slap her mouth, but honestly, she couldn't think straight sitting so close to him. Adam Torrey wasn't just a man. He was a chunk of granite. An unbelievably sexy rock, and brimmed with so much male power that it leached out of him and into her.

He spelled trouble with a capital D. A. N. G. E. R. He was not so much forceful, though he had been that in his anger, but more, a force to be reckoned with. He was that point of reference on a map that said, "You'd damned well better start here if you know what's good for you."

Shannon sensed that he didn't so much work for Alex as with him. That theirs was an employer/employee relationship built on mutual respect and trust. Better yet, that neither could be swayed by influence, power or gain. That one would willingly die for the other.

Anger breathed from Adam's flared nostrils across the table to her sweaty palms, and damn, she'd spoken before she'd thought. This man had every right to question his mission, before, during, and after. Unintentionally, she'd put him in his place, the last thing she meant to do. He'd only voiced his opinion, which made perfect sense. But she'd slammed the door in his face as soon as he'd opened up. The shades were down, and his true feelings shuttered. She'd won the battle, but lost the war.

The blank stare commenced again. Adam straightened, rolled his neck once to his shoulder, and reacquired his civil but indifferent expression. "As I stated in the final report, which you have a complete copy of, I landed at precisely oh-two-forty-five on August thirtieth, per the specific directive of the Reagan Industries contract. I retrieved the HH drone, verified the serial number, and walked back to my rucksack to attach the airlift harness. Before I signaled the pick-up drone to assist, an armed assailant fired at me from a motorized paraglide. In order to return fire, I set the drone on the ground inside the LZ. I charged the individual firing at me—"

"Wait. Armed assailant? Someone shot at you?" Not once had her father mentioned that very important detail. "Were you hurt?"

Adam drew in a breath and released it slowly. He continued, his voice tight and his gaze distant. "I attempted to overtake the individual who fired at me. A male. Yes, shots were exchanged. At the same time, a woman in another motorized paraglide was able to secure the drone."

"Because you left it on the ground," she clarified.

"No." His clenched fist hit the table. "Because the contract specifically demanded one agent for this son-of-a-bitchin' mission. Because one person couldn't possibly defend himself against multiple attackers with automatic rifles. It should've been a simple pick-up, just like your father insisted it would be. It wasn't. But you already know that, don't you?"

Alex interrupted calmly. "I questioned your father when he insisted on the HALO jump. That's an extreme request in our line of business; one we don't take lightly. He also insisted this be a one-man mission. At that time, I chalked it up to the whims of an eccentric inventor, but given the way everything turned out, I no longer believe that to be so. I stand by my agent. Adam was set up."

Hostility radiated in waves off the angry man at her right. Shannon didn't need to look at Adam to see its intensity. She didn't dare.

"And to answer your question, Shannon..." Mark Houston nodded to Adam, now pushed farther from the table, his arms folded over his chest. "Adam was seriously hurt during the altercation. Whoever intercepted him left him to die. If he hadn't activated his distress beacon, we'd be at Arlington today instead of sitting here."

"And..." David Tao spoke up, "you need to understand that Adam is hands down the best HALO jumper in the country. We're lucky he works for us."

Harley nodded. "He's got more guts than me, I'll give him that. I hate jumping out of a perfectly good airplane."

He almost made her smile with that gentle twang. Shannon glanced at Adam, but he'd purposely turned his chair toward the opposite end of the table. It was hard not to notice the jut of a proud man's chin. His tongue traced his bottom lip, drawing her eyes to his mouth. He was so angry, but those lips.

Her heart stuttered at the fierce but glorious profile. If she were brave, she'd grab hold of that tight muscular forearm and give it a friendly squeeze to let Adam know she held no hard feelings. That she was only there to help. But she didn't. He looked so angry.

Shannon swallowed hard and tried to breach the barrier between them. "I had no idea you were hurt," she admitted quietly. "Where were you shot?"

Her genuine concern fell flat. His clenched jaw told her he wasn't sharing that personal information. Not with her.

"Who... who do you think did it?" she asked, ashamed for her part in this charade.

"We're investigating," Alex said, "but that's not why you're here, is it?"

Her mouth had suddenly gone drier, if that was possible. She had a message to deliver from the man who it seemed had set this in motion. Paul Reagan expected an answer when she returned, only it seemed wrong to ask.

Alex leaned forward, his palms flat on the table, his long, slender fingers strumming, but not out of nervousness. More from pent-up energy. "You may not know this, but I've already received your father's demand for damages this morning. To be perfectly honest, I expected him to come in person, since he requested this meeting. I'm surprised he sent you to fight this battle for him. By rights, our attorneys should be having this discussion, not us. Once again, he misled me."

Shannon should've felt defensive or outraged at that carefully crafted jab at her father, but she didn't. Alex had accurately pegged Paul Reagan. She swallowed hard. "He, umm, has an offer for you."

Alex's eyebrows spiked. "An offer? His written demand stated very clearly that he wants five million in replacement damages for the drone and another five in punitive. I don't call that much of an offer, considering it was my agent who was shot and left for dead."

Shannon honestly didn't know those details either, but there she was, trying to hold her father's business together like the good little simpleton he must've thought she was. She pressed forward, needing to save her reputation if nothing else. Pulling another contract from her folder, she slid it over the polished tabletop toward Alex. "He will forgo the aforementioned settlement on one condition."

Alex took the single sheet, his signature block already typed and dated in advance. God, her father was arrogant to assume Alex would snap to at his command.

He barely skimmed the document before he handed it off to Mark at his left. "Why would I do that?" he asked her, his blue eyes drilling through what was left of her confidence. "To be brutally honest, Paul Reagan hasn't been straight with me since day one. I don't trust him. Give me one good reason why I should agree to this offer."

Why indeed. *He hasn't been straight with me, either.*

"Please. Call me Shannon" was all she could think to say. At least, she'd be on a first-name basis with Mr. Stewart if no one else. Ah, Alex. But damn, she couldn't come up with any reason why he should enter into another agreement with

Reagan Industries. He had nothing to prove, but her father had some explaining to do.

"Shannon." Alex leaned forward, his fingers interlocked up to their knuckles, and damn, this guy was drop-dead gorgeous in an older-man kind of way. He had to be in his mid-thirties. "Do you know what's in that contract you just handed me to sign?"

"Yes," she whispered. That was the only thing she'd made sure she understood before coming there. It seemed simple to her. Apparently, Alex thought otherwise.

"Do you? Because you're asking me to provide a two-man security team to transport four more prototypes to Joint Base Pearl Harbor-Hickam within two days. What assurance can *you* offer that this operation won't end the same as the South Dakota op?"

Oh, for a bottle of glacier-fed spring water! Her tongue was parched all the way to her toes. She made the only bargain she could think of to get this second-chance contract off the ground and signed, and to prove her good faith. "Because I'll accompany the prototypes to Hawaii with whomever you decide to send."

Alex studied her, his eyes hard and calculating. He could've cut multi-faceted diamonds with that look. David Tao slid an unopened bottle of water across the table to her. Nodding her thanks, she unscrewed the plastic cap and took a sip before she could face Alex. He looked unyielding, his expression indecipherable. It took all of her willpower to lift the bottle to her lips and take a sip, her hands shook so hard.

There was no way for her to add any more incentives to what she recognized as a blatant attempt at blackmail. *Really,*

Father? Get this man to sign up for more abuse, or you'll sue him?

She wished she'd known all the facts before she'd agreed to attend this meeting. *Oh, wait. I didn't agree. I got railroaded, and now Mr. Stewart's getting railroaded, too.*

Alex didn't blink. She gulped, sure he wouldn't accept. He shouldn't. By the looks of this place, he made good money. He had to also employ a good attorney. Besides, he was right. She had no business speaking with him, much less threatening him with this stupid contract.

"I'll do it." Adam's sudden response came out of nowhere. "It's my fault, Boss. Send me. I'll finish this."

"None of this mess is your fault," Harley muttered, his hands flat to the table but his eyes on Shannon, "and we need to discuss this latest contract before we sign anything else with this Reagan guy. I don't like it."

It seemed the world stopped turning while everyone waited on Alex. Shannon nearly cringed, sure he' would toss her out the door, and her father's idea of a viable contract with her. He should have, but he didn't. Alex took the document from Mark's hand while Harley shook his head and growled in quiet protest. With a quick scrawl from the silver pen he'd taken from his pocket, Alex signed the contract, obligating himself and his company to ensure that four more drones would be safely delivered to Joint Base Hickam.

Shannon breathed a sigh of relief, certain that she could make this one thing happen if it was the last thing she did. Delivering drones wasn't in her repertoire of job responsibilities, but she'd seen the fire in Adam's eyes when he'd said it was his fault. Junior Agent Torrey was a man of pride and honor. Well, she was honorable, too.

At last, Alex said, "You do realize that your verbal offer is not part of this written contract, Shannon."

She cringed. He was right. His signature only obligated him. Not her. Shannon extended her hand in a simple gesture of good faith. This man had to know he could trust a Reagan, and she meant it to be her. "You have my word. I'll go to Joint Base Pearl Harbor-Hickam with whomever you decide to send. I'll make certain this operation goes smoothly."

Please say yes...

Icy blue lasers skewered her clean, clear through. "I believe you will. Fine. It's a deal," he said calmly, releasing her grip after a good, solid shake.

"Thank you, Mr. Stewart, ah, I mean Alex." *I'm never going to get that right.*

Shannon stuffed her folder into her briefcase, her hands visibly shaking, her knees the same. She needed to get out of that Sit Room before she totally fell apart. "I'll be on the tarmac at Andrews Air Force Base the day after tomorrow. Good day."

But then Alex made it worse. "Adam, would you please see Shannon out?"

Chapter Four

"Ma'am." Agent Torrey held the Sit Room door open while Shannon took her leave. She felt like running to the elevator; it was such a relief to get out of there. She'd never been so intimidated in her life, but satisfied, too. She had made the deal, and it was a good deal.

Alex had signed her father's contract. He might not like that she'd volunteered to accompany the drones, but that's what trusted assistants did. They made tough decisions and they got the job done. This way, Alex would get what he wanted, too. In a couple days, she'd be on the sandy beaches of Hawaii and this distasteful business would be far behind her.

She stumbled, suddenly dizzy, her head buzzing. Agent Torrey 's hand cupped her elbow and held her steady, but she flattened her palm to the wall anyway. He didn't really want to touch her. She could tell. A swirl of blackness enveloped the hallway. Shannon lowered her head, waiting for it to pass. *Great. My big break and I faint. Breathe. Just breathe.*

"Are you okay?" Agent Torrey almost sounded concerned. Yeah, right. Good deal or not, he pretty much still hated her and her father. "Can I get you anything? Another bottle of water?"

"No," she answered quickly, determined not to embarrass herself more than she already had. Alex Stewart had seen right through her. All of them had. She was nothing more than a pawn in this wheeling-and-dealing business world, her, a literary scholar with not one shred of negotiating skill. If she'd had any sense, she would've told her father to jump in the lake when he'd coerced her into accepting this devious mission. She should have.

"I'm fine." Shannon squeezed her eyes tightly shut and gathered her wits, intent on making it to the solitude of the elevator before she did something more stupid, like pass out. Agent Torrey 's grip tightened on her elbow anyway. She took a shaky step forward, and focused on escape. *Air. I just need air.*

He didn't say another word, but neither did he release her. Finally, at the elevator, he let go long enough to press the ground floor button, but he didn't go far. Oh no. Her silent sentinel waited at her side. It was an awkward distance for the man she'd all but accused of intentionally losing the Hummingbird. Not her best move.

She kept her face forward and her mouth closed until the elevator pinged, and its doors slid quietly open. "Thank you. It's been nice meeting you," she said, putting as much genuine courtesy into the goodbye in lieu of the relief she felt.

"It's been nice meeting you, too." His hand moved from her elbow to the small of her back. "I assume you have a chauffeur waiting for you at ground level?"

"Yes." What he really meant was, *'Don't all daddy's girls have a chauffeur?'* "You don't need to accompany me. I'll be fine."

"No problem."

Damn. He stepped into the elevator and to her side.

"I'm serious. Raul's waiting for me. You don't need to follow me."

"I'm serious, too. You're my guest until you're safely in your limo."

Just great. She gulped, still feeling dizzy and a little queasy too, definitely not a good combination in the presence of a handsome guy with an attitude. She had to give Agent Torrey that. He might hate her guts, but he still maintained a polite demeanor. And he really was to-die-for handsome. She couldn't help but notice.

This big, tough guy had laugh lines at the corners of his eyes, and gentleness in his manly grip. When his big hand had all but enveloped hers in that one handshake, some odd sensation resonated deep within. An ember flamed to life. She ignored it, hoping all those odd feelings would go away before they gave her something to believe in. She'd had enough of fairy tales.

The ride to ground level was short, but vertigo hit when the doors opened. All four walls spun. The entire lobby tilted sharply to one side. She leaned her palm to the edge of the door and took one shaky step forward, determined to get as far away from Agent Torrey as she could.

No such luck. The dizzy sensation intensified. Another very unwelcome feverish wave washed over her. Her stomach lurched. Shannon groaned to the depths of her very embarrassed soul. *Not here. Please. Not now.*

Too late. She doubled over, her hand to her poor stomach, projectile vomit on its way. Agent Torrey jumped back, but in the middle of retching, and crying from embarrassment, she also noticed one of his wide palms rested gentle at the small of her back, his other lifting her long hair away from the mess she seemed unable to stop spewing.

Earth, please swallow me up. Make it stop. Let me die.

"I'm... I'm..." Tears rolled over her cheeks. They had to be crimson by now; they were hot enough. Words got stuck within more ragged retching. She stopped trying to speak. Doubled over and throwing up like she was, she could barely catch her breath anyway.

"It's okay," he said soothingly.

She coughed, her throat burned and sore from the abhorrent exercise of purging. At long last, her stomach settled. The retching ceased. She could stand, but she couldn't face Agent Torrey. Not only had she thrown up in front of him, but she'd planted her butt against his muscular thigh for balance instead of the elevator wall. Would this awful day never end?

"Ember." Somehow he'd managed to call his office while he still held a handful of her hair in a ponytail. "Clean up in the lobby. Tell the janitor to bring a bucket." He paused. "Yeah. Something like that." He hung up and slid his phone into his jeans pocket. That was another thing. Why did he look so good in denim while she looked utterly pitiful in Jimmy Choo heels?

She straightened, wiping her mouth with the back of her hand, and burning with humiliation. "Sorry," she squeaked. Sorry was such a worthless word. Somehow it didn't begin to encompass 'mortified,' 'embarrassed to death,' or 'I suck' like it should've.

"Don't worry about it. Everyone gets sick. It's no big deal." He sounded so gallant as he released her hair finally with one last stroke to make sure it stayed clear of her face.

Yeah, but not everyone throws up in front of a handsome guy who thinks they're a pain in the neck. She cringed, wishing she were home, showered, and smelling better.

"Hey." He peered into her face, but she didn't look up. From out of nowhere, he offered a tissue, which she promptly used to wipe her mouth and blow her nose. "You're still a little green. Let's sit down while we wait." He motioned her to the stone bench beneath the American flag, the absolute last place she wanted to be with a good-looking guy and the reek of vomit in the air.

"No. No, thanks." She glanced out the spotless glass windows, looking nervously for Raul. "My driver. He's waiting for me."

"Are you sure you're going to be okay?" Agent Torrey sounded genuinely concerned, his hand still warmly capped on her shoulder.

She nodded. *Never been so sure about anything in my whole life.*

But his grip told her he wasn't going anywhere, which was a pretty good thing. He might not like her, but she needed help walking to the limo that had just pulled alongside the curb. Finally! Raul was there. He scurried to the front door, reaching for her arm as she all but stumbled onto the sidewalk with Agent Torrey still holding her steady. "Miss Reagan! What did they do to you?"

"Nothing. I'm fine. Honest," she reassured him, focused on getting inside that limo before she made a bigger fool of herself.

Raul held the door while Agent Torrey assisted her wobbly procession to the limo. Darned if he didn't pull her snug into his side at the curb. The rock-solid feel of his hip and thigh didn't go unnoticed. Neither did that manly fragrance of Old Spice, a very pleasant change from what she smelled like.

Shannon ducked her head and climbed in, ready to put this humiliating day behind her. Leaning back on the buttery soft leather upholstery, she finally faced the junior agent who her father claimed had bungled his operation. Wrong move. A tender gaze skated over her ugly, red, sweaty face.

Agent Torrey ducked his head and shoulders through the limo's doorway, and she thought for a split second he might hug her. She sure needed one. Instead, he stuffed more tissues into her trembling hands and winked. The angry man was gone. "Are you sure you'll be up for a fifteen-hour flight the day after tomorrow?"

All that Old Spice entered the limo with him. Afraid she'd burst into tears, she offered up a resolute, "I'll be there. You'll see."

What is it about throwing up that always makes me cry?

He actually smiled. It wasn't more than a tug at the corner of his lips, but it was enough that butterflies swarmed in her stupid, nauseous stomach. She clamped a palm over her poor belly before they decided to fly out of her mouth, too.

"Ember will call you to coordinate the flight plans. See you then," he said as he shut her door, and stood back on the edge of the curb.

Shannon breathed a sigh of relief as Raul pulled away, but like the traitors they were, her eyes skated over her departing view of the agent she'd never be on a first name basis with. He'd turned to his building. Broad, muscular shoulders. Tight backside. Long legs. Check, check, and triple check.

Mortified, she sunk deeper into her seat as the limo left Agent Torrey behind. Her stomach had settled down, but she needed a bottle of industrial-strength anti-nausea medicine before she boarded that Air Force transport in two days. She would *not* be embarrassed like this again.

"Are you sure you're okay?" Raul studied her anxiously in the rearview mirror.

"Yes. Can we stop by the drugstores on the way home? I need something for an upset stomach." *A really bad upset stomach.*

"You bet." Raul made a left turn off King Street and headed north to Crystal City. "I'll get whatever you need to help you feel better, Miss Reagan."

A new life would be nice, she thought bitterly. *This one sucks.* Obstacles confronted her at every turn, and they were all men. In two days, she would travel a long way to try to please one of them—'try' being the key word in the promise she'd just given Alex Stewart.

That had to be why she'd gotten ill. She already knew her father wouldn't condone her method on negotiating. Well, whose fault was that? If he'd taken her under his wing instead of throwing her under the train, maybe he would've gotten his way. Maybe none of this would've happened. Darn. Her stomach pitched in protest. Carsickness was well on its way. She swallowed a noisy gulp, hoping to stave it off.

Raul pulled into the nearest drugstore's parking lot and left the car running while he ran in. She took the small box he handed her when he returned and check the dosage instructions. Grandpa Denver's words flashed to her mind. There in print was a warning for pregnant women.

What now? Take the medicine or throw up all the way home? And yet… What if? That one awful night… *Oh, God no.* Her quivering heart pitched at the thought.

"I bought some water." Raul handed the already opened bottle over the seat. "Just in case you want to take that medicine now. You're still pale."

"Thanks," she said quietly, mulling over the slim possibility that Grandpa Denver's prophecy was right. Of all the ways to become pregnant. *Please God. Not now.* She'd been so humiliated. So violated. Spousal rape was not how she wanted to conceive her first child.

What to do… Suffer the nausea… Or make sure… She swallowed hard. There was no choice. No baby, even one as small as this one had to be, if there really was a baby, deserved a selfish, careless mother on top of an abusive father. "I need to go inside. I'll be right back."

"Why? Are you sick? Do you need to—?"

"I just do, Raul. I… I… Oh, never mind. I'll be right back." She slid out of the car, her knees knocking.

Of course, kindly Raul thought he should accompany her.

"No," she insisted. "Keep the car running. Really. I can do this."

He pulled his cell phone from his front pocket. "You call me. For anything."

"I'll be fine," she lied. Was there really such a thing as mother's intuition? There had to be or she wouldn't have that sneaky feeling that it wasn't just the stressful day making her sick.

She bought two kits just in case, then barricaded herself in the handicapped restroom stall, her hands shaking as she performed the first test. *Shit.*

Frantically, she tore the second box open, and amidst tears and whispered prayers of "No, no, no. This can't be happening to me..." Shannon found out it could happen to her. She was pregnant.

"Everything okay?" Raul asked from the front seat when she'd finally composed herself enough to return to the limo.

"Do you have time to take me to Dr. Remy?" she asked, biting her bottom lip and unable to meet Raul's questioning eye. He'd see right through her. He'd know.

"Of course. My time is your time." God bless Raul, her one bright spot in what had become a really bad day.

Dr. Remy's big smile of congratulations, along with his, 'You're going to have a baby!' proved the pregnancy tests were right, damn it. She left his office with another appointment in a month, a handful of *You're Going To Be A Mommy* pamphlets, and a couple samples of anti-nausea medicine for morning sickness.

"What can I do to help?" Raul had the patience of a saint, but Shannon couldn't answer. Not yet. Her world had just imploded, and she needed a minute to process it. Or a month.

She was expecting. Her. A recently divorced woman. The unwilling CEO of a defense contractor. An inexperienced, unqualified businesswoman. Tears welled. Even now, a parasitic, miniature Brit Paxton was growing inside her body, and it would probably look like—him.

The freedom she'd so briefly enjoyed crashed to an end. She'd be bloated for months, but worse, she'd be tied to this child's selfish father for the rest of her life. She'd have to tell him. Brit had a right to know, but the thought of all those future entanglements with the man who'd lied and cheated on her, made Shannon want to vomit for an entirely different reason.

Raul's warm gaze in the rearview mirror waited an answer.

"I'm pregnant," she whispered.

His eyes reflected her sadness. This news was nothing to celebrate. He knew all she'd gone through. Stoically, Raul kept his opinion to himself as he backed out of the parking stall and headed to her gated singles community.

She stared out the window in mute wonder at her pitiful life. Her father, Paul Reagan, maintained a distant relationship with her, always too busy to bother with his only child. Then there was Brit Paxton. She'd recognized her naïveté in marrying him long ago. He was her father all over again. Arrogant. Remote. Selfish. Yet her father had praised her for the smart choice she'd made in accepting Brit's proposal. He must've recognized something of himself in his future son-in-law. That was why they got along. Paul and Brit were clones.

Shannon clenched her hands over her traitorous stomach. First vomit, now a fetus. She couldn't stop the tears. All her dreams were dying inside.

Chapter Five

"The proper command is, 'sit.'" Harley held his palm forward to the charging canine.

Adam watched, amused that Harley thought he could get this hardheaded Irish Setter youngster to settle down with one word. But sure enough, Seamus screeched to a smiling halt, planted his butt, and sat at Harley's foot as if he'd understood.

"How'd you do that?"

Harley grinned. "Easy. He's a smart dog. You picked a good one."

"He's been a monster since I bought him—more like an out-of-control kid."

The redheaded child in question sat demurely watching the conversation with bright brown eyes, his long tongue lolling.

"Nah. He's still mostly puppy. He'll learn. Dogs need to know exactly what you expect from them. That's all."

Adam blew out a big sigh, not so sure. Dog training looked easy when Harley did it. "You sure you're okay watching him for a couple days?"

"You bet." Harley ruffled the dog's red-brown fur, brushing the long skirt free of a few leaves he'd picked up running like the crazy puppy he was. "We've got plenty of room."

Adam glanced over the five-acre farm Harley called home. It boasted an elegant A-frame house, two rambunctious twin boys, and an out-building where a couple of German Shepherd litters awaited training and socialization. The Mortimer kennels only bred the best. Sometimes Adam wished he'd selected a different breed, maybe one of Harley's pups. He should have. Harley's dogs were intelligent and quick learners. At eight months, Seamus was still more moose than dog, all legs and boundless energy that didn't fit in Adam's busy life like he'd thought it would.

He had an apartment. All the late-night jogs in the world didn't compensate for a big dog left alone too long during the day.

"You're not giving up on him, are you?" Harley asked.

"No," Adam admitted quickly, "but I am thinking of moving. He needs an outdoor kennel and room to work off some of his energy. Besides, we're both tired of city life. I need a place like this."

"There's an empty building lot down the road for sale. Think about it while you're in Hawaii. It's been—what? A year now?"

Adam nodded, surprised Harley remembered the date of the debacle with his ex, Shirley. But he should've. Harley was the one who'd taken him in with all his broken belongings, gave him a rack to flop on, and made him part of his family.

The day in question came back to his mind.

He'd returned home from a successful but long operation in Southeast Asia. The flight alone was torture enough, but then he'd seen the disaster waiting for him. Everyone else saw it, too. Shirley, his live-in girlfriend of two years, had decided to divest herself of him. What a Looney Tune. The woman threw *his* stuff off of *his* balcony. *His.* Not hers.

He'd lost a lot that day. Besides boots and clothes, she'd tossed his prized *Les Paul* guitar, his Derek Jeter autographed baseball, his Bose brick, a MacPro laptop, and various other audio and video equipment.

But what hurt the worst was watching Granddaddy's antique 1860 Colt Army revolver fall from the third story balcony, followed quickly by his fifty-caliber Springfield 1866 Trapdoor rifle, similar to the one Custer might have used at his infamous last stand. Adam intercepted the rifle, but missed the revolver by mere hundredths of an inch. It literally brushed past his fingertips before it shattered to its death.

Those things might have been good investments to a collector, but to Adam they were part of his family history, priceless gifts given by a man now buried but never forgotten. Thankfully, the police showed up. She stopped chucking things over the balcony then, not like it did much good. Adam's belongings were already splattered and shattered. It took less than ten minutes for the fine officers to escort his ex to their patrol car. Oh yes, her girlfriend, Tamara, too. No wonder Shirley was spun up. Tamara was her bipolar match made in hell.

So there he was, just home, tired as hell, with a duffle bag full of dirty laundry and his apartment mostly stripped bare. One of the two had doused his walls with obscene graffiti. Yeah. Two bi-polar witches on a rampage? Not a good thing. At least they hadn't gotten his big screen to the balcony. Things could've been worse.

Oh, wait. No, they couldn't. Someone caught her antics on their cell-phone camera. If local humiliation wasn't bad enough, worldwide was better. Even now, the YouTube video of him trying to catch his property while it rained down from above garnered hundreds of views a day. Adam Torrey's life became a freaking reality show.

Luckily, Harley offered a free room and board while a clean-up crew repainted the apartment, but it was dammed hard moving out the day Adam got his place back. Leaving Harley's little boys, Alex and Georgie behind ended up being more painful than Adam expected. Saying goodbye to Harley's dogs was, too.

Enter Seamus. Life hadn't been the same since.

The mission to South Dakota eight months later should've helped. It didn't. Waking up in the local hospital with a bullet hole in his chest and a failed mission to his credit sucked. Murphy's law ruled. What could go wrong did.

"Sit." Adam tried the command that worked for Harley. Instead of sitting, Seamus slapped both front paws to the ground in play, his butt raised high, his tail wagging, and a 'let's go' grin on his silly, happy face.

"Sit," Harley commanded. Same word, but damned if Seamus didn't drop that wiggling backside to the ground and sit. He glancing back at Harley like a good dog, his eyes half-closed and his nose on point. On Harley.

Adam huffed. "See what I mean? He listens to you. How did you do that?"

"I'm hearing you tell him to sit, but you don't say it like you mean it," Harley offered. "It's all in your voice. Try again."

Adam turned away from Seamus, which only meant the dog would follow. Sure enough, the long-legged, over-sized pup nudged his hand playfully as they walked ten feet or so from Harley. Adam pivoted on his heel, raised his palm flat to the dog's face, and told Seamus in no uncertain terms to "sit."

Lo and behold. Seamus obeyed, his longhaired ears perked up and listening for a change.

"Now give him his treat."

"Why? You didn't."

"Because you need to incentivize him. I don't. Dogs are no different than little kids, Adam," Harley said quietly. "He's dying to please you, but Seamus doesn't know the rules yet. That's where you come in. Tell him what you want, and mean it when you tell him. Reward him when he gets it right. Wash. Rinse. Repeat. I'll run him through basic dog-training while you're gone. That'll help."

Adam tossed a puppy treat to good boy Seamus, certain that funny red-haired guy could smile.

"Now tell him, 'go play.'"

Adam repeated the command, and Seamus took off alright, after a bushy-tailed squirrel. Seamus ran fast, but Mr. Squirrel ran faster. Life didn't get any better. Adam had lost out to a rodent.

Harley grinned. "Wait 'til you have kids. You train 'em the same way. Tell 'em the rules, enforce the rules, and let the testing and pushback begin. It's taken me a while to figure it out, but if you say what you mean, you'd better mean what you say. Draw a hard line. Just make sure Seamus knows where it is."

Adam watched his lame-brained canine pursue another squirrel with equal abandon. Somehow, this obedience lesson sounded more like childrearing than dog education. "I don't have kids, Harley. Just a bonkers dog with two ears that don't always work."

Harley shrugged. "Puppies. Kids. They're pretty much the same at this stage. Are you planning on spending a few days on the island?"

"No. Once the UAVs are signed for, I'm out of there. I've had enough of Reagan Industries."

"Miss Reagan was a nice surprise though."

"Yeah. Right." Adam remembered the *nice surprise* in the elevator that almost got all over his boots. "Guess you could say that."

"You made her nervous."

"Me?" Adam shook his head. "Nah."

No high-class woman would be intimidated by a man the likes of him. She was Niemen Marcus to his Smith and Wesson. Heck, the fancy, high heels she'd worn that day probably cost more than his entire wardrobe.

That Harley had noticed Miss Reagan's nerves made Adam smile. Good. He'd meant to make her nervous. It was his reputation her father had impugned; she should've been a whole lot more than just nervous. Shocked. Maybe indignant, if that innocent act of hers was genuine. Outraged, if she really planned on confronting her father over his failure to tell the truth. Adam doubted both scenarios. Miss Reagan might have shown for the meeting, but her old man pulled the strings. There would be no apology.

Still, she did seem more like a lamb to the slaughter than a woman on her way up the corporate ladder. Even her remark about Adam leaving the drone unguarded seemed more naïve than insinuating. She'd just asked the first thing that had popped into her head.

When he'd heard Reagan's daughter was a writer, Adam thought he'd be meeting with a sharp-tongued harpy from the press, not a pretty little gal who actually seemed to care what happened in South Dakota. Paul Reagan had never asked about the gunshot wound. Not even once. Shannon had. Hell, she'd stopped the show with her concern.

Her sincerity had almost blown Adam to the wind. If she'd touched him like a lot of women would've at that point, if she'd laid just one hand on his wrist in true sympathy, he'd have folded the game. A caring woman's touch meant a lot. But when she failed, he'd focused on the bastard part of the equation. Paul Reagan wasn't much of a man, much less a good dad. What guy sends his little girl to do his dirty work?

Of course, her getting sick all over the lobby embarrassed her, so Adam had no choice. He let her off the hook. Maybe he had gone overboard with his 'tough guy' routine. Maybe not.

Shannon wasn't what he'd expected, and she did have a cute way of chewing her bottom lip while she negotiated, at least while she thought she was negotiating. She hadn't done much of it. For the most part, Alex ran the show. He'd put her on the spot at hello, and manipulated her into accompanying the drones instead of accepting carte blanche Paul Reagan's preposterous second proposal. Alex was pretty clever.

Adam considered apologizing until she'd pursed her pink lips in an attempt to slow her breathing. That's when he'd really looked at her and recognized the signs for what they were. The sheen of perspiration above her upper lip. The sudden pale skin. Eyes wide and too big. The poor thing was about to faint or puke.

Dealing with a powerhouse like Alex had to have been tough enough, but Adam made it worse. He'd bullied her until she broke, and he honestly felt bad. He'd deserved that comeuppance in the elevator, but her getting sick gave him an unexpected opportunity to delve all five fingers through those luxurious tangles of hers, streaked with browns, golds, and blonde. A man didn't get a chance like that often enough, not without inviting trouble.

Miss Reagan was different. Intelligent, but naïve. Trusting. Traits alien to most modern businesswomen. Despite her unfortunate display of nerves, her hair was smooth, sleek, and cool to the touch. He couldn't let it get in the way, could he? *Nah. Poor thing.*

Adam licked his lower lip at the thought of her lush body in his hands.

He'd noticed other things too, especially when she'd backed into his thigh before she'd lost her cookies. The pleasant plumpness in all the right places. The luscious breasts trapped and heaving in a lacy, beige bra under the cut of her expensive business jacket. Sassy hips that were more than a bony handful. Warm, sensual curves that surely led straight to Heaven the way they'd pressed into him for support. Long legs made longer and a ton sexier when she'd planted her high heels wide, which in turn made her skirt tighter across her butt.

There she was heaving her guts up, and his all-male mind was down and dirty in the gutter. But then she'd made it worse. She'd burped. She'd straightened and swiped the back of a dainty hand across her mouth, and with tears in her eyes, she'd apologize for getting sick. What the hell?

That sweet apology did him in right then and there. Shannon needed a defender in her corner, and damned if it wasn't him.

The men stood in silence watching a happy, hairy dog bounce circles across the fenced-in acreage like a little boy high on sugar. Seamus looked the epitome of ecstatic, his normal attitude about life in general. When he wasn't tearing around, he was sound asleep. The dog had two speeds—off and out-of-control.

"Who's going with you?" Harley asked.

"Connor and Izza. Donavan, too."

"The Mahers? I thought Reagan only wanted two agents this time around."

"I don't guess Alex cares what Reagan wants." Adam nodded, his eyes still on his dog. "The boss decided to send the Mahers when Miss Reagan announced she was going. Guess he thought a married couple should accompany a single woman."

"Why Donavan?"

"He's just bumming a ride home. He's got family on the big island."

"You remember the serial number to the drone?"

"UVZ172661. Why?"

"Just a thought. If you can, check all the serial numbers before you take off tomorrow. Write 'em down. Alex has a gut feeling. He thinks Paul Reagan's got something up his sleeve, or he wouldn't have sent his daughter."

Adam rolled his shoulder where the wound from South Dakota still healed. "I hate it when his gut starts talking."

Morning sickness could wait. Shannon needed to get smart in a hurry. Determined to be knowledgeable, sharp, and professional the next time she faced anyone from The TEAM, she pushed her persistent nausea aside and fired up her laptop.

After absorbing all the publically accessible Hummingbird Hawk UAV data she could find, she challenged her father's secretary for a higher-level security clearance. It was late afternoon by then, and she was tired, but Shannon couldn't hide her surprise when Ms. Brant refused her request without hesitation.

"If he wants me to take over the business someday, he'd better change his mind. I need full access, and I need it now."

"It's proprietary, Miss Reagan. You don't have a need to know," Ms. Brant replied firmly.

"But you haven't even asked him yet." What could be so top-secret that her father kept it from his daughter? The one he'd just publicly promoted without her knowledge?

"I don't need to ask him. This is common protocol."

"Is he there? Put him on." The more she talked with Myrtle, the more Shannon's aggravation grew. Her father was a puzzle, saying one thing, then doing another. What? He expected her to assume his responsibilities carte blanche without knowing everything about the business? There was no way he was winning this contest. He'd made her look like a complete idiot at Mr. Stewart's office today. That wouldn't happen again.

"He's busy. He's with a client."

"That client wouldn't be Alex Stewart, would it?" That would make sense. Alex seemed like a guy to confront his problems head-on.

"No, ma'am. Mr. Stewart is not on the calendar today."

"Myrtle." Shannon heard the uncustomary ice in her voice. "You tell my father that he's got one minute to call me back." She gulped. Or what? She had no 'or what' to threaten his with. There was no reason he'd return her call just because she'd said so, but now that the demand was made... She gulped again. Might as well see what happened next. All he could do was ignore her. She was used to that.

"Yes, ma'am. I'll give him your message."

Interesting. Ms. Brant just called me ma'am.

Shannon replaced the phone in its receiver, doubting it would ring again.

Setting her frustration aside, she had to give her father credit. Despite his reluctance to share information on it, the HH was an impressive weapon system. It was similar to its competition, the very deadly MQ-9 Reaper, a predator drone built by another heavy-hitting defense contractor. Compared to the sixty-six-foot wingspan of the Reaper, the HH, with its less than two-foot-long tail fins, really was a hummingbird.

She had yet to understand how such a small airborne vehicle could carry munitions though. The much larger Reaper boasted a maximum payload of nearly four thousand pounds. If the information on the Reagan Industries website was true, the HH weighed in at less than twenty-five pounds, and that included its high-tech docking station. There was no way the drone could accommodate much in the way of explosive ordnance.

While she waited for her father's return call, she continued comparing MQ-9 specifications to the HH. By the time she was through listing differences in engines, airframes, fuselage, payload capacity and overall endurance, her pride in her father's genius knew no bounds.

The success of the tiny HH seemed to hinge on the innovative solar battery that stored enough compressed energy to support the Hummingbird's high-powered laser beam. That explained the lack of a heavy payload. If the industry claims were accurate, Shannon's father had pulled off a tremendous technological coup.

She could've danced at what she'd discovered. This tiny drone carried its own death ray. It didn't need bombs or ammo. Combined with its state-of-the-art targeting system, it was nothing short of phenomenal.

Shannon kept digging. Another claim she found interesting, if not a little terrifying: Each Hummingbird was capable of completely autonomous flight. It required no human contact or intervention once it lifted up from its docking platform with its mission pre-programmed into its tiny brain.

Designed to serve in remote war zones where armies or secret operatives couldn't go, the HH was programmed to dock intermittently with its docking platform. There it recharged and hooked into the main computer at Reagan Industries to receive further intelligence or instructions.

The docking station could likewise be set up remotely. An uplink with the Department of Defense, the CIA, or any other government entity was possible, but had yet to be tested. All RDT&E (research, development, test, and evaluation) had thus far been done in-house with Reagan Industries satellites and their mainframe only. Further testing would take place at Joint Base Pearl Harbor-Hickam in Hawaii. In two days.

Wait. My father has satellites? Shannon didn't know that, either.

She thought she'd had enough until she came across a heart-stopping phrase. *Artificial intelligence.* That required closer scrutiny. Shannon didn't understand everything in the technical article, but if it meant what she thought, the HH had been designed with the ability to perceive threats to its environment or hardware, and to adapt accordingly. Shannon read faster. The tiny creation could develop solutions to that perceived threat. Worse. It could select defensive strategy based on previous directives, performance and mission outcomes. The tiny drone could alter its prime directive.

Oh. My. God. It can think.

A full-on body shiver slammed her with images of science-fiction movies with robots rampaging across the world and killing mankind. The darling little contraption named after a sweet little bird had just taken on an entirely new perspective. *What if something goes wrong with the HH brain? How do you stop a drone with a license to kill?*

Maybe it should've been named Pterodactyl Hawk.

Her desk phone rang before she could think of a solution to that scary scenario. She cringed at the name on her caller I.D. *Darn. It's him.*

"You don't need Delta level clearance," her father roared when she'd no more than lifted the receiver to her ear. "It's math, not literature. You'll never understand the complex schematics or the engineering involved behind HH technology no matter what clearance you have."

He might as well have told her she was brainless. She took the hit gracefully. Yes. He was the math genius. One point in his favor. She opted for open dialogue instead of verbal warfare. "Am I to understand the HH can make decisions? That you've empowered this drone with artificial intelligence?"

"What do you think? It's an intelligent system," he shot back. "More so than most humans."

She gulped. Point two went to him with that nasty volley. She tried warming him up with praise. "Frankly, I'm not sure what to think. It sounds as if you've created quite an astounding weapon if the HH can actually problem solve. That's so—"

"What do you mean 'if'? The Hawk's design is ingenious. It builds complex mathematical algorithms based on incoming data—not that you'd understand what I'm talking about. Of course, it can problem solve."

"Which means...?" She let her question trail away, not sure she'd comprehend his explanation, but needing to hear him verbalize precisely what the drone could do. Unless he wanted something, Paul Reagan had no use for her. She got that. He'd proven it within the last eight hours. The real question was why she'd ever thought she could please him. For a man who'd recently declared to the world that he wanted her to take over his business, he had a funny way of showing it.

"Which means..." He blew out a big sigh of exasperation. "I don't have the time to waste educating you in the field of mathematical deduction and cybernetics, *little girl.* Take my word for it. You don't need access to secure files because you won't have a clue what you're reading. It's science, hypothetical, and far above your head. It's cold, hard logic, not fairytales and bedtime stories."

She winced. That hurt. His sarcastic, condescending tone hadn't helped.

"I want access to all company files, Father," she said firmly. "I'm far more capable than you give me credit for, and if there's something I don't understand, it's time I learn. When I have questions, I'll ask you. If you can't answer or don't have time, tell me who does. Sound fair?"

"You…" he hissed, "had to divorce him."

What? That came out of nowhere. "Brit was abusive, Father. What would you have had me do? Put up with a man who—"

"He knew how to get things done!"

Shannon gathered her courage. "He… he cheated on me. He lied." She swallowed hard. This was not the time to tell her father she was pregnant. "I refused to live like that. Why should I?"

"Everyone lies, little girl. Get over it. Life's hard, and it really is a dog-eat-dog world."

"Don't call me little girl," she said, shaken at the harshness slithering over the phone. "What's wrong, Father? Tell me. You're not feeling well, are you? I can tell. Why don't you ever talk to—?"

Another deep breath in her ear followed by a clear, crisp "no." And the phone went dead.

Shannon closed her eyes, chastised once again, but angrier than she'd ever been. He pushed her in two very opposite directions. *You're my heir. Come join the business.*

But when she tried, *Oh wait. You're not smart enough. Do as you're told. Look pretty, little girl. Just don't get in my way.*

Shannon made up her mind. No more bullying. *Ever.*

Returning her house phone to its charger, she snapped her laptop shut. The only reason she'd forge ahead with this final duty was because she'd promised Mr. Stewart. Someone in the Reagan family ought to be a man—or woman—of their word.

Grandpa Denver's warning came back to her in a whisper. Maybe it was time to leave. Everything and everyone.

Chapter Six

"You've got to be kidding me." Adam stood at the rear hydraulic cargo door on the starboard side of the silver Gulfstream twin-engine jet aircraft. Not at all what he'd expected.

"Thought we were flying Air Force?" he asked the gray-uniformed pilot. "What happened to the C-130?"

The man looked ex-military, his hair trimmed high and tight. "Mr. Reagan prefers dependable transportation," he replied without a break in his granite composure.

Adam shrugged the dig against Air Force travel off and turned to Conner Maher and his wife Izza, also junior agents for Alex. "Looks like we're flying in style this time."

"Works for me." A spitfire Hispanic who could always dish out trouble as good as she gave, Izza smiled that dazzling smile of hers and gave him a knuckle bump on her way into the jet. "You guys go check the cargo. I'll see what's on the in-flight movie."

Adam nodded toward the open cargo door, but Connor was already headed in that direction. He offered a striking contrast to his sassy wife. She looked the part of an edgy South American jungle guerrilla, her long, black hair pulled into a tight ponytail, her cargo pant pockets full of who knew what, and a camouflage gear bag slung over her shoulders.

Her signature clothing statement—two tank tops beneath her half-open shirt—added to her tough chick persona, while laidback Connor sported a brightly flowered Hawaiian shirt and knee-length shorts. Flip-flops. Sun-streaked blond hair. Tanned from his last operation in the Mid-east. He always looked ready for vacation. Izza looked ready for war.

"Crap. They're palletized," Connor muttered out of the side of his mouth. "Doesn't that figure? Reagan won't like us opening these babies just to jot down serial numbers."

"I don't care if he likes it or not." Adam stepped into the cargo compartment where two crates stamped *REAGAN IND* sat wrapped in cellophane on a single wooden pallet. Red nylon packing straps ran like Christmas ribbons around and over them.

A fierce-looking guy inside the hold jumped to his feet. "You punks got no business back here. Move it."

The guy was Stallone on steroids, thick-necked and big-chested, with cold, black eyes, and a Remington Rangemaster bolt-action rifle strategically positioned at chest level. He handled that weapon like he meant to use it. Adam went for the soft sell of diplomacy. "No, sir, I'm responsible for these drones making it safely to Joint Base Pearl Harbor-Hickam. I'll be inspecting each of them before take-off."

Mr. Steroids took a menacing step forward, his rifle sideways. "You're not responsible for anything. I am, now get outta here."

Adam planted both feet, not going anywhere. Connor stiffened beside him. The guard glared, and Adam prepared for trouble too soon in the day.

"It's okay, Ramsey. I'm good with it. Open the pallets up and let him look."

Adam glanced up to Shannon Reagan walking toward them in all her glory. Dressed in khaki slacks, a cream-colored blouse, and sandals, she looked the part of a rich woman. On vacation. Dark glasses concealed her light blue eyes, but she had a lot more color on those pretty cheeks than the last time he'd seen her, and none of it was green. Honey-streaked brown hair spiraled down her back, held away from her face by two gold clips tucked high at the sides of her head.

Hot babe came to mind—and a couple other body parts, too. He brushed the tantalizing thoughts away. No sense revving those engines. This hot babe wouldn't be flying with him. Not in *that* way.

The breeze on the tarmac toyed with the few loose tendrils of hair around her face, adding to her allure. Her rust-colored scarf lent an elegant air to her already regal demeanor. Full, red lips framed a pleasant smile. High cheekbones drew his attention back to her wide-framed dark glasses. Miss Reagan employed that minutia of a woman in complete control very well, the message in her eyes hidden while the rest of her long, elegant body commanded awe, if not respect.

He lowered his Oakleys and peered over the frames in case he'd missed anything. He hadn't. She didn't resemble the nervous chick he'd met two days earlier. Even the chauffeur following at her heels with a small woman's carry-on suitcase validated she knew how to give orders. With her hands relaxed and comfortable at her sides, all Miss Reagan needed was a riding crop in her hand, and her command would be complete.

The sway of her hips was new, though. *Captivating.* Damned if his southern boy pride didn't stand up and take notice with a healthy dose of 'aw shucks, ma'am.' Adam shifted his stance to, hopefully, adjust his crowded jeans without notice.

"Not going to happen, Missy Reagan," Ramsey objected, "not as long as I'm running the show. These seals are not to be broken except by your father's hand at Hickam/Pearl, and that's the way they're going to stay."

Adam caught the condescending title. *Missy Reagan? What an ass.*

She boarded the cargo ramp in two quick steps, slightly out of breath, and straight away faced her father's guard. "I said open them, Ramsey. These gentlemen have every right to inspect the cargo they're obligated to protect. Please? It's okay. I'll speak with my father."

Adam stepped back to watch the drama. In all his military time, he'd never seen anything that matched it. There she stood, toe-to-toe with an employee, her chin stuck forward with determination. No chief or boss commanded with polite language or by asking, and this man obviously didn't respect Miss Reagan. This was her plane and her cargo. She didn't need to ask. She was brave, though. She took another step inside Ramsey's testosterone zone. He squinted down at her like she had no authority over him. Like she was a bug he could squash.

Showdown.

When she took another half-step forward, the jerk had no choice but to back up. His square jaw clenched. His top lip curled.

"I won't ask you again," she said, quietly maintaining the dignity this whack-job so did not deserve.

At last, Ramsey glanced sideways, lowered his rifle, and whipped a USMC Night Stalker Bowie knife out of his boot holster. When he flashed the double-serrated, twelve-inch stainless-steel blade too close to Shannon's chin, Adam's fists clenched of their own accord. One more display of male attitude, and he'd knock Ramsey on his butt. Men just didn't treat a lady like that where Adam came from.

"You open all your mail with that?" Connor joked.

Ramsey turned on him. He hadn't raised the blade, but the threat was clear. *Stay out of my way.*

Happy-go-lucky Connor shrugged it off, deflecting the bully's attempt to engage. "No need to show me what that snazzy steak knife can do. Heck. I'm just making conversation."

With a grunt, Ramsey sliced the almighty Reagan foil seal, cut the plastic wrap, and undid the straps, while Connor carried out introductions behind Adam's back. "Good to finally meet you, *Miss Reagan*. I'm Junior Agent Connor Maher. My wife, Izza, is already onboard. Glad you could join us."

Leave it to Connor. Did he or did he not just politely emphasize the correct way to address Miss Reagan? A sudden need to break Ramsey's line of sight with Shannon propelled Adam forward. He stepped between her and the man she should most definitely fire. Spoiled boss's daughter or not, she didn't deserve the hostile attitude emanating from this 'roid freak.

Ramsey didn't offer further assistance with the palletized drones once he cut the wrap, so Adam did what any covert surveillance specialist would do. He leaned down and pulled his own twelve-inch blade out of his ankle holster and popped the top off the wooden crate. Only he did it without drawing attention to the weapon. It was a tool, not a statement.

Securing the blade back where it belonged, he pulled the nearest drone up from its wooden cradle within the crate. There was that feeling again—that he was holding one of the coolest babies on the planet. With it lying snug along his forearm, he smoothed his hand over its nose and committed the serial number to memory. UVZ172662. One digit different than the missing drone. Easy to remember.

When he turned to show it to Connor, his elbow hit Miss Reagan square in the middle of her chest, smack dab between two very plump breasts. Soft but firm. Hardly any jiggle. His masculine mind noticed. *Yup. Hot babe.*

Nonetheless, a quiet grunt escaped her lips as she took the impact.

"I'm—, I'm sorry," he apologized. *Kind of.* "Didn't know you were standing so close to me, ma'am, or I—"

She smiled mischievously back at him. "It's okay. You didn't hurt me."

"I'm sure sorry," he repeated, biting his lip while a heatwave coursed up his neck and flamed over his cheeks. What was the proper thing to say to the woman you couldn't help but notice? *Sorry I elbowed your boobs, ma'am? May I rub them better? Please, oh, please?*

Again with the cute grin. "No, it was my fault. I was in the way. I just wanted to see a Hummingbird up close."

Damn. How could a woman change so much in two days? He'd noticed her plenty back at the Sit Room, but he'd been primed for battle with her father then. When she'd shown up, he'd taken it out on her. But now, standing this near and making accidental intimate contact like he just had, well, he wanted to do it again.

She'd taken her dark glasses off and twirled them by the stem. Her face lit with wonder, like she'd never seen one of these babies before. Perfect little dark angel wings over soft blue eyes batted back at him. Wait. Was she flirting?

"Would you like to hold it, ma'am?" He had to ask.

"Yes, please." There was that word again. *Please.* It bugged him. Aggressive, rock 'em, stomp 'em businesswomen simply didn't use it. Who exactly was this gal, anyway?

Adam transferred the baby bird into her arms, careful to not brush her breasts when he did it. She accepted the drone eagerly, licking her lower lip and looking very much like a little girl getting ready to taste an ice cream cone for the first time in her life. His body sprang to attention.

Connor stood looking over her shoulder, taking it all in. He winked at Adam. For all intents and purposes, they were just two big guys and a pretty little lady with a very deadly toy in her arms.

"Wow. It's so light. I thought it would be heavier. And it's small," she murmured, her hand skimming over the smooth titanium surface while she cradled it like a baby. There was no other word for it. Shannon Reagan was downright adorable.

"And deadly," Adam said, to distract himself. "These little babies are the killer bees of the future. Our enemies won't know what hit them once these UAVs are deployed."

Shannon met his eyes, and he was speechless. Light blue with tiny gold flecks. Bright and wide with innocence, and what? Joy? Reverence? Adam could only stare.

Until Ramsey grunted, "Lock 'em up, boys. Playtime's over."

Did he just call me boy? Adam closed his eyes and counted to ten. This guy was asking for it, but not today. Not in front of Shannon. He forced his mind back to the reason he'd opened the crates in the first place. "Let's see the other three. I want serial numbers."

Ramsey huffed through his nose, challenging. Instead of reacting, Adam eased the HH from Shannon's grasp, again without making any other intimate contact.

When their fingers tangled in the transfer, an embarrassed smile crossed her face. She scrunched her shoulders, and that little-girl persona peeked back at him. "I don't want to drop it," she admitted shyly. "I'm a klutz sometimes."

"I've got it," Adam assured her, once again surprised at the transformation he'd just witnessed. She'd dropped the woman-in-charge façade the moment he'd opened the crate. Or maybe it had happened because she was no longer dealing with Ramsey. Or maybe...

He pushed other possibilities out of his mind. She had *not* changed just because he'd bumped her boobs. No man could be that lucky.

Returning the drone to its wooden cradle, Adam secured it before he performed the same inspection on the other three, conscientiously making an effort to keep his elbows to himself, and committing all serial numbers to memory. Alex's gut was wrong if he'd thought the lost Hummingbird Hawk was in one of these crates, damn it.

Adam shot Connor a quick glance of 'no go' when the last drone was restored. Connor caught the covert message with a barely perceptible nod, and offered Ramsey a "Thanks for your customer service."

Ramsey grunted, the knife still in his hand. What was the deal with this guy anyway?

"Hey! Wait up!" Donavan Easton ran panting up to the Gulfstream, a full-sized suitcase in his left hand and a huge smile on his face. He'd dressed like Connor, ready for a vacation. "Am I late?"

"Yes," Connor drawled at the bottom of the aircraft stairs, ignoring Ramsey's continued evil stare from the cargo hold. "You missed us. We already took off. We're in the air."

"Huh?" Donavan Easton was an easy mark, not stupid by any means, but prone to open his mouth too quickly. "Oh, yeah. Guess I'm right on time, huh?"

The gangly junior agent angled his rucksack up the ramp and into the aircraft, one step ahead of Connor and chatting all the way. "Hey Izza! Sure glad you guys don't mind me tagging along. I told my mama I was coming. She's baking..."

Adam stopped listening. He still stood with Shannon on the tarmac while Donavan's voice faded away. Ramsey had finally quit glaring and closed the cargo door. Where the man went after that, Adam hadn't noticed, and he didn't care as long as Ramsey wasn't coming aboard with them.

The plane engine was revved and ready to go. It was a sunny day to travel, but Shannon hadn't made a move to go inside. "I'd like to apologize," she began.

"About what?" He gave her a way out, feigning ignorance. There was no sense crying over spilled milk, and no need to apologize. Life happened. Move on. He had.

"I wasn't feeling well the other day," she offered contritely.

Oh, that. He allowed a small smile. He'd lost his anger with her over the missing drone before she'd lost her lunch in the elevator. "Think I caught that same bug. I wasn't feeling too good either, ma'am."

She'd caught his drift. A real smile blossomed over her face this time. "And I'm sorry you were shot in South Dakota. Honestly. I didn't know about that until the meeting. I would've visited you in the hospital if I'd known sooner."

"No problem. It's all in a day's work," he offered easily, secretly pleased she'd given his injury a second thought.

She hesitated, biting her lip.

Here we go. She's going to ask—

"Where?"

He tapped his shoulder with his index finger, wishing she'd let it go.

"Is that why you, umm, didn't want to shake my hand? Does it still hurt?"

Now she'd gotten personal. Either way, he was caught. He'd never in a million years admit his arm hurt when she'd shaken his hand as firmly as she had. She was just a little thing, and frankly, her solid grip had surprised him.

What then? Admit that he didn't want to touch anything related to Paul Reagan? That he was flaming mad because her father dragged his good name through the mud? Adam settled for diplomacy. "No, it doesn't hurt. Guess I just didn't appreciate the way the SD Op ended."

"I'm not my father," she said softly. "I hope you realize that."

"I understand," he admitted, "but you are Reagan Industries. You represent him and you speak for him."

A shadow darkened that pretty smile. She sighed. "Yes, you're right. I guess I do. Well, on behalf of Reagan Industries, I'm sorry you were hurt while employed by my company. I will personally look into covering all of your medical costs. If I had known sooner, I promise, I really would've visited you in the hospital. I'd have brought cookies, too, or something. I would have told you a long time ago how sorry I was, I mean, I am."

He narrowed his gaze, needing to understand why she felt the need to make amends for something she wasn't responsible for. "Hospital's already paid. Thanks for the thought." He ended the conversation and motioned toward the stairs. "After you."

"You have to let me do something to make it up to you." She persisted.

Options sprang to mind. There were other ways she could repay him, but he dragged his stupid male brain out of the gutter. Not her. Despite her powerful name, she obviously had no idea what she'd just said or how most men would've taken that offer. How the heck had someone as innocent as this pretty woman come from Paul Reagan's loins?

"Time to go, ma'am." He nodded at the open passenger door again.

She relented, and he followed her up the steps. Shannon was full of surprises, not the least of which was the very pleasant view of her feminine backside swaying with each step. Adam stifled his very masculine response to reach out and pat one of those firm round cheeks. Maybe squeeze a handful of her ass.

By the time he closed the door behind him, he knew one thing for sure.

This was going to be an interesting flight.

Chapter Seven

"The Molokai express?"

Donavan nodded emphatically. "Yes, ma'am. Darn near got myself drowned that time."

Shannon couldn't get over this gentleman's wild tales of growing up on Oahu. "I'm guessing you joined the Navy?"

His eyebrows arched. "No way. I've seen enough saltwater to last a lifetime. Always wanted to be a Green Beret and see the world. I joined the Army."

"Cool. So you're a Green Beret."

He shook his head. "Not quite. When I aced the ASVAB—umm, that's the Armed Services Vocational Aptitude Battery test, ma'am. Anyway, I scored high in math and mechanical comprehension, so they kinda helped me decide my MOS—umm, that's my military occupational specialty, in case you didn't know that neither. Plus I can shoot a pea out of a peapod at a thousand paces without blinking an eye. Guess it's a gift. I don't know. So I kinda volunteered for Ranger School. The rest is history."

She relaxed into her comfortable leather seat. Donavan had an easy-going way about him, and he told the funniest stories. One minute he was being rescued from the strongest current in the world just off the island of Oahu, and the next he was tangling with a feral mother pig and her piglets near a sugar plantation.

"What's the difference between being a Ranger and the Green Beret?" she asked. "I thought they were the same."

"Nope. Any eighteen-year-old dumb butt—umm... geez. I'm sure sorry I said that, ma'am," he apologized quickly. "I mean, pretty much any kid joining the Army can apply to be a Ranger when he enlists. It don't always mean he gets to be one, but a guy can try. Rangers are mostly light infantry. They handle 'most everything the Green Berets do, like all the raids and ambushes and stuff, but to be a Beret, you got to serve three years first. It ain't for lightweights and mama's boys. Nosirree. Them guys go through tough training for guerilla warfare and subversion and stuff like that. Course there's also the Delta Force guys, but they're just plain scary. I didn't want to be one of them. I just wanted to shoot."

"Geez, Donavan. Give her a break," Izza spoke up from the row behind them. "You're talking Miss Reagan's ears off with all that Army mumbo-jumbo."

Shannon glanced over her shoulder. Izza smiled back, her dark brown eyes inviting girl-talk. "Haven't you had enough of all his stories yet?"

"I'm learning a lot about the Army," Shannon admitted.

Izza rolled her eyes at that understatement. The team Alex Stewart had put together was unlike any Shannon had worked with before. A definite air of camaraderie replaced the pettiness and power struggles she'd witnessed when she travelled with her father's entourage. She wasn't sure who was in charge of this team, Adam, Connor, or Izza. They were all on a first-name basis and one acted as casual as the next. They all picked on Donavan, but he didn't seem to mind.

"You got any kids?" Izza asked.

"No, ahh, I don't." Shannon cringed. *Why would Izza ask such a thing? Do I already look pregnant?* "Do you?"

"Yeah. Come back here and sit with me. I've got pictures."

Shannon looked to Donavan to explain why she was changing seats, but his eyes were closed and he had his earphones on, his head bobbing. She moved to sit with Connor's wife.

"See this one?" Izza handed her cell phone to Shannon. "That little stinker there is my first. Jamie. She needs glasses already, and she's only three."

"Oh, my gosh. She's adorable." Shannon studied the dark-haired little girl who looked exactly like her proud mother. Jamie sat in a cart full of bright, orange pumpkins, dressed in jeans and a pink T-shirt, her arms around the pumpkin in her lap, and a huge grin on her face. A child's pair of wire-rimmed spectacles balanced crookedly off her upturned nose. A little girl couldn't have looked cuter.

"And this is Braxton." Izza scrolled the screen to the right. She was just a proud mother, her voice soft and sappy. Cutie-pie Braxton, also dark-haired, sat on a small red tricycle in jeans and a T-shirt, a baseball cap that proudly declared *Daddy's Little Helper* over the brim.

"Aww, he's darling. You and Connor make beautiful babies." Shannon relaxed. Maybe she'd find herself sharing pictures of her baby with a complete stranger some day too.

Izza ducked into her side like she was just another girlfriend. "Connor's the best thing that ever happened to me," she confided. "Don't know what I'd do without him, but don't tell him. Stuff like that always goes to a guy's head, know what I mean?"

Shannon glanced across the aisle to where Connor and Adam sat chatting about some upcoming NASCAR race in Richmond, Virginia. Adam was a sight for sore eyes. He made those denim jeans and that black polo look good. A solid ten. He filled that comfy recliner passenger seat, too. The second she looked his way, his eyes caught hers. His whole face it with a genuine happy-to-see-you smile. She gulped, jerking her gaze away. All of a sudden, she was back in high school stealing one of *those* glances. Her face flushed all the way to her toes. An embarrassed shiver scrunched her shoulders. *Does he like me?*

"Are you okay?" Izza's bright perceptive eyes didn't miss a beat.

"I think I might still have a touch of the flu." Shannon wasn't going to admit to anything. "I'll be right back."

"Uh-huh, yeah. Bring a couple Cokes and maybe some peanuts or pretzels, okay? I'll show you my wedding pictures."

"Sure." Shannon eased out of her seat, gripping the armrest for support and making sure not to look in Adam's direction. The sight of that man did things to her libido she couldn't explain. Besides, she was pregnant. Unhappily maybe, but definitely carrying another man's baby. Nothing interesting was going to happen in *that* department for a long—long—time.

Thankful for the smooth ride of her father's specially designed jet aircraft, Shannon made her way easily to the restroom in the rear of the plane. Unlike commercial airlines, this bathroom boasted more room, a porcelain sink and toilet bowl instead of the stainless-steel version. Just beyond the restroom, the galley sported a suicide bench for the sole flight attendant.

She smiled at the young man sitting there. "Hi. I haven't seen you before. I'm Shannon. You are..."

"Mr. Dillon Lorenzo, at your service, ma'am." He jumped to his feet, offering a mock salute with a big cheesy grin. Black curly hair topped his head, but his green eyes caught her attention. "Everyone knows you, Miss Reagan. Let me know if you need anything."

"I will. Thanks."

"Oh, and just so you know, I'll be serving a light lunch in a few minutes." He winked as he flirted. "Would you prefer the herb-crusted lamb or the filet mignon?"

"Do you have any soup onboard?"

"Yes, ma'am." He pulled the small refrigerator open. "Let me see what's in here today. Looks like French onion, lobster bisque, or roasted tomato. Which would you prefer?"

"The tomato, if you don't mind."

"No, ma'am. No trouble at all."

She lingered at the restroom door. This young man seemed so eager to talk, and she didn't really need the facilities anyway, just to get away from Izza's female intuition before she honed in on Shannon's pregnancy. "So, Mr. Dillon Lorenzo, what do you do when you're not accompanying me and my guests to Hawaii?"

"I've got big plans." He grinned, his arm relaxed on the open refrigerator door. "After college, I plan to join the Air Force and be a pilot."

His enthusiasm touched her heart. "That's a good plan. What kind of fighter jet do you want to fly?"

He rolled his eyes. "Not fighters, ma'am. You'll think I'm crazy, but I'd love to try my hand at one of those K-135 refueling tankers. I know they're not as glamorous as the F-16 Fighting Falcons or the F-117 Nighthawks, but it's the plane for me. I'd be serving my country and all those hotshot fighter pilots, too. Seems like the best of both worlds, if you ask me."

"Are you married?"

Again with the cheesy smile. "Are you asking me for a date? You interested?" he teased, and she had to laugh. Dillon was charming.

Just then, an odd ripping noise sounded from the tail of the plane. Dillon must've heard it, too. He'd glanced behind him. It seemed something hit the side of the plane, jolting it sideways in the sky. Oxygen masks dropped from the ceiling compartments above all passengers. The refrigerator door slammed shut.

"Ladies and gentlemen," the pilot's voice boomed over the loudspeaker. "Please return to your seats and fasten your seatbelts. Do it now."

Shannon gripped the restroom doorframe, not sure she could make it back to her seat with the airplane vibrating like it was. She turned up the aisle, staggering like a drunk and hanging onto each seat along the way. The aircraft bucked, nearly throwing her to the ceiling. She gripped the back of Connor's seat to keep her balance and her feet on the floor. He'd moved to sit with Izza, their heads ducked together.

Dillon had already strapped himself into his lonely little drop seat.

The plane jolted, shook like a wet dog, and tossed her sideways. Losing her grip, she fell across Connor's vacant seat. Adam grabbed her wrist and pulled her down. He had her strapped in and secured before she knew it.

"Prepare for crash landing!" the pilot commanded.

Shannon turned to Adam. "We're crashing? In the ocean?"

He never got the chance to answer. A loud explosion outside his window drew their attention to the left engine. Sputtering black ribbons of smoke trailed in the wind. Instinctively, she placed her right palm over her stomach. *My baby. He's going to die.*

Adam grabbed her left arm up to her wrist. "Hang on!"

The Gulfstream shuddered as it tipped forward into a dizzying spiral. Everything not permanently attached or strapped down flew through the air. Cups. Plates. Magazines. Momentarily suspended as downward motion hesitated, then resumed. The worst rollercoaster ride ever. Straight down.

Shannon straightened her arms, shoving back into her seat. Nauseous fear climbed up her throat. An image of everyone she'd ever loved or cared about flashed before her eyes. Her father. Raul. Connor and Izza's cute babies. Fun-loving Donavan. Stoic Adam.

He interlaced his fingers with hers on the armrest between them. Their eyes interlocked. A tender warmth reached out to her.

"Are we going to die?" she asked, her heart in her throat and the answer clear as day.

"Maybe. Maybe not," he admitted, his voice a quiet note of reality in the maelstrom. His fingers tightened around hers.

Someone screamed, "Brace for impact!"

She hung on tight, Adam's grip in one hand, the armrest in her other. It was happening. She was going down and her unborn child with her. Possibly to drown. Maybe to die. Here. Now. Before her son had the chance to draw a single breath.

So much noise! Howling wind roared through the aircraft. Grinding metal. Shrieking. Whistling. Screaming! Panic stabbed up her entire body like a massive blade until the Gulfstream hit the water, then—

Silence.

Chapter Eight

Darn dog.

Seamus kept licking his lips, like the crazy, persistent mutt he was. Licking. Sucking. Drooling all over Adam's chin. More licking. More standing on his chest. The beast needed to go on a diet. Had one big paw in the middle of Adam's ribcage, weighing him down. Felt like concrete.

"Get... off…" Adam batted him away. "Leave. Me. Alone."

Seamus didn't take the hint, just kept annoying the living hell out of him. At last, Adam opened one bleary eye, not sure why he couldn't see out of the other at the moment. A big blur hovered overhead. Through the haze, Seamus almost appeared—human. *Too human.*

Wait. Shouldn't he be at Harley's?

An actual human nose nearly poked Adam's eye out. Wet dirty blonde. Panting. *Who's licking me?* It took another minute or two to sink in. Not Seamus. *Oh shit. Connor?*

"Get the hell off!" Adam shoved at his buddy's chest and tried to lift up onto his elbows, but Connor pushed him down. "You good now? You gonna keep breathing?" he asked, his chest heaving like he'd run a marathon.

"I will if you back off and give me some room." Adam turned his face to avoid the mouth-to-mouth resuscitation that felt a lot like being kissed by a guy. *Holy hell. Where am I?* Despite the sounds of surf and seagulls overhead, this was not paradise. *Damn. We crashed. Now I remember…*

Connor gasped into the side of Adam's face, still breathless. "You've got to help me. I can't find the girls."

Adam nodded, his head pounding so hard he couldn't make sense of what Connor wanted. "The girls?" *What girls?*

Connor looked away, one hand still pressing Adam flat to the beach while he shielded his eyes with the other and stared out at the water. "I can't find... Izza. She's gone."

Adam groaned. *Those girls.* Izza and Shannon.

The crash came back to him in bits and pieces. Shannon falling into his arms. It would've been perfect it the engine hadn't failed. The Gulfstream pitched and bucked, but finally nosedived. At the end, it hit a concrete wall of black water. Then sand. Then more water. He thought he'd smelled fire mingled with the suffocating odors of aviation fuel and diesel. Shannon screamed something about... what? *A baby?* That made no sense. No matter. All at once, she'd stopped screaming.

He craned his neck toward the sound of crashing waves. Sure enough. They'd crash-landed in the middle of the ocean.

Adam pushed Connor's hand off his chest and rolled to his side, resting on his elbow while he shook off his body-aches and got his bearings. Sand stretched beneath and all around him. Palm trees swayed to his right, making the postcard effect of the island seem surreal. Iridescent turquoise blue water to his left broke the expansive gold floor. The elegant Gulfstream lay scattered in pieces on the beach.

He remembered everything now. His last thoughts had been for Shannon. He'd strapped her into her seatbelt before she hurt herself, but by then, she was scared, and so was he. The aircraft had lost power and they were going down. Somehow the pilot had leveled off just before impact.

Adam shoved off the sand, swaying for a moment and blinking furiously at the crush of pain in his head and chest. He wasn't bleeding, but every muscle protested. Every bone, too. Standing took more effort than he'd expected. An iron grip stifled his breath. Broken ribs? Punctured lung? He couldn't tell. One was as bad as the other.

Connor stood beside Adam staring at the ocean, his Hawaiian shirt half-open and his clothing soaked. "I don't see her. Do you?" He cupped both hands to his mouth. "Izza!" he called to the noisy ocean. "Izza! Where are you?"

Adam took a hard look at his friend. Still panting. Licking his lips. But no sign of the highly-trained and fast-thinking ex-Marine. "Give it a rest. She can't hear you over the surf, buddy."

He turned on Adam, tears brimming. "But I have to find her. Don't you see? She's lost, and Jamie needs her. Braxton, too. Who'll read them bedtime stories?"

And you're hanging on by a thread. Without asking, Adam took hold of Connor's elbow. "Come on. Let's go find the others."

It was then he realized that Connor had no shoes. His flip-flops were missing. Adam stared at his bare feet. *Where's my boots? My socks?*

He checked his weapons. Both gone. The holsters, too. *Damn. Alex is gonna be pissed. I lost my piece. A SEAL never loses his weapon. It just doesn't happen...*

Adam shrugged off the rambling rant in his head, a sure sign of his own wretched condition. He steered Connor toward the beach at their right. They had work to do. It didn't take long to locate the copilot, crumpled beneath the broken wing of the craft, both bobbing in the shallow surf. One glance told Adam everything. He'd have to dig a grave.

"He's dead," Connor stated the obvious.

"Yeah. I see that."

Connor's behavior revealed a man running on fumes. He'd either suffered a brain injury or was in shock. Either way, Adam didn't trust him alone. He didn't need another fatality. Still fighting to inhale one good, deep breath, he pulled Connor along and scanned the beach for the rest of the flight crew, for Shannon, Izza, or Donavan.

Panic began a relentless tapping at his shoulder. *Where could they be?*

A choking, gagging sound drew their attention to the edge of the jungle where a long scorch mark darkened the sand. Together, they found the young flight attendant still strapped to his seat, leaning against a palm tree like he'd meant to be there. Smoking twisted metallic debris lay next to him. Blood poured down his neck and over his chest. The boy blinked wild green eyes up at Adam and Connor. The desperate fear on his face sucker-punched Adam. He never spoke, but the message in his frightened eyes was clear. *Save me. Help me. Don't let me die.*

There wasn't enough time. The kid had a hole in his throat, and the quick mercy of bleeding out. Within seconds, Adam pressed his fingertips to the young man's eyes to close them forever. Whoever he was, he never stood a chance.

Panic added a frenzied drum roll up Adam's spine. *Where the hell are they?*

"Are you hurt?" Adam asked Connor as he steered him away from this desperate scene.

"No, I... It's just that I..." Connor seemed at a loss for how to answer.

"Come on." Adam clutched his buddy's arm tighter, determined to find survivors, damn it. "The girls are here somewhere. We'll find them."

"Do you really think so?" Connor asked, his question curiously child-like.

"Yes." Adam pulled him farther down the beach, fighting his own fear. "I'm sure of it. We'll find Donavan, too. Can you run?"

"Yes." Connor pulled away as if he was going to do that, just run.

"*With* me." Adam didn't release his buddy's arm. "Run with me. Can you do that?"

"Yes," Connor answered quickly.

"Come on then. Let's find our guys. Let's build a camp for the night. Let's catch something for supper. Got that, sailor?"

"Yeah. Yeah." Connor's head bobbed. "But I just want Izza."

"She's not the only one missing."

"I know. I know." But Adam doubted Connor knew much at the moment. Together, they ran the beach. It made sense. He and Connor had washed ashore. The girls should have, too. Right? *God, I hope so.*

Adam searched the edge of the water, but came up with nothing but airplane parts and debris. "Let's go back the other way."

"Why?" Connor asked.

Adam couldn't answer. Strength faded with every step. He steered Connor in a quick turn about-face, and they headed back toward the other side of the crash zone. Facing into the sun made it harder to see. Sweat poured into his eyes, stinging and blurring his vision. He had to be seriously hurt or his body wouldn't weigh more with every step. Too soon, rest wouldn't be an option. He'd collapse. He couldn't let that happen before he found every last survivor.

"Look. I see... I see..." Connor pointed to where a lone seagull hopped along the edge of the beach. Something lay half out of the water. The nasty bird pecked at it. Connor jerked out of Adam's grasp, running pell-mell to the bird and the human body beneath its clawed feet. "Izza!"

Adam had never heard more pain infused into a single word. Connor dropped to his knees in the sand to pull his dead wife into his arms. "Aw, Izza," he cried. "Not you, too."

God, no.

She must've lain there a while. Probably washed ashore. One of her pant legs was torn open from the hip down. The ugly gash below her knee had been washed clean by the water. Her long ponytail lay in the sand, stark contrast to her white, lifeless face. Again, her boots were gone, somehow lost in the force of the crash-landing.

Connor buried his face in her chest, sobbing, "No, no, no. Baby, not you. I can't live without you."

Adam looked away, fighting the godawful hopelessness of their situation. Tears brimmed. Damn it to hell. Izza was the tough one, the one who had more reason to live than him. Why her? She had kids. He had a dog. Why the hell her?

He choked back his grief, needing to be strong for Connor. This would kill him. *Shit, it was killing him.* Adam cast his gaze to the whitecaps rolling ashore, lapping against the far side of the Gulfstream. Rocking it. *Shannon baby. Talk to me. Where are you?*

Suddenly, Izza sputtered. She smacked at Connor with a very limp hand. "Damn it, get off me. What you trying to do, kill me?" she muttered weakly.

He cradled her like a baby, rocking forward and backward too quickly for her injuries. "Oh, God. You're alive. Izza. We crashed. The copilot's dead. We can't find anyone else."

"How bad?" Adam knelt alongside her, scrubbing a hand over his face in relief.

"That you, Adam?" She squinted into the sun. "Man, I need a drink."

Adam shifted to shade her with his shadow. "I'll get you some fresh water as soon as I can, just tell me. Can you wiggle your toes? Your fingers? How bad are you hurt?"

"Been wiggling them a while now," she said weakly. "That damned bird kept trying to eat me. Pretty sure there's nothing broken. Back hurts though. Just can't move too fast."

"Whiplash." Adam hoped he was right. That would explain his body aches, too. They'd all been run over by a freaking Gulfstream. He glanced around for some kind of shelter to retreat to. Izza needed shade and relief from the gull's incessant pecking. Even now, it hadn't moved far.

Spotting several palm trees close to shore, he thumped Connor's shoulder, pointing to their next destination. "Let's move her out of the sun."

Connor lifted his face, his eyes filled with grief and shock. "I can't live without her."

"I know that, but can you carry her?"

"Who?" he asked tearfully, but that sad off-the-wall question activated Izza.

"Get me out of the ocean, Connor," she ordered. "Move it. I'm not dead, and you're making me mad. Jesus Christ, what's the matter with you?"

Connor eased her into his arms, and Adam was thankful for all that martial arts, muscle-training Connor had apparently received from his kickboxing wife. Even befuddled, he seemed to understand he'd better act upon Izza's orders or risk her ire. She found herself resting in the shade in no time.

"You seen Shannon or Donavan?" Adam asked.

"Uh-uh," Izza grunted as she made friends with the hard palm tree behind her. "You guys are the first. Ah. That feels better."

"Can I leave Connor with you?" he asked quietly, his head reverberating with flashing lights at every move. There was still time. Shannon was out there, Donavan and the pilot, too.

"I got no problem keeping Connor while you look for the rest of us," Izza said with her eyes full of tears. She stretched a hand to her bewildered husband, still looking out to sea and now wringing his hands. "I'm cold, Connor. Come keep me warm."

His eyes narrowed as he sank to her side. "I thought I'd lost you," he whispered, clinging to her hand like a lost child. The minute she pulled him into her arms, he choked, and Adam looked away. He'd have cried too if he'd had the time, but he didn't. Connor was no help. Izza neither. *Damn it, Shannon. Where are you?*

"I'll be back," he muttered as he stood and walked away. Returning to where they'd found Izza, he scanned the shoreline. The annoying gull was gone. The ocean stretched, its endless blue now punctuated with smoldering wreckage and a far-reaching oil slick. The reality of a plane going down in the Pacific was a damned hard fact. He might never find the pilot, Shannon or Donavan. They might have already washed out to sea. *Or worse.*

Every sailor knew the gruesome history of the USS Indianapolis, the flagship of the Fifth Fleet. Torpedoed by the Japanese Imperial Fleet on July 30, 1945, it went down with three hundred crewmen. But those guys died fast compared to the nine hundred survivors left topside to face dehydration, exposure, delirium, and—sharks.

By the time Lieutenant Wilbur "Chuck" Gwinn and his copilot spotted the survivors from their fighter plane three and a half days later, only three hundred and twenty-one men were left, all of them in wretched condition.

Adam scanned the waves for signs of dorsal fins, his gut filled with acid. Izza's blood, maybe Shannon's and Donavan's, had already scented the water. It wouldn't take long before the ocean's clean-up crew showed up. Time was running out.

He turned back to the crash site. The bright red Reagan Airlines logo didn't look so proud anymore, not with the aircraft's smoking guts strewn up and down the sand. Sparks flashed from the nose of the plane, its port side leaning hard onto the beach. The passenger door was still closed. Adam stared at the wreck, trying to make sense of it. *How'd we get out? How are we even alive?*

He saw the pilot then, dead at the stick, still strapped to his seat. The gaping hole on the starboard side of the cockpit explained how the copilot got out, and why he died elsewhere. It possibly explained how the rest of them had gotten out as well. Adam's brain strived to fit the puzzle pieces of this awful disaster. Engine failure? Bird strike? Lightning? What could've brought down such a well-designed aircraft? The explosion off the port side flashed back to his mind. Yeah. That would do it.

The pilot almost looked asleep at the wheel except for the staring eyes of a dead man.

"Where are they?" Adam asked stupidly, as if the corpse would tell.

A faint "Help me…" drifted over the waves.

He jerked around, sure he'd heard her. "Shannon!" he called. "Where are you?"

"Adam… Here..." It was so soft, he couldn't tell where it came from. Too much pain and ocean noise vied for the last of his energy.

"Shannon!" he yelled louder this time.

Nothing. No whisper. Was it an illusion? Shock? Hope? A gull floated overhead, its plaintive cry oddly human-sounding. That could've been all he'd heard. Not Shannon. Adam dropped to one knee, near to passing out and his head reeling. He stared at the lying bird. "You're wrong. She's not dead. Not... not yet."

Struggling back to his feet, he faced the pilot again. "She has to be close to the plane. I just heard her," he declared to the corpse. *And now I'm losing my mind like Connor. I'm talking to a dead man. Shit!*

He staggered to the nose of the plane, wiping the sweat out of his eyes and trying hard to differentiate between what was real and what wasn't. Rounding the seaward side, he stood there panting and trying to catch a breath, the water up to his knees. Despite the bright tropical sun overhead, darkness pressed upon him. He shook it off. Now wasn't the time to fail.

"Shannon!" he called, his heart in his throat.

A small movement near the belly of the craft caught his eye. There she was, clinging to what looked like the mangled aft cargo door, her mouth barely above water. The tiny movement he'd seen was her fingers lifting off the door to signal him. Thrashing through the debris-filled waves, he shoved all the things that had once been inside the plane out of his way as he hurried.

"Adam. It's really you. I was scared. I thought that..." she paused, sputter and sucked in a quick breath before the next wave washed over her face, "I thought I was going to drown."

The ocean was deeper on this side of the plane. Circling her with his left arm, he attempted to lift her against him. "I've got you now. Let's get you out of here."

"Ow. Don't pull." She winced, stretching her arm over the smooth, flat door, her fingertips searching for a better grip. "I'm kinda stuck. Can't hold on much longer. Can't get away, either. Is everyone else okay?"

"We're still looking for Donavan," Adam muttered. He ran his hands down her body, feeling for whatever had her trapped. His fingers tangled in cargo netting wrapped around her legs, the kind he'd seen draped aft when he'd inspected the drones prior to take-off. From the hip of her right leg and downward, she was caught. The netting had no give. Something beneath the plane held it fast.

"Izza and Connor are okay, though?" she asked.

Adam nodded. Shannon didn't need to know any specifics just yet. He ducked underwater and dove to the bottom, hoping to see what needed to be done. No such luck. Too much foam and flotsam clouded the view.

Rising back to the surface, he sucked in another gulp of air and returned below the waves. His chest burned with the strain of the shallow dive on his tender ribs, but he'd seen enough. Working his hands and fingers alongside her thigh and knee, he freed all of her except one foot. The netting had wrapped itself around her ankle and held her tight, her leg stretched taut by the rising tide.

Damn. He needed air and he needed more time. Topside again, he found himself clinging to the cargo door beside her, more tired and weary than he'd ever been. She was really stuck. Cords of shuddering pain wrapped wickedly around his chest, limiting what little air he could suck in. Even if he could dive again, he couldn't break the nylon without a sharp tool.

"How are you holding up?" He gasped, wiping the spray out of his eyes. "Still with me?"

Shannon nodded, but fear shadowed her face. Yeah. She was scared, and he was scared for her. She blinked the saltwater spray out of her eyes. "Are you hurt?"

"No." He shook his head. "I'm good. Don't worry about me. I'm not leaving. I'll get you out of here," he promised, reaching his hand to smooth the sodden hair out of her eyes. Not only was she stuck, but every swell of the ocean also splashed saltwater over her face and into her already bloodshot eyes. She wouldn't need to sink in order to drown. The ocean would do it for her.

"I'm really stuck, huh?" she said, the light in those pretty eyes dark even as she tried to act brave.

"Yeah. You are, but..." He looked around for some piece of wreckage sharp enough to cut the nylon. "I won't let you drown, Shannon. I'll be right back."

With a desperate lurch, she let go of the door and clutched his wrist, her fingernails digging into his skin for dear life. "Don't. Please don't... go."

"Hey." He covered her hand with his, wanting to instill hope where there was damned little to offer. "I need something to cut the net off your foot."

She stared, her eyes bleak. This girl didn't believe him. He hoped she wasn't right in that conclusion. His ribs were on fire. Breathing had become an extremely difficult mechanical effort. *Suck air in. Push air out. Pray to be able to do it again.* She might be right, but he'd never tell her that.

"Shannon." He brushed another handful of wet hair out of her face and pressed his forehead to hers. "Trust me. I'm coming back, if it's the last thing I do."

She let go of him, her cheek flat against the only thing that kept her afloat and blinking with those big sad eyes as the ocean splashed another drowning wave over her. Coughing it out of her mouth and lungs, she looked gray and utterly without hope.

Damn it. The only way to convince her that he meant what he said was to act, so Adam turned his back to her and swam for his life, intent on finding the first sharp thing he could. He staggered to shore, holding his right arm tight around his ribs to control the pain while he searched. Some of this debris had to be small enough and sharp enough. At last, he grabbed a shiny piece of jagged metal. It would do.

He'd turned back to the water when he spied the tip of a black handle sticking up from the sand. He looked twice. Could it be? A Night Stalker Bowie? Crouching to one knee, he pulled it up and looked down the beach with different eyes. *Where the hell was Ramsey?*

Since the confrontation before takeoff, Adam hadn't thought twice about the ornery bastard, much less that he too might need rescue. It made no sense that he'd be there. No one in his right mind would've remained in the cargo hold during the flight. Between the high altitude, freezing temperatures, and hypoxia, Ramsey had to have known he'd never survive without specialized equipment.

Sabotage.

Adam stopped that train of thought dead in its tracks. He now had two missing passengers to find, one he actually cared about. But his strength wouldn't last much longer. He headed back into the waves. Shannon came first. Then Donavan. Maybe Ramsey. Or not.

He heard them before he saw her. Small, sad whimpers. When he rounded the nose of the plane, she had her face pressed into her arm. Shannon was crying. She hadn't believed.

"Hey." He went straight to her, angry she had so little faith in him.

She lifted her sad face. "You're back?"

The question stabbed him. He must not have inspired much confidence. "Told you I'd be back," he growled. "Damn, woman. Don't you trust me?"

He gave her no time to answer. The tide had come in fast. Sucking in as much air as his screaming lungs would allow, he ducked underwater, and felt down her leg for the netting wrapped around her calf and foot. Pushing one hand between the fabric of her pants and the nylon, he sliced the netting. Resurfacing, he boosted her higher onto the cargo door while he caught his breath. *Goddamn, that hurt like a son-of-a-bitch.*

She clung desperately, gasping for air. "Th-thanks."

"Put your arm around my neck. Easy now. Hold on tight." He circled her waist, tugging her into his side. She slammed into his ribs, clutching his neck and holding on like he'd told her to. But damn! Pain sucked the breath out of him. It took a moment to shake it off. He gritted his teeth, sure they'd splinter under the force of his clenched jaw.

Focus, Torrey. Just focus.

Shoving away from the wreck, he took her into the waves with him. The weight of her body warmed as much as it hurt. He wanted to shove away from her, too. Every pressure stabbed. Every touch jolted. Deep in his chest, the ends of what had to be broken ribs grated against each other. At least he hadn't coughed up any blood. Yet.

Staggering through the littered surf, they tumbled onto the beach. It took all his willpower to conceal his pain when he fell to his knees and rolled to his back. Damn, inspiring confidence took a helluva lot out of a guy. With her trembling face pressed against his chest, he kissed the top of her wet head, focusing on the pleasant feel of her instead of how difficult it was to breathe. She smelled of aviation fuel and ocean, but she was alive.

The chore still ahead seemed insanely huge for a guy running on empty. *Three safe. Two to go.*

"You're hurt." The instant she touched his cheek, he closed his eyes, wishing she hadn't done that. A woman's touch meant so many different things, and all of them good, but he wasn't ready for it. Not skin to skin. Not sweet. Not yet.

He pulled away. "No, I'm not. Let's get you with the others."

She didn't argue, but he saw the hurt in her eyes. Shannon knew a lie when she heard one. She didn't press the issue.

He headed toward the palm trees. "Connor and Izza are over here. Maybe you guys can help each other set up camp while I—"

"Where are you going?" She limped along beside him, her bare feet bruised and scraped from fighting the cargo net. One of her shirtsleeves was ripped away but hanging by a thread, her left arm swollen midpoint between elbow and wrist. Possibly broken. Thankfully not a compound break.

"Still looking for Donavan. Ramsey too."

"Ramsey? He's... he's here with us?" She glanced over her shoulder.

A man would have to be an idiot not to notice how she stepped in closer to him. Shannon Reagan was scared of Ramsey and Adam wanted to know why. She hadn't seemed scared of him before takeoff. But that mystery had to wait. He held up the knife he'd found. "Yeah. He's here. Somewhere. Either that or his knife made the trip without him."

She didn't say more, and by then they'd arrived at the gathering place beneath the palm trees, so Adam let the puzzle of Ramsey and his knife go. Tired beyond tired, he eased Shannon into a sitting position alongside Izza and sank to the sand with her.

"You look like crap," Izza muttered. Connor lay sound asleep in her left arm, his body stretched alongside hers, his face pressed into the side of her neck.

"How is he?" Adam chose not to acknowledge her astute observation of his ragged condition. They *all* looked like crap.

"He's got a good-sized hematoma on the back of his head. I can feel it." She ran her fingers through her husband's hair. "It's right here."

"You shouldn't have let him go to sleep. He might have a concussion"

"Now how was I gonna stop him, huh?" she snapped, instantly angry. "It's not like I had a choice. Besides, what if he's...? What if he's...?" Her eyes brimmed with tears.

Adam heard the word she'd left unsaid. *Dying*. Izza was a tough cookie, but holding her husband while she was scared to death he might die was a damned hard thing to endure. Climbing to his knees, Adam crawled to Connor's side, knowing full well the man displayed all the signs of shock and concussion. Death *was* a very real possibility. He shook Connor awake, needing to see into his friend's eyes. "Hey, buddy."

Connor grunted. "What? Who? Aw, leave me alone, Adam."

"Just checking your hard head. How you feeling?"

"Like crap." He rolled back into Izza's neck. "Let me be."

Adam ran a hand over his friend's skull. At least Connor had answered as if he'd understood the question this time. Adam wanted to question him further, but he was spent. Besides, there wasn't much to be done but keep a careful watch on him. Izza had already figured that out.

Shannon stared anxiously out to sea. "Where are we?"

Adam stood to leave, forcing the throbbing fire in his chest to back off. "Don't know."

"Where are you going?" Shannon seemed so fearful, but then why not? She was one of few survivors.

"I've still got to find Donavan and Ramsey. Need to bury a couple others. And we need fresh water or none of us will survive."

"Who died?"

Adam stared at her. The answer seemed painfully obvious. The dead were the ones not present, the passengers still missing. It was easy to figure out, but he understood why she'd asked. She was just trying to get a grip on the awful turn of events and doing it as gradually as her brain would allow. Sometimes, knowledge helped a person deal with reality. Not today. Denial slowed the process.

He turned toward the beach, too tired to come up with a polite answer. She'd have to figure it out for herself.

"Check back here, Adam." Izza pointed behind her palm tree. "I heard something running around in the bushes. Think I heard splashing, too. If we've got rats on this island with us, there might be fresh water."

Adam doubted he could be that lucky, but Izza was right. When he investigated the edge of the jungle, he located a green, algae-filled stream oozing through a sandy channel. It wasn't deep enough to bathe in, but the water appeared clean. He knelt, ladling a handful to his lips. Sweet and clear, he sucked up another mouthful, thankful for Izza's sharp ears. Greenery sheltered most of the stream. Small animal tracks lingered in the soft, wet ground just like Izza had said. *Good. Dinner and water.*

His thirst quenched, he needed a way to transport the water to the other survivors. Wearily, he trudged back to the shore and found two plastic water bottles bobbing in the surf, both unopened, another plus. The more he walked, the more certain he was of at least one broken rib, maybe more. Breathing was tight, but he wasn't bleeding. Not tasting blood, either. Both damned good signs, considering how awful he felt.

He stood again at the palm tree where he'd deposited his fellow passengers. They now had water and a way to get more. Wiping the sweat off his face, he surveyed what was left of his team. Izza and Shannon were both injured. Connor, too. His shirt had been wrapped around Izza's gash, and it would've made a difference if Connor had done that. But Adam doubted it. The guy was hurt bad.

Shannon held one of the full water bottles up to him. Man, she looked like heck, her hair straggly, and one eye black and blue. Her pants were dirty but in one piece, her blouse in the same shape. She offered a small smile. "You should stay here and rest. Just for a minute."

Tired and fading fast, Adam couldn't allow his own fatigue. He hadn't found Donavan yet, but he paused. Her simple, thoughtful act was as sweet as the water in her hand. Sinking to his knees beside her, he landed on all fours. "Can't stop yet. Donavan's out there."

"I know. I'll help you find him." She held the bottle to his lips, and like a dog, he sucked the cool drink down. Parched, he couldn't seem to get enough.

Shannon placed a tender palm to his chin, wiping the dribbling water away. "You need to rest, Adam," she said softly, "before you collapse. You're hurt, too. I know you are."

She was right, but he shook his head out of sheer Navy SEAL bullheadedness. "Got to go. Donavan's out there."

He meant to push away. Really, he did, but his arms failed to oblige. His elbows unlocked, and down he went, face first. Only this time, he landed on something soft and sweet and—*Shannon.*

Chapter Nine

She slept for hours. More like, she passed out along with Adam and everyone else.

Like four scarecrows, the survivors seemed more comatose than alive, but Shannon knew different. When she awoke, Izza and Connor seemed to breathe in sync with each other, both regular and steady in their inhalations and exhalations. Connor had groaned once, and Izza muttered something into his hair. Shannon couldn't translate the softly spoken endearment exactly, but she was fairly certain *te amo, baby* meant *I love you, baby*. Izza knew the way to her man's heart even in her sleep. Connor had stilled, and that was the last she'd heard from the Mahers.

Adam snored quietly, his body sprawled in the sand next to her, his head on her lap. It was a gentle sound on such an awful day, the breath of life in the middle of death and disaster. She'd run her fingers through his hair when he'd first fallen, as much to give him comfort as to take it. Her head hurt and her arm, too. It had to be broken, but the tactile sensation of his scalp beneath her fingertips brought a measure of peace. His hair was dirty, but his head was warm. This man had risked death to save her life. He'd come back for her, just like he'd said he would. And then she'd fallen asleep with her fingers nestled in the short hair of her exhausted savior.

His sweaty head lay still as a stone on her lap and as heavy as one, too. Now that she'd awakened, she needed to readjust her position, but didn't. He needed rest more than she needed comfort, so she endured the ache in her lower back and contented herself by watching the ocean swell beyond their sanctuary. Birds fluttered in the palm fronds overhead, and those pesky animals Izza had mentioned made their little squeaky noises. The leaves rustling announced their passage to and fro. They were small. No heavy footsteps or growls met her ears, so Shannon wasn't afraid. With Adam sound asleep and almost lying in her arms, she wasn't afraid at all.

She studied the drop-dead gorgeous man. He'd rolled to one side, facing her stomach. Even in sleep, he moaned deep in his throat, and she knew he had to be suffering. Nothing showed except for the cuts and abrasions most of them had on their faces and arms, but falling out of the sky had come at a cost. Adam wouldn't have dropped to his knees like he had unless he was concealing an injury.

With her fingers already on his head, she traced her thumb over his brows and down the side of his face to his clean-shaven jaw. Dark eyelashes fluttered against his cheeks at her touch. He sighed, so she did it again, offering a gentle caress not intended to wake him, only to comfort. After another deep sigh, he settled. Shannon was glad to have given something back to the man who'd saved her life. He seemed to like it.

Guiltily, she continued her frank observation. There was more to Adam Torrey than she'd noticed before. His squared-off jaw culminated in a masculine chin that jutted forward even in repose. Sandy-brown hair trimmed his neckline, not the buzz cut of a military man, yet there was military in his posture and mannerisms. She'd already detected that dimension to him. He had that ultra-polite, *yes ma'am, no sir,* ingrained habit of most of the military personnel she'd met. Even as angry as he'd been during their initial meeting, he'd still been the perfect gentleman. Actually, he'd been more than that. She didn't know many men who would've dared to come as close as he had to a woman heaving her guts up, just to hold her upright and keep her hair out of the line of fire.

How mortifying to have thrown up in front of the man you'd just verbally sparred with. Ugh. Just the thought of what he must've seen brought a hot flush of embarrassment. She shivered, but brushed the unwelcome memory off. That moment would forever stand as one of her worst, and yet... he'd stood resolutely at her side.

Unlike Brit...

Her mind seemed determined to size her ex-husband up against this unexpected new man in her life, but there was no comparison. Brit was *Esquire*, his hands smooth, his wardrobe impeccable, and his motives forever self-serving. He whined when his plans went awry. He berated and belittled for petty reasons, and heaven forbid that his wife stepped out of line or caught the attention of the press instead of him. She couldn't put her finger on it, but there'd always been something quirky about her ex. Something borderline—creepy.

But Adam? She honestly didn't know which magazine suited him. Maybe something sports related? Maybe fitness? His hands were wide and rough; his nails trimmed but his cuticles were ragged. A working man's hands. A little worn, but capable of tenderness. That one moment of being crushed to his side there on the curb in Alexandria had nearly tossed her poor stomach from the sheer pleasure of it. Even angry, he'd been thoughtful. Concerned for her, the daughter of a man who had proven to be more enemy than friend. And Adam was strong. Rugged, hot-damned—hot.

Shannon continued investigating the man in her rams who had more nerve than most. How odd that a dimple pinched his left cheek. He wasn't smiling, but he looked peaceful and the dimple persisted, a reminder that a boy lay deep inside this heavy, male body.

The sensation that she'd met him before lingered. Where on earth would a meek writer like her meet a man of action like this one? Only in a war zone, and she didn't do stories or exposés on the military. Besides, she had no idea what service he'd been in, whether Army, Air Force, or... *oh, my gosh. Navy?*

Her heart thudded to a complete stop. *That's where I've seen this guy before. In my dream.* He was *that guy*, but how could he be? What did it mean? Her fingers trembled when she traced that soft indentation on his cheek again. Leaning forward, she sniffed for the telltale sign of wintergreen. When she didn't catch any hint of it, she shook her head at her foolishness. *Reality check. You, Shannon, are losing your mind. It was just a dream. Don't be stupid.*

There were a lot of similarities, but Adam wasn't *that* guy. No way.

"Are you awake?" Izza asked from her prone position beneath the palm.

Shannon startled, hoping Izza wasn't somehow intuitively able to read her idiotic thoughts. She turned to Jamie and Braxton's mother. That was who she saw now—those two cherubs from Izza's cell phone, faces smudged by love, waiting for their mama to come home and play. Only Izza resembled a zombie now, her eyes sunken and too dark, her beautiful olive-colored skin too pale.

"Yes, I'm awake," Shannon whispered in reply. "How do you feel?"

"I'm good," Izza answered quickly. "When these guys wake up, they're going to be hungry. We need to be thinking about finding them something to eat."

"Okay," Shannon agreed. Izza probably meant scavenging or hunting, but Shannon had no experience with cooking much less foraging, so she thought about the dinner Dillon had offered instead. Did anything in the galley survive the crash? She might be able to swim out to the wreck to get some food.

"How's Adam?" Izza asked quietly.

Reality struck. Dillon hadn't survived. He was one of those bodies Adam still had to bury. Shannon bit her lip, ashamed. Here she'd been worried about dinner while poor Dillon laid dead on the beach somewhere. Tears blurred her tired eyes.

"Shannon." Izza's sharp whisper jolted her back to the moment. "Listen up. It's just you and me right now. How's Adam? Is he bleeding anywhere?"

"Not that I can see." She smoothed a hand over his bicep, eager for his warmth under her fingertips. Touching him brought a level of secret pleasure and strength, so she smoothed her hand over the same strong muscle just to feel it again.

"Lift his shirt. Check him out. Is his chest or stomach bruised? Any swelling? Tell me what you see."

Carefully, Shannon lifted Adam's still-damp shirt, feeling timid for all of two seconds. It didn't take long to get confident. She tugged his shirt up farther to see more of this handsome specimen. He seemed built of squares and planes, from the defined pectoral muscles and the relaxed furrows of his abdomen to his thick biceps and hefty forearms. Ropes of hardened musculature, thick and powerful, lay relaxed at the moment. He made two of her. Easy. But blackened and purpled bruises colored him from his collarbone all the way to his belt.

"He's got massive bruising," she told Izza. *And he's smooth-chested,* she thought. *And, oh, my gosh.* A thin trail of hair that began just above his navel marked his abdomen, running down beneath his belt. She squelched her desire to take advantage of him in his sleep, maybe unbuckle that belt and see if he was injured anywhere else. That might be important.

"He's not bleeding though, is he?"

"Not that I can see," Shannon whispered, remembering she wasn't alone. Sharp-eyed Izza was watching.

"Shannon!"

She looked up into Izza's annoyed face. "Y-yes?"

"I asked you if he's bleeding. From his mouth? His nose?" Izza snapped. "What's the matter with you? Did you hit your head, too?"

"No. Sorry. I'm fine." *But he's handsome and hurt, and when he wakes up, he'll think he needs to save the world. He'll leave me. I may never get another chance like this.*

Dutifully and also lovingly, Shannon tipped his face gently to the side so she could see his entire mouth. No blood, just two tanned lips pressed together in deep slumber. He huffed a breath at the disturbance. She traced the skin below his bottom lip with her thumb, telling herself she needed to be sure there was no blood, but wondering how his mouth would taste. How a kiss from this guy would feel.

He moaned softly, but didn't move away. Neither did she. Her palm cupping his chin felt warm and perfect.

"No." She looked directly at Izza so as not to betray her feelings. "He's not bleeding. Just badly bruised on his chest and down his side. I think he might have a broken rib, though. He seemed to have trouble catching his breath before. How's Connor?"

"I'm fine." With a big stretch, Connor rolled out of Izza's arms and flopped onto his back in the sand. He groaned out a long yawn. "Crap. What a landing."

"How's your head, honey?" Izza asked, her voice full of worry.

He slowly pulled into a sitting position, his arms on his knees as he grimaced and squeezed his temples. "Hurts like hell. How's yours?"

"I'm good," she said again, but this time Shannon really looked at her. Izza hadn't moved from the trunk of that palm tree other than to lie down beside it with Connor. She'd answered far too quickly, too.

"Izza?" she asked. "What's wrong?"

"Nothing," Izza replied just as quickly, but Shannon saw through the lie this time.

So did Connor. He knelt over his wife, his hand gentle on her shoulder. "You're hurt, aren't you? Damn it, where? Tell me."

Tears welled up in Izza's angry eyes. She was fighting whatever pain she had. "My leg's cut, but mostly... would you look at my back? I think something's stuck inside of me."

Carefully, Connor eased her to her side to face Shannon. Lifting her soiled top, he winced and closed his eyes. It had to be real bad. "Can you hold her steady? Don't let her roll over."

"Sure." They were lying close enough that Shannon reached for Izza's arm to keep her still, while not disturbing Adam. "Hang onto my hand, Izza."

"This is going to hurt, baby. Sorry." With a grunt, Connor pulled something about three inches long, thin, and silvery out of Izza's back. She shuddered, clutching Shannon's hand, but she didn't scream.

He leaned over to kiss her cheek while he pressed his palm into her back. "I'm really sorry. It wasn't deep, but that thing had to come out."

She nodded, her eyes squeezed tight and tears running down her face. "What was it? The wing off that Gulfstream? It felt big enough."

He didn't spare a smile at her poor attempt at humor. "I don't know for sure, maybe a piece of metal molding or something. I can't believe you let me sleep this whole time with that thing in your back. What's the matter with you?"

Poor Izza squeezed her eyes shut and choked. "I couldn't... let you go."

"Baby," he growled, lifting her gently against his chest, his own face awash with tears. "I'm not going anywhere. Neither are you. We'll get through this."

Shannon's eyes overflowed. She looked away, touched by the depth of emotion around her. The beauty of this island paradise was nothing compared to the love between Connor and Izza. And she had—Brit.

His snide remark when she'd called the night before the flight flashed to her mind. As usual, he'd acted as if he had better things to do than hear her out. Instead of showing any interest in the news of his impending fatherhood, all he'd said before he'd hung up on her was "So? Take a pill. Get an abortion. I don't care which, just get rid of it."

It. Her baby and hers alone. He'd called it—*it.*

Her eyes went instinctively to her stomach, where a man's weary head rested against the child growing deep inside of her. Deep blue eyes gazed tiredly into hers. Adam lifted his hand to her jaw, his thumb warm and gentle on her cheek. "Hey," he muttered hoarsely.

"Hey." She returned the simple word. Somehow it was enough.

"How long?" he asked, his fingers stroking her still.

"You slept for a couple hours," she answered, leaning into his touch. "We all did. I guess we were tired."

He breathed out a long sigh, lowering his hand back to his chest. Holding him seemed natural. She didn't want him to leave, despite the fact this was probably not the most comfortable position for him. But the temperature was perfect and he needed his rest. And a foolish woman could hope.

He snuggled his face against her stomach, his arm curled around her backside, pulling her close like a pillow. She ruffled her fingers through his hair and watched his heavy eyelids close. His breathing returned to slow and steady, so she closed her eyes. Too soon this magic moment would end, but she let her foolish romantic feelings linger. He seemed content to stay. She wished he would.

They slept again. It seemed the sun would never set, but gradually the day ended. When it did, both Adam and Connor were suddenly energized.

When Adam woke this time, he must have been more awake than the first time. He pulled slowly away from Shannon, his eyes dark and hooded. He lingered when he was back to his hands and knees beside her, and her breath caught. It was the perfect moment for a kiss. Did he feel it, too?

"Damn," he hissed as he shot her a look she couldn't translate. "I've got to find Donavan. I should never have lain down. Why'd you let me sleep so long?"

"You didn't lie down," Shannon corrected him. "You collapsed. We all did."

He didn't argue, just sprang into action despite his injuries. "How are you guys doing?" Adam asked his teammates, brushing the sand off his hands and jeans.

"I'm good," Izza said quickly.

Shannon stifled the urge to correct that cover-up. None of them fit the definition of good, but these people all seemed intent on denying their injuries. What was up with that?

"Better," Connor answered. "Let's see if we can find the others before it gets dark."

Shannon looked away when Adam turned his back and walked toward the wreck with Connor. She had no reason to expect more, but his leaving left her chilled.

"You hungry?" Izza's hand on her arm distracted her.

"Not really," Shannon replied, but obviously Izza was. This was the second time she'd mentioned food.

"Damn. Look at you. Your arm's broken."

Shannon glanced at her purpled, swollen arm. The pain was more like a dull ache that wouldn't let up. "Yes, but it doesn't hurt. I feel better now that I've slept."

With her other hand for support, she worked her way up the trunk of the tree, making sure she was strong enough to stand before she let go. Her clothes had dried except for where she'd been sitting on them, and her hair was dry. Smelling of fuel and dirt, but dry.

She pushed it out of her face. Fresh water to rinse would be nice. She itched all over. Another drink wouldn't hurt, either. "Guess I'll look around for something to eat. Do you think there are any berries on this island?"

"Yeah. Big ones." Izza pointed directly overhead. "They're called coconuts."

Shannon glanced up. Big brown *berries* attached to a very long trunk and stuck in the sky like these were didn't offer much hope. "Let me see what else I can find."

Unsteady on her feet, she took a few tentative steps toward the stream behind them. Water meant vegetation. Hopefully, some of that leafy greenery would be edible. Her injured limb reminded her it was truly broken, so she clasped it against her chest to minimize the pain.

Any other day, she would have been enthralled with the magnificent colors the fading sun splashed across the tropical sky. Not today. Their life-and-death struggle had effectively sucked away the simple pleasure of a sunset. Plenty of trees and bushes enclosed the center of the island. Shadows lay long in the fading sun. She headed into the green.

"Don't go far," Izza cautioned.

"I won't." Shannon called over her shoulder. "There's some kind of a trail in here though. Are you sure you'll be okay while I'm gone?"

"I'm fine, but you be careful. It's probably an animal trail. Maybe deer. Don't get lost."

"I won't," Shannon promised. She took another step, remembering that tiger from *Swiss Family Robinson*. He'd followed a trail, too, hadn't he?

A large bush farther along the trail overflowed with white berries, but when she reached it, the white berries turned out to be tiny puffs of downy flowers. The sound of the surf receded while the twittering of birds grew louder. She startled a flock of small brown birds that scattered at her feet instead of flying away. Looking back at her path, Shannon kept careful track of how far she'd gone from Izza. So far, so good. The stream was no longer visible, but trickled beneath the shrubbery.

She took a few more steps, still cradling her arm. Holding it eased the throbbing ache. Considering everyone else's injuries, she'd gotten off lucky.

Glancing up, she spied what looked to be clusters of big green fingers. Bananas! Proud of herself for locating food, she planted her feet and prepared to bring home the groceries. She stretched both hands toward the biggest bunch, intending to break several clumps off. Even with one broken arm, she could still haul enough for everyone to get a taste. *Way to go,* she congratulated herself. *While Adam and Connor are looking for Donavan, I found something to eat, and—*

Plop. Something landed on the back of her outstretched hand. Something big. With legs. The darned thing was so big it nearly covered her hand. Two furry fangs snapped at her, right before it danced up her broken arm like it was after her.

"Spider! Spider!" she shrieked, shuddered, and shrieked again. Shaking her hand to send that creepy insect flying didn't work. Pain from the break radiated up her arm. The huge hairy insect wouldn't let go. Another blood-curdling scream let go all the way from deep in her gut. "B-b-big s-s-spider!"

She stomped the jungle floor. Long yellow legs with clusters of tiny black hairs clutched her arm with the longest stabbing feet. The hairy beast took calculated, mechanical spider steps up her arm, each leg lifting up and stepping down with precise intent until—

It... it stopped.

Tilting its ugly yellow body upward, it faced her like it intended to run straight up her arm, over her shoulder and into her hair. It wanted to build a nest. That's what it meant to do. It was a mother, too. And now it would wrap her up in a fuzzy cocoon and make a nest out of her and feed her body fluids to its gazillion, creep, crawly babies, and...

Oh. My. Gosh! It... it has a thousand eyes. It's looking at me!

Twisting her hair into a ponytail, just in case, Shannon squeezed her eyes shut. Out-of-control goose bumps shivered up her back and into her scalp. That thing was still attached to her arm. It wouldn't let go!

She couldn't breathe. She couldn't move. Spiders could bite. Some were poisonous. The things had fangs! She couldn't bear to look. It was coming. *Sticky! Icky! Scratchy!*

Another scream crawled up her throat, and—

"Shannon!" Adam burst into the small clearing where she stood frozen and still screaming her guts out. He spun her around, her back to his chest with one fist lifted to protect her.

She gasped. He had to be blind not to see the ten-pound monster on the verge of sucking every last drop of her blood out of her hand. Her broken arm hurt when he'd grabbed onto her, but she didn't care. She kept her insect-laden arm paralyzed and stuck straight out in front of her. That thing could be laying eggs on her skin right this very minute. May be inside of her! Pretty soon there'd be thousands of tiny, hairy, hungry, baby spiders running all over her body and— Ewww!

"Shannon. What the hell's wrong?" he growled against her head.

"It's... it's a spider!" she shrieked, her eyes closed and her head turned into his neck, so she didn't have to look at it. "Get it off me!"

His body tensed. She thought he might be scared too, but when he didn't respond fast enough, she peeked one eye open. Bemused blue eyes stabbed hers. He grinned, tipped his head back to the sky, and... *Darn him!*

Adam laughed.

There she was, under attack by what had to be the biggest spider ever, and he laughed. She tried to elbow him away, but he groaned when she bumped his ribs and she thought she'd hurt him. "I'm sorry. I hurt you, didn't I?"

He shook his head. "No. I'm good. Found her," he hollered over his shoulder.

She wouldn't have gone far anyway. There was no way she'd leave the warmth and safety of the solid male body she was planted against, not unless he took her with him.

With a quick flick, he reached out and brushed the huge spider off her arm. He'd actually touched it. *Ewww!* Just that fast, it was gone. Adam didn't even blink, but she shivered all the way down to her toes. *Just great. It's on the ground now.*

She pushed her backside harder against Adam, her eyes riveted to the jungle floor. That thing was down there. Walking. Stalking. Her! She couldn't see it, but something fluttered over her neck. She slapped a hand to cover her bare skin as a burst of goose bumps travelled at the speed of light up the length of her body. Adam had the nerve to chuckle, right before he blew another teasing puff of air down her neck.

"You're laughing at me," she said petulantly, her heart rate still climbing.

He shook his head, but there was a definite playful light in his eyes. "No. I'm laughing *with* you," he said in mock seriousness. "Honest. I'd never laugh *at* you, especially not if you keep pushing your butt against me like that."

Connor crashed through the banana fronds, a hefty stick raised over his head. "What was it? A wild pig? Where'd it go?"

Adam smiled the most glorious smile. It literally cracked his serious face wide open. Shannon wanted to bask in it if not for that remark about her butt, and the fact that he'd laughed at her. Embarrassment warmed her cheeks. Kind of. It *was* a really big spider, but it was hard to stay angry with

Adam after that butt comment. He liked it? She noticed he hadn't let go of her, so she pushed again.

"It could've been a tiger," he teased, his chin in her neck. "It was black and orange like a tiger, wasn't it?"

Another shiver slithered up her spine. "And it had furry legs. Really long legs."

Connor's brows wrinkled. "Long legs?"

"Don't forget there were eight of them," Adam added.

"Quiet, you." Shannon felt her lip sticking out. There she'd thought she was the conquering heroine, only to turn into the damsel in distress. "There was this giant spider, Connor, and it landed on me, and it was really big."

Annoyed disbelief flickered through Connor's eyes before he outright laughed at her, too. Adam still held her tight, but somehow it didn't feel as good as it had before. *Darn men.*

"Don't ever come into the jungle alone again," he scolded, his breath warm and moist in her ear. "I'm not kidding. There might be more than spiders out here. Wait until I have a chance to look around."

"But I found something to eat." She pointed with just the tip of her index finger at the clumps of bananas overhead, no doubt still protected by tiger spiders with hundreds of sticky, hairy legs. She'd learned her lesson. No sense in extending a whole arm when one finger would do.

"I see that. You did good, Shannon. Scared the living hell out of me, but you did good."

"Crap. All that noise over a stupid bug." Connor rolled his eyes, grumbling when he stepped forward and hacked an enormous bunch of bananas from the tree with Ramsey's knife. "It sounded like someone was dying out here."

Shannon kept her mouth shut while Adam escorted her back the way she'd come. They had to walk single file through the bushes where every branch and every leaf could hide another eight-legged beast. She held her breath and kept going, her gaze ever watchful over the top of Adam's head, and her fingers gripping his hand.

Covered with goose bumps, she finally faced Izza, her eyes bright with curiosity. "What was that all about?"

"I found some bananas," Shannon offered weakly, pointing at the rack of green fruit slung over Connor's shoulder. Just looking at the possible spider nests setting on his bare back made her shiver again.

"And..." Adam looked expectantly at her, one brow lifted and his eyes lit with mischief.

Connor still seemed annoyed, his foot tapping.

Shannon bit her lip. "And I found a really big spider. You had to be there. Honest, it was huge."

Darn it. Even Izza laughed.

Chapter Ten

"A tree house? Really?"

Despite their tenuous circumstances, Adam smiled at Connor's question. He looked stricken at the thought of building anything long-term on the island, but something had to be done. All of them were injured. Adam's broken ribs allowed limited movement. The only thing that kept him going was the very obvious fact that he had no choice.

After Shannon's spider incident, they'd returned to the beach to search for more survivors. In the process, they got a better feel for the place. The island they'd crash-landed on was a hundred-acre sandbox in the middle of the Pacific. Palm trees, vines, and shrubbery filled the center; white sandy beaches filled everything else. Night was coming on fast. A pinkish glow already lit the darkening western sky. Except for rescuing Shannon from Spider Man, it seemed an innocuous place to spend a night or two. Or three.

Adam didn't want to entertain the thought that this disaster might extend beyond that. Not with four missing drones and two missing people out there, one who might be dangerous.

The Gulfstream drifted in the shallows as much as a downed wreck could drift. Sparks still lit up the fuselage from time to time, and Adam really wanted to extract the pilot's body and get those three graves dug, but a man could only do so much in one helluva day. The women were their first priority. The dead could wait.

They'd discovered a shallow cove a couple of hundred yards beyond the wreckage. It was no larger than a backyard swimming pool, but there were fish there, and that meant a ready food source. A waterfall would've been a nice touch, but the banyan tree sheltering the innermost curve of the cove was better.

Extensive branching from the parent tree had created a crescent-shaped temple-like structure around the crystal-clear pool. Each of the prop roots were more tree than root, some extended into the salty water. The trunks closest to the edge of the cove had died. That indicated to Adam that the cove was a fairly recent development, or else the whole tree would've been dead.

Jungle vines strangled the columnar trunks of the banyan, but a little hacking might create a suitable ladder for the ladies. At least a shelter on the lower levels would get everyone up off the ground and away from creepy crawlers and snakes, if there were any.

Aside from the knife, there'd been no sign of Ramsey. Donavan, neither. After hours of searching, Adam and Connor were forced to assume the worst. Their flight had suffered a fifty percent casualty rate, and they were lucky to be alive.

In the meantime, the women needed to be cared for, and maybe Connor, too. He still displayed moments of extreme disorientation, as if he didn't remember what had happened. And he'd gotten paranoid, a definite sign that something was amiss in that hard head.

"Think about it," Adam said, hoping to sway Connor to his point of view. "A tree house makes sense. We might be here awhile."

"Nope." Connor was adamant and edgy. "We're getting off this island, if it's the last thing I do. My kids aren't going to be orphans."

Adam bit his lip. He missed his dog, but children were a whole different heartache. "We need shelter, Connor. If it was just you and me, I'd stay on the beach, but we've got the women to—"

"Yeah. I know. I get it." Connor blew out a big sigh. "Heaven knows Miss Reagan can't sleep on the beach with spiders and bugs like the rest of us."

That didn't go as well as Adam had hoped. "You don't want Izza sleeping in the sand, either. She's hurt. She needs a decent place to recuperate."

"No, you're right. Crap, I get it." Connor still seemed agitated. He kept slapping his palm to his thigh. "Let's start on it tomorrow. I don't want to think about it. Not tonight."

"I'll rig a fish trap in the morning," Adam offered. "We'll need more to eat than bananas."

"Yeah." Connor let out another big sigh and another slap. "Bananas."

"Are you feeling okay?"

"Yeah. No." Connor shook his head, cringing as if that simple motion hurt more than his skull. "It's Izza. Her leg's bad, and she's running a fever. I've got no antibiotics. Crap. Everything went down with that plane. I don't have anything to clean that cut. She needs stitches, too."

That explained part of Connor's foul mood. He was worried.

"Let's get back to the ladies," Adam offered. "It's late. We'll search the plane tomorrow."

"I pulled a metal thing out of her back. Damn woman..." Connor's voice tightened. "She's laying there suffering while I'm out of my head. She needed me, and crap..."

Crap. Connor's cuss word of choice. Adam hadn't known about the thing in Izza's back until then. *That stubborn woman.* He clapped a hand to his buddy's shoulder, still hoping to derail Connor's angst. "You're the one who gave me mouth to mouth, remember? We'll be okay."

"Me?" That got Connor's attention. "Damn. Don't tell anyone."

Adam allowed a small smile. "Don't worry. I'm a firm believer in *don't ask, don't tell.*"

Connor shrugged away from Adam's hand, but Adam couldn't leave it well enough alone. "You are my hero though. Just want you to know. I'll always be thankful for that kiss of life—"

"Shut up!" Connor punched Adam's arm, which hurt his ribs, but made him grin, too.

Their circumstances were pretty darn bleak, but there *were* four survivors, and three of them *were* SERE trained and damned good sharpshooters. Their gear might be at the bottom of the ocean, but all that survival, evasion, resistance, and escape training would count for something. Except for the knife Adam had found, they were unarmed, but no SEAL was ever helpless. No Marine, either. Shannon was the only one they'd have to watch out for.

The way Adam figured, cannibalizing the wreck had better be their next order of business. They'd use what they could to set up a decent camp, establish an around-the-clock guard routine, and hunker down until help showed. He picked up a small tree limb from the sandy beach as they walked. Even that small movement sent a painful reminder to his ribcage.

Approaching their camp, which was simply where they'd left the ladies, Adam spotted the glow of a fire. It was small, but a definite surprise. Did Izza have a lighter he didn't know about? He waved Connor to stand back in the shadows with him. Together, they listened and watched who they'd thought was the weaker sex.

Shannon sat cross-legged at Izza's side, leaned over and peering down, her brows knit in concentration as she worked something around Izza's leg. Drawing in closer, Adam saw that Shannon had torn the sleeve off her very expensive designer blouse. She'd used it to make a decent bandage for the slice on Izza's leg.

Izza leaned against the tree with her fingers knitted together over her chest, quietly watching while Shannon tied bows to hold the bandage in place. Adam couldn't help grinning. Bows. Three of them. Everything Shannon did was ultra-feminine and just plain adorable.

Both women were bruised and exhausted-looking. She probably didn't know it, but Shannon boasted a black eye amongst the bruises on one side of her poor face, and Izza looked as pale as a Hispanic ghost.

"There now, you're all set." Shannon patted Izza's leg carefully. She leaned back and cocked her head while she surveyed her handiwork. "That ought to hold you. Just don't go running around. The cut looks pretty clean. I'll check it first thing in the morning to make sure it isn't getting infected. Does it hurt?"

"No, but I wish I'd shaved my legs today," Izza muttered. "How's your arm?"

Adam couldn't help but smile when Shannon flexed her broken limb like she was showing off her bicep. Only a very dainty arm showed up for the drill. "It hurts, but I'll live."

"You know, in some parts of the world, people eat spiders," Izza teased.

Adam saw Shannon shiver from where he stood. Her shoulders scrunched, her head shook, and she stroked her sore arm as if she'd gotten chilled. "Ewww. I couldn't do that. Could you?"

Izza shook her head. "I was just kidding, but we might get that desperate. You might not have a choice."

"Uh-uh. No spiders. No bugs, either. And don't go telling me how they eat chocolate-covered grasshoppers in some parts of the world, either." Shannon sounded adamant. "I don't do crawly things, but if the guys go fishing in the morning, I'll steam whatever they catch. Course they'll have to clean it. And cut its head off. I'll need some nice big banana leaves, too. Stuff like that."

"I almost killed a turtle once," Izza replied dreamily. "Me and Connor were lost in the desert and starving. Figured I could make turtle soup out of the old critter."

"But you didn't?"

"Nah." Izza crossed her arms behind her head, watching the fire. "Connor named the darned thing. I couldn't kill a turtle named Homer."

"Why were you starving? How'd you survive?"

Izza grunted. "We tangled with the Sonoran cartel. Not smart. We got ourselves dumped in the desert. It was tough, but we made it. Connor trapped jackrabbits for food. I would've died without him."

"Ewww," Shannon whined. "You ate bunnies?"

"Let me tell you what, girlfriend. When you get hungry enough, you'll eat anything. Besides, these weren't cute, little, fluffy bunnies. They were tough, rangy jackrabbits with long radar ears. I had to boil 'em twice just so we could chew on 'em once."

"In their skins?" Shannon sounded appalled, and Adam smiled. This girl was a breath of pure, fresh air. Naïve to her toes maybe, but as honest and sweet as the day was long. She had to be adopted. In no way did she take after her nightmare of a father.

"Oh, my hell, Shannon. What are you thinking? Of course I didn't cook 'em in their fur. I skinned 'em first." Izza sounded just as appalled as Shannon. "Good grief. Haven't you ever gone hunting before?"

Shannon shook those dirty blonde curls of hers. "Never had a reason to."

"You've never fished or anything in your life?"

Shannon shook her head again. "I'm a writer, Izza, and I own my own publishing company. Plus, I know some pretty good restaurants. I could recommend a few if you'd like."

"What the hell on earth have you been doing all your life, girlfriend? Living in a rich bitch bubble?" Izza sounded harsh, but Shannon lifted both shoulders and giggled. The crystal-clear lilt in her voice caught Adam by surprise. She had a beautiful laugh.

"My gosh, don't you read the tabloids? I've been raised by the megalomaniac of the century. Why would I need to worry about where my next meal's coming from? All I've ever hunted is a way to stay clear of the media frenzy my father creates."

"You do have an interesting dad."

"You could say that."

"So how'd you know about steaming fish in banana leaves then?"

"Discovery Channel."

Shannon's simple answer damned near pulled Adam's heartstrings out of his chest. This was a woman accustomed to the lap of luxury, not living off the land. She shouldn't be there, but there she was, learning to survive and making sure her fellow survivors were cared for even though it meant facing a *really big* spider.

He couldn't take it. He and Connor stepped into view. "Hey. We found a better place to camp. Plan on moving after breakfast tomorrow."

Connor went straight away to Izza, pointing at the fire. "You got matches or something I don't know about?"

Izza looked to Shannon. "It's all her fault," she teased. "She did it."

"How?" Connor asked bluntly, his brows furrowed and an edge to his question.

Shannon smiled shyly. "It was easy. There was a fire in the cockpit. It was still smoking, so I found a long, dried branch and used it to make a torch."

"Yeah, but she had her tinder and firewood ready before she went swimming, so all she had to do when she got back was light it up," Izza said proudly, her palms to the cheery flames. "Nice, huh?"

"Damn it. You went out there all by yourself? In the dark?" That surprised Adam. He didn't know whether to kiss Shannon or spank her. Going into the jungle alone was dangerous enough, but sharks lurked in the shallow surf, not to mention the danger of getting too close to the burning wreck. Didn't this girl know anything? "Don't do it again."

She shrugged. He'd embarrassed her. "Okay."

"You made that fire and you... you helped Izza? Why?" Connor's bewildered question drew Adam's attention back to his buddy. Connor wasn't coping well. Adam understood the feeling. It had been a tough day, but the guy sounded stretched to the limit. Maybe beyond.

"Izza's leg needed to be covered, so it wouldn't get infected. I just wanted to help," she explained.

"Here. Since you're so good at doctoring, I brought you something." Adam changed the subject, holding out the small branch he'd picked up off the beach to Shannon.

The cutest puzzled expression passed through her eyes when she took it. He saw a completely different look when he pulled his shirt over his head. Her heated gaze fastened to his chest and slid quickly down his abdomen. She blinked once, glanced up at him, and blushed.

He looked down at his banged up body. "Damn," he breathed, taking in the sight of all his bruises for the first time. "Guess I should've kept my shirt on. I thought I was going to impress you. Guess not."

Shannon took a step toward him. "You're hurt."

"No. I'm fine," he muttered, one palm forward, halting her advance. "Sit down. Here."

He motioned to the palm tree across from where the Mahers sat. Obediently, Shannon knelt, the stick still in her hand. Adam knelt with her. With one hard tug, he ripped his shirt at one of the side seams, and then the other. Taking the stick from Shannon, he broke it in half and positioned her broken forearm gently between his upper arm and his side, binding her arm to the sticks with more strips of the shirt. It was primitive, but it would work.

"Oh," she said softly, scrunching her shoulders. "It's a splint. Thank you."

"Not a very good one, I'm afraid, but it'll do." Folding the large piece of shirt in half diagonally, he fashioned a sling. "Here. Lean in so I can tie this around your neck."

Shannon pulled her hair to one side so he could reach. The moment her hair brushed against his skin, he felt the current. Tingly sparks danced up his arm. She must've felt it too. Her breath hitched. So did his.

All at once, tying a simple square knot was a very difficult maneuver for a guy with ten thumbs. She leaned in closer, her head bowed, holding her breath. It didn't help. He couldn't get his fat fingers to function properly with her almost tucked against his half-naked body like a lover. The skin at the nape of her neck that she'd just bared looked soft. Kissable. He wondered how she'd taste. If the touch of his tongue might send shivers through the rest of her body. If she made small noises of pleasure when she—

Torrey. For God's sake, stand down.

He forced himself to focus on something else, anything besides that loveliness within reach. *Think knots.* Half hitch. Anchor hitch. Rat-tail stopper. Rolling hitch. Anything but the ivory skin presented to him now.

It took long enough, but at last the knot was square and tight. He gave it one last tug before she straightened and let all her hair fall over her shoulders.

"There," he said hoarsely when he could see her eyes again, glittering with the orange from the fire.

"There," she repeated sweetly. "I feel better already."

He felt better, too.

"My turn." She reached for the shirtsleeves he'd tossed aside. Still joined at the back yoke, they made one long ragged strip. She leaned in with the piece stretched wide. "Lift your arms. Up you go."

He winced as that simple movement sent lightning bolts of pain through his chest.

"Your ribs are broken, I think," she said.

He grunted. "One for sure. Maybe two."

"They hurt?"

Adam nodded. "A little." God, a man had better be careful getting too close to those pretty eyes. He might slip and fall in and never be seen again.

"This should help." Shannon angled her knees between his to get in closer. Inadvertently, her kneecap touched the inseam at his thigh. It wasn't like she bumped his crotch on purpose, but she blushed at the personal contact, and he couldn't take his eyes off of her. The luscious body right in front of his nose beckoned him closer. Rosy-cheeked and flustered, each ragged breath of hers matched his.

He didn't mean to make her feel uncomfortable, but he could tell he did. The sensual tension between them escalated. He caught himself leaning forward, wanting her to bump him again, but Shannon was intent on her task. Reaching behind his back with both arms, her cheek almost touched his chest. Her arms trembled as she looked up. He blinked, amazed at the pleasant storm coursing through his veins and rushing over him.

There was no come-on in her eyes, no *'hey big boy, wanna play'* smirk on her face like the promiscuous hang-arounds at SEAL hideouts. Only innocent concern glimmered there. "Am I hurting you?"

Like she was in any way big enough or strong enough to hurt him. So tiny. So much like a little girl. "No. Not at all," he answered, shocked at the grit in his voice.

Shannon pulled the cuffs of the sleeves around him and together at his chest. Tying the ends together, she leaned over to reach the other half of the stick. When she inserted it into the loop of sleeves, he understood. She meant to tighten that bandage to keep his broken ribs from grinding against each other. Maybe she *was* strong enough to hurt him after all. To borrow Connor's favorite word, *'Crap.'*

He gulped. This next part would to be painful. He wished she'd smooth her fingers over his chest before she started. That would go a long way toward easing his pain. But then again, maybe not. "Go on," he muttered. "Do it fast. Just get it done."

She nodded, her eyes wide and serious. "I will. Take a deep breath."

He tried, but managed only the same shallow intake he'd been able to inhale since the crash. When she twisted the stick once, he saw the fear in her eyes, only this fear was for him. She didn't want to hurt him. "Still okay?"

He nodded, stifling a groan. This kind of pain was nothing.

Staring at him, she twisted the stick quickly, three times in all, her tender gaze never leaving his face. The homemade wrap tightened until a shudder he couldn't control escaped. Sweat trickled down his temples. His spine. She bit her lip, twisting the stick one last time. No slack remained in the improvised bandage, just tension. Just pain.

"More," he ground out, not breaking eye contact. "The tighter, the better. You know it. Get it done."

A tear glistened off her lower eyelid. "But I'm hurting you," she whispered.

"S'okay." To prove he meant what he said, Adam covered her slender hand with his and gave the torture device two more quick, sharp turns that proved her right. Agony roared from that stick straight through his body. His clenched jaw hurt, his teeth too, but she wouldn't see him acknowledge a couple of measly broken ribs. No way in hell. He stared her down, daring himself to break eye contact first. SEALs don't cry, damn it.

"I'm sorry." The tear fell, and pain or not, Adam pulled her close. It hurt like a son-of-a-bitch, but the sadness in her eyes hurt worse.

"No." He breathed as shallow as he could. "Really. I'm okay."

Clasping her close so she couldn't see, he allowed his eyes to close as fire swept over him in a sickening wave. There was only one thing left to do, but he waited until he could move again. The sweat trickling between his pecs betrayed the calm he meant to portray. With her in one arm, he took his other hand and jammed the stick in between his chest muscle and the now tightly wrapped sleeve. It hurt like hellfire, but that primitive support needed an anchor to keep it from unraveling. Like it or not, all this suffering would help him heal.

"You've been hurt so bad." Her fingers moved light and gentle on the foam bandage still covering his healing gunshot wound from the failed South Dakota op. "I'm sorry someone shot you. I wish I had known."

"It's okay," he said again, finally allowing a deep sigh. He'd forgotten the hole in his shoulder. Closing his eyes against the awful day, he tucked her under his chin and focused on breathing. This broken rib was nothing. That gunshot wound was just as insignificant. But the tenderhearted woman in his arms?

Definitely something.

Chapter Eleven

Zombies looked better.

Staring across the campfire at the other survivors made Shannon very aware how lucky they were. She only wished Donavan had been there. A few of his crazy stories would sound good. Where could he be? It seemed odd that everyone else inside the plane was accounted for but him.

And Ramsey. Was he really on this island, too?

She rubbed another cold shiver off her biceps at the thought. An ex-Army soldier, the man had always given her the creeps. He did things. Horrible things. She didn't know exactly what those things were, but that was the feeling she got in her few dealings with him. He came across as over-protective and always too forceful, as if he'd kill at the slightest provocation if it meant keeping her safe. Or something. The way he looked at her made her feel like a mouse, not safe as much a tasty snack in the paws of a very hungry predator. Or a toy.

The last time she'd seen his knife, it was tucked into a knife sheath on his belt, right alongside his gun holster. She couldn't remember if he'd climbed onboard the Gulfstream or not though, and that missing detail bothered her. She scanned the dark shadows beyond the cheery campfire. Where

Ramsey went, his knife went. Was he really out there? Watching?

To make matters worse, the much anticipated dinner was a bust. Yes, everyone ate, mostly because they were starving. The bananas tasted good enough, but they weren't sweet, and their flesh wasn't smooth like the pretty yellow ones in stores. She rubbed the bitter, fruity taste lingering in her mouth with a sore tongue.

After the first bite, she'd given serious thought to fasting, but her hungry stomach had other ideas, so she'd peeled her banana and ate a tiny portion, and then another. Before she knew it, the piece of fruit was gone, and Adam tossed another her way. It lay unpeeled in her lap while she worried the unpleasant sensation lingering on her tongue and palette from the first course. There had to be something better to eat.

"What do you think? Is SAR looking for us yet?" Izza asked from her tree with Connor at her side.

"Search and rescue," Adam quickly interpreted. He'd chosen a spot between her and the Mahers to sit. That act of distancing himself from her bothered Shannon. One minute it seemed like he cared enough to get in close, the next, not so much.

For now, he sat cross-legged, his elbows on his knees while he suffered through another banana. The poor guy still couldn't take a deep breath, though. Shannon felt bad for him. Her attempt to help had also hurt him. His attitude about pain amazed her. He just kept on going, like an army tank with no off switch. After she'd wrapped his broken ribs, he'd gathered more firewood. The only reason he'd stopped searching for Donavan was the dark—that and he had to be exhausted. She was, and she hadn't done one tenth what Adam had.

"They might not be searching for us yet, but I'll bet Alex is," Connor said.

"How?" Izza turned to her hubby.

"Same as always, babe. GPS." Connor pulled his cell phone out of his shorts pocket and wiggled it at her. "Don't worry. He'll find us."

"Yeah. Know that. Just wasn't sure our cell phones would still work after a crash like this." She glanced at the dark ocean and shivered. "I lost mine in the water. I think."

Connor leveled his phone to his nose, his brows wrinkled. "Crap. I thought it would, but it won't turn on. How about yours, Adam? Do you have any bars?"

Adam shrugged. "I doubt there's coverage out here, but no. I've got nothing. No phone. No pistol. It's all at the bottom of the ocean. Shannon?"

All she could do was shrug. She didn't know where Raul had stashed her carry-on.

That drew a moment of somber silence until Izza glanced over her shoulder at the moonlight off the ocean. "I wonder where Donavan is."

The silence turned downright gloomy. With night falling and no cover, Shannon didn't relish the thought of falling asleep. Too many things scurried in the dark, and they sounded larger than spiders or rats.

"What do you guys think happened to our plane?" She tried to change the subject, but caught the averted glances from one agent to the next. Even Izza looked away instead of answering. Yeah. Shannon might have crashed and survived with them, but she was still the outsider, and, oh yeah, Paul Reagan's daughter.

"I looked at the fuselage when I went out there to light my torch," she offered, hoping for some discussion. "Half the cockpit's missing."

"That reminds me," Adam said somberly, staring at the fire. "We've got three men to bury. We'll hold funeral services first thing tomorrow morning after Connor and I retrieve the pilot."

"Do any of you know his name?" Connor asked, looking directly at Shannon.

She shook her head. She'd never thought to ask. He was just another nameless member of her father's staff. Paul Reagan went through employees quickly. It was hard to keep track. As soon as she knew them by name, they were gone.

"The flight attendant's in the jungle directly opposite the starboard wing." Adam added quietly. "I would've buried him, but I ran out of daylight."

"That's Dillon," Shannon said. "Dillon Lorenzo."

"Guess one out of three isn't bad," Connor remarked drily.

She caught his sarcasm. He'd gone from grateful to rude, and she didn't know why. Just because she didn't know the names of all her father's employees didn't make her cold-hearted, like he'd implied. She bit her lip. The balmy eighty-degree weather pattern hadn't changed—just the company.

"He wanted to be a pilot," Shannon continued, feeling like she had to prove she wasn't entirely thoughtless. "He took college classes at night. After work."

The problem was she did care. His green eyes flashed to mind. Dillon was full of life, and a charmer from the ground up. She didn't want to go to his funeral. She wanted to attend his graduation and make sure he flew that Air Force tanker like he'd wanted to. But there was no use trying to make conversation.

Brit's last words lingered, adding to the depressing end of the day. *Take a pill. Get an abortion. I don't care.*

Well, I care. Interlocking her fingers over her barely rounded tummy, Shannon stared into the flames. So much death, and in the middle of it, this little spark of life rested safe inside of her. Dr. Remy had said she was six to seven months along. That surprised her. She was a little bloated, but except for that one horrific moment in front of Adam, she'd never had a hint of morning sickness. Without a regular monthly cycle, she'd had no way to know she was pregnant, either. Wasn't a pregnant woman supposed to turn into a blimp?

That last eight minutes of endurance sex on the floor weighed on her now. She should have fought harder. Maybe kicked and bit, but honestly, she'd never fought for anything in her life. Until now…

She should be happy. Birth was an event to be celebrated. Shannon wished she'd read all that pregnancy information her doctor had given her instead of wasting time researching her father's drones. It would be good to know if this little person tucked safe and sound within her womb was old enough to have all five fingers. Was he sucking his thumb? Did he know how to smile?

Brit was the real dilemma, the poison in the baby's blood. The thought of him squashed any inclination to celebrate or share her good fortune.

Connor pulled Izza into his side as they lay facing the fire. Shannon glanced at them, but just as quickly, looked away. His lips were in Izza's ear. She'd smiled, and Shannon was suddenly aware the she was very much alone. Connor and Izza loved each other. It showed. She had no one but the tiny boy or girl nestled deep in her womb. Eventually that would show, too.

Braiding her hair into a single manageable but dirty bundle, she faced the truth. She was a single mother. That was all. Her father didn't know he would be a grandfather. After his curt response to her request for access to company files, she hadn't felt like sharing her unexpected but lovely secret. Now she wished she had. Happy about it or not, he deserved to know.

Adam pushed to his feet and walked outside the circle of firelight, toward the shore. He'd seemed more and more withdrawn as the night grew darker. *He might be sick*, she thought. *I need to pay attention. Maybe he's hurt more than he knows. Maybe I made that wrap too tight.*

She glanced into the jungle behind her one last time. Ramsey might be there, but he might not. Just the fact that he'd lost his knife seemed to indicate he was no longer as scary as she'd thought.

And if there were more spiders out there, they'd better be afraid of fire. But that thought led to another sad truth. Even the spider belonged somewhere, even if it was just in a bunch of bananas. All she had was a tiny creature inside of her, maybe the size of a gummy bear, maybe smaller. She didn't know. A tear trickled out of her eye, the day at last too much to bear.

"Hey." Adam crouched beside her.

Startled, she jumped. She hadn't heard him return with another armful of branches and driftwood. Hurriedly, she wiped her eyes and turned a brave face, hoping he hadn't seen.

"Hey," she answered hoarsely.

"Mind if I sleep here?" He nodded toward the tree she sat beneath.

Shannon blinked. "Here?" *With me?*

"I mean, you're tired, and I'm tired, and..." He smoothed the sand beside her. "I just thought a little company might help tonight. We could keep each other warm."

She fidgeted, her fingers twirling around each other and over her stomach. Over her baby. Could he tell she was expecting? Did he know what a mess her life was? Did he— care? The awkward moment stretched.

"Hey, it's okay. If you'd rather not—"

"No." She reached for his wrist. "Please. I mean, yes. It makes sense. It won't mean anything. We've already kind of taken a nap together."

That dimple of his deepened and darn. He was adorable when he even hinted at a smile. "Don't worry. I'll keep the fire going all night long."

"Thank you," she said quietly. Pulling her braid over her shoulder, she lay down and faced the flames. He lowered himself to the ground and leaned in behind her.

Shannon steeled herself not to notice the feel of his body. She needn't have worried. Adam placed one big palm politely on her bicep. That was all. Not another part of his body touched hers, not even his knees. Of course. He wouldn't want to get too close to Paul Reagan's daughter. She should've known. Adam was just being kind like he'd said. Nothing more.

It happened slowly. The longer she laid so close to him and still so alone, the more tears eked out between her squeezed tight eyelids. She caught a self-pitying sob just in time.

He must've noticed. "Hey." He pulled her into his chest, his lips suddenly at her ear, and the length of him tight against her. "Don't worry about Connor. He's not usually like that. You did good today. Real good."

All she could do was nod in silent misery, the warmth of Adam's strong body more than she deserved. Brit had soured the whole concept of happily-ever-after. Besides, no one knew about the baby, and she intended to keep it that way.

"Don't cry, Shannon," Adam whispered into her neck. "You're quite the adventurer. Most women wouldn't have a clue what to do out here." He tightened both arms around her, one bicep for a pillow and the other for a blanket. He had to be hurting to do that, but she accepted the comfort he offered.

"I'm not brave," she said, thankful he couldn't see her face or read her expression. She didn't feel like an adventurer. More like a bumbling fool with a scarlet *P* branded on her forehead for '*Danger! Pregnant lady coming through.*'

"Then how is it you're the one who found food and fire for the rest of us, huh?" He was teasing. She could hear it in his voice.

"I'm only trying to help. I didn't want to be a burden."

He squeezed her ever so slightly, his breath in the crook of her neck. "You, Shannon Reagan, are no burden. Trust me. I'd know."

She relaxed, enjoying the calm reprieve. The warmth of his body heat wasn't so bad, either. Spooning might be an odd way to spend the night, but she was glad to be there.

"I need to apologize," he murmured. "I was kinda hard on you a couple days ago."

"No. It's okay. You were fine."

"I was an ass," he muttered. "You didn't deserve that."

"You didn't deserve what happened to you in South Dakota, either."

"No," he sighed. "Sure didn't."

They lay in silence watching the flickering fire, and she wondered how she had come to this point, wrapped in the bear-like arms of a kind man on a deserted island in the middle of the Pacific. He didn't deserve to have the truth withheld from him, either. No. Adam wasn't Brit. He was a good man. Shannon knew it to her soul.

Taking a deep breath, she decided to be the adventurer he thought she was, and tell him about her baby. Now. Before he made assumptions she couldn't deliver on. "Adam?"

"Huh?" he responded dreamily.

"There's something you should know." She wanted to turn and face him, but his arms were connected to his ribs. She figured she'd already hurt him enough. "I'm pregnant," she said softly over her shoulder.

"Hmmm," he breathed. "That's... nice..."

A gentle snore growled against her neck. Didn't it figure?

Adam was sound asleep.

Sea breeze and Shannon. No better fragrance in the world.

Adam opened his eyes to the soft caress of a woman's breath on his chest. Sometime during the night, Shannon had turned into him. She lay sound asleep, her left hand cupping his neck and her head tucked under his chin. It didn't escape him that his left arm was wrapped beneath her, cradling her gently and more than a little possessively. His other palm rested easily on her ribcage, as if it belonged there. The feel of her slender body pressed against his set his heart to pumping. It seemed so natural, as if they'd lain like this a thousand times before. He wished.

Ah, yes. It rained during the night. That was when she'd snuggled into him, and even though it'd hurt, he'd welcomed the warmth of her lush body. The rain hadn't lasted, but Shannon had.

A twitter overhead drew his attention skyward. Palm fronds, birds and blue sky welcomed another day. Soon she would wake, and she might be embarrassed at their intimate hold on each other. He hoped she wouldn't, but just in case, he played it safe. He closed his eyes and let his mind wander to the loveliness of the soft woman in his arms. Her breath. Her uniquely feminine scent. The way her petite frame molded perfectly into his. With her ankle rested between his legs and her knee between his knees, he wished they were tangled beneath sheets instead of across the sandy way from the Mahers.

The day promised more work and maybe more troubles, but for this one single moment, the island did feel like paradise.

Chapter Twelve

"Are you seeing what I'm seeing?"

Adam looked to the black sheet bobbing in the surf at Connor's question.

Morning came bright and early on a deserted island with the glare of tropical sun off the. miles and miles of reflective water. They'd already collected the copilot, whose nametag identified him as the late Frederick Stankowski. Pilot Irwin Bell laid beside him on the shore, both men now face up and their arms crossed over their chests. They'd cut the ends off some empty soda cans bobbing in the surf and used those pitiful implements to carve three graves into the far end of the sandy beach.

Adam and Connor were about to retrieve poor Dillon Lorenzo from the jungle, but Adam's ribs were on fire from the steady activity. He wanted this ugly business of recovery and burial over. A long nap wouldn't hurt, either.

"Crap. It looks like…" Connor splashed into the waves and grabbed the black canopy out of the water for inspection, "…another parachute? Didn't we already recover two from the cockpit?"

Adam nodded. They'd tossed plenty of debris ashore as they'd combed the crash site for a body, or at least, body parts. He still prayed to find Donavan alive. So far, no such luck. But yes. Both cabin parachutes lay on the beach, still in their bags.

Connor dragged the soggy thing to shore, its suspension lines snarled with the nylon canopy. Sleep seemed to have helped him, but his good humor wouldn't last. Adam had seen the cracks. Like now. Connor seemed pleased with his find instead of suspicious like a covert operator ought to be.

But Adam was damned suspicious. His internal warning system flashed to life when he'd first caught sight of the parachute. It could've been an extra that had come unraveled in the chaos, but still. He'd checked when he'd boarded the Gulfstream before he'd taken his seat. That was what HALO jumpers did. They checked in before they strapped in, and he'd found vests and flotation devices, yes. No parachutes. This one was different than the other two. Solid black, not red and white. And it had been deployed.

Connor held his hand out. "Give me that knife, so I can cut three funeral shrouds. We'll save the other parachutes. Who knows? They might come in handy."

Adam bit back any comment, not up to arguing. Connor was right. Concealing the corpses was a good idea. Shannon and Izza didn't need to see that, but this third find spelled trouble. He glanced over his shoulder and back at camp. *Where was that 'roid freak, Ramsey?*

Connor cut through the tangled lines and sliced three portions the size of bed sheets, then rolled the remaining nylon into a ball and tossed it onto dry sand. "Come on. I'm tired. Let's do this."

Adam blew out a slow breath through pursed lips. "I'm with you."

He followed Connor, fighting his weakened physical condition. It had been a long time since he'd hurt this bad. He meant to get the bodies wrapped as quickly as he could, but the sunny day couldn't quell the prickly sensation that someone was out there. Watching.

The pilot had done a decent job bringing the jet down, although it had lost both wings, probably sheared off when they hit. How the copilot ended up beneath the one wing was a mystery, but in all honesty, they couldn't have asked for a better crash landing—the fuselage dug into the sandy beach of their own private island paradise. What were the chances?

Couple that with what obviously were three explosions—one inside the cockpit, one that eliminated the jet portside engine, and another aft. From the cargo door back there was nothing. The tail was completely gone. Adam weighed possibilities and scenarios that this could've been just an accident. Just engine failure. *Bullshit.* He'd seen enough Black Hawks and Osprey brought down by enemy fire to know the difference. This was sabotage. Maybe espionage, too. Maybe worse.

Connor interrupted his silent analysis. He'd halted in mid-stride, the nylon sheets in one hand, the knife in the other. "This mess is all your Miss Reagan's fault."

"What?" Adam took a step back, not sure what had just happened.

"You heard me."

"Yeah, but I'm not sure I heard you right. Why would Shannon be behind the crash?"

"She's the only reason we were in that jet in the first place."

"So?"

"So think about it." Connor faced him now, his usually calm blue eyes as hard as ice and the knife pointed at Adam. "Would Paul Reagan and his men have gotten access to an Air Force bird the way they did this one? And the only reason we flew Reagan One is because at the last moment, she decides she's coming with us."

"Give me a break." Adam couldn't believe what he was hearing. "The only reason Alex agreed to Reagan's demands is because she stepped up and did his dirty work for him."

"Bullshit!"

"Are you saying Shannon is responsible for the crash?"

"You bet I am. Miss Reagan comes to mind in a hurry."

"Knock it off, Connor. What would she have gained? She could've died just like the rest of us."

"But she didn't, did she?" Connor took a step backward and handed the blade handle first to Adam. "How can you not see what I'm saying? It as clear as mud."

Relieved, Adam took the knife from Connor, but *clear as mud?* He looked closer at his friend.

"Don't give me that look," Connor muttered. "Think about it with your big head for once, not the little one in your pants."

Adam bristled. "What's that supposed to mean?"

"I saw you last night. You're getting too close to *Missy Reagan*, Torrey. Every time I look at the two of you, she's in your arms or climbing all over you. You need to cool your jets. Back off."

That was another thing. Connor never called his fellow teammates by their last names. And that *Missy Reagan* jab? Name-calling was unlike easy-going Connor, too. Adam forced a calming breath. *Here we go again.* "Are you okay, man?"

"Just think about it, would you?" Connor pointed to the wreck bobbing in the surf, a hint of hysteria creeping into his tone. "And stop defending her. She's behind this. You know it as well as I do."

Adam didn't argue. The more Connor talked, the more Adam was certain the man needed some serious medical help. Connor was right about a couple things. They'd flown Reagan Air because of Shannon. To make the point for his twisted thought process, she'd stepped to the back of the plane just prior to the rear explosion. That didn't explain the port engine flaming out like it had, or the cockpit damage. It didn't really explain anything at all except that she was onboard, she'd used the restroom, and she'd spoken with Dillon Lorenzo before the trouble started.

"Not Shannon," he muttered again. They were halfway back to retrieve poor Dillon by then. "She only came with us to prove a point."

"No kidding!" Connor blew up, stopping in his tracks. "And she made it, didn't she? She's nothing but a spoiled rich diva who thinks she can snap her fingers, and the world bows at her feet. Her father sure did!"

"That's not what happened, and you know it." This whole conversation had gotten tiresome. "The only reason she came with us is because Alex didn't trust her old man. You weren't there, so you wouldn't know, but that's how it went down."

"And he trusts her now because she wants a tropical vacation? Alex fell for that?" The more Connor talked, the more spun up he became, and the crazier he sounded.

"No. He trusts her because he believed her, and..." Adam bit his lip as he deliberated for a split second. He didn't want to bait Connor, but loyalty was a weakness of his. Right then, he had an enormous loyalty for a certain woman at camp who didn't know he was talking about her behind her back. "I believe her. She's nothing like Paul Reagan. Give her a chance. For hells sake, she's done nothing but try to be useful."

"Yeah, right." Connor rolled his eyes.

"Knock it off. If I were you, I'd be worried about where Ramsey is. He's the dangerous one, not Shannon."

"Why should I worry about a dead man?"

"Because I'm not sure he's dead, are you?"

Connor parted the thick fronds concealing the flight attendant's body. "You know what? I don't care. Let's get these guys in the ground so we can talk in private. We need a strategy, and I don't want her around when we—holy crap!"

"What?" Adam peered around him into the thick foliage.

Poor Dillon still sat slumped forward in his harness, his back against the palm tree, but now, an ominous message had been carved in deep, jagged lines across his forehead. *1 X 1.* Black drips of blood etched his cheeks. Both eye sockets were empty. Only gaping bloody holes stared back.

Adam spat to the side. *Shit.* It had been awhile since he'd seen mutilation like this, and then it had been in a third-world country where barbaric enemies fought with brutal measures. Whoever'd carved on this poor kid meant it as a scare tactic. They were damned cruel, especially if they—or he—meant Shannon to find it.

"Someone just did this." Connor took one step forward, peering closer. "The blood's not dried yet."

There were three sets of footprints in the sand, still damp from the overnight rain, and two of them were theirs. It had to be Ramsey.

Adam's heart stopped. The women! Broken ribs or not, he couldn't run back to camp fast enough, Connor close on his heels.

Izza looked up in surprise. "You guys look like you've just seen—what's going on?"

Connor went to her side of the fire, and Adam went to Shannon on the other. He crushed her into his chest, panting in a full-blown panic he hadn't felt in a long time. His chest burned with the exertion he'd just put himself through, but the thought of Ramsey hurting her hurt worse.

He fisted her long hair in his hands and smothered her under his chin, scanning the brush and nearby jungle for that bastard, Ramsey. Damn it! The knowledge that she'd gone blithely by herself into the jungle scattered his wits again. She'd purposefully followed that error in judgment by swimming out to the wreck to retrieve a spark of fire from the cockpit, again all by herself. She wasn't brave; she was foolish.

Adam couldn't hold her trembling body tight enough or long enough. It could've been her forehead that Ramsey had just carved a warning into. Her pretty face he'd defiled. Her blue eyes he'd gouged out. This woman put herself at risk without any thought to her own safety. What the hell was wrong with her?

She didn't resist his embrace, not like it wouldn't have mattered if she did. Right then, he needed to know she was present and accounted for. All of her, damn it.

"Connor?" Izza asked, balancing on her one good leg even as he held her tight. "You guys are scaring me. What's wrong?"

He glared over his wife's dark hair at Shannon. "Who'd you meet up with yesterday in the jungle, Miss Reagan? You didn't just go looking for bananas, did you?"

"Knock it off." Adam turned his back to shield her from Connor's steely gaze. "You know damned well she wasn't meeting anyone out there."

"What's he talking about?" Shannon asked. "I just went to find—"

"Yeah. Bananas. Right." Connor snapped. "And then you went out to the wreckage all by yourself, didn't you? Why'd you really go alone? Were you meeting someone there, too?"

Adam didn't give her a chance to respond. "You saw her in the jungle. Did she look like she was having a covert meeting with that spider, screaming like she was?"

Connor didn't blink. "I didn't see no spider and right now, I'm not sure what I did see. All I know is that every time we turn our backs, she takes off to places unknown. Why don't you tell us everything you know about your man, Ramsey?"

Shannon peered around Adam to confront Connor. "*My* man? But he's—"

Her heart pounded as hard as his. All these wild accusations weren't helping. With her broken arm against him, the splint dug into his tender ribs. He didn't care. Connor needed to shut the hell up, and they all needed to come up with protective measures.

"He's worked for my father for a long time. Before that, I think he was in the Army, and, umm..." She leaned back and glanced up at Adam. "He used to be some kind of a special ops guy. Why? What's the matter?"

Adam shot a look to Connor, calculating how much he should share with the ladies, but Connor took that for a license to tell all.

"Because some bastard just carved a message into one of your father's employees." He spat the words out. "If it wasn't you, it was someone who works for you. It was Ramsey, wasn't it? He's here, isn't he?"

"Connor. Stop it," Izza muttered, her palm to his chest. "Shannon wouldn't do that."

"Well, someone sure did!"

Connor had never sounded so unlike himself. Usually the most laidback operator and the biggest tease on the team next to Harley, he'd changed into a mean, paranoid man, his eyes as sharp as daggers. All the signs were there. Hyper-vigilance. Paranoia. Connor was suffering from post-traumatic stress. Big time. And he was taking it out on Shannon.

"W-w-what...?" She shook so hard she could barely speak. She tried again. "W-what did it s-say?"

"You know what it said. Don't play your lying game with me. One by one. He's coming for us, *Missy Reagan.*" Connor mimicked Ramsey's condescending greeting for Shannon yet again. "One by one. Did he come up with that clever line all by himself, or is that what you told him to carve?"

Adam took a firm step around Shannon, his fists clenched, and tired of Connor's unwarranted attack.

"Shit, Connor," Izza cursed again, but Shannon's knees buckled. Adam went to ground with her.

"He... I..." She huffed, her head down. "He always says that. It's like his motto or something. When I divorced Brit..." Adam still had hold of her, his arms and legs wrapped around her in an awkward embrace. "He said... he said he'd keep everyone away from me... one by one... if that's what it took. He used those same words, Adam. He did this."

Ramsey was a total nut job, but his thinking he was in love with Shannon might explain his bizarre message. Still, why carve on Dillon? Out of revenge? Ramsey had no idea she'd spoken with the flight attendant. He was either in the hold by then and geared up for a parachute jump or... what? Setting the timer on the bombs he'd placed in the cabin? Blowing the aft hatch and stealing the drones after take off? Then why the hell was his knife on the island? The more Adam analyzed what he thought he knew, the more questions he had.

"Was that jerk infatuated with you? Did he stalk you?" Adam had to know.

Shannon shivered in his arms. "Gross. Oh no, so gross. He always gave me the creeps when Father assigned him to escort me."

Adam glared at his buddy, expecting another unfounded accusation, but Connor only sneered back. *Keep it up, buddy, and I'm going to knock your head off.*

"Was it... was it...?" Shannon blew out a big breath. Finally, she faced Connor. "Was it Dillon?"

"Yes." He spat the one-word bullet at her.

She bowed her head and whined. "No, no, no. He was a nice boy. He was supposed to go to school. He wanted to be a pilot, and... no!"

Despite his burning ribs, Adam held her tighter still. "Dillon didn't suffer, Shannon. You remember he died from the crash, don't you?"

"I know but…" she drew in a long, quivering breath, "he didn't deserve that."

"None of us did, Missy Reagan," Connor growled.

Izza pushed gently away from her husband, her hand on his cheek. "Why are you being so mean to Shannon? You don't feel good, do you?"

Connor's jaw dropped. He looked at her with something akin to horror. "I'm just trying to take care of you."

"But you do know I can take care of myself, don't you?" She ran her fingers through his hair. "Come here, baby. Let's sit down and talk about this. Shannon's our friend. She wouldn't hurt us. You know better than that."

Just that fast the fight was over. Connor sank to the sand and Izza sat on his lap, her injured leg stiff in front of her. Adam pressed Shannon against him, still not willing to let her go. Ramsey *was* out there, and this island was small. He could be watching them this very minute and planning his next move.

"You're not to go anywhere by yourself from now on, do you hear me?" he muttered into Shannon's ear. "Never again. You go; I go. That's the rule, and you damned well better follow it."

"I was just trying to help. Everyone's hurt, and I thought… I just thought…" She choked back a sob. "You're all so capable, and I'm just a civilian, and I wanted to help."

"I know." Adam held her tight, wincing as he did. *Damned broken ribs.* "And you did exactly what I would've done. You helped all of us, just don't do it again."

He pressed his forehead to hers. Soft teary eyes blinked back at him. The woman in control he thought he'd seen a day ago was gone. "Ramsey is out there, Shannon. Don't go anywhere alone. Promise me."

She nodded, wiping her face, and the truth sprang up within his heart. It was happening. He had to keep her safe. There was no way this tender woman was guilty of the insinuations Connor had just leveled against her. Izza didn't seem to think so, either.

Izza faced Adam, her arms still wrapped around her husband's neck. "Let's get those bodies buried, then we need a better position than this beach. It's too open."

Adam nodded. "We found an inlet. It's shallow, but it's full of fish and there's fresh water nearby. How's the leg?"

Izza smiled at Shannon. "Ask my lady doctor-friend there. Whatever she did, it feels a lot better."

"I just cleaned it," Shannon whispered. "That's all." Carefully, she pushed out of Adam's arms and wiped her face.

Izza offered that cocky smile again, the most reassuring thing on the island at the moment. "Let's keep our eyes open."

"I will too," Shannon said quietly, like she was part of the team. *His team.*

Her answer made Adam smile. Between the three of them, they could handle Connor. With a war-hardened Marine like Izza, and a city girl willing to take chances, it was just a matter of timing before they handled Ramsey, too

Any sniper knew that.

Chapter Thirteen

Seven days already. One week. And still no sign of search planes. No sign of anything.

The funeral laid the dead to rest, but it created more questions, too. Adam hadn't noticed the true cause of death to the pilot, copilot, or flight attendant until he and Connor moved Dillon's body. All the blood pouring down the poor guy's neck hadn't come from massive internal bleeding or any injury relevant to the crash. The young man's throat had been cut.

They'd hurriedly checked the copilot's body then. He hadn't died from the crash, either. Neither had the pilot. Both were stabbed. Apparently, Ramsey had been real busy once he'd landed. He'd taken out the experts in crash survival first. If it was Ramsey.

Damn it, Adam knew a killer when he saw one, and Ramsey fit the bill to a T, but the guy wouldn't have parted willingly with his prized weapon, nor would he have simply lost his knife. Special operators didn't lose anything, not unless they meant to.

The mystery deepened. If it wasn't Ramsey running the show, then who? The puzzle of the missing drones nagged just as much. Where the hell were they and were they armed? Not one night had gone by he hadn't fought sleep, half expecting one or all four of them to show and lay waste to their pitiful camp. That annoying itch between Adam's shoulder blades never let up. Someone was watching. Maybe the drones…

The only carry-on Adam and Connor had located so far was Izza's, which proved a good thing. Like any mother and wife, she'd over-prepared. Tucked under one of the passenger seats instead of stowed in an overhead compartment, her carry-on hadn't turned into a flying object. The darn thing didn't even get wet.

While it lasted, they had a first-aid kit with Ibuprofen, a couple of antibiotics, and sunscreen. She'd also brought a travel-sized sewing kit, and now sported a nicely stitched leg wound, thanks to Adam's skill with a needle and a piece of the nylon filament pulled from the parachute. So far, so good. Her leg was healing, her back didn't bother her, and she was on her way to being herself again.

Connor was another problem altogether. One minute he was cheerfully helpful, the next, adversarial and combative. Exhaustion seemed to trigger his tantrums. It was the day after the funeral, when he'd helped Adam drag one leather recliner from the Gulfstream through the surf that he'd turned on Izza. Even Shannon stopped in her tracks to watch that mistake.

"I'm sick and tired of you telling me what to do," he'd bellowed. "Back off!"

"Come on, Connor—" Adam had tried to intervene.

"You, too! Stay the hell away! You're all after me; I know it. You think I can't hear you talking behind my back? You think I don't know you're gunning for me?" Connor had backed into the surf like he was surrounded, but Izza never hesitated, not even once. She'd marched right up to him.

Adam worried that Connor might hurt his wife. He towered over Izza, but whatever she'd said took the fight out of him. He'd spent most of the time since then sprawled on the cover of a banana leaf floor and sound asleep. The man was hurting. Adam just hoped rest was all Connor's brain needed. Adam didn't want to bury anyone else.

Dire necessity had become the mother of innovation. Their limited arsenal consisted of Ramsey's blade, two pocketknives, Izza's pocket-sized Beretta, which she'd had the good sense to pack in her carry-on, the cockpit crash axe, and a handful of Chinese stars, also courtesy of the deadly Mrs. Maher. The woman knew how to pack.

The utility tools on the Swiss Army knives provided a means for Adam to remove wall paneling from the wreck. The crash axe allowed him to split several downed trees and turn them into primitive planks.

So far, he'd improvised three separate three-sided enclosures, one for the Mahers, one for Shannon, and one for the head, discreetly located far enough from the cove for the sake of privacy, yet close enough to hear a scream if trouble came calling.

For himself, Adam opted for nothing more than a higher lookout in the banyan to keep watch over all. The tree's branches were sturdy, wide, and comfortable enough.

A freshwater shower or a waterfall would've been a godsend, given the harsh effects of saltwater on a person's skin. He intended to remedy the lack of that convenience when he could, but for now they relied on the fresh water from the two island streams. One emptied into the cove, the other at their first campsite. Adam fully intended to explore the entire island when he had time, but he refused to leave his compromised friends to fend for themselves.

When his ribs complained too much, he rested. When they barely complained, he pushed harder. Work had to be done. For now, they reminded him with every swing of the axe that they weren't healed enough for the strenuous work he put them through. He ignored them. Too many things could happen. Ramsey was still out there. A storm might hit the island. Pirates. Anything and everything seemed possible.

Dressed in her slacks, now reduced to cut-offs, Shannon stalked the cove with a sharpened wooden spear for those pesky fish. Adam had fastened a sliver of metal debris from the Gulfstream into one end of her weapon for added killing power, then rigged the nylon netting between wooden stakes at the mouth of the cove. He pulled the net aside every night. When the tide came in, the day's catch came in with it. He closed the trap and on most days, Izza went fishing and they ate fairly well.

Today Shannon took over that chore. She hadn't actually caught anything yet, but he had to give her credit for trying. The woman didn't seem to have it in her to sit down and feel sorry for herself. She'd had a couple of weak moments. Who hadn't? Her broken arm kept her off-balance, but she didn't complained. Not once. And she looked good trying to be helpful yet again. Damned good.

Izza puttered around the camp, scavenging when something useful washed close enough to shore, reorganizing their 'stuff' when she couldn't scavenge. The woman knew how to repurpose and make do.

Once she'd become mobile, she'd gone into the waves time and time again to retrieve everything and anything she could, including both of Adam's boots. She only found one of Connor's, a decent trade considering most of the heavy work fell to Adam for the time being. Her storehouse of scavenged stuff lined the area where they'd first camped. Connor kidded it would all blow away in the first tropical storm. Izza just smiled.

For now, they had stuff. Lots of stuff. Including a pan for boiling water, plastic containers for fresh water, and four of the recliner-style passenger seats from the Gulfstream around their fire pit by the cove. If she'd had her way, the refrigerator from the galley would be front and center of their cozy camp, but that project required more muscle than Adam had at the moment.

With one eye on the women, he pulled his mind back to the necessity at hand. Eventually, he planned on a tree house, but for now, each rough-hewn board he hacked out of the downed trees would be used to strengthen their flimsy camp with better walls. Maybe fences. All those civilized things folks back home took for granted.

The parachutes had become a handy resource. Three braided strips of the nylon fabric made a decent rope to secure the boards until Adam could figure out something stronger. Little by little, the banyan was becoming home, sweet home. Well, home anyway.

Wiping the sweat from his forehead and eyes, Adam took a moment to catch his breath. It never failed. If he wasn't worrying about Ramsey, he was thinking of Donavan. Where the hell was he? Adam would've preferred digging another grave than the confounded pain of not knowing.

That missing detail would make breaking the news to Donavan's parents more difficult. *Lost at sea* was just as vague and twice as useless as *missing in action*. Both left loved ones wondering for the rest of their lives. Of course, that only mattered if and when they were rescued. Until then, they were all lost at sea. Every last one of them missing in action.

The glint of a reflection far out at sea caught his attention, and Adam stopped again to catch his breath. He stretched the ache out of his back and neck muscles. Whatever it was— ocean-liner, cargo ship, or fishing trawler—the shiny glint of hope was too far away to get excited about. He stared at it until the glitter dropped over the horizon like the others over the past days. Without any way to communicate with a passing freighter, there wasn't much more to be done. That this little speck of an island wasn't in any major shipping lanes had already become abundantly clear.

"Got it!"

Adam turned at Shannon's delighted voice, followed by a lot of splashing. She was in the cove, dancing like a little girl with her spear stabbed into the sandy bottom of the cove. "Look, Izza, I did it. I caught one."

"Don't just stand there. Toss it on shore before it gets away," Izza advised.

Adam smiled at her childish joy at catching her first fish and froze. A gray-striped blur of bunched muscle and fur pounced just as she lifted her neatly speared catch out of the water and held it high. She was still celebrating her success when the animal flew past her head, snagged her prize, and disappeared into the jungle.

Izza laughed. Not Shannon.

"Did you see that?" she asked in awe, but then her voice hardened. "He stole my fish."

By now, Izza had to hold her stomach, she was laughing so hard. Adam tried not to chuckle, but Shannon didn't do angry very well. She turned to him, her eyes blazing. "Did you see that... that thing?"

He couldn't hold his grin back. This woman was just plain sweet to the core. "I did."

"You're laughing at me, too? But I'm trying to help and... and..." She turned away, and damn. He'd hurt her feelings again. She seemed more sensitive with every passing day. Like the man he was, he dropped his axe against the log he'd been jacking on and splashed his way into the shallow cove to make amends. "I'm sorry."

"Never mind." She turned away. "I'll show you guys. I caught one fish and I'll catch another, and when I do, I'll show that flying cat creature, too. We're having fish again today, darn it." With that said, she raised her spear over her shoulder, once again stalking the mighty fish of the dangerous, two-foot deep waters.

Izza winked at Adam, so he joined her at the edge of the cove. "Is he any better?" he asked, his eyes on the audacious Amazon warrior.

"The swelling's gone down," Izza said, "and he isn't having those headaches anymore. I think we're past the worst of it."

"Good."

"You do know it took her all morning to catch that one fish," she muttered quietly out of the side of her mouth. "Think I should teach her the right way?"

Adam shook his head. "Not yet."

No reason to spoil the show. Shannon looked prettier every day, and it was more than just the blonde streaks in her hair or her deepening tan. The now sleeveless blouse hanging over her waist added to the mystique. Her tongue sticking out while she concentrated on stabbing another fish didn't hurt, either. She glowed, an odd development considering their meager diet of fish, fruit, and coconuts. It had to be all the sun.

"You like her, don't you?"

He nodded. Liking Shannon wasn't the problem. His feeling went far beyond that simple emotion. He couldn't ignore the fierce trumpet call to protect her that had sounded deep inside his gut. Other body parts, too. Anymore he hardened at the mere sight of her. The slightest sigh from her lips. The slightest brush of her fingertips on her bronzed skin or through her hair.

He chose to be more careful. Sharp-eyed Izza had already picked up on it. Connor too. The only one who didn't seem to know how much he cared was Shannon. He'd caught her shy looks in his direction on occasion, but other than the day she'd wrapped his broken ribs, she had yet to reciprocate. Either she wasn't interested, or she thought she was too good for him.

Whether he wanted to believe it or not, that assessment was likely true. Until this crash, Shannon and he had travelled in different circles. Their singular need to survive was the only common thread between them at the moment. Rescue would break that thread. She'd go her way. He'd go his, and that would be that.

Maybe...

Leaning back on his elbows, Adam stretched both legs and watched. Shannon may not be interested in him, but he was interested in her. He couldn't seem to catch a breath when she was around, and it had nothing to do with the limited capacity of his lungs.

A covert operator spent a lot of time alone stalking his prey, and Adam had never minded the solitude. Until now. The magnetic energy from her slight frame pulled at him like the moon did the tide. Even now, he wanted to go to her, wrap her up in his arms, and show her how to hold that spear and how to aim. He wanted to teach her where to strike, and where to hunt those skittish fish, how they hid in the shadows. Guide her arm when she struck. Hell, he wanted to kiss the breath out of her. Who was he kidding?

He'd sensed the difference between him and her that day in the Sit Room, but attributed it to the power of her family name. Seemed he was wrong. The compelling draw of her spirit had nothing to do with her being a Reagan, but everything to do with her soul.

Shannon believed in the inherent goodness of people. Even Connor's. She had yet to engage in his tirades, just let Izza handle him when he spouted off. How she'd escaped her father's manipulative nature amazed Adam, but she had.

Her gullibility made her dangerous to her teammates, though. She'd put them at risk twice now by innocently walking into danger. What if Ramsey had gotten to her in the jungle instead of that silly spider? What if a shark had attacked her on her quest for a nice cozy campfire? In both scenarios, Adam wouldn't have thought twice. He would've risked his life to save hers. She could've gotten him killed. Maybe Connor and Izza, too.

Adam brushed a quick hand over his face wishing it provided a mask. He'd altered their sleeping arrangement in direct proportion to his awareness of her tempting body. Instead of spooning like they had that first night, he now kept a respectable distance and his hands to himself. Close quarters could make two strangers best friends or nasty enemies. He couldn't take the chance. It might also make them lovers.

He suffered in hard-on agony most nights as it was, and a goodly portion of most days. That thin excuse for a blanket he'd fashioned out of a parachute wouldn't stop him if he'd been inclined to have his way with her. Or if she'd so much as hinted that she wanted him. But she didn't, and he wasn't the kind of guy to take what wasn't offered.

So he watched the pretty lady of the cove, the huntress who didn't know she was brave. The warrior who'd faced a hostile business world without being sucked into its cynicism. The tender woman with the spear who was quickly becoming his whole world.

No way!

Shannon caught the movement to her left out of her peripheral. Something rustled just beyond the bushes. Then silence. It was him. That darn cat thing. He'd returned, and he was creeping in for another easy catch that she'd worked for. He thought he was pretty clever.

Well, two can play this game, Mr. Wildcat. I've got news for you. I'm hunting you, too.

She took two cautious steps toward her furry foe, crouching low, her arm cocked, and her trusty spear poised to strike and strike hard. *Now we'll see who's the better hunter.*

The lacy fronds at ground level moved ever so slightly. She froze. He knew she was there. She allowed a smile at this feline's curiosity. *Not this time kitty-cat. It's you or me, and I'm...*

Two dark eyes stared out from beneath the leafy undergrowth. Human eyes. A man's blackened face pressed through the leaves. Bare shoulders supported by bloody arms and dirty hands followed.

"It's a... It's a..." She couldn't get the words out. Shannon spun around, and ran face-first into Adam's rock-solid chest.

He shoved her behind him. "Donavan?" he rasped, his head cocked as he set her aside. "What the—"

"Donavan!" Izza charged past them, splashing through the cove and dropping to her knees beside the man. "Where've you been? Oh, my hell, you're..."

He collapsed against her. "Water," he croaked.

Shannon ran and retrieved a plastic bottle filled with fresh water. Charging back through the cove, she handed it to Adam and stepped back. He'd already rolled Donavan to his side and cradled him in his arms while Izza checked him for injuries.

"Here you go, buddy." Adam held the bottle to Donavan's cracked lips.

Donavan drank greedily, squeezing the bottle tight and sucking it dry. When empty, he sagged against Adam. The man was filthy, covered with sores. He stared at her, then Izza, and finally returned his gaze to Adam. "He's got... the drones."

The shiver she'd gotten from the spider was nothing compared to the chill that sluiced over her rattled nerves. The drones. The solar-powered, forward-thinking, decision-making Hummingbird Hawks. Pterodactyls. Hunter killers. Even Adam had called them killer bees. And they were there on the island. With Ramsey.

"Where?" Adam asked. "Where is he?"

"The caves..." With a groan, Donavan clutched Adam's bicep. "He's coming for her."

Adam brushed a gentle hand over Donavan's cheek. "Come on, buddy, take it easy. What caves?"

Donavan blinked desperate eyes at Adam. "She's not... who we think she is," he ground out.

"Who isn't who we think she is? Shannon?" Izza asked, her palm to Donavan's forehead. "Come on, big guy. You're burning up with fever. What are you trying to tell us?"

With a groan, he went limp before he could answer.

"Help me move him," Adam ordered.

Shannon sprang into action. She lifted one of Donavan's legs, and Izza the other while Adam carried him by the armpits, and together they transferred him through the cove to where Connor lay sound asleep. Once on his back again, Izza busied herself undressing Donavan, while Adam checked for injuries. They looked like they knew what they were doing, so Shannon stayed out of their way.

"He's been undercover," Adam said. "That's why we couldn't find him. He used some kind of reddish tint, berry juice maybe to camouflage his body. That's why he's so dirty. The streaks on his face are ash, probably from a campfire."

Shannon rubbed the goosebumps off her sore arm. They had a campfire. Could Donavan have entered their camp without them knowing it? While they were sleeping? Had Ramsey?

"Adam." Izza sat back on her legs, pointing to a nasty black line on Donavan's upper thigh.

"Damn," Adam muttered. "He's been shot."

"Creased." She traced the two-inch long wound with her fingertips. "It's not septic yet. Shannon, get the first-aid kit. I need more water, too."

Glad for the opportunity to help, Shannon ran to the stream for more water. It took a few minutes to stoke the embers in their fire pit and get the water boiling, but the moment she'd sterilized one of the Swiss Army knives, she handed it to Adam.

Deftly, he opened the wound with one quick flick of his wrist. Donavan didn't move. Izza cleaned and flushed the wound, while Shannon folded one of the linen napkins from the Gulfstream for a bandage.

Half asleep, Connor raised to one elbow. "What's going on? Crap. You found Donavan?"

"More like he found us," Adam muttered. "He's been shot. Give me a hand. I need to stitch this wound."

Connor joined in, and Shannon was amazed at how well these three agents functioned as a team. One minute Adam was giving orders, the next Izza. Even Connor offered up a terse "Hold him still, damn it." In no time, Donavan's wound was stitched and dressed.

Adam convened a team meeting at their friend's side. He motioned for Shannon to join them, so she sat cross-legged next to Izza. Adam cut to the chase. "Ramsey has the drones. If he knows how to activate their homing stations, we're in trouble."

"Do you think he can, though?" Connor asked. "How would a security guard know how to control that level of technology?"

"There's no way to know for sure, but once their batteries are fully charged, yes. Ramsey's perfectly capable." Adam looked to Shannon. "That takes what? Seventy-two hours for a full charge?"

She nodded. He'd taken command without a word, and Connor and Izza let him. There was no arrogance or condescension in Adam. He was gathering his forces, not stepping on them. Shannon listened while he led. He seemed to be a natural-born leader.

"Wait. He's got to have a visual feed to see what those drones see, doesn't he?" Izza asked.

"He's got a laptop. I saw one in the cargo hold," Adam replied.

"But even a laptop needs a power source, unless it's solar-powered, too." Connor looked to Shannon when he said that. "Well? Is it?"

She shrugged. "I honestly don't know, but it makes sense. My father developed the solar-energy technology the drones run on. If he can do it for drones, why not computers?"

"Then we need to acquire that laptop," Izza continued.

"Agreed," Adam shot back. "How?"

"That's why Donavan was out there," Connor said thoughtfully. "He must've intercepted Ramsey after we crashed. Maybe witnessed the murders and followed him."

"And Ramsey took a shot at him," Adam added. "Donavan mentioned something about caves before he passed out. I know we didn't cover the entire island, but did you see any cave while we were scouting?"

Connor shook his head.

"Then it's got to be subterranean," Adam said quickly. "Izza..." He paused, looking at her long and hard, like he couldn't decide what to say next.

She must've read his mind. "We go out two by two, Adam. You know the rule. No one hunts alone. Not even for a bloodsucker like Ramsey. No."

He sighed, and Shannon understood his dilemma. There were only two capable covert operators right now—Izza and Adam. Connor might be feeling like himself at the moment, but Adam didn't trust him alone with Shannon. No, Izza needed to stay with Connor to keep him calm, and she, Shannon, was pretty much deadweight. Adam had already made sure she understood she wasn't to go anywhere by herself.

"There's something else." Shannon bit her lip. Instantly, all eyes were on her, but her friends needed to know. "I didn't find out until the night before we took off, but these drones were built with artificial intelligence."

"They what?" Connor asked. "They have a brain?"

"Yes. Each of them has a fully functional microprocessor. It's how they can be programmed to work together. Like you guys. Like a team."

"Ha," Izza snorted. "More like a hunter-killer team."

"Are you telling us they know how to think?" Connor asked.

"And make decisions," Shannon answered.

Adam stared at her before he blew out a deep sigh. "Damn. That's bad."

"We're sitting ducks," Izza breathed a low growl. "He's got four armed drones with lasers that can vaporize us on sight, and we've got nothing but a couple knives and a gun."

"I know the code to shut them down." Shannon blurted it out before another word was spoken. Again, three sets of piercing eyes drilled hers. Connor shot a dark glance toward Adam. He probably still thought she was working with Ramsey, but right now, she didn't care what Connor thought. Adam had faith in her.

He proved it when he brushed his hands on his knees and stood. "Then it's settled. You're coming with me."

Chapter Fourteen

Adam would've preferred Izza's company over Shannon's on a covert operation. Izza knew black ops down to her soul. She could and had taken on bad guys twice her size and made them cry for their mommies. She just didn't know drones.

But then, gearing up to go dark used to mean strapping on NVGs, as in, night-vision goggles, loading up a dozen flash bangs, as many clips or magazines as he could carry, maybe a garrote, and always—as in always—a sharp knife and another gun or two. Make that three. Maybe a compressed parachute if there were any chance things might take an aerodynamic spin.

Tonight, it meant that Shannon dressed in one of Izza's black TEAM shirts and zero-dark-thirty cargo pants, while he smeared soot from the campfire over his face and down his neck and arms. It was interesting that Izza had brought work clothes on what should have been a second-honeymoon, but that was Izza. Always ready for trouble.

While Shannon changed clothes, Adam made a muddy concoction of berries and ash. He smeared his bare chest, his arms, up his neck and face while Connor covered his back. No skin must show. Not tonight.

Then it was Shannon's turn to get dirty. Any surface or flat plane of her bare skin, any part of her that would catch moonlight, had to be concealed. She held her breath and trembled beneath Adam's fingertips. It would've been a whole lot nicer if he'd been doing something a little more intimate than covering her with cinders. Like coconut-scented suntan lotion. Whipped cream. Sweet chocolate syrup. Maybe some honey. Anything but getting her ready to go undercover for her first black op.

Big, scared eyes blinked up at him while he applied ash to her forehead and down her nose. "I can do this, you know," she declared bravely.

He nodded in the affirmative, fighting the urge to dip his fingers below the collar of her T-shirt and cup the soft, sweet mound of her breast. That was the kind of dirtying-up he and she should be doing. Drawing closer. Talking. Touching. Exploring each other's bodies instead of infiltrating a dangerous killer's lair.

With no time to second-guess his decision to take her with him on the hunt for Ramsey, Adam sat her down between Connor and Izza, and together, they'd bombarded her with one piece of black ops advice and know-how after another.

At last, he felt sure she understood how every breath and sound might be the difference between life and death. How buddy teams moved in sync, never alone.

At least, she'd heard enough to be minimally capable. There was no other way. They didn't have the luxury of time. The drones had to be disabled.

"What are you thinking?" Connor asked quietly while Izza checked Shannon's paint job one last time.

Adam lifted his chin at the jungle. "The usual. We'll stick to the edge of the jungle. Keep a low profile. Find the bastard."

"Just recon?"

"Maybe more. Depends how many we find with him. If Ramsey's alone out there…" Adam let Connor fill in the blanks. When Ramsey moved, Adam intended to follow. If the gods of war and chaos were on his side, he intended to give Ramsey his fancy knife back, too.

"She's no operator," Connor murmured, his gaze fastened on the women. "It might be better if you stick to the jungle and don't engage. Track him to his camp if you can. See how many are working with him. Then tomorrow we leave Shannon with Donavan and the three of us go after Ramsey."

Connor actually made sense. As much as Adam needed to locate Ramsey, he needed to take care of his team more. "Agreed," he said softly, scanning his partner one last time. Shannon had donned Izza's black canvas sneakers. She'd have decent foot protection in the jungle. No flash of white showed anywhere. *Good girl.*

"I'll be waiting for you," Connor declared at their departure, his hands on his hips. His eyes seemed clear for a change, but something in Adam refused to change the roster and take Izza instead of Shannon just because Connor was having a good night. Call it male ego. Call it jealous pride. Adam wanted Shannon at his side, and no one else's.

"Take care of him, Shannon," Izza said, with a firm nod. "He's our best flying squirrel."

"Look for us at dawn," Adam answered. "If he's prowling our camp at night like I think he is, we should at least know where he's holed up and how many he's got with him. Take care of Donavan."

"You got it," Connor murmured. "Later."

Adam stepped out with Shannon at his six.

The moon was high in the east. Creeping from shadow to shadow, Shannon did a good job of keeping up and keeping quiet. He recognized the banana tree where she'd encountered her spider. If they could get past this shadowy den of a thousand screams, they could make it anywhere. She stiffened when it came her turn to pass. That was all. No gasp, and no scream. *Good girl.*

They were well past the spider tree when a small creature scurried through the brush beside them, then stopped. Adam halted and signaled Shannon to do the same. A frightened animal might squeal, squeak, or raise an alarm. Before he moved another foot, that creature needed to decide there was no danger in the jungle tonight and to walk away. It didn't. The darn thing was curious.

It rustled closer until it stopped at his boot. Small, short-eared, and bright-eyed, a sliver of moonlight made the creature visible in the dark night. A long snout pointed up at him. The thing was friendly. It sniffed the cuff of his jeans, but when it rested a paw on his boot like it meant to climb aboard, it was time to discourage the little guy.

Adam would've moved his foot to scare it off, but the nervy rodent did a quick about-face and shook its tail. Damned if it didn't pee on his boot before it squeaked and disappeared back into the brush. He was officially marked territory. Adam's heart flew homeward to Seamus. The goofy dog would've had a field day chasing the pesky rodent.

Stealthily, they skirted the island, a boot-shaped piece of rock and sand with a narrow spur that jutted into the sea at the southwest side. The jungle was alive with insects, a good indicator that all was well. Nature tended to quiet down in the wake of large predators, and Adam banked on that tonight. All five senses were hyper alert and tuned to the slightest signal, a brush of skin or clothing against leaf, the snap of a twig or the crush of sand or gravel beneath a heavy foot. But no such noises came to him.

Shannon proved as silent as he was, maybe more so. He could hear and feel the throb of his pulse. Not hers.

On the opposite side of the island, he called a rest stop within the temple columns of another Banyan. Shannon didn't say a word, looking out at the deserted beach and the waves rolling to shore. The quiet moment begged a kiss, one he considered giving her, but that kind of thinking got an operator in trouble. He pushed the temptation off.

There was still no sign of Ramsey. Nothing to indicate any human being had been there. No campfire. No marks in the sand. Just the great wide Pacific aglow with moonlight. Adam jerked his head toward the jungle. Shannon offered up one quick nod and followed. There was more than one way to skin a cat, and if they had to sit all night to wait Ramsey out, Adam intended to do it.

Deeper into the jungle they went. When he figured they'd gone far enough, he signaled Shannon to lower into position. Gradually, she crouched to her knees. He signaled her to sit. She didn't bat an eye, but sat cross-legged. Now for the hard part—keeping still while the jungle life investigated you.

He'd done this long before he was ever a military operator. Deer hunting in his home state of South Carolina with his dad had taught him plenty about lying still in the mud while centipedes, ants, and spiders checked him out. It had been a tough lesson, but it paid off. The best time of his life had to be the day he'd shot the two-hundred-and-five-pound, ten-point velvet buck. Talk about beginner's luck. He'd just turned sixteen. It was his first deer. Nearly his last.

Adam and his dad had lain for hours waiting in the muck for the chance. In a county full of large corn, soybean, and peanut fields, it was just a matter of time. Sure enough. Lying there on his belly, all smelly, itchy, and wishing he could swat the pesky flies and ticks off his neck and face, along came the granddaddy of all deer. Even though his heart was pumped full of 'Wow!' Adam had done everything just right, exactly what his dad taught. *Be patient, Son. Be still. Don't get all excited. And most of all, don't shoot until your target's close enough.* Words of wisdom Adam lived by still.

He remembered the day perfectly, a clear blue and downright chilly morning. Ever so slightly, he'd raised his bolt action Winchester M70, the one he'd gotten for Christmas the year before. The mythical creature advanced. Adam's teenage heart very nearly stopped, it was ramped up so high on adrenaline. What would all his friends say? He would have been a hero if he'd shot the monster buck. So cool!

But a funny thing happened. Liquid brown eyes looked straight into his soul, and Adam's heart failed. He'd never considered the personal cost of taking a life until then. This benign creature lived in the same wonderful world he did. It drank from the same cold streams. It breathed the same frosty air. And it had survived to ten-point maturity because it was the wise one in the forest. Not Adam. He was just some punk with a gun.

More than most, it deserved to live.

Killing this regal king wasn't cool. It was wrong.

The buck snorted softly. It had to have sensed something out of sync with the universe that morning. It had to have known a cold-blooded killer lay waiting to end him.

Adam's dad never made a sound. He didn't offer one word of advice or make a suggestion. Truthfully, Adam had forgotten his dad was lying there beside him in the dirt. For that split second, his universe consisted of three things only. Himself. The life-ending round in the chamber. And the most beautiful creature on earth.

It was then that reality intervened, reminding Adam life was hard for all living things. The only reason he and his family hunted in the first place was to put food on the table. They weren't rich city folk who strolled into a store and bought meat in plastic wrap without ever once thinking about where it came from, or what it meant to take a life. They raised their own beef and they lived off the land.

He remembered that he'd whispered, "I'm sorry," before the lightweight rifle in his hands fired true, and the stately king fell.

Adam crossed a line that day, the line between Bambi and manhood.

All the guys at school were ecstatic. Even the girls.

Adam wasn't.

From that day on, killing was a hard necessity without a speck of joy in it.

So, yeah. He'd never forgotten his first deer.

He glanced at Shannon. Shirley would've never been caught dead sitting in the dirt with him, not even to save another. Yet Shannon, a wealthy man's daughter, hadn't batted an eye when he'd declared she was coming with him.

She looked like crap with all that ash and mud smeared across those sun-kissed cheeks. How could he not notice when her breasts heaved the second his fingers touched the flat wall of her chest when he'd painter her up, how she trembled and looked shyly away? He would've kissed her right then and there if they'd been alone. Then they would've really gotten down and dirty.

She must still feel like an outcast, though. Connor, Izza, Donavan and he were the war-hardened agents. On a good day, they wore tactical gear. Shannon wore Gucci. They knew what it meant to kill. She knew what it meant to shop. Yet there she was, broken arm and all.

Dirty. Willing. Waiting.

He thinks I'll scream. I'll show him. I can be brave. I think.

Shannon sat focused and still, the quietest she'd ever been in her life. Adam had moved more than a few feet to her right before he'd lowered into the brush. The jungle seemed dense, but he'd quietly cut several fronds for an extra layer of concealment over her. She could still see him, though.

He'd made the same screen for himself. And now they waited, breathing their only body movement, and she suppressed that as much as possible, taking slow, shallow breaths like she'd been told. She also paid close attention to what she did with her fingers, hands, elbows, knees and feet. If this was the only way to catch Ramsey then she'd do it, even if it took all night.

A foot long centipede with a million legs all in perfect working order marched up her thigh, over her knee, and kept going in between her legs and over her other thigh. Her first impulse was to scream, but she shivered instead, and focused on her last conversation with her friend, engineering genius Terrence Moore. It helped take her mind off that icky bug and her aching back. Sitting still this long was tedious.

"Just call me Terrence," he'd cajoled when she'd called him that final night before the flight. "You know me well enough. Heck's sakes, Shannon, I remember when you were still in pigtails and braces. You always were my favorite."

"It's so good to talk to you," she'd replied. "How are you?"

Calling an older man by his first name seemed a major social blunder, especially when he was old enough to be her father, but that was the difference in talking to him instead of her dad. Terrence never failed to make her feel like there was no one else in the world he'd rather talk with.

"Never too busy for you," he'd answered with genuine warmth in his voice. "But you didn't call just to see what's on my social calendar, did you? What's going on?"

"I'm going to have a baby!" she'd all but squealed. Even now, sitting on a desert island in the dark, she didn't know why she'd done that, other than she needed someone who actually cared about her to be happy about the baby.

Real joy travelled all the way from the phone in his hand to her hungry heart. "You are? Well, good on you, Shannon. Congratulations! That's the best news I've heard in years."

And she'd relaxed. His happy reaction was all she'd needed to feel good about being pregnant. Somehow, Terrence Moore got her. He actually listened.

"When's the happy day, if you don't mind my asking?"

"In three months. Maybe less."

"Oh." He'd grown quiet. "Then I guess that means..."

"Yes, it's Brit's child."

"Does he know?"

Her emotions caught up with her. She couldn't repeat Brit's ugly words, so she said nothing.

"I take it Paxton doesn't care one way or the other, does he?" Terrence already understood. He'd never cared for Brit like her father had. He'd never made excuses for him, either.

"No, but that's okay. I'm keeping the baby, not him."

"Well, of course you are. Do you know if it's a boy or a girl?"

"Not yet. I just found out today that I'm expecting. It's been crazy. My doctor said he can do a blood test later to find out, but I'm not sure if I want to know."

"I'm happy for you, Shannon. I know you. You'll be a fine mother."

"Hmmm, I don't know about that. I've never been around many children."

"You wait. You'll be just like your mother," Terrence had grown almost reverent. "Olivia loved you so much. I wish you'd gotten the chance to know her."

"I do, too."

"What'd Paul say when you told him?"

"You know him, Terrence. He's too busy with work. I haven't told him yet." She'd downplayed her father's probable disgust at her good news, but that had allowed Shannon to segue to the subject of the drones, and what little she knew about them. She'd mentioned how she was going to Hawaii the next day and why. That had seemed to surprise Terrence, but it gave her a chance to elaborate on the drones' capabilities.

"To tell you the truth, they sound scary," she'd admitted.

"That was the idea. These little fellows were created for the defense of our nation. They're not the welcome wagon, my dear. Not by a long shot."

"But they can think for themselves, can't they? Doesn't that worry you? I mean, what if lightning hits one of them and fries its circuits? What if they go, umm, what's it called?"

"Rogue?" He'd laughed, and she'd been so glad she had called. Hearing the warm acceptance in his voice reminded her of how much she'd missed and loved him all her life. He'd adored her as a child, and she'd worshipped him. But something happened between him and her father. She never knew what. Terrence still worked at Reagan Industries, but one day he was family and friend; the next day he wasn't.

"Did you know I always wanted to marry you?" She'd interrupted their serious discussion.

"You did?" He'd loved hearing that. She could tell he was smiling.

"I know it sounds silly, but when I was in first grade, I had our wedding all planned. You were my hero."

"You and your other always were my favorite Reagans," he'd said quietly.

She'd caught the tone of longing in his voice, and instantly repented for being such a poor friend. She'd not spent any time with him lately, and she'd regretted it. "I need to visit you when I get back from Hawaii. Would you be able to get away for dinner one night? Just me and you?"

"My treat," he'd said.

"It's a deal!"

That had seemed to make his day, but he'd grown serious at that point, too. "If one of these drones were to go rogue, which is very unlikely, but let's say it happened. Let's pretend one of our enemies intercepted a drone with a bullet or something like that. Let's also pretend they hit and damaged the microprocessor. It's highly improbable, but I guess it could happen. There's still a kill code, Shannon. I wouldn't agree to prototype testing, much less real-world utilization without an easily accessible failsafe protocol."

"Whew," she'd sighed. That was yet another thing about this dear friend. He never failed to set her mind at ease when she needed it.

"Your father fought me tooth and nail over this. He's been darn secretive. There's a lot I still don't know about the top-secret solar contraption he created, but you're nearly ready to take over the business. It's time you knew. If that doomsday scenario you're concerned about ever happens, and if these weapons went crazy, more people than just your father and me should know how to stop them. You're right. In the wrong hands, they could cause a lot of trouble. I'm getting old and..."

He'd let his words fade, and she'd held her breath, exactly the same as she was holding it now. Staring across the way at Adam, she thought how ironic the kill code to disable the drones should be so simple. It was no algorithm, no entangled calculus formula like she'd expected from her father. Terrence must've thought of it. The kill code actually reminded her of Adam's boss, Alex Stewart.

God bless America.

That was all.

Adam let out a slow, quiet breath across the way, and Shannon worried about the effect on his ribs of sitting so long. He must be tired, yet that single slow exhalation was all she'd heard from him since he'd sat down. The endurance of this ex-military man was amazing. But what branch of the military had he been in? She hadn't the slightest idea.

Shannon eased her aching spine to the left and then to the right as carefully and as slowly as possible. Now wasn't the time to let Adam down. Knowing he'd done this kind of boring surveillance as part of his job before gave her an insight into him. He was extremely patient, controlled, and determined.

So am I.

Something was terribly wrong. Adam could feel it in his bones. It had been a miserable night spent hiding in the wrong place at the wrong time. Ramsey never showed, only bugs and a few nosy rats. The moon was still fading in the west when Adam called it quits. He and Shannon had barely stepped out from their jungle cover when Connor's anguished, "No! God, no!" shattered the air.

Casting caution aside, they ran to camp. Connor and Izza looked up from Donavan's prone body, both startled to see them and ready to fight.

"He's been here," Izza spat. "That ass was here. Right in our camp!"

Donavan still lay asleep on the ground only he wasn't asleep. A trickle of blood ran into his closed eyes from the hole in the side of his head. He'd been shot.

Shannon mumbled something incoherent before she fell to the sand in a dead faint. Adam couldn't get to her in time to catch her.

Connor stabbed a finger at the beach. "Look what Hell washed up last night."

Holy shit. Another body lay at the edge of the beach. Could this nightmare get any worse?

Chapter Fifteen

"Tide must've washed her in. She was already there at sun-up. We went to the beach the minute we saw her," Connor explained. "Man, we were only gone five, maybe ten minutes. Never heard a thing."

It had been a helluva day and Adam was weary to his bones. He and his team, Shannon included, had gone from one problem to the other. First to puzzle over the female corpse on the shore, then back to poor Donavan.

"The son-of-a-bitch." Izza glanced warily around the many trunks of the banyan tree where they'd regrouped. "Ramsey must've been here the whole time, just waiting for us to leave. Used a silencer. Damn him, anyway."

"Do you recognize her, Shannon?" Connor asked, his snarky tone gone. Maybe he felt sorry for her since she'd hit her head when she'd fainted, or maybe he was finally back to normal.

"No," she whispered, glancing toward the surf where the bloated corpse bobbed. The dead body's extremities and face had been pockmarked in the way of human fish food that had been in the water for too many days. An awful, ugly sight.

"Remember that parachute you found?" Adam asked.

Connor gave him a puzzled look. "No. Sorry. My brain's kind of fuzzy. What parachute?"

Adam nodded toward shore. "I'm not saying it's her, but two people intercepted me in South Dakota, and that gal could be the same one who snagged the drone. Same general height. Black hair. Want to bet she worked with Ramsey?"

Connor shrugged, not sold on anything he couldn't recall.

"We gotta get him," Izza ground out, her eyes narrowed and canvassing the shoreline. "The son-of-a-bitch came right into camp, right under our noses, and..." She growled instead of finishing.

"Why go after him, though?" Shannon asked weakly. "Why sit in the jungle all night waiting for someone who obviously knows where we are? Why not set a trap for him right here? Why not bait him and make him come to us?"

Adam acknowledged her sound reasoning. "I didn't want the bastard fouling our camp, that's why, but now..." He glanced at Donavan. "It doesn't matter, does it?"

Shannon had been a trooper during their stakeout. Despite her logical argument, she seemed to be falling apart this morning. The black smudges on her face didn't hide the panic in her eyes. Furtive glances to Connor and Izza always ended back at Adam before she'd jerked her face and look the other way. A sheen of sweat clung to her forehead. She kept cringing, and damn it, the last thing he needed was a crying woman on his hands.

"Are you going to be okay?" He needed to know now if she wasn't able to man up. This was no time to faint or throw up, damn it.

"Yes," she whispered again, glancing toward the wreck and away just as quickly. "I'm okay."

Adam forgot her and turned to where Donavan laid, his eyes still open and unblinking. He pushed off the ground to kneel alongside his friend, and for the second time, he closed a young man's eyes in death. Only this guy he'd played basketball with, worked with, and told lies with.

This was the kid who'd showed up at Harley's night after night just to check on Adam's state of mind when Shirley pulled her crap. This was simple, happy-go-lucky Donavan. More kid than man. More friend than most. The poor guy hadn't had a date in months. All the agents kidded it was because of that heart tattoo on his arm with 'Mom' neatly inscribed in the middle of it. Shy, backwards, goofy Donavan. Gone.

Like Izza, Adam wanted Ramsey dead. The man had weapons and most likely, a means of communication. Worse, he had four robot assassins he could unleash at any moment. The rules in this damned game had to change and Adam meant to change them.

"Connor." His one hoarsely spoken command brought Connor immediately to his side, like the loyal friend he was. Connor understood what had to happen next. Men's work, pure and simple.

"Stay with Shannon," Connor said to Izza. "Don't take any chances while were gone. Got it?"

Already with knife in hand, Izza sent it flying blade-first into the nearest banyan trunk. "You know it, honey. I see him, and he's going down. If you need me, whistle like you mean it."

"No, I'm going. I can help," Shannon offered.

"No. Stay with Izza," Adam growled, not up for a woman who obviously needed to rest.

"No, Adam," she insisted. "Donavan was my friend, too. Let me help."

Whatever. Adam had no strength to argue. He wasn't proud of it, but he'd morphed into a hard-assed sergeant, task driven and ready to kill or be killed. He glared at Izza, but she shook her head. "No. I'll stay here," she murmured. "Just don't take all day."

Connor kissed her forehead, and the task at hand hit Adam hard. He steeled his jaw, and blinked the tender feelings out of his eyes. Without another word, he and Connor carried their friend to the growing cemetery on the far end of their beach while Shannon followed.

The three of them dug another goddamned hole.

Sand fell from the improvised scoops. Within a foot, the powdery grains gave way to a layer of damper, colder sand. Then black, gritty dirt. Shannon helped at first, but then she groaned and leaned back. It was difficult for her to reach the bottom of the grave. Adam didn't care if she helped or not at that point. This was his friend he was laying to rest. Not hers.

He couldn't seem to stop digging. The corners needed to be squared off, neat and trim. Proper, damn it. A man shouldn't have to rest for time and all eternity in a sloppy grave. Donavan should be honored. Respected.

He should still be alive!

Adam blinked harder as he completed the only act of service he could do for his friend. He smoothed the bottom of the square-cornered hole until it was flat and even. He tamped the loose soil with his palm. Connor stuck with him until the last speck of loose dirt was flattened into a fitting floor. It was a final gift of sorts, but so worthless for a man so brave. The futility of his efforts galled Adam. The grave was cold. Barren.

"Adam."

He looked up to Shannon, the pain of the moment etched on her dirty face. Tears coursed over her drawn and still smudged cheeks. He blinked his own grief away and bit his lip hard, not willing to give in to the sucking hole in his heart that he saw reflected in her teary eyes. He'd seen men fall before. Donavan wasn't the first. He wouldn't be the last. But it would always hurt.

Connor knelt silently beside Donavan, sweating in the tropical sun with the same wretched agony on his face. It was time. With duty pushing his heart out of the way, Adam joined Connor in the final act of friendship.

Grasping Donavan by his armpits while Connor lifted his legs, Adam laid his friend very tenderly into the hole, and together they laid their friend down to his eternal sleep.

It was a tight fit. Donavan was a tall kid. Adam wanted to extend the grave by a few inches, but the futility hit home. Those few inches didn't matter. Not to Donavan. They laid him down at an angle, his head in one corner, his feet in the opposite.

"I should've put his shirt on him," Connor said. "His Hawaiian shirt."

"It's okay, Connor. This way he looks like a crazy kid again," Shannon whispered. "Like he's ready to ride the waves."

Looking out to the unforgiving sea, Adam stifled his heart at her tender assessment of a good man down. She had a way of seeing the real Donavan in that hole. He'd been born to ride the wind and the surf. It almost seemed fitting he'd lie down forever surrounded by the ocean he'd loved.

No, damn it!

Adam clenched his jaw so hard it hurt, the rock of a scream stuck in his chest, and mad as hell. This wasn't where or how a hero should be buried. Not out here in the middle of nowhere, and certainly not where his parents couldn't come cry over their lost boy. A soldier who'd fought valiantly and served his country with honor deserved better. Donavan didn't even look peaceful. He looked sad. Abused. *Murdered.*

Red-hot rage licked at the walls of Adam's gut. *I'm coming for you, Ramsey.*

Shannon's sniffle jerked Adam out of his angry reverie. He blinked his anger away and saw his friend again. This was the part he was never good at—the stepping away part. That was why Shirley'd thrown his things out. He never knew when to quit.

Even now, Connor and Shannon knelt waiting on him to commence filling the hole. The breeze off the ocean wafted over them, bringing with it the fresh fragrance of wide-open air and surf. The waves pounding the shore had become mere background noise, but today, in this single moment in time, they sounded melancholy. Lonely. So damned desolate that Adam wanted to bawl.

Shannon cleared her throat, asking permission in her timid way. "I want to say a few words."

Adam gave her the go-ahead nod. Connor had already gone to her side and taken her hand. It was a small thing, but it choked Adam. Yeah. Connor was himself again. Adam wasn't. All the digging and lifting had wrenched his tender ribs, but he was glad they hurt. He needed the pain. Used the anger. It kept the tears at bay, kept him hard and cold. He didn't want to be himself right now, not when he had killing to do.

The thought of the final act of burial suffocated him. Pretty soon he would cover his friend with sand and dirt. Once again, he'd be caught in the claustrophobic sensation of being buried alive in that hole with Donavan. Displaced empathy, the awful tendency to become the other person, always did him in. He knew it well. All the sand in Donavan's face and nose, the confinement of the walls of the cold, wet grave—just the thought sent panic crawling up Adam's already dry throat, choking the life out of him and closing off his air.

He cursed his internal weakness and channeled anger instead. Not now. Maybe not today. But the time would come when he'd let it all out. And Ramsey would die.

"We are gathered here today," Shannon began softly, "to remember and honor our friend and companion, Junior Agent Donavan Easton. I didn't know him very long, but he seemed like a man who loved everything in his life. He lived it to the fullest."

"He loved his mom," Connor said quietly. "He was a good kid."

No one spoke for a moment. It was Adam's turn, but he didn't speak. Couldn't. There were no words for times like this.

"And he loved the Army. I could tell by the way he talked to me about when he enlisted. He was proud to serve his country. I'm thankful for all of the ways that he served me,"

Shannon said. "I bet he was the best sniper the Army Rangers ever had."

Adam could barely stand to look at her. She wasn't afraid to let her feelings show. Tears streamed openly down her face. There she was again, stepping up to the challenge of the day like it was no big deal, and doing a bang-up job.

"He must've been a really good friend, because that's all I see here today," she whispered, blinking hard. "Good friends. Loyal friends. His brothers. A couple sisters, too."

Adam clenched his fists, and God, he tried, but the tears fell anyway.

"A man can't ask for a better way to be laid to rest," Connor finished the eulogy as quietly as Shannon, "than to be surrounded by brothers and sisters who knew him and loved him."

"God bless him." Izza's edgy voice ended the eulogy. It was just like her to come late to the graveside, fighting her tears. Izza hated to show weakness, and God bless the fool who made her cry, but there she was. Standing behind the others. Wiping her cheeks. She let her anger out with a vow of vengeance. "Let's get the bastard who killed him."

"Amen." Adam bowed his head. That was something he could pray for. *The only easy day is yesterday.* His motto. His promise now to Ramsey. *I'm coming for you. You'd better run for your piece-of-shit life. Every day will be hell for you because I will find you. You're going to die.*

Adam stiffened his back and squared his shoulders. He cocked his arm and smartly raised his right hand, his fingers stiff and straight to the edge of his right brow. With his heart in his throat, he cast his gaze out to the wide Pacific, afraid if he made eye contact with the others, his tears would fall. He saluted his friend with pride for noble service humbly rendered. There should've been a twenty-one-gun salute. There should've been a bugler and the plaintive call of Taps. Damn it. Ramsey should've been in that grave.

And suddenly, Adam did have something to say. He came to parade rest, his hands clenched behind his back, his feet spread. With the breeze in his face, he cleared his throat, then closed his eyes and recited the words of an old Navy poem, "Bury Me With Sailors," Author Unknown.

It was five simple verses, a pitiful tribute to his friend, but they captured his own death wish. To lie down among friends when his time came. To spend eternity with like-minded men who'd given all, and who knew what it meant to "face the guns and die…"

The last verse rolled reverently off his tongue.

> *So bury me with Sailors, please,*
> *Though much maligned they be.*
> *Yes, bury me with Sailors,*
> *For I miss their company.*
> *We'll not soon see their likes again;*
> *We've had our fill of war.*
> *But bury me with men like them*
> *Till someone else does more."*

"Amen," Shannon whispered, and Adam swallowed hard, his all given. Damned if she didn't clear her throat and surprise the hell out of him. "This poem was written by John Masefield, and it was published in 1902. It's called 'Sea

Fever,' and it reminds me of Donavan. I thought you guys would like to hear it."

She coughed again, and lifted her voice above the background music of the gulls and the surf. Adam couldn't take his eyes off her. He'd never heard anything lovelier than those three poignant verses of a man's longing for the *lonely sea*. For the *grey dawn*. For a *sweet dream* when life ended. He could have kissed Shannon for the depth of her insight of a man she'd only just met. That poem was Donavan down to his bare feet and his suntan.

"Amen," Izza said quietly when the poem ended. "Thanks, Shannon. That was real nice."

But at last, it was time. A gull cried overhead, mimicking the sorrow in Adam's soul. Like death and life, the great Pacific crashed relentlessly to shore. Together, the four friends dropped to their knees in silence and pushed the soft white sand of a deserted island over their honored friend. When the last of it was tamped down good and proper, Adam pushed up from the beach and extended a helping hand to Shannon. She came easily into his side.

Connor already stood with his arm around Izza, her eyes hard but rimmed with tears. "You two stay here and rest," he said quietly. "Izza and I are going to take a look around."

"No," Adam growled. "Like you said, all four of us need to—"

Connor stopped him cold. "No, Adam. You and Shannon have been out all night. You need to eat and rest. We've decided. It's our turn. We won't be gone long."

"We won't rest long, Connor. Damn it, mark my words, I'm going after that son-of-a-bitch." Adam knew he came across harsh, but he didn't care. War had come to this island paradise, and he meant to win it.

He couldn't rest. Too angry to eat, all Adam did was plant his butt in the sand and plan how he'd do it. Unless Connor and Izza beat him to it, he *would* take Ramsey down. There was no doubt in his mind. He meant the man to suffer. He almost hoped Connor and Izza weren't successful, but he was also smart enough to know they very well might be.

They were the ultimate hunter-killer team, this husband and wife duo of ex-scout snipers. At least Connor was. Izza was an ex-Marine security cop—like that made a difference to her shooting prowess. Connor admitted it often. She hit her targets more often and with better accuracy than he did. The woman was steady as a rock, with eagle eyes. Meaner, too.

If Connor was up to par, they might just return with Ramsey's head on a post. But Adam wanted to be the one who did it. He wanted the satisfaction of plunging his knife hilt-deep into Ramsey's neck, slicing it open, ending him like the bastard had done to poor Dillon. It galled Adam that he was confined to camp. He didn't need rest, but he couldn't leave because Shannon was obviously running on empty. Evil rankled strong and hard in his blood while Adam wrestled with right and wrong. Part revenge, part self-defense, this was his clearest plan ever.

"Ah, Adam."

Glancing at Shannon, Adam didn't really see her, much less hear her. Despite her very gracious prayer over Donavan, her timid voice irked him now. This was a day for strength. For war whoops, face-paint, and death. Ramsey needed to be afraid. *Very afraid.*

Adam's palms itched for the molded grip of his Sig Sauer P228. Ramsey had a gun; Adam wanted his trusty nine-mil, his weapon of choice. He'd slept with it often on missions and in the service. He wanted it now, but it laid at the bottom of the Pacific.

Instead—he had Shannon. She was too gentle and too nice for this place. If he couldn't act on his death wish, Adam needed to strike back. He couldn't, not with her sitting nearby and watching. The ugly, hard side of his soul had to stay hidden and restrained. For now. Soon, he'd let it out. No leash. No rules. No holds barred.

"Umm, Adam."

Again that gentle, nagging voice broke through the angry roar in his head. She didn't understand what he'd become. He hoped she never would. Right then, a thousand demons screamed inside his skull to act, to move, to do something. *Anything!* Not being able to follow through was half his problem. Frustration stoked his rage, but it also clarified his plan. He breathed a slow, measured breath. *I need to be the one who—*

"Umm, Adam?"

"What?" He snapped at her this time. She sat in their lousy excuse for a camp and she looked scared again. With his mind caught up in murder, even that pathetic look on her grimy face irritated him. This woman was scared of everything. With her hand stuck in her side, she looked like she had runner's cramp, the way she twisted her body and arched her spine. They both needed to wash and eat, but he couldn't sit still long enough. He had a killer to hunt. Now wasn't the time for a timid, whiny woman.

"I think my water just broke."

That got his attention. "You what?" he roared.

He'd heard right. The pain-filled eyes of a woman in labor met his. She grimaced, nodded, and blew out a shuddering breath. Of all the stupid, poorly timed—

"You're pregnant? Shit! Are you sure?"

Stupid question.

"Ahhhh, yes, I am." She tipped her head back and groaned, clutching the small mound of her belly, a belly he hadn't really noticed until now. He took a closer look. She had no gut on her. No baby bump. Well, not really. That small mound didn't look big enough for a nine-month pregnancy. There was no way this was happening. Not there. Not now. He scrambled to her side. "For hell's sake, Shannon. You're having a baby? Here?"

"Yes-s-s-s." With a deep hiss, Shannon leaned back, the wrinkles on her forehead knitted. "Ahhhh... it hurts, Adam. It really hurts."

"Then lay down... or something." He pressed her flat to the ground, looking around, for what he didn't know. Bleeding wounds and broken arms he could handle. Burying bodies, killing Ramsey, sure, but a baby? Here? Now? In the middle of all this? What was she thinking?

She gripped his hand. *Tight.* "Help m-m-me. Please."

"Well, yeah. Sure. Okay then." His mind pinged back to all he never knew about childbirth. Contractions. She must be having contractions. That was why the death grip with fingernails digging into the back of his hand. Shannon was in pain. Her jaw clenched so tight he could hear her teeth grinding. He calmed. Kind of. She needed help. He was the only one there. *Oh, shit.*

"How far along are you?" He knelt at her side, concern breaking through his befuddled anger.

"S-s-s-six. Maybe s-s-s-seven months. Oh, God. Ouch!" She bore down again, crunching his fingers. He wasn't sure if that was a good thing for her to be doing or not, but she was doing it. He counted. One-one thousand. Two-one thousand. Three-one thousand. Four-one thousand. She released the pressure, but didn't let go. Okay. That seemed like a strong contraction. He guessed. It sure hurt him.

"Six months?" he asked, hoping she was talking out of her head, and really, oh God please—really—meant more like eight or nine. Six months seemed way too early to be having a baby, wasn't it? No wonder she had no gut on her.

Shannon nodded, gulping great breaths now that she could breathe again. "Maybe seven."

"My hell. Why didn't you say anything before?"

"I just... a-a-ahh..." Man, this woman's grip was strong. A light sheen of sweat covered her dirty face, and he wished he had time to clean her up. But things seemed to be progressing pretty quick. *What the hell am I going to do?*

"Shannon. Are you sure you're in labor?" he asked again.

Her scorching look was answer enough.

Duh, Torrey. Of course she is. A woman would know that kind of thing. Oh shit!

"Okay then." He sucked in a deep breath. His mind snapped to attention. A new plan for the day materialized. Ramsey would wait. "We're going to have a baby."

Another evil look glanced over her face before her features transformed into wrinkles and sweat. When that contraction eased off, he scrambled out of her grasp to grab what was left of that parachute. It was the only thing large enough in camp to serve as a sheet, and, oh hell, whatever else he needed.

Slicing a big square of the flimsy nylon fabric, he was back before the next pain, and just in time. She grabbed hold of his forearm while he tried to position the sheet beneath her backside. Adam and Shannon were face to face, his heart pounding fast and furious.

"You okay?" he asked, for want of something better to say at the moment. What *does* a dumb jock say to a woman in the throes of labor anyway?

She nodded, but she kept arching her back and whimpering.

"Breathe, Shannon," he said softly. "Nice and easy. Breathe."

"It hurts," she ground out. "My stomach, my back— God! Everything hurts."

And then it dawned on him. Her pants had to go. Off. Oh, yeah. He ran back for another piece of that damned parachute.

The baby was coming way too fast, and Adam was scared. A preemie born in the middle of nowhere was the worst possible scenario. Could it survive? He didn't know. Babies weren't his thing. Guns and HALOs were. Yeah, he'd raised a few baby animals during his boyhood days. Chickens. Puppies. He knew basic human biology, and how things worked, but this was the last thing his team needed. He'd buried too many on the beach already.

God, not a baby, too!

Chapter Sixteen

"I... I don't want it."

"Your baby?" He had to ask. That wasn't what he'd expected to hear from someone as sweet and thoughtful as Shannon Reagan. Cursing the insanity of what was definitely about to take place, he hurriedly rinsed his hands with spring water before he rushed back to her.

All pregnant women about to deliver probably said they didn't want their kid, didn't they? Her eyes were wide and distant. She shuddered, clearly in pain. Maybe out of her head. It seemed a natural response.

Kneeling at her side, he took her shoes off and eased his fingers beneath the waistband of her pants. "I'm going to slide your pants down and off. Can you lift up and help a little?"

"Sorry. No, damn it," she mumbled, as another contraction hit. Grabbing his shoulder, she dug her fingernails in deep. He flinched, then stiffened to endure the shooting pain in his ribs. This delivery might just kill him before Connor and Izza returned.

The contraction ended, and Adam blew out a big breath along with Shannon. By now, he dripped with sweat, too. This was a different kind of battle, and it scared the hell out of him. Women died during childbirth. They bled out. He recalled those dangers now. Sometimes they got infections that made them sick, then they died. Or the baby was born dead. Or they both died during delivery. And this dirty, stinking island was the furthest thing from a sanitary hospital room.

She sucked in a deep breath and groaned, reaching for his shoulder. He dodged just in time, offering his hand instead.

"Son-of-a-bitch! I don't want it!" she screamed this time.

"Okay. Okay. Calm down. You're doing good. You don't want it. I heard you, but it's still got to come out." She needed to be pacified, so he pacified.

Very gently, he pulled her shoes off and clothing down. He covered her with the parachute sheet, hoping to get her situated before another contraction hit. Casting her wet clothing aside, he wished again he'd cleaned her pretty face. The first sight a newborn saw should not be the blackened, sweaty face of its warrior mother. Blowing out a big breath of sheer nerves, hyperventilation set in—with him. He was in way over his head. *What a helluva day, huh?*

"I mean it," she whispered sadly, her voice tight and quavering.

"You mean what?" He couldn't remember what she'd said. "I'm sorry, but I need you to bend your knees, spread your legs, and—" He lifted the sheet to take care of business. Not a second too soon. The tiniest head of dark brown hair had crowned, as well as a trickle of blood and...

Shit. It's coming. What do I do? Adam clamped down on his bottom lip as he watched the miracle of childbirth. *Man, that's gotta hurt.*

Shannon writhed, clutching her backside with both hands. She leaned forward and—

Whoosh. Adam caught the smallest human being he'd ever seen in his life, a very tiny, very perfect baby boy. The world flooded with light, but it wasn't from the sun. Oh no. This light was more pure. Brighter. Whiter. It seemed to pour straight down from heaven on this warm, wet, bloody, and reverent man-child. Brilliantly, awesomely precious.

Adam held his breath, afraid to disturb the spirit this birth had brought with it. Time stood still. Hallelujahs bubbled up in his heart with this fragile, little guy in his big, callused hands. The perfect juxtaposition of light and dark, this newborn life so pure and clean in his scarred, ruggedized warrior's hands. Hands that had taken life. Fingers that had pulled the triggers of more guns than he could recall. Now holding this perfect child. This brand new—life.

The tiniest feet he'd ever seen in all of his years nestled snug against a skinny butt, the infant still very much in the fetal position. Adam wanted to sing for joy, but the child hadn't made a sound. He held the baby's chest to his ear and listened intently. No breath. Not even a whisper. He panicked. *Not on my watch.*

Carefully, he turned the boy face-down in his hand. Adam spread his fingers so the infant's head and neck were supported between them, his mouth and nose exposed. Very gently, he massaged a tiny circle between fragile shoulder blades. "Come on, little guy. Breathe for me. You can do it."

Nothing.

No! Adam commanded the universe. *Not today. This baby will not die.*

Yet he trembled at the very real knowledge that Shannon might have delivered a stillborn. "Come on, little guy," he whispered against the babe's bloody cheek, massaging what he hoped was life into this man-child. "Breathe. Your mama really needs you."

Shannon whimpered. "Is it alive?"

A tiny gasp answered. A sputter.

"Talk to him again, Shannon. He knows your voice."

"No," she murmured softly. Sadly. "You're wrong."

The infant jerked in Adam's hand and wiggled like that gentle touch on his back was extremely uncomfortable. "Good boy," Adam crooned. "You can do it."

Another careful circle with just the tip of his index finger, and finally, the baby sputtered and coughed. He opened his eyes and cried. THEE best sound in the whole world.

Adam grinned. Turning to Shannon, he raised her son up so she could see him. "It's a boy," he said proudly. "You have a son, Shannon."

She shook her head and refused to look. "No."

He remembered then. *Oh, yeah. She doesn't want this baby. We'll just see about that.* "It's okay. It's perfectly natural. Don't worry. Let's get you cleaned up."

Adam laid her newborn child on her stomach. He had work to do, even though he hadn't a clue exactly what that work was. He knew the basics; he'd seen the movies. There was still an umbilical cord, and a placenta, but real life was different. Shannon needed to be cleaned, but more importantly, she needed to want that baby. The sooner, the better.

Man, was he pumped. A baby! A beautiful baby boy!

He hurried back to Izza and Connor's three-walled hut and brought Izza's first-aid kit to Shannon's side, along with another piece of the best damned parachute on the planet. The tiny child still lay untouched and unloved. His hands and feet jerked. He whimpered.

Adam kept one eye on the newest addition to his team while he tied off the umbilical cord and severed son from mother with a quick slice from Ramsey's knife. The little guy mewed with such a scratchy voice. He didn't sound much like a baby at all, more like a creaky door.

Shannon hadn't made a move, other than to cross her arms over her chest. In doing so, she'd effectively created a wall between herself and her son. She tucked her fingers into her armpits, and closed her eyes. She wasn't sleeping though. No sleeping woman bit her lip like she was biting hers. If she'd only touched that tiny baby boy, Adam knew she'd fall in love with him. He bided his time.

The placenta came next. Adam quickly removed it from the scene. Very discreetly, he finished cleaning her, which probably added to her embarrassment. She'd covered her eyes with one forearm, so Adam hurried. He wiped her down and applied a nice thick bandage-type pad to her female parts. He had no idea how to hold it in place, but once she lowered her legs, the problem solved itself.

The beauty of the moment didn't escape Adam. His initial panic had evolved into a tremendous feeling of honor at assisting this frightened new mother in delivering such a perfect little man from her body. It was a miracle, plain and simple. He wouldn't trade it for anything, not even his best HALO jump.

New life had brought an unexpected rush to an otherwise downer of a day. His heart pumped like a happy beast in his chest at what he'd witnessed. Adam turned his attention to the still unclaimed child.

"One of those linen napkins from the galley will make a good baby blanket. What do you think?" He tried to keep the conversation light. After her heartwarming prayer over Donavan's grave, this side of Shannon wasn't what he'd expected. She was better than this. He needed her to come to that conclusion on her own, but how?

After washing the tiny fellow with the lukewarm spring water, he dried him gently, using Shannon's stomach for a changing table. She might as well get used to it. Her son was there, hopefully to stay.

The linen napkins made perfect baby accessories. Adam easily fashioned another into a diaper, but he had to cut it in fourths, and even then, it was still too large for this preemie. The tiny guy squirmed and let out another creaky, crabby screech.

"You know what? I'm going to call you Squeaks," Adam told the little fellow as he tucked him into his first and only baby blanket. It seemed fitting that the linens were embroidered with an elegant R in the corner. R for Reagan. "Squeaks Reagan. Yup. That's your name from now on. That's who you are."

He'd learned long ago that the best way to win an argument wasn't to argue, so Adam sat next to Shannon with Squeaks bundled in the crook of his arm. Snuggling a three-pound baby boy, if he weighed that much, was a feat unto itself. The bundle took up all of six inches of Adam's muscular arm. It felt as if he were snuggling a hamburger instead of a football, and not a quarter-pounder, either.

Squeaks was a plain burger. No cheese. No pickles. No lettuce or onions.

"How are you doing?" he asked the unwilling mother.

"Fine," Shannon whispered, her voice tight, and her eyes still closed.

"I'm guessing you didn't know you were pregnant, did you?"

"I found out," she said sadly, "the day I met you."

"So that's what morning sickness looks like. You were pretty green." He meant to tease her out of this conundrum she'd gotten herself into.

"I guess."

"Well, you done good, Shannon. Real good. This little guy's smaller than one of my old coonhound's puppies, but he's breathing, and he's going to be just fine."

Adam thought back to Mable Lou, the best coonhound in South Carolina. She hadn't wanted her first litter neither, just ran around the yard scared, yelping and dropping her puppies as if they were what she usually dropped in the yard. Of course, he'd run behind her, collecting every little puppy in his mom's laundry basket until he could corner Mable Lou and get her settled down. It had taken a few minutes, but once she'd decided those ten puppies weren't so scary after all, she'd been the best mother. It just took her a spell to wrap her head around the notion of motherhood. That was all.

The same thing was going on with Shannon. She'd been plenty brave and tough for days now. She was just tired and overwhelmed. She'd come around.

He gazed at the tiny new life cupped in the palm of his hand. Squeaks lay with his arms crossed like skinny hockey sticks across his chest, all five fingers on each hand stretched wide. He looked more like a miniature old man, his translucent baby skin full of wrinkles. Tiny blue veins spider-webbed over his bald head. Now that he was breathing on his own, Adam checked for toes and fingers. He relaxed. The skinny little guy had ten of each, all except for that other little guy part. He only had one of them, and Adam was proud as hell. Squeaks had a big one for such a little guy.

Pressing the boy against his ear, Adam held his breath until he heard the soft pitter-pat of another heart. He closed his eyes, grinning like a fool. Who wouldn't? This brand new heartbeat was the coolest sound on the planet.

Adam couldn't help himself. The songs bubbled out of him, a stream filled to overflowing breaching its banks. First, a soft version of "When Irish Eyes Are Smiling," then "Danny Boy." Squeaks calmed with the crazy choice of music.

Adam racked his memory for others, settling for "Itsy Bitsy Spider" when he couldn't remember the beginning of "The Minstrel Boy." Squeaks sputtered once, then yawned, and Adam's heart was full. Despite everything else that had happened on this speck of sand in the Pacific, this was a good day.

A damned good day.

Shannon knew it would be a boy. Somehow, she just knew.

She couldn't win. It was here, and Adam was loving it as if it were the dearest thing ever. Only it wasn't. It couldn't be.

It was Brit's son. She thought she'd feel different when it was actually born, but the spot Brit had killed in her heart was still dead. The thing in Adam's hands couldn't bring it back to life. It would only make everything worse. *Stop hugging it, Adam. Set it down somewhere. Walk away. Let it go.*

The baby wasn't supposed to be due for two, maybe three months. She'd planned to be rescued and home before this happened. Why was it here now? Why did it come so early? She hadn't gotten used to the idea of being pregnant yet, and now this? It wasn't fair.

Adam sang to it with the deepest, softest baritone that all but melted her heart. His southern drawl had barely surfaced until now. She looked twice at the gentle man streaked with ash and grime singing so sweetly to what was most likely a dying infant. And yes, beast and baby made for an awesome tender sight, despite the bleakness of the day. Strange. He actually knew lullabies, singing '*too-ra-loo-ra-loo-ra*' as if it was no big deal for a grown man to nurture a child, then "Rock-A-Bye Baby" like he meant for the boy to live.

Shannon stilled. Adam seemed an unlikely gentle giant. He'd been built to play tackle football, charge through walls, and fight to the death. Yet he held the child as if it was the most precious thing ever, and he sang to it as if it could hear him. He had his nose pressed into the linen napkin, softly crooning with his lips on its forehead, rocking back and forth and smiling.

How long could it live? Maybe hours? Days? It's awfully small. Nothing that tiny can live for long. Can it? Will it?

Adam started the sweetest version of "You Are My Sunshine," his voice mellow and rumbling. The way he sang those familiar words, as if he poured his heart into every sweet note from his throat, touched her. He wasn't just *singing* to it. He was loving it. Encouraging it to live. The tender melody came from deep inside of him, like a promise. A vow.

Shannon wriggled against the ground, her shoulder blades uncomfortable and her back sore. How embarrassing. And yet, her unseemly declaration that she didn't want this little boy child embarrassed her more. She'd wanted that sweet little gummy bear before? Why not now that it was here? She honestly didn't know, except that it came so fast. So unexpectedly quick.

Note by note, Adam's deep baritone dripped honey and warmth into her soul, drawing her into the tiny circle he'd created for himself and that little boy-child. She didn't want to go into that circle with them. It would hurt. It had *always* hurt, the abysmal natural order of things, of man, woman, and child. All of her life it had done nothing but hurt. Her mother died. Her father rejected her. Brit rejected her. Family meant nothing but pain and loneliness and hurt and yet…

She craved it most of all, and she knew that she did. It was a hunger she'd lived with most of her life, an unquenchable thirst to belong—somewhere. To be unconditionally loved by someone instead of just her chauffeur.

When a tiny pink hand jerked into view above the linen napkin, all five fingers stiff and straight, Shannon couldn't look away. Something was happening and she was caught in the ebb and flow emanating from Adam. Tendrils of his gentle but very masculine call to order had breached her defenses, and flooded the barren place inside of her, that hard spot deep in her soul where her father's deceit and Brit's lies lingered, reminding her of pain and heartache. The unwritten story of her life. *That place.*

Adam started a quiet chorus of "Ninety-one Bottles of Beer on the Wall," still smiling that glorious smile she'd only seen once before on his handsome face. He'd been holding her in his arms then. And now he held—it.

Was there any possible scenario where this could be a good thing? Where it could survive such an early birth? Where she could turn the cursed Reagan luck into something better for this next generation?

Its tiny fingers reached up to the edge of Adam's whiskered chin, and her heart melted. Those five little fingers clutched the man who'd saved its life, and it seemed to recognize that fact. It made a tiny sound, but within the scratchy infantile voice of Brit's offspring, she heard the plea intended for her. *I am so little. The world is so big. Where's my mama?*

Inexplicable warmth surged through Shannon's heart, igniting a firestorm of maternal instinct. That tiny hand with five tiny fingers belonged to *her* son. She wanted it—*him*—to live. *He's my son. My baby.*

It hit her hard. She'd called her baby *it*, just like Brit had. What was she thinking? He was Squeaks, not just an *it*, and he'd never be anything like his father. No. He'd be like Adam, if only because Adam was the man sitting there with him, pouring his love into that tiny newborn chalice that had just breathed his first breath. And her baby boy drank it in, the same as she did.

"You named him?" she asked, ashamed of her confused feelings.

Adam turned to her with that otherworldly light in his eyes. He grinned and held her baby boy alongside his cheek. "You see that pretty lady there, Squeaks? That's your mama. Isn't she the most beautiful woman in the world?"

Adam's blue eyes were red-rimmed and extra shiny. He'd been crying. Rivulets of tender emotion dripped off his chin. With the back of his hand, he wiped them away, but it only smeared the black mask of a warrior. Her heart stuttered. No man had ever looked as masculine as he did then and there.

Hunger for that little child in his large hands roared through her soul.

"Hey, Mama. Don't cry." Adam leaned in with the baby carefully secured in the crook of his arm. "It's okay to be scared. Us boys are scared, too. It's not every day we get to do something great and wonderful like this, you know. You wanna hold him?"

She nodded, feeling like the biggest failure on the planet. "Yes, please. Give me my baby."

Passing the boy into her shaking hands, Adam bowed his forehead to hers and kissed her nose. "Congratulations, Shannon Reagan," he said huskily. "He looks just like you."

She choked at his kind words, more so when the weight of that tiny infant nestled safe and sound against her. Like a mother bear, she wrapped her firstborn son inside of her arms and breathed the smell of him into her soul. *My son.*

"I have a son, Adam," she announced to the man who already knew, a catch in her voice. "Thank you."

"Don't thank me," he muttered. "I'm just the wide receiver. I caught what you threw. You're the quarterback."

She honestly didn't have a clue what he was talking about, but it sounded wonderfully masculine and exactly like Adam. He'd not only caught Squeaks, he'd caught her. "I love you," she said, her heart full and her lips loose.

"You do, huh?" Adam still hung over her, his elbow in the sand beside her and his face warm and tender and close. "I meant it, you know. You are beautiful."

Very slowly, he leaned in. She moved Squeaks to the side and watched Adam descend, his dark blue gaze full of that same glorious light of love. He palmed her cheek and his thumb wiped the tears out from under her eye. She prepared as much as she could, her barriers breached and her heart willing to try again, but he paused, and she couldn't understand how he would want to kiss her. Not then. Not after she'd rejected her child.

"May I?" he breathed huskily.

She'd barely nodded when his lips were on hers, soft, warm and exquisitely tender. His tongue traced her mouth while his breath warmed her soul—not what she'd expected from the man who'd witnessed her cowardice. But then he lifted her and her baby onto his lap. She was a mess, but he didn't seem to care.

Adam pressed her under his chin, and rocked her and Squeaks as if it was his place to do so. Like he was father and husband. He smelled of sweat and sand and this forsaken desert island. Squeaks smelled of blood and birth, but both scents were the same. They were life. Nothing more. Nothing less.

Shannon snuggled her tiny firstborn child against her heart, amazed at the swell of motherly love for him. And then she heard it. Mingled with the steady beat of a very strong man were the soft strains of an old English melody. "Greensleeves." Only he sang the Christmas version. "What Child is This?"

Chapter Seventeen

Adam couldn't stop smiling. His cheeks seemed pinched in perpetual bliss. Not his child. Not his wife. Still—best day ever.

He'd heated more water over the coals and got Shannon cleaned up again, this time with some of that body wash Izza had packed into that carry-on of hers. That woman had literally thought of everything, and Adam was glad for the very feminine trait. Most guys would've maybe packed enough underwear and socks. She'd packed a little bit of everything.

The grime was gone from Shannon's pretty face. She glowed like a new mother should.

For his part, he'd gone down to the surf to wash. He knew she watched when he stripped out of his jeans down to his boxers, and that made him smile, too. All of their dealings had somehow ended up on an intimate level. Why stop now?

In a wild moment of abandonment, he dropped his boxers before he strode into the waves with his clothes in hand. Maybe seeing him naked would alleviate some of the discomfort she'd felt when he'd stripped her clothes away for the delivery. He hoped. Despite the extenuating situation, his male mind planned another intimate encounter with Shannon in the not-too-distant future. Somehow, some way, it was going to happen. Let her watch.

He scrubbed his hands with the fine powdery sand until he was clean enough to handle baby and mother again. No doubt about it, that boy had been in a hurry to get there. Maybe he should've named him Speedy instead of Squeaks. Adam scrubbed his clothes in the sand, too. The incoming waves made for a decent agitator and the sand would do for detergent.

Keeping an eye on Shannon, he waved, and she waved back. That girl had the biggest smile on her face, too. Breakfast was next on his agenda. Then a nap.

Casting his eyes down the beach to the graves, he thought of Donavan and the still undone chore of the day. That strange woman's body had to be buried next. Another grave. That made five.

But not Squeaks.

His happiness tempered, Adam went commando. He donned his wet jeans and stuffed his underwear in his back pocket before he walked to Shannon.

"Hi," she said shyly.

He crouched near mother and child, knowing full well she'd watched him bathe in the buff. "Hungry?"

Light blues scrolled over his chest and down to his unbuttoned pants. A different kind of hunger glittered in her pretty eyes, one that would have to wait, but yeah. She'd seen and she liked.

Shannon made like she was going to get up from her cozy parachute bedding, her elbows stuck in the sand behind her.

"Give me a break." He pressed a hand to her shoulder and leveled her back to earth. "I'm cooking today, Mama. My treat. What would you prefer, the peeled bananas or the sliced papaya? Our chef dried a lovely sea bass on a stick, or maybe it's filet of flounder. Your choice?"

"You know what I'd really like?" Her eyes filled, dark and misty.

He read her mind, if only because he wanted the same. Eventually. But there was no reason not to taste now.

"I think I know," he whispered on his way to her lips. The problem was that taste would only whet his appetite, and she was in no shape for more. He kept this contact chaste. "We really should eat. Food," he qualified.

She giggled coyly, and the easy feeling settled between them. She wasn't pushing him away anymore or blocking him with that invisible, hands-off wall.

"You know what I'd settle for?"

"Sushi?" he teased.

"No. I'm sick of fish."

"Me too. I just didn't want to say it out loud."

"I'm thinking cheeseburger with a dill pickle." She rolled her eyes like she was in heaven, and he could've sat there and watched her forever. This was the real Shannon, and she was delightful. "Extra fries. Those spicy-coated fries they have at Dinah's Diner. And ketchup. I know it sounds crazy, but I want lots of ketchup on my fries."

He laughed. "How about a chocolate shake?"

"Yes, but..." She deflated. "Fish and fruit will do. I guess."

"I could trap one of those rats we've seen shinnying up the coconut trees. They might taste good roasted over a slow fire."

That put a stop to the pity party. "Ewww." She punched his bicep gently, and the camaraderie of that simple act felt good.

He tapped the end of her nose. "Don't go anywhere."

In no time at all, he returned with enough of their current menu items to at least fill them. But he'd interrupted something very important. Shannon was trying to nurse an uncooperative preemie. She covered herself and turned away, red-faced.

"Is he eating?" Adam asked, going for the nonchalant approach. He'd seen enough women breastfeeding in his jaunts across the world. He wasn't embarrassed by it. She shouldn't be, either.

Shannon shook her head. The squirming infant in her hands arched his head back and let out a scratchy mew. "I think he's hungry, but... I don't know how to get him to, umm, open up."

"He might be too little to suckle," Adam said softly. He'd heard the plaintive note in her voice. "Won't he latch on?"

She blinked up at him, and he'd embarrassed her again. But honestly, he could help if she'd just let him. Adam set the banana leaves loaded with fruit and fish on the ground. Breakfast could wait. Squeaks needed to get the hang of nursing first.

"Try this." He held his first two fingers up like a scissors. "Take your nipple between your fingers like this."

He wanted to show her what he meant, but figured hands-on training would push her over the edge. She'd already cringed just baring herself. Blinking up at him, he could tell she was mortified to let him watch, but a man had to do what a man had to do. Once this little guy started nursing, Shannon would get over it.

Adam gulped. But was he going to live through the effect of the sight of her lush naked breast on his male body? That was all she needed to see—him horny and loaded for action. He brushed his damp jeans to lessen the hard-on springing to life. Not happening.

Shannon was too preoccupied to notice. She'd pulled her baby in close, her tongue working her lower lip and her brows knitted in concentration.

"Yes," Adam breathed softly, watching the Squeaks brush his sealed tight lips over her delectable mauve-colored tip. *Breastfeeding is simply and perfectly natural. It ensures the survival of the species. Yeah, right. With the right woman, it can also turn a guy on.*

He groaned for the strength to endure.

But the little guy didn't grasp the concept. Squeaks arched his back and moved his head back and forth like he was searching, but never really opened his eyes or his mouth to find his mama. Shannon whimpered and…

The big guy in command sprang into action. Without thinking, Adam's fingers were on the soft pillow of her breast. Very gently, he lifted Squeaks' head and steered his mouth to his mama's dripping nipple. The little guy was stubborn. Adam more so.

At last, Squeaks offered a soft grunt at being tortured, but in the process, he opened his mouth. His cute face scrunched into a frown. Because Adam knew how things worked, he squeezed Shannon's breast very carefully, milking it. A tiny stream dribbled over the baby's lips and into his mouth. He brushed his head back and forth and opened up. Adam tucked her in between the boy's lips, and just like that, Squeaks figured it out. He latched on.

"You see, he's got a tiny mouth right now, and—" Adam made the mistake of looking into her eyes. She wasn't embarrassed anymore, but he was. Heat swarmed his cheeks at the intimate liberty he'd just taken.

"You make it look simple," she said coyly. Her full lips blossomed into radiance.

"It is," he said, but right then he didn't know if he meant her nursing her baby or him having sex with that baby's pretty mother.

"You have very soft hands." Her eyes glowed. He looked down to where he still cupped her. Her hand rested calmly over his. The moment stormed him, and he was falling. Hard.

"Shannon..." His heart banged inside his chest.

"Yes?" She waited breathlessly. Squeaks suckled, and Adam couldn't think. In the twinkling of her pretty blue eyes, she'd become his sun, moon, and stars.

He brushed his thumb over her bare breast while Squeaks managed a couple more heartwarming grunts. The most incredible sense of protectiveness filled Adam's soul. Words came to him; words that fit the moment perfectly; words he should say.

He didn't.

"I had a dog once. Ah, I mean..." He stumbled over the size-eleven foot in his mouth. "Mabel was a new mom, and she didn't know what to do, either, and..." He looked away. *Tell me I didn't just compare Shannon to a dog. Way to go, Torrey.*

"Did Mabel's puppy live?"

He nodded. "All ten of them."

"Wow." Shannon's eyes widened. "That's a lot of puppies."

He relaxed. She wasn't offended.

"I'm sorry about before, you know, when I was...." She paused. "I kept thinking of my ex, that this is all his fault. And it happened so fast. I barely found out I'm expecting a baby, then I'm in labor and I've never had a baby before, and I just... I just..."

"You just survived a plane crash." He reminded her. "That's a miracle all in itself. It's probably why you went into early labor, too. Give yourself a break, Shannon. Were you in labor sitting out there in the jungle waiting for Ramsey to show?"

"I didn't think so. My back hurt, and I ached, but... I don't know. Maybe."

"And you didn't move? You just stayed out there all night with me? On the hard ground?"

"You said not to move."

"And then you helped bury Donavan?"

She nodded. "What else could I do? He was a good person. I wanted to be there for him… and you."

Adam shook his head. This girl was incredible. She'd taken everything he'd thrown at her to heart. This woman was champagne and caviar. He was beer and pizza. What could they possibly have in common? He intended to find out.

"Don't forget. I brought food." Reclaiming his hand, he settled alongside Shannon and her child. Adam offered her a slice of papaya off the edge of his knife. "So tell me about What's-His-Name."

"Brit Paxton?" Her countenance clouded as she took the fruit. "He's a handsome man, intelligent—cavalier when he wants to be. He's every woman's dream. That about sums him up. He's in foreign relations. A lot of them."

Adam caught the sad pun. The man was a cheater. "He know about Squeaks?"

"Yes. My father doesn't, but Brit does, only he doesn't want children. He told me to get ride of it."

Adam's fists clenched at the disgusting notion of ridding the world of an infant as pure as Squeaks. Brit Paxton was a damned ass. The world could do without him.

"I'd still be with him, but..." Shannon looked out to sea. "You're going to think I'm crazy, but I had the same dream three times in a row, one right after the other. That's when I knew I had to leave him—that he'd never be home and want to be with just me."

Adam couldn't imagine not wanting to be with Shannon. She had a way of making everything—better.

"It was a message from his grandfather, only..." She sighed. "I'd never met the man. He died before Brit and I were engaged, but in my dream, he told me to leave Brit and to think of the baby.

That got Adam's attention. What a crazy dream.

"He was right about everything." She bit her lip like she was debating her next words.

"Your ex wasn't all bad." Adam nodded to Squeaks, hoping she'd smile again. "He got this little guy right."

There was an entirely different world in the depths of those sad blues of hers. He leaned in for another kiss, and she met him halfway. With his hand gently at the back of her neck, he pulled her to his mouth, softly tasting the most delightful woman he'd ever met—strong, courageous, and innocently vulnerable at the same time. The thudding in his heart morphed into a consuming fire. Rolling to his knees, he cupped her face between both hands, worshipping his new true North.

"Thank you, Adam," she breathed as they broke their tender hold.

"For what? I'm just an overbearing frog who thinks he knows everything, even about nursing mothers." Forehead to forehead, he chuckled. "Maybe I ought to become a maternity nurse. I could teach, what's it called, lactation?"

"You do look cute when you're embarrassed."

His heart soared. *She thinks I'm cute.* How silly. How sweet. How odd that he felt like he was sixteen, and about to become a man all over again.

"So what about you?" she asked. "What's your sad story?"

"Not sure I have one." He settled beside her again. "I grew up in South Carolina. Dirt poor. Guess I've had my share of bad luck, like everyone else."

"Do you still have family back there?"

"Yes. Granddaddy moved in with my folks a couple years ago. Got a big family and a couple dogs, cats. You name it, we've had it at one time or another."

"Any brothers or sisters?"

"One sister. Two Nieces. Three nephews. Sandra married one of the good ol' boys from Clemson. Lives down the road a-piece."

"Clemson?"

"Clemson University. Home of the Tigers. Best football team in the world."

The smile on her face melted his heart all over again. Whatever was happening between them, he didn't want it to stop.

"Were you their quarterback?" she asked with something akin to awe in her voice.

"Nah." He shrugged it off, knowing a lady of her upbringing probably wouldn't understand the sport anyway. "Wide receiver."

"What does a wide receiver do?"

He winked. "They catch pigskins and babies."

Shannon offered another embarrassed smile. "So, umm, no ex in your life?" she asked, a hint of anxiety to her question.

"Heck no. My last girlfriend was bad enough. I came home from a three-week op and had to call the police just to get into my own apartment. She'd thrown all my things out."

"She threw *you* out of *your* place?"

"Did I mention she was demented?"

"How could she do that?"

"Beats me. Guess she'd had three weeks to get herself worked up. Enough about me. I've got a question for you." His heart vacillated somewhere between *God, I love this girl* and outright pounding like the Clemson U drumline before a homecoming game. One minute he could think; the next he was tongue-tied and trying real hard to remember what he'd wanted to ask. "Would you let me take you to dinner when we get off this island?"

"Yes."

He liked that she'd answered quickly. With one last long and lingering kiss, he settled closer to Shannon and her baby, never wanting to be separate from them. The feeling Adam had always thought impossible surrounded him now.

It felt like happily-ever-after.

Chapter Eighteen

"Hey! Look what we found." The sun was high overhead. Connor and Izza were on the beach, dragging something behind them in a long gray sheet. They'd been gone all morning, but it looked like they'd been successful.

"You stay here. I'll be right back." Adam pushed up from the ground beside Shannon.

They'd been discussing names for little boys. He'd been reluctant at first to share his opinions since Squeaks wasn't his son. Still, she'd insisted, so at last, he'd acquiesced. His father's name was James. His grandfather, straight off the old sod, was Malone.

She tried it on for size. James Malone Reagan. Jimmy. It fit. Like she and Adam seemed to fit. That he'd memorized a poem as long as "Bury Me With Sailors," then delivered it with perfect diction and reverent inflection to his lost teammate, had taken her by surprise, but it also connected her to him at a fundamental level. This man of brawn and muscle, the guy who thought he was responsible for the troubles of the world, had a definite tender side to him, a side that cherished a sweet lullaby and the written word as much as she did.

He'd made a magnificent sight standing there against the endless blue of the ocean, his arms behind his back and his head bowed. His shoulders squared and deeply tanned. His bare chest heaving and the breeze in his face. More than once, she'd thought he might break down at the raw emotion in his voice, but he'd held it together for the entire poem, and Donavan got a sendoff the angels would have been proud of.

But that voice. How rare indeed. She could listen to Adam all day and not grow tired of the rich honey in that rugged, manly baritone, sprinkled with a touch of southern charm. His drawl didn't come through often, but when it did, it soothed her soul as much as it plucked at her heartstrings and toyed with her libido. The man was pure magic with that sexy, smoky voice. Step aside James Earl Jones. Adam Torrey was in the house.

"Hey." Adam crossed the beach to Connor and Izza, peering down at the thing they'd dragged back. It had to be an animal, though she'd not seen any that large on the island yet. Maybe a small beached whale? A seal? It was big enough. Whatever, it was dead. She covered Jimmy's face with her hand. He didn't need to be inhaling the stench blowing upwind.

A mountain of clouds piled high in the northern horizon added to the pleasant sight of two bare-chested men, tanned and getting tanner every day. They'd gotten scruffier, their hair always tousled. Connor and Adam dragged the thing to where the woman's body still lay.

Izza had stepped away from the two men, shielding her eyes and looking toward the opposite end of the beach and the wreck. Her ponytail ruffled in the breeze. She lent the scene an exotic air with her deeply bronzed skin and tank top, as if maybe they weren't really castaways on a deserted island, as if maybe this was all a dream and they'd all wake up on a Caribbean cruise with piña coladas.

Jimmy Malone stretched, and Shannon forgot about the rest of the world. She counted his toes and fingers, each one perfectly formed and so miraculously tiny. When she looked up, the three agents stood over the woman. Connor nudged the corpse with his boot while the other two bent to take a closer look at it.

Shannon cringed. There was no way she'd touch anything so gruesome or that decayed. Ewww. A shiver raced up her neck at the notion. But Izza did. She pulled something up and out of the body, holding it pinched between two fingers, and looking up at the men like it was important. She had a plastic bag in her other hand, and that was so like Izza. She'd brought a whole new depth to scavenging. Where Shannon saw garbage floating in the water, Izza saw something else.

A gal could learn a lot hanging around her. Maybe from Connor, too. Adam for sure. There was a bond there, a link. Shannon felt it as sure as a rope tying her to him, and it wasn't just because he'd delivered her son. Her universe had changed since the moment she'd stepped foot inside The TEAM.

All at once, Izza's head jerked up. Jamie's and Braxton's mother zeroed in on Shannon like a lightning bolt about to strike the only tree in sight, and *oh, oh*. Adam must've told her about Jimmy. A very passionate, hot-blooded woman now knew there was a newborn on the island, and she was on a mission, stomping straight to Shannon.

"Oh, my heck. He's beautiful," she half-growled, half-whispered when she sank to her knees where Shannon sat with her son. Izza's dark eyes turned to melted chocolate fudge. "Aww, why didn't you tell me?"

"Probably because Shannon wasn't planning on delivering in the middle of the Pacific," Adam teased. He still grinned like a Cheshire cat. "This trip is like Gilligan's three-hour tour, remember?"

Even grumpy Connor's scowl quickly turned to a smile. "Go boil some water, woman," he urged his wife. "Wash your hands. You know you want to hold him."

"Aww, I do." Izza still knelt at Shannon's side. Her eyes lit with fire as she leaned into admire Jimmy. "But you should've told me," she scolded again. "Connor. Get one of my shirts out of my bag. He needs something softer than that old napkin for his first baby blanket."

Connor returned with a soft blue T-shirt, which he promptly tore into halves. He knelt beside Shannon, his eyes glistening. "I put some water on to boil. Wow. He's as small as our Jamie was when she was born. She was a preemie, too. Congrats," he said huskily. "You're sure full of surprises, Shannon, but this one's the best."

A hint of sadness colored his compliment, and the thought of two other little children waiting back home for the mommy and daddy they might never see again tempered Shannon's joy. But she'd also noticed that he'd used her first name.

Izza leaned into her husband, her eyes full of tears. "We're going to get home. I know we are. Don't cry."

He brushed the back of his hand over his eyes. "I'm not crying."

"Well, I am," Adam declared gruffly, swiping his face. "This little pipsqueak stole my heart the second he showed up."

"What are you going to name him?" Izza asked.

"I'm still deciding." Shannon wasn't ready to share the name that meant the most. She glanced up at Adam, by now the only man standing. "Adam calls him Squeaks."

Adam winked. That small, intimate connection filled her with desire. The tropical heat couldn't stop the shiver that raced over her body. One glance, one wink and her heart took flight—to him.

"Hey there, Squeaks, my man. Oh, you're so cute, I could eat you up." Izza changed from a tough street fighter into a sappy mom.

"So what'd you guys find? What did you drag home?" Shannon asked finally, scrunching her nose. "A shark? A deer? You guys aren't going to roast it for dinner, are you? It smells really bad."

Adam shook his head in disgust. "Hell, no. It's Ramsey."

The look on Shannon's face was priceless.

"Yes, Ramsey." Adam answered her unspoken question. "Looks like he's been dead for a day or two."

"Then who killed Donavan?" She looked fearfully around their camp.

"We don't know," Connor added, "but we brought this jerk back for a decent burial anyway. We found another parachute and his skydiving gear, so we know for sure he was in the Gulfstream with us. It's just possible that woman out there on the beach was his partner. Will you gals be okay while we dig a couple more graves?"

"We'll be fine," Izza said, without looking up. She'd made herself comfortable on the sand beside Shannon, cross-legged and obviously dying to hold that baby.

It was all Adam could do not to take Shannon in his arms and kiss her goodbye. The die was cast. This woman was in his heart to stay.

Connor bumped his arm, signaling time to go. Adam gathered their homemade digging implements. He and Connor left the women behind. They used a couple banana leaves in lieu of gloves to transfer the woman's remains to the tarp alongside Ramsey's.

"You found this by the body?" Adam asked, fingering the gray tarp. It looked damned familiar

"No, we found Ramsey already in it. It's what you think it is. It's got Reagan Industries stamped on the other side. Ramsey must've wrapped the pallet before he jumped and took it with him. That could explain the extra parachute."

"So could she." Adam dropped his eyes to the dead woman. "Are you thinking what I'm thinking?"

"That this crash was a set-up? Been thinking it for days."

"You don't still think Shannon was in on it, do you?"

Connor grunted as they dragged their load toward the cemetery. "Nah. I was out of my head. That little lady couldn't hurt a flea. Sorry I was a dick. I owe you one. Her, too."

Adam let it go. He'd seen enough concussions and traumatic brain injuries come out of combat. Connor was lucky he hadn't been hurt worse.

"At first, I thought Bell was in on it," Adam admitted, "because he dumped the Gulfstream on a damned tiny island in the Pacific, but now I'm not sure. Maybe he was just lucky."

"Pilots who fly the ocean often enough might know where to land in case of emergency. You saw the wreck. You know the difference between engine failure and sabotage. I doubt Bell would've rigged a bomb in the cabin."

"No, that's on Ramsey." Adam dragged in silence, relieved that Connor offered sound logic instead of paranoia. He had no doubt Ramsey killed the crew, not after the cryptic '1X1' mark he'd carved into poor Dillon. It was possible Donavan interrupted Ramsey, that they struggled. Ramsey lost his knife. Donavan gave chase. So who killed Ramsey? Better question, who had the damned drones?

After they arrived at the cemetery, Adam dropped his corner of the tarp to kneel at his friend's grave. He smoothed a hand over the sand, wishing with all his heart for that elusive *one more day* with Donavan. "He saved our lives, Connor, but why didn't he let us know where he was? If he'd come back to camp sooner, we could've saved him. Protected him."

"You know Donavan. There must've been a good reason." Connor nodded at the corpses. "It'd sure be good to know if she was stabbed or shot."

"What difference would that make?"

"Then we might who she was working with—the jerk with the knife who killed the crew, or the guy with the gun who shot Donavan. It sure wasn't Ramsey."

"On a good day…"Adam glanced at the scattered wreckage, "I carried both. So did you. Knowing how she died doesn't mean anything. We've still got a killer on the loose."

"I know you've been a little busy with Shannon and the baby and all, but me and Izza found the cave."

That was a surprise. "You did? Where?"

"On the other side of this rock. You could walk to it in thirty minutes if you took the long way around. Forty tops. And you were right. It's a subterranean hole in the ground, maybe an eight-foot drop straight down through solid rock. Looks volcanic. Our fresh water streams run from there. Plenty of boot tracks in the mud around it, too."

"You see anyone there?"

"Just Ramsey. Someone dragged him to the beach, probably thought the tide would take him out to sea."

That raised Adam's brows. "Why didn't you say anything before?"

"Because that new mama back there doesn't need more stress." Connor said the right words, but Adam caught the well-intended lie.

"And because she's Paul Reagan's daughter," Adam said bluntly as he got to his feet. "You still don't trust her, do you?"

Connor hemmed and hawed. "Actually, I do. Now. I don't believe she's directly responsible, but she's involved somehow, maybe just because of her last name. I do think her coming with us put a wrinkle in the plan. So where the hell are the Hummingbird Hawks? Why haven't we seen them yet? If they're so bad, Ramsey could've evaporated us in our sleep that first night. Why didn't he?"

"Damn, I'm glad you're feeling better." Adam smacked his friend's shoulder. "Don't think I haven't been asking myself the same question. Either the drones are still hidden on this island with us, or—"

"Or they didn't survive the drop," Connor finished for him, "which changes everything. Why kill Donavan if there are no drones? Why kill anyone?"

"But he said they were here. He must've seen them."

Connor looked upward, his brows lifted as stretched both hands over his head. "Crap. This mess is one damned big, ugly onion. You peel one layer, and what do you get?"

"Enough shit to make your eyes water," Adam answered.

"You're getting close to her, huh?"

Adam grunted at that shift in conversation. "Kinda hard to miss, isn't it?"

Connor glanced at the graves. "Izza's convinced Shannon walks on water, and I have to agree. She's quite the woman. Come on. Let's get this done."

Adam wasn't about to lay Ramsey next to Donavan, so he started digging on the other side of Dillon's grave. After a few cans full of sand, that decision felt wrong, too. The poor boy deserved better company in the hereafter. Adam sat back on his legs. "I don't want to bury this bastard here."

Connor looked up from digging with a so-now-you-tell-me look in his eye. "Then where?"

Blowing out a deep sigh, Adam stared at the sea. The usual mountain of clouds piled high to the north promised another breathtaking sunset he had yet to appreciate. Maybe a thunderstorm by the dark looks of them. He glanced farther down the beach to a fallen palm, grayed with age and salt, its narrowed tip pointed straight into the surf. That tree would mark a definite wall between the decent and the indecent.

"There." He pointed to where he meant. "Let's bury them over there."

Connor shrugged. "Fine. I don't really care. Let's just get them in the ground. They reek."

In short order, they lugged the bodies to the other side of the palm tree and dug one extra-wide grave.

"I'm going to make some grave markers one of these days," Connor said when the hole was deep enough. "You want to help?"

"What will we call this one? Madame X?" Adam nudged the dead woman's foot. Mostly denuded of flesh, her skeletal leg rotated to the side and her foot fell off, the waterlogged boot with it. He intended to roll the leg into the grave with the rest of her, until a thin, black case fell out of the sole of her boot. He opened it to reveal ten one hundred dollar bills neatly folded alongside a cylindrical piece of metal. "Whoa. Check this out."

"What the hell?" Connor's jaw dropped. "An antenna?"

"And get-out-of-jail-free cash," Adam said, referring to the money a covert operator carried behind enemy lines. Bribing the locals might work, or might not. It never hurt to be prepared.

His inner sniper sprang to life. Finding an antenna meant a radio. Maybe in the other boot. As carefully as possible, he pulled it clear of the slimy mess. Thankfully, that foot bone stayed connected to her leg bone.

"Gross," Connor muttered.

Something rattled inside that sole, too. Pressing his palm to the slimy rubber Adam exerted pressure. The sole slid open. A cell phone dropped into his palm, only this was no ordinary cell phone. He lifted it to Connor. "Lookee here.

"Crap. Does it still work?"

"Oh, hell yeah." This baby was a fully functional satellite communicator, waterproof, dustproof, and impact-resistant. Adam had used one before. It wasn't meant for vocal conversation, only for sending emergency calls. Best yet, GPS coordinates pinged along with the SOS.

He texted Alex as fast as his fingers and thumbs could fly. *Boss. Torrey. Mahers. Reagan. Request immediate pick-up. Get us the hell out of here!*

The color screen gleamed bright and beautiful in his hand. He held his breath. The power of this thing was amazing. Even now, it should've been pinging a distress call to a satellite far above earth's orbit. He hoped. A twenty-four-hour monitoring center should already be relaying the message to local responders while the text hit Alex's phone in Virginia at the same time.

He really hoped. Alex was technically challenged, but he usually kept his phone on him. He'd goddamned better have it on him today.

The minutes stretched. Connor got antsy. "Here. Try it with the antennae." He screwed the pencil-thin antennae into the top of the communicator. Just as he did, the handheld device vibrated and pinged an alert.

Alex had answered. *Sit tight. On our way. ETA in twenty-four hours max. Casualties?*

Adam sank to the sand, emotional beyond belief and so damned happy. The fact that he hadn't slept in more than twenty-four hours didn't help. He typed, '*Donavan and flight crew dead. Mahers, Torrey, and Reagan good. Baby boy good, too.*'

Alex's response came quick. *Whiskey. Tango. Foxtrot? Baby boy?*

Adam laughed at his boss's military version of swearing. He could've bawled like a baby. Connor sank to the sand beside him. "Tell him we need real food, and a few weapons wouldn't hurt."

Need food. Weapons. Unknown enemy combatant on location. Killed Donavan. Bring the rain.

"Good job." Connor thumped Adam's shoulder. "That'll get his attention."

Alex answered back. *Message received. Harley in transit soon. Watch the sky.*

Copy that, Adam typed. *Damned good to hear from you, Boss.*

Another message came quickly. *Hawaii. Tomorrow night. My treat.*

The fact that Alex had just specified a specific time hit Adam hard. Their nightmare was almost over. He fumbled an answer. *Copy that.*

"We're saved," he told Connor, like Connor didn't already know. "We're going home!"

Chapter Nineteen

"When I get home, I'm taking a day long bubble bath," Izza said coyly to Connor. "Want to join me?"

He still held her tight in his arms after spinning her around like a ragdoll when he and Adam had returned. Instead of answering, he kissed her long and hard. They'd turned into lovebirds. First Izza had screamed and cried. Then Connor. Then they'd cried together as if they were the only two on the whole island.

Shannon looked away. It was hard to watch. She wanted to hug Adam, but since he'd returned with that communicator device, he'd been sitting off by himself, playing with it. He didn't seem as happy as the Mahers.

"Hey guys." Adam interrupted their merry-making. "You need to see this."

Shannon joined the huddle around him. Baby Jimmy was sound asleep. Izza had devised a sling that kept the baby pressed to Shannon's body and at the perfect level for feeding. She'd also explained a lot about babies and nursing. A woman's tutelage was so much easier to accept than a man's. Still...

Shannon's eyes went to the tense neck of that very helpful man now focused on the phone he'd found. The memory of his hand on her breast still tingled. He'd looked so genuinely distressed when he'd realized what he'd done. She wanted him to do it again.

Connor sat cross-legged next to Adam with Izza on his lap. Bright blue eyes smiled like there wasn't anything Adam could say that would make him unhappy. Izza's brown eyes smiled, too. Shannon took a position next to Connor and Izza. She would've preferred snuggling with Adam, but he seemed—busy.

They'd no more than settled to the ground when a steady buzzing sound caught Shannon's attention.

"Shit, hold still!" Adam commanded, his gaze focused beyond her.

She froze. The sound came from more than one direction. Apprehension shivered up her back and over her shoulders. If those buzzing things were bees, they were really big bees. She clenched Jimmy to her chest.

Adam motioned with his palm for everyone to stay down. No one had moved, anyway. She stopped breathing, watching his expression change from disbelief to fear to anger. His jaw clenched tight. Adam glanced at her and held her gaze. Shannon cringed, expecting the sting of a thousand killer bees at any moment. Covering Jimmy with both arms, she vowed she'd die before they touched him.

Closer. Closer. The buzzing turned to a mechanical hum. Her heart thudded to a dead stop. *Oh, no. It's drones. Not bees.*

With a whisper, one hovered directly in front of her. The sleek titanium Hummingbird toggled its tailfins as it maintained an even keel, almost as if it looked at her. From her late-night crash course in UAVs, she recalled that most of the auditory and visual sensors and cameras were encapsulated in the black polycarbonate nose. The drone was, at that very moment, evaluating everything about her, from her height, weight, and body mass to her temperature, and if she was armed or not. And it was thinking. Planning what it needed to do next. Deciding if she should live or die.

"Easy," Connor whispered at her side. "Take it real—"

The drone pivoted toward him and Izza. Shannon shuddered. A ripple of air on her bare shoulder made her cringe as another drone passed by. Everyone scrambled to their feet. Adam held up three fingers. Three drones. Terror shivered over her.

Where's the fourth?

The second Hummingbird lowered into the same hovering position in front of Adam. A third came to rest in front of Shannon, while the first maintained surveillance on Connor and Izza.

We are going to die.

The harder her heart beat, the tighter she clutched Jimmy. Intense emotion flooded her heart. If this thing was studying her, then it was also studying her son.

Study this!

Shannon didn't think. She just balled her fist and punched the snub nose of that snoopy, man-made piece of trash. It hurt. She winced, but she also caught Adam's surprise. He winked, lending her courage. She covered Jimmy defiantly with her arm, ready to knock that thing out of the air if she had to.

"Easy," Connor murmured beside her. "It might be armed."

Number Three, the drone she'd punched, resumed its previous position. It clicked once, then two times in quick succession. Another click, and—"Hello, Shannon Reagan."

Her jaw dropped. It talked? "How do you know my name?"

"Protocol search engines retrieved a ninety-nine-point-eight percent match with the Reagan Industries database and federal databases. Therefore, you are Shannon Reagan. Daughter of Paul Reagan and wife, Olivia, now deceased. Ex-wife of Brit Paxton." The drone pivoted to Connor, Izza, and Adam in turn. "You are Conner Maher. Isabella Maher. Adam Torrey. Employed by The TEAM in Alexandria, Virginia."

"What do you want?" Shannon tensed, remembering the solar-powered lasers that could melt a man in seconds. Number Three rotated another full circle before it tilted down toward Jimmy.

Adam made a motion with his raised hand, prompting her to say something. She couldn't tell what until he pantomimed shooting a gun with his thumb and index finger.

Oh, the kill code. "God bless America," she blurted out.

Number Three whined then quietly settled to the ground. The other two powered down, too. The standoff was over.

"You hit it!" Adam took hold of her hand, the biggest grin on his face.

Connor blew out a big breath. "I didn't know you could do that."

"Me neither." It hadn't dawned on her to just say the kill code. She thought she'd have to activate the onboard keyboard of each drone and type it in, or something just as difficult. Ha. The difference between how authors' and an engineers' minds worked. Amazing.

"Now we've got problems. The murderer will be looking for his drones when they don't return." Izza jerked her thumb toward the communication device. "What were you going to tell us?"

Adam held it up for all to see. "This little thing can connect to any social media site on the planet. And I mean any. It's got email, too."

"Then who was that dead chick, and who was she talking to?" Izza demanded. "You got a profile picture? A name?"

"That information isn't posted, but she did communicate regularly with someone at Reagan Industries."

All eyes turned to Shannon. "Don't look at me I didn't do it."

"No. Not you." Connor clapped a hand to her shoulder. "You're not behind any of this crap."

Adam held up a hand for silence. "Listen to this e-mail between TM and JB."

TM: Drop zone is prepared for your arrival.

JB: Good. Pawn is in place.

TM: Queen is open?

JB: Yes. Queen is open. Consider everyone collateral damage.

TM: Say again. Queen, too?

JB: Yes. Yes. Queen, too.

TM: HH will survive?

JB: Most assuredly. You'll have it within seven days.

TM: How can you be sure?

JB: I'll be there.

Adam looked up at Shannon from the screen. She got it. She was the queen. "Someone inside Reagan Industries deliberately planned this crash," she whispered. "They meant to kill me, and steal the drones." Her father's calculating face flashed to mind. He was underhanded enough, but to murder his daughter? No. Absolutely not. He wouldn't.

Then who? In a flash, anyone and everyone who worked for her father became suspect. Well, all except Raul. He'd been through thick and thin with her. He wouldn't be behind this.

"You know any JBs or TMs?" Connor asked.

A breath hissed out of her. *Oh, my. TM? Could he? Would he? What have I done?* "I told him everything."

"What, Shannon?" Adam asked. "Who did you talk to?"

"I don't know if it's him. It couldn't be him. He's elderly, and he's..." She gulped. "Those initials. TM. I called him the night before we took off. It couldn't be him, but—"

"Who?" Connor asked, his hand gentle on her shoulder again. "Who do you think it is, Shannon?"

"My friend, Terrence Moore. He's an engineer on the drone project. My father refused to give me access, so I called Terrence. Oh, Connor. You're right. I did it. This is my fault. I told him everything. Only that doesn't make sense. He cares about me and he gave me the kill code. Why would he do that if he wanted me dead?"

"How old's this Terrence dude?" Connor asked

"He's close to fifty or sixty, I think."

Connor rolled his eyes. "Wow. That old man's got to be something if he HALO dropped onto our little island, killed

Ramsey, murdered that gal we found, and sent the killer drones after us. Crap. You're right. We're screwed."

He made Shannon smile. He wasn't so bad.

"Are you two finished?" Adam asked, his brow raised at her snuggled in Connor's arm. "Because whoever TM is, he's signing off with a DPRK officer designation. He's a captain."

"You sure?" Connor released Shannon to peer into the screen.

"That's the Democratic People's Republic of Korea's flag alright," Izza declared. "I'd recognize the red star anywhere."

"If TM is a North Korean spy, we're looking at some serious espionage," Adam muttered. "Whoever JB is, he's selling top-secret weaponry to an enemy."

"And it's possible TM and JB are both on our island with us," Connor added.

"Then let's go back to the cave and finish them." Izza had changed into a hardened warrior. A handful of Chinese stars splayed like playing cards in her hand. "That JB jerk is going to come looking for his drones if we don't. You coming, Connor?"

He shot her a devil-may-care smile. "I'm whipped, I admit it. I'll follow you anywhere, woman, just point the way."

"And you…" Izza took a step into Adam's space. "You keep Shannon and our little boy safe. Can you handle that, *Junior Agent*?"

Shannon had to smile. Diminutive Izza had her finger poked into the chest of the hulk towering over her. Adam could've easily pushed her aside and done as he'd pleased, but she looked like a mean bantam rooster, ready to take him down if he dared argue. Her chin jutted forward with defiance. For lack of a better word, Adam looked—obedient?

"I'm not leaving her," he said the words Shannon wanted and needed to hear as he circled an arm around her waist. "You two stay safe. Don't let this JB person get past you."

"We won't. Let's go," Connor said. "We're taking the pistol. Remember. Keep an eye on the sky. Help's on its way."

Izza snorted as they walked away. "One if by land, two if by sea, and an archangel by sky if I know the boss."

"Shouldn't they wait until this storm passes?" Shannon asked, her eyes on the billowing thunderclouds stacked to the north. She edged in closer to the muscled warmth of Adam's body. "I don't think help can get to us through that storm. It's going to be a bad one. Shouldn't we look for cover?"

Adam nestled his nose into the crook of her neck. "Shannon baby, I am the storm."

Chapter Twenty

"Hang on tight!"

The roar of the wind drowned out Adam's command. With no way to escape the rain, he and Shannon huddled within the shelter of Banyan tree trunks. Squeaks was safe inside her shirt, wrapped in his sling and warm beneath the nylon windbreaker, another miracle item that Izza had packed for her *tropical* trip. Adam zipped Shannon and Squeaks up tight.

The flimsy three-sided huts had already taken flight. Lightning crackled sideways in the sky and through the stacks of clouds. The driven rain pounded relentlessly.

She should've kept her head down instead of looking up, but she didn't. Water dripped off his head and into her upturned face. Adam had never beheld a more perfect picture of trust.

In one fluid motion, he caught her to his mouth, plundering the sweet treasure she offered. She grasped his shoulders, maintaining enough distance not to crush the baby, but pouring everything into that simple contact of flesh on flesh and heart on heart.

His tongue traced the seam of her lips then tangled deeper. She melted into him. The storm wailed like a banshee, but a more magnificent thunder pounded in his soul.

Trembling, he broke the connection to cup her rain-wet cheeks between his palms.

"Shannon," he whispered reverently, knowing she couldn't hear him above the storm. No matter. It needed to be said, and he intended to say it a thousand times more. He mouthed them to be sure she got the message. "I love you."

She tipped her forehead into his lips, and he understood why she wasn't afraid. Love was like that. It made her strong. It made him brave. Let nature rail around them. Let the howling wind bend the trees. As long as he and she were together, they were greater than the fury of any storm.

"Beat it! Shoo!"

Adam smiled at the change in Shannon. Motherhood was a good fit.

For now, she rested with him and Squeaks beneath the shade of the banyan tree. The storm had passed quickly, but not before Mother Nature had stripped most of the leaves from the trees, tossed their cozy campsite-by-the-cove, and scoured Izza's carefully collected *stuff* from the beach. Everything was gone, except what clever Izza had tied to the tree. Her half-empty carry-on. The metal pan. Half a dozen empty water bottles. Connor's lonely boot.

The recliners from the Gulfstream were now in the bushes, but still salvageable. Again. But those flimsy shacks Adam had wasted time and effort on? Gone like kites. The disabled UAVs still lay where they'd fallen, but the fire pit was a puddle of mud. It was a good thing Harley was on his way. Adam didn't relish rebuilding what had been, at best, a hovel.

Out of sheer exhaustion, Shannon slept until the baby fussed, but now she batted one spider after another out of her way. The eight-legged crawlers seemed to have come out with the rain, but the second they dropped down from the branches, she gave them a good flick of her hand and sent them flying. Her squeamishness was gone with the wind, too.

The intimacy of holding her while she nursed sparked an overwhelming feeling in Adam. Was it fatherhood or family? He honestly didn't know, but wow. It had happened fast, and it hit him hard. One moment, he was a throwaway boyfriend. The next, he was ready to fight the world for the woman he loved.

"I saw when you took your clothes off," she whispered shyly.

"Planned it that way." He nestled his chin into the crook of her neck, pleased she'd mentioned his brief moment of nudity.

"I'd like to see it again."

"It?" he teased.

The reddest blush consumed her face. "I meant your butt, maybe *it*, too."

Cupping her jaw, he angled for another taste. They were at the kissing stage of their relationship. Tastes and nibbles of each other that couldn't wait. The moment they parted, he wanted more, so this time he let himself get lost in the flavor of her heated mouth.

Her quiet moan splashed fire through his veins, which he instantly quelled. Squeaks needed her. Adam stilled his aching desire, breaking their contact. Heart-poundingly tempting with a babe at her breast, Shannon smiled demurely, her hand soft and gentle on his jaw.

"Adam," she murmured, and he was lost. He blinked, but the spell of this woman entangled his soul, pulling him in deeper.

"Shannon," he said huskily, not sure what his mouth might say next. If he didn't get his feelings under control, it wouldn't matter that she'd just given birth. He'd be ravishing little Squeaks' mother right there in the sand. Breaking the gentle connection, Adam settled for his nose in her hair and bland conversation that wouldn't throw sparks. "Tell me about yourself. What do you do for a living?"

She sighed. "I used to be a writer and a publisher."

"Oh, yeah? That's cool."

"It was. I owned a small boutique press. I was living my dream."

He heard the wistful note in her voice. "But your daddy had different plans for you. I got the impression you were out of your depth that day in the office."

"What gave me away? Throwing up all over your boots?"

"You didn't throw up on me," he whispered. "You just looked like you had your back against the wall, like you thought you had to fight us all."

"You were so mad at me."

"No, I was angry at your father. He'd leveled some pretty damning charges against me, but then he didn't have the guts to show up and say them to my face. He sent you to do his dirty work."

She scrunched her shoulders. "I'm supposed to take over the company. He thinks throwing me into the fire will help me learn."

"He's a bully. He's just trying to control you, Shannon. You shouldn't let him. Tell him 'hell no' once in a while."

"It's easier said than done." Her voice grew quieter.

Adam cupped her chin, turning her to meet his eyes. "Listen. You're a strong woman; you just don't know it. Who braved the giant spiders to get food for the rest of us?"

"Me." She blinked up at him, and darn, he wanted to kiss her again.

"And who brought fire out of the ocean so we could roast those godawful bananas?"

"We didn't roast bananas." She scrunched her shoulders again, and that little-girl quality wasn't lost on Adam. The spark he'd been fighting sprang to life.

"And who..." He groped for some of the other things she'd done, but logic faded fast. "Oh, yeah. Who cleaned Izza's hurt leg? Who wrapped my broken ribs?"

If she wasn't convinced of her strength, he was. Industrial strength. That was Shannon through and through, and he was swept along with her. A ray of reflected light off the horizon caught his attention. *Could it be?*

"Look there. Do you see it?"

She followed his direction. "What is it?"

They both leaned forward. The glitter grew into a ship, and then another, this one farther west, but approaching as rapidly as the first.

"Adam. Look up there. In the sky." She pointed overhead where a man dangled from the canopy of a white parachute.

Adam tensed, unwilling to assume friend over foe. The intruder drifted down, and with a running step, landed on their beach. Dressed in a gray flight suit and black helmet, there was no way to know who'd just landed. The man promptly unfastened and dropped the rucksack strapped to his back. The minute he peeled off his helmet though, Adam took off running. "Harley! Damn, man. Is that you?"

"Hey!" Harley caught him in a thumping man-hug. The guy never looked so good.

"How'd you get here so fast?"

"Been in Hawaii since you guys went down. The whole world's looking for you." Harley Mortimer was a danged welcome sight. He leaned his chin into the two-way radio pinned at his shoulder. "Touchdown, Boss. In contact with Adam. He looks good."

"Keep me advised," Alex's disembodied voice crackled.

"Copy that." Harley reached into a rear pocket and pulled out two pistols. He tossed one to Adam, quickly followed by a couple of extra magazines, while he scanned the island.

"Is he in Hawaii, too?" *Unbelievable.*

"Hell, no," Harley nodded at the smaller boats now fast approaching, one from each ship. "You know Alex. He's been on the USS George Washington for a couple days now. Least he was. He might be in one of those utility boats headed our way. You know how he is."

Adam's brows lifted at that impressive statement. He'd been on the GW, a Nimitz-class nuclear-powered super carrier only once in his career in the Caribbean. That the United States Navy was there on that specific aircraft carrier meant the President was prepared go to war to protect the drones, but also—that Alex cared enough to personally search for his missing agents. It put a lump in Adam's throat.

"Donavan's dead?" Harley asked.

Adam swallowed hard and got back to the business of being rescued. "Connor and Izza went after his killer. The bastard's on the other side of the island. He sent the drones after us, but Shannon disabled them." While Harley peeled out of his harness, Adam rolled his parachute into a manageable bundle and stuffed it into the bag hanging from Harley's belt.

"Damn." Harley's gaze rested on the mounded graves. "Is that him?"

Adam sobered. "Yes, and the flight crew. Ramsey and the Korean gal are farther down."

"Let's get off this beach. It's about to get crowded. One of those boats coming ashore is Navy, most likely with Alex onboard." Harley glanced over his shoulder. "The other's North Korean. GW's commander already told them to stand down, but they refused."

"They're after the drones," Adam stated.

Shannon stood in the shade of the Banyan, one hand shielding her eyes as they approached.

"Well, well, well," Harley chuckled. "It's sure good to see you again, Miss Reagan. Alex said there was a new baby boy in town. What's his name, darlin'?"

"James Malone." Shannon glanced shyly at Adam. Her choice of names only intensified his feelings for the little guy and for her.

"He's as small as a June bug." Harley caressed the baby's cheek with the back of his index finger. "I've got twin sons, Sponge Bob and The Beast."

"Oh, my. What kinds of names are those?" she asked.

"Wait until you meet them," Adam said, "then you'll know. They're just like their dad."

Harley took the hit with a lopsided-grin. "And what's wrong with being handsome-as-hell and a better shot than you with a long rifle?"

The normal banter was a welcome relief. Adam could've spent more time chatting, but it had to wait. "We've got trouble, Shannon. One of those boats headed our way is North Korean. The other's Navy."

Harley pulled a small baby blue package out of his rucksack and tossed it to Shannon. "This is for your little guy, some diapers, a blanket, and stuff. Nothing fancy—it's just something to get him ready to travel. We don't have a lot of time."

He pulled several more pistols, a sawed-off, and a dozen more magazines from his rucksack. "Listen. Technically, we're in international waters. This island doesn't belong to any country, but our President would prefer the North Koreans don't take the drones with them when they leave." He tossed Adam a plastic carton of grenades, two noise-cancelling headsets, and two gas masks. "Time to gear up, Adam. Shannon, if things get ugly, keep your headset and mask on. Take cover. Got it?"

She trembled as Adam secured both items around her neck, but damn it. She *would* wear it. This was crunch time, that moment when rescue was so close you could almost taste it, but bad things still happened. He'd known too many guys who'd been shot on their last duty day and worse, when they were in the chopper and flying home.

"You're worried," she told him, her eyes soft and dewy despite the approaching danger.

"I am," he admitted. Worried those boats and ships out there might bring war to their shores. Worried he'd lose her when this adventure ended. That he'd never see Shannon or Squeaks again. That she really was too good for him.

"Here's protection for the baby." Harley pulled out a tiny helmet for Squeaks from his rucksack, complete with chinstrap and a full, face shield. "One of my Navy friends made it when he heard there was a baby involved, but damn. He's small. Hope it fits."

Adam didn't have time to double check. A distant gunshot sent a flutter of birds through the palms. Shannon clutched his forearm. "What about Connor and Izza?"

"They have a gun?" Harley's face jerked toward the sound.

"Just Izza's Berretta," Adam's eyes riveted to the jungle, "and her Chinese stars."

Harley pushed to his feet. "Anything I need to know before I leave? Any snakes? Lions? Tigers? Things that will eat me before I get to where I'm going?"

"Not that I've seen, but you'll make better time if you cut through the middle of the island. The cave's directly opposite this beach on the other side," Adam replied. "That's where Connor and Izza were headed."

Harley nodded once. "Stay here."

Chapter Twenty-One

"This is crazy," Shannon muttered, her hand smoothing over the sleeping babe in her sling. "We sit here all week and nothing happens. Now look. Everyone's showing up."

She'd gotten anxious since Harley left, pacing their cove one moment, then sitting beside Adam, only to jump to her feet and do it again. The waiting game wore on his nerves, too. He'd never been the kind of man to stay behind and tend the home fires.

"It's because I activated the communicator. The Koreans knew they were made when I texted Alex, that something happened to their agent."

"I'm glad this is nearly over. It'll be good to get out of here, I just wish I knew who got shot."

"Me, too. It might've been nothing," Adam muttered, wishing he could be so lucky. That single gunshot ate at him. His guys never wasted a shot if they didn't have to. Just how many people were on this damned rock?

That brought Shannon back to him. She folded her body at his side, her hand on his knee while they faced the ocean. "Your boss is something else."

"He is that," Adam agreed. "I really thought he was in Virginia when I sent that text, not in Hawaii."

"At least he came for you," she said wistfully.

So that's the problem. Adam lifted her hand from his knee to his lips. Despite how he treated her, a part of Shannon was still that little girl trying to please her father. Tenderly, Adam planted a kiss on each of her knuckles, his eyes locked on hers. "I'm sure Alex has kept your father apprised, Shannon. He's probably in Hawaii right now waiting for you and wondering where you are."

Her lashes came down. "Hmmm."

By then the sound of the two approaching motorboats lifted over the waves. "We need to get you somewhere safe," he said to break the tension.

"No, you don't," a gruff voice growled from the shadows of the Banyan.

Adam scrambled to his feet at yet another unknown quantity in the game of drones. He stepped between him and Shannon, blocking her with his arm, his weapon on target.

The guy ducked around the trunk of the Banyan, a polished steel Glock wavering in his unsteady hand. Whiskered and dirty, his beach shorts and open shirt looked in as rough shape as him. This had to be the bastard who'd killed Donavan, maybe the woman and Ramsey, too. "My, my, don't you two look cozy?"

Shannon angled around Adam for a better look. "Brit?" she asked in disbelief. "What are you doing here?"

Adam growled but let her have her say. He already despised this slimy bastard for what he'd done to Shannon, and indirectly, to Squeaks. Knowing that Paxton had to be the guy who'd murdered Donavan cinched his fate. The Glock was a good pistol—almost as good as Adam's Ruger. But justice always came down to the man behind the gun.

Paxton's leered at Shannon, his eyes skimming up her body like they had a right to. "I made a deal, and I plan to keep my end of it, unlike you, you lying bitch. You ever heard of *'til death do us part*?"

"Did *you*?" she shot back at him. "At least I'm single. How many times did you step out on me while we were married?"

Every male muscle in Adam's body clenched with the need to end Paxton. He could fully deliver on the death part of that one-sided marriage vow. "Back off. There's no way this'll come out in your favor."

The red laser dot from Paxton's weapon danced over Adam's chest. "I don't want to kill either of you, but I'll do it. I need the activation code, and she's got it."

"Not going to happen," Adam breathed. *Not only no, but hell no.* He didn't need a cute little laser to shoot straight. His sixth sense and years worth of muscle training had already locked his pistol sights into place. He steadied his hand, aimed dead center of Paxton's forehead. There'd be no body shot today. Adam meant to blow his fucking head off.

"No, Adam." Shannon's hand settled on his shoulder blade, but he instantly shrugged it away. *Don't touch me. Not at zero-minus-time-to-kill. Not when I'm standing between good and evil. Not now.*

Squeaks offered a scratchy cry into the tense standoff. The infant's tender voice inflamed Adam's full-blown protective instinct, but it also drew Paxton's attention. "What the hell's that? You got a monkey?"

"This is your son." Shannon took a step around Adam. She raised Squeaks to her ex-husband's view, just enough for him to see the infant's face. Adam couldn't believe she'd done that. She couldn't still have any feelings left for this murdering liar, could she?

"Don't you want to see him?" she asked softly. "He's a perfect little boy. Our son."

Paxton spat to the side. "Never should've crawled into the sack that last time."

"The only place you ever crawled was into every other woman's bed. Now look at him!" Shannon's voice turned to steel. "Look at the child you created the night you raped me, so I can honestly tell him his damned father met him."

Paxton rolled his shoulders. "*You* look at him. I don't have time for this."

"Your grandfather was right." The steel had changed to calm. "You've never appreciated what we had together."

"What *we* had? Would all that '*what we had together*' crap be the privilege of being married to *you*, the richest bitch on the East Coast? Would it be watching *you* rise to the top of Reagan Industries while I worked my guts out at a two-bit job? Give me a break. There was no us. It was always about you. The only way I could make your old man notice me was to..." He stopped bellowing, like he'd caught himself from saying too much just in time.

Adam growled. "You're JB. You used Shannon's I.D. to get inside Reagan. It was you communicating with the Korean agent, wasn't it?"

"So? Might as well be the best spy in the business, don't you think?"

Adam didn't get the connection. Best spy in the business? What the hell did that mean? JB didn't mean anything, except for... *Holy shit.* Brit Paxton just took the idiot of the year award. "You honestly called yourself James Bond?"

"What if I did?"

"Did you kill that Korean woman, too?"

The hint of a shadow flickered across Paxton's face. "No, Ramsey killed Tia. I... I loved her. I had to kill him. It was self-defense."

"You don't know the meaning of the word love, you liar. It was you, wasn't it? You sent the drones to kill me. I was nothing but another pawn in your—"

"You were the queen! God, Shannon, don't you get it? With you I could've—"

Shannon was quicker on the uptake. "*The* queen, Brit, but never *your* queen. Why did you want me dead?"

"Was this just about money?" Adam asked. "Sell the drones to Korea? Kill your ex-wife? I get the get-rich-scheme with the drones. Korea's willing to pay big bucks for that technology, but why kill Shannon? It can't be for the insurance. She's smarter than to have you listed as her beneficiary. What then? Revenge?"

Paxton's upper lip lifted in a sneer. "Wouldn't you like to know?"

"Who wants Shannon Reagan dead?" Adam growled, the Ruger sure as Hell in his palm. Was there more than sabotage going on here? Was this a two-fer? A hit and treason?

"None of your damned business," Paxton ground out. The sweating imposter might think he held the upper hand because he'd killed Ramsey, but in no way was Paxton bad assed enough to follow through with shooting Shannon. He didn't have the heart for it, not the way he kept licking his lips and peering beyond Adam and Shannon to the trouble off shore. "I'm not asking again. Give me the damned codes!"

"I wouldn't give them to you even if I could," she declared. "I'm no traitor."

"Give them to me! Those UAVs have to be up and running before Mia's team lands, or we're all dead. Shit, if Id known you could disarm them, I never would have sent them after you."

"So why did you?" Shannon asked, her lips to her sweet little boy's fuzzy head.

"To scare you!" Paxton bellowed, the barrel of his pistol sideways to his forehead in a stupid move of pure frustration. He leveled the weapon again. "Now give me the code, or so help me, we all going to die."

Adam pushed Shannon behind him again, his weapon never moving off target. Paxton wouldn't kill Shannon as long as he thought she had the codes. "You're already dead."

Paxton's eyes flashed to the shore, and then to the three docile drones slumbering in the sand. He whined. "Come on. They're coming. I'll split the money. Fifty-fifty. It's millions."

As if money made any difference. Adam would've laughed in Paxton's face if he hadn't been holding a gun. A nervous man still might kill a guy.

Adam knew exactly when the first boat landed. Paxton's gray eyes widened. He ducked his head into his neck. He was about to get his comeuppance, and he knew it. His weapon wavered as he took a bold step forward. "I need the code," he growled between clenched teeth, his pistol lifted to aim around Adam. "Give it up. Now."

"She's not giving you anything. Drop your gun or so help me, I'll send you to hell," Adam promised.

Paxton whined in the way of a desperate man. He straightened his arm with a nervous, "We'll see who sends who to—"

And Adam could take no more bullshit. BOOM! Thunder vibrated the air.

Shannon shrieked, strangling him for dear life. "Adam! Not you. God, not you!"

His ribs crunched from the impact. He dropped to one knee to catch her, more because he couldn't get his arm around her fast enough, not with a loaded weapon in his other hand. But it was Paxton who fell dead, his brain matter coating the jungle behind his doomed final stand.

Hysteria gripped Shannon hard. "I thought... Oh, God, I thought..."

Adam breathed into her hair, his hand cupping her head to keep her from seeing the carnage. "Not me. No way. He would've killed you. He had to die."

She was all over him, feeling his neck and jaw and cheek with frantic fingers that seemed to need to validate he still breathed. He pulled her closer, careful not to squash poor Jimmy Malone in the process, but needing to absorb the concern this sweet woman offered.

Her lips grazed his chin. "He killed Donavan," she moaned.

"I know, but it's over." Adam wanted to kiss her for her endless compassion, but the sound of boots on the ground drew near. She might not hear them, but he was very aware of the uninvited guests headed their way. Amazingly, Squeaks hadn't made a sound.

Adam pushed off the ground with her in his arms using the wall of his body to keep her from seeing Paxton. Four fierce Korean soldiers approached the Banyan trees rapidly, their rifles aimed, but one glance at what remained of Paxton, and they stopped short.

One stepped forward, his pistol on Adam. Obviously, an officer. Obviously in a hurry to get out of there before the Navy arrived. "You will drop your weapon," he demanded in stilted English. "Now or face the wrath of my country."

Big talk for a man with a losing hand. Adam recognized the drill. He'd once worked inside Communist North Korea on an especially dicey black op. He'd seen the effects of all that nationalistic *wrath*. The country literally called their years of starvation in the 1990's the *Arduous March* in honor of its ruthless leader at the time. Close to four million North Koreans died. *Arduous, hell.*

He'd been in Pyongyang since then. He'd seen the workings of the North Korean propaganda machine firsthand, the posh disguise of luxury at one corner of town intended to fool the world, while skinny children begged for a crust of bread on the next. Even now, the effect of a life lived in hunger was easy to see. Every last one of these soldiers was thin to the point of gaunt. Malnourished. And eyeing the coconuts in the trees.

Adam let the Ruger twirl off his thumb to the sand. Poor Shannon's breathed hitched, but he wasn't worried. Alex would be ashore soon, and this problem would only get better—or worse. "Don't worry," he assured her quietly. "We're okay."

"Move!" The Korean jerked his weapon toward the drones. Dark eyes narrowed when they scanned over Shannon and the baby.

Adam kept her under his arm, nodding his chin at the docile UAVs. "Take them. They're yours. I'll help you load them."

"No, Adam," Shannon argued. "You can't do that."

"Sure. Why not? It's obsolete technology. Everyone but these guys knows that."

The officer studied Adam, one brow lifted in suspicion. "What you mean? Obsolete?"

Adam shrugged, hoping he appeared more bored than he felt. "You know how it is. Technology changes fast these days. Reagan Industries developed something smaller and faster. You guys are too late to the game. These particular drones are USA leftovers, but if that's what you want—"

"You American. You lie," the Korean officer snapped. He scowled at his troops, and immediately, his soldiers slung their rifles over a shoulder, and each picked a Hummingbird up carefully from the ground.

Adam waved them off. "Good riddance. I'll be glad to see them go."

The officer's lip curled. "Where are docking stations? Where is controller?"

Which revealed how little this guy knew about the drones. There was no controller.

Time to stall. Alex had just landed and five men piled out of the landing craft with him. The Koreans knew it, too. They were outnumbered and out of time. The soldiers glanced nervously toward the beach. They couldn't hang onto the UAVs and manage their weapons, too.

Adam used the extra chaos of the Navy landing to back away from the showdown with Shannon, still shielding her from the view of her dead ex-husband. When bullets started flying, he needed her out of there. "Go," he whispered. "Take Squeaks into the jungle. Remember the earphones and mask. Keep our little guy safe."

She stepped away, her fingertips reluctantly skimming his hand. "I don't want to leave you."

"It's okay," he murmured, his gaze riveted to the Koreans. "Don't go far. I'll be right behind you."

When she hesitated, he gave her a gentle shove. The Koreans were too busy with their own troubles to notice her getaway, but gradually, her footsteps faded, and Adam's angst calmed. No matter what went down now or who fired first, she'd be out of range.

The Korean's tenuous bargaining position worsened when heavy-breathing Harley, Connor, and Izza materialized behind them, their weapons locked and ready.

"It's about time," Adam hissed. "The party's already started."

"Yeah, well…" Harley muttered, glancing at Paxton. "Your dead friend there set a booby trap."

"Damned near hit me with that piece of crap Punji stick," Izza growled after one look at the body. "Glad you got him or I would have."

"We did bring something back for you, though," Connor added, nodding behind him at the missing fourth drone.

"You guys have been busy," Adam murmured. "The boss just got here."

"Stop right there!" Alex bellowed, his weapon up and trained on the Korean officer as he approached rapidly. "These drones are United States property and you will not take them."

"No!" the Korean leader bellowed right back. "You stop! They Korean property now. Come no closer."

The pressure lifted off Adam's shoulders when two more US Navy landing craft scraped ashore and a dozen more sailors jumped onto the beach. Izza was right. Alex had brought the whole damned fleet.

He took command, but didn't lower his piece. "You, sir, are out of your coastal waters. The Shantou class patrol boat you arrived in is right now under the cross-hairs of the United States Seventh Fleet's carrier strike group. They've been running Sea Wolf exercises in these waters. Why are you here?"

The Korean didn't answer, his hopeless dilemma etched his weathered face. He was obviously nervous, glancing from Alex to the American reinforcements on the sea behind him, then back to Alex. He didn't seem like a man to be intimidated, but his belligerent stance had shifted one degree toward diplomacy.

Alex stepped forward and holstered his piece. "Your men won't be fired upon as long as they release the Hummingbird Hawks voluntarily. Tell them to do it now before things get out of hand."

The Korean soldiers, now surrounded by U.S. sailors, shuffled their feet, but still the officer stalled.

Alex played the winning hand. "The commander of the USS George Washington is waiting on your answer, sir. What shall I tell him? That you're amenable to compromise or that he's cleared to blow your ship out of the water?"

The sound of an outboard motor drifted across the waves, probably a flanking maneuver by the Navy to further prove they meant business. Given the powerful aircraft carrier offshore and its awesome firepower, not to mention the sailors onshore, the Korean's never stood a chance.

The officer in charge took a step back and lowered his weapon. His lip curled at the sight of Paxton's body. "This man was an American spy."

"Did you know him?" Adam asked.

"Captain Gangjeon worked with him, strictly on humanitarian issues, you understand."

Humanitarian drones? Yeah, right. Bullshit.

The Korean spat to his side. "Americans are not to be trusted."

And Korean officers must save face above all. Adam rolled his shoulder, still pumped from the confrontation with Paxton, but ready for another if this blowhard kept badmouthing the U. S. of A.

"Yes," Alex agreed diplomatically after a quick glance at Paxton, "some Americans can't be trusted, but in no way did that man represent The United States. My president will take your gracious act of peace into consideration."

Adam held his breath. He couldn't remember Alex using so many carefully crafted words all at one time before. The man had a short temper most days, but *what's this gracious act of peace bullshit? Give me a break. The Koreans hadn't assisted in anything other than showing up to steal U.S. property.*

The Korean officer stiffened his chin and stared at Alex. He'd been offered a way to save face if he was smart enough to take it. After a moment's fierce stalemate, he nodded curtly to his men. They set the drones down, their eyes on their leader. With one more nod, he signaled them to retreat.

Well done, Boss.

"I trust you'll require no further assistance," Alex said, the implication clear as to what *assistance* he meant.

Adam nearly grinned. Was Alex taunting this guy? Egging him on? It certainly sounded like it.

The Korean turned his back to Alex. His men retrieved their rifles, and in minutes, the sound of their patrol boat motor faded in the noisy surf. Izza holstered her pistol and ran into Alex nearly taking him down. "Damn, am I glad to see you!"

"It looks like we got here just in time." Alex took a full step back to catch his balance, then shook Connor's and Adam's hands while Izza disengaged and surveyed the scene. "Where's Shannon?" she asked.

"Safe." Adam thumbed at the jungle behind him. "I'll go get her."

He stepped away to do just that. This whole mistake of an operation was done. The Hummingbirds were safe. Before the day was through, he'd be eating lobster and steak in Hawaii with the woman he loved. Maybe dancing with her soft body rubbing against his. Definitely kissing those sweet lips again and again. Bedding her. Making love to her all night long. Damn, it was a good day. Did the sky just get bluer?

He brushed more island vines and brush out of his way, his heart swelled with love. After a layover in Hawaii, he intended to court the beautiful Miss Reagan, and he'd do it right. Little Jimmy Malone would know what it meant to have a real man in his life, and then... well, Adam would know for sure if what he and Shannon felt for each other was meant to last. He was in deep, and she needed to know it.

He tried the words on again for size. He'd said them before, but she might not have heard with all the thunder banging in the sky at the time. "I love you," he whispered, flinging fronds and branches aside as he marched to the woman of his dreams. She wouldn't have gone far, and if she overheard his declaration, so much the better. It was time he reminded her. "I love you," he whispered again. *Oh, man, do I love you, Shannon. You and Jimmy Malone.*

"Shannon," he called quietly. "You're safe now. I have something to tell you. Come on back."

When a flock of birds scattered at his approach, the first hint of apprehension pumped up his heart. "Shannon? Where are you?" he called louder

Harley and Connor thundered up the path behind him. "I thought you said she was right here?" Connor asked.

"She is. I sent her to hide, so she wouldn't be in the line of fire," Adam explained, pushing more greenery aside as he picked up his pace and began to run through the jungle. "She should be right here."

"Shannon!" Connor yelled. Izza joined the search. Alex, too.

But no Shannon. No Squeaks.

In minutes, Adam and his buddies burst through the trees on the other side of the island. The entrance to the cave beckoned to his left. Harley's hand on his shoulder brought him around. "Hold up. I found this."

Adam clutched Squeaks' baby blanket.

"Over here!" Connor called out. "Got something."

Adam joined him at the edge of the shore. Two sets of booted footprints marched into the surf with a smaller set of bare feet between them. His heart sank. That was what the sound of that outboard motor was. Not the Navy at all, but someone taking Shannon off the island. Who? Pirates? Another one of Paxton's buddies? Ramsey's?

Alex growled, his chin in the two-way radio on his shoulder. "Request electronic counter measures. Are there any other watercraft in the immediate vicinity besides the Koreans?"

The answer came back promptly from the GW. "Negative, sir. Just what appears to be a pod of humpbacks."

"Location?"

"Twenty knots due west of your position."

"Copy that." Alex turned to Adam, regret clear on his face. "I'm sorry, son."

No! Adam refused to believe. He had plans, damn it, but by the time he'd made two more frantic sweeps of their island, he had to face the truth.

Shannon and Squeaks were gone.

Chapter Twenty-Two

"Let me go!"

Shannon spat her demand at the heavy-handed bouncer with a death-grip on her bicep. The enormous watercraft he'd hustled her onto hurtled west across the ocean and away from Adam. Whoever owned it had to have a lot of money. A smoked Plexiglas windshield wrapped around the black and gray metal boat, screening her from the wind as much as blocking her view. The boat's meticulous interior and plush cushions revealed no indication of its owner. No sign of the diabolical madman behind her abduction, either. *Nothing.*

Already sitting with her hands tied behind her back, fear rattled over her. The men who'd taken her away from Adam were three buzzed-cut, square-chinned behemoths. All white males. Possible pirates, though she doubted it. They'd moved with precision when they'd grabbed her, as if they'd done this kind of thing before. One drove the boat. Another sat beside her on the bench. Across from them, another buzz-cut held Jimmy in one hand like a football he might spike at any moment.

Poor Jimmy whimpered in that same weak, scratchy preemie voice, but the man didn't seem to care. Shannon forced her fear down. With the ocean so close, Buzz-Cut could easily toss her baby overboard if he wanted to.

She peered around the massive chest of her bodyguard to Buzz-Cut. "I want my son. Give him to me."

Neither man so much as twitched. They might as well have been stone deaf, their faces impassive and their eyes cloaked behind the anonymity of dark sunglasses. Both stared straight ahead. She recognized the type. They were like her father's butler, Hubbard. *Just doing their job*. And then she was really scared. Whoever these guys were, they could drop her and Jimmy into the ocean if she made too much trouble, and no one would ever know.

She chewed at her lip and faced the bottomless, deep blue sea, her heart throbbing over her predicament. She hadn't even heard them until it was too late, but they'd been waiting for her, like they'd known exactly when she'd stepped away from Adam.

"He needs to eat," she said more calmly. "He's too small to go long without nourishment for long. May I feed him? Please?"

The man beside her grunted and shook his head.

"Come on, you guys." She appealed to their humanity, hoping they had some. "He's not even a day old yet, and he's two months premature. What could it hurt to let a tiny guy like him nurse? It's not like either of us are big enough to hurt you."

Again, the negative shake of her buddy's square head. *Damn him.*

"Please." She tried one last time. Jimmy's fragile cry tugged at her heart. Her baby needed her.

Without a word, Buss-Cut holding Jimmy grunted and handed him across the narrow aisle. The other guy reached behind her back and unlocked the cuffs that held her. He didn't touch her baby, but he did lean out of her way so she could grab Jimmy.

Greedily, she gathered her baby into her arms, shaking with relief and checking him for injury. Satisfied he was okay, she slid him back into the sling Izza had crafted, then turned away and nervously slipped her shirt over her shoulder to nurse. The moment his lips touched her breast, she stilled. Adam's bright smile came to her mind, the smile he'd had just this morning when Jimmy was born, the one that told her the world was full of hope after all.

That smile.

It seemed so long ago. Tears rolled down her cheeks. She bowed her face to the top of Jimmy's head. "It's okay," she soothed. "Mama's got you. Adam will come and get us. We'll be okay."

Shielding her nursing son with the thin material of the sling, she turned back to the unwanted bodyguard at her side. "Where are you taking me?"

He ignored her, so she settled in, thankful for the tiny guy in her arms. He reminded her of Adam, not Brit, and Adam *would* come for her.

The ocean flew by. More and more watercraft shared the sea. Then a massive gray Navy battleship. Apprehension skulked across her shoulders when their boat passed the breakwater at Hilo Bay. She was in Hawaii. Her father had a plant near Hilo. *Shit.*

"You men work for Paul Reagan," she stated flatly. "He sent you to kidnap me, didn't he?"

It all made sense. The pricey boat. The hired muscle. The abduction. What would these guys have done if they'd had to face Adam? Kill him?

There was no more reason to talk. These hired guns wouldn't listen to her any more than her father did. A righteous dose of indignation stiffened her spine. How could he treat her like this?

Glancing at the ocean behind her only stabbed at her heart. Adam was out there, and she was hours west of him. He would've searched the entire island frantically for her. He'd be out of his mind, but he was also smart enough to figure out what happened. He would've seen the tracks in the sand. He'd be mad.

A knot as big as that small island swelled in her heart. Paul Reagan had skated on her good graces and her need to believe in him for too many years. He'd not only overstepped his fatherly bounds with this awful interdiction, but he'd endangered his premature grandson's life as well. A mother's last straw.

His highness, Paul Reagan, was in for a rude awakening. She meant to contact the Navy. They'd put her in touch with Adam. He'd stand by her. Izza and Connor would, too. Then she intended to fly off this rock and start her life over again. She'd done it before. Reagan Industries could fall back into the darkest shades of hell, for all she cared.

At last. The boat sidled up to the long private dock of Reagan Industries just like she knew it would. It was him alright, dear old Dad waiting on the dock, all dressed in nautical blue and white, from his fake captain's hat to his practical boat shoes. A surly woman in a stark white nurse's uniform stood at his elbow, her fingers clasped over an ample waist, and her hair buzzed-cut short. She was obviously another Reagan employee. Shannon instantly branded the woman an enemy and traitor, someone not to trust.

Just like him.

"Shannon!" Paul Reagan beamed as if he was glad to see her. *The liar.*

"You did this," she hissed.

While one of her captors secured the boat's moorings, the other offered a meaty hand to help her disembark, which she had to accept because her other arm was full of Jimmy. What she really wanted to do was to knock that jerk off his feet and dropkick his ass overboard.

"If you're referring to your rescue, well of course I did it. I've been worried sick since your plane went missing." Her father made this abduction sound noble.

Shannon stepped onto the dock, but stood her ground. "How dare you send your lackeys to kidnap me? What were you thinking?"

"Now, Shannon." He persisted with the caring father routine, but he hadn't even looked at the bundle in her arms. Little Jimmy lay serenely unaware of the drama about to unfold.

"Don't you *'Now Shannon'* me." She planted her feet. "There were four of us on that island, and right now, they don't know where I am. We've been through hell this last week, and the only reason I'm alive is because they took care of me. Why didn't you rescue them?"

Her father shrugged, almost succeeding in looking apologetic. "I wasn't sure who was on that island with you, and to be honest, I couldn't take the chance that I might lose you. I sent my best men to bring you safely home. Come. Let's get you cleaned up and fed. I have a reservation at—"

"No!" She lifted Jimmy into view to make sure this arrogant excuse for a father got a glimpse of the grandson he might never see again. "You know damn well who was on that island with me. It was your plane. Your idea. Your manifest! And look what else. They helped me with the premature birth of your grandson! Have you even thought to ask where this baby I'm holding came from? Didn't you wonder? Just a little? Were you in on the sabotage of your Gulfstream? Did you make a deal with the Koreans?"

"Shannon, Shannon, Shannon." He tsked his annoyance at her. "Of course I'm curious about that child. Who wouldn't be? But what's this about sabotage. And what Koreans? My goodness, you might have a touch of sunstroke. Let's get you inside and—"

"No more, Father" she declared. "I'm done playing your games. I'm done with you and Reagan Industries, too. It's not my dream, it's yours, and you can keep it. I'm headed home as soon as I can reconnect with Adam and schedule a flight out of here." She folded the sling back around her baby. Paul Reagan would never change, but she already had.

He glanced at the two men who until then, had stood at the edge of the dock, their hands clasped behind their backs like good little soldier boys. One stepped forward and restrained her again, his hands firmly attached to her biceps.

"What you're going to do, *little girl,* is speak to the press."

"No, I'm not." She glared at her father, but then it got worse. The other man eased the sling over her head, twisted her arm and lifted Jimmy away. "No! Don't take him!" She struggled, her eyes fastened to her child. "You can't do that! Give my baby back!"

The man handed him off to the gruff-looking woman. A snarky smile lifted her lips as she enfolded Jimmy in her arms. *Her* arms! Shannon seethed, hating her with all her heart. "Father! What are you—?"

"Don't you dare *'father'* me," Paul Reagan mimicked, his imperious tone a slice of sharpened ice.

Shannon's mind pinged in desperation. She'd do anything to get Jimmy back. She sought eye contact with the woman, but the thief's face was a sublime mask of motherly attention focused on the tender babe in her hands. She smiled and cooed at him as if she wasn't stealing another woman's child at that very moment.

Resolved to do whatever she needed to get her son back, Shannon ceased struggling. "Fine. What do you want? Tell me."

Through hooded snake eyes, Paul Reagan studied her, his words clipped and cold. "This is what will happen next. Linda will take over the childcare of this boy, so you can assume a more active role in Reagan Industries."

"That's what this is all about?" Shannon's heart thundered. "Fine. I'll do it, just give Jimmy back."

Her father snorted with unblinking disgust. "Jimmy? For a Reagan? Where did you come up with that redneck name?"

She stared right back at him, offering a defiant chin lift in the face of his condescension. "From the man I love. Now give him back, or there's no deal."

"That's where you're wrong. You will speak with the press, and you will respond appropriately to every last question they ask. They've been highly interested in your whereabouts, more so because of the valuable cargo that was lost at sea when my jet went down."

"The drones weren't lost." She corrected his erroneous assumption. "They're—"

"They're lost!" The sharp edge was back in his eyes. "Do you understand? That's the official Reagan statement. All four UAVs were lost in the unfortunate accident at sea, and you'd better make it sound good."

"I'll speak to the press," she agreed quickly. Talking to them was akin to a fox and hound chase. She'd done it enough in the past. One only had to keep a step ahead of the pack and backtrack once in a while to keep them guessing, but tell them an outright lie? Only for Jimmy. "Is that all you want? Where are the reporters?"

"They'll be here in a moment."

Okay, that didn't seem so difficult. She'd gladly tell whatever lies he wanted until she had Jimmy back. At that precise moment, Linda coughed. The child-stealer had the nerve to walk away. She cooed to Jimmy as she disappeared into the stretch limo waiting on the dock.

"Father! Wait! What are you doing?" Angry desperation snapped out of Shannon before it gave way to all out terror. "Tell me. What do you want me to say? I'll do anything!"

He smiled knowingly. "Only the truth, *little girl*. Just tell the world the truth."

"Where is she?"

Adam couldn't sit still. The trip to Hawaii was long and anguished for a man with his heart in his throat. The Navy stayed behind to retrieve the bodies from the beach graveyard, while the outboard utility ship that had come ashore with Alex hurtled westward. Every crashing wave only took Adam farther from the island. Even though Shannon wasn't there, the need to be in the place where he'd last held her persisted. Unquenchable apprehension choked him. Who had her? Why? But mostly, how could he have sent her into the jungle alone with an infant? *What the hell was I thinking?*

Harley, Connor, and Alex were engrossed in conversation up front with the boat's skipper, their heads tilted together. Izza stood at the rail with him, watching. Hawaii was coming up fast in the west. Soon they'd swing south and make their way into Pearl Harbor. Too soon.

"God," he groaned. "Where is she?"

"We'll find her," Izza promised, fighting her own tears. "That little boy of yours, too."

Adam didn't argue over her choice of words. She was right. Shannon and Squeaks were his. The gaping hole in his heart proved it.

Connor joined them on Adam's other side. "Want to bet her father's behind this?"

"Paul Reagan?" Adam asked in surprise. "But why kidnap his own daughter? No, that doesn't make sense."

"Me and Connor been talking with Alex," Izza said. "He had Mother do some checking into Brit Paxton. The son-of-a-bitch cheated on Shannon the whole time they were married."

"Yeah. I know that, but it doesn't prove her father's involved."

"No, but the fact that he's been paying Paxton on the side, does," Connor stated. "Alex doesn't know why yet, but he's digging into Reagan and Paxton. He'll find out."

Adam scrubbed a hand over his face in frustration. Neither Reagan nor Paxton mattered. One was dead, the other a flaming bastard. Shannon wasn't where she was supposed to be—with him. That's what mattered.

The claustrophobic sensation he'd dealt with when he buried Donavan was nothing compared to the monstrous darkness he fought now. The need to strike back welled up from his soul, a surefire source of nuclear energy brimmed to overflowing. It could save lives as easily as it could lay waste.

He'd relied on it, nurtured it, called on it as needed on black ops across the globe. And he needed to unleash it now. To run to her rescue, or to fight the world for her. Yet there he stood, his fists clenched at his side. Doing nothing. He crossed his arms over his chest, breathing hard. Not knowing where Shannon and Squeaks were was hell, pure and simple.

Oahu came into view. The boat reduced speed and puttered into the channel toward Pearl Harbor. Adam had been there before on too many assignments to notice the sights now. Ghostly images of Shannon and Squeaks overlaid every shoreline and every picturesque postcard view. Maybe she was safe, but *where, damn it? Where?*

Connor placed a foot to the side of the boat and stepped onto the dock. "Alex has a car waiting. Let's go."

"Right behind you." Izza followed. Connor latched onto his wife's elbow as he safely helped her off the boat. He pulled his wife into his arms and planted a quick kiss on her cheek. "We're safe."

"I wonder what Jamie and Braxton are doing right now," Izza said, her voice brimming with emotion. "I can't wait to get home. They'll be so happy to see us."

Adam swallowed his heart and turned from the happy scene, his lips tight and the reality of his loss slapping him down again. This was no welcome home. Alex clapped him on the back. Harley stood at his other side, and together they walked to the waiting Navy shuttle.

"We've got a flight out of here in four hours. You ready to go?" Alex asked.

Adam turned to his boss, steeled to answer like a man. "Yes, Boss." His hoarse voice betrayed him.

"I've got everyone looking for Miss Reagan. Mother and Ember are both pulling down satellite images. The whole office is engaged. We will find her."

Adam nodded, mutely fighting the desolate storm sweeping over him.

"Think about it. Whoever had the means to take her also knew exactly where to do it. And when. Surveillance like that takes someone with guts and power."

"And a lot of money," Harley added.

Adam glanced at his boss. "Do you really think Reagan would abduct his own daughter?" It made no sense.

Icy blue eyes gentled the moment they made contact. "Let's go home, son."

"Adam! You've got to see this!"

He'd just stepped out of the shower when Harley bellowed at the hotel bathroom door. He wrapped the closest bath towel around his waist. He joined everyone gathered in front of the television. CNN's reporter on site, Milani Kekoa, had just announced that billionaire Paul Reagan's elite search-and-rescue team had recovered the missing heiress, Shannon Reagan.

Adam's heart stopped at the sight of her at her father's elbow. *Thank God. There she is. She's okay.*

The camera zoomed in for a close-up of two stony-faced tough guys, then panned the dock for a shot of the rescue boat. Sleek, off-black from stem to stern, it looked like one of the many military ops boats that had transported Adam into and out of dangerous ops. Designed for stealth and rigged for assault, they were the best at infil and exfil—infiltration and exfiltration to civilians.

"That bad boy's not government issue," Connor muttered, stabbing a finger at the screen.

"And they're not your regular search-and-rescue guys, either," Harley added.

"That boat's experimental. It's designed to avoid radar detection," Alex growled. "No wonder the GW only detected a pod of humpbacks."

Adam stared, needing to see Shannon and Squeaks, not the boats.

Dressed in black T-shirts and pants, the square, muscular bodies and military stance of the men behind Shannon gave them away. They were Paul Reagan's muscle. Nothing but. But why'd he need to send ex-special ops guys after his daughter, and why didn't Shannon look happy? Better question, where the hell was Squeaks?

Shannon kept her eyes focused on the dock when her father pushed her toward the reporters and beamed over her shoulder. He seemed to be prompting her, his hand gripping her bicep while he leaned around her into the camera. Her drawn face didn't portray any joy at being reunited with him. She had yet to smile, and she'd been crying. Her eyes were puffy. Her lips thin.

Adam's heart ached for her. She'd had one helluva day, but this was not the way he'd wanted the day she gave birth to Squeaks to end. *Where the hell is he?*

"Miss Reagan, how did you survive without decent food and water all this time? What was it like out there? Whatever did you live on?"

"Were you alone?" another reporter interrupted. "Did anyone else survive?"

When Shannon didn't respond to those questions, her father whispered into her ear. He offered the camera a stifled smile while he obviously gave his daughter a hint. Or a threat. She flinched, but mumbled, still without making eye contact, "We did what we had to do."

"Where the hell is Squeaks?" Adam demanded, his blood pressure climbing higher the more that question went unanswered. Nothing about the interview struck true, and Shannon looked as forlorn as the day she'd gotten sick in the elevator.

"We understand from your father that you gave birth to a son while you were stranded. Congratulations! How did you manage a premature delivery by yourself? Weren't you scared?"

He voice quavered. "Jimmy's very small, b-b-but he's—"

Adam ran both hands through his hair. *God, where is he?*

Her father leaned into the mic and took over the interview. "As you can see, my poor daughter is still in shock. She's dirty. She's been living on next to nothing. She's confused, and it's been a trying day. Please, give her time to recover."

"Where's your baby now, Miss Reagan?" the reporter persisted, shoving the microphone back under Shannon's nose. "And where are the others who were on that plane with you? Was anyone injured? Did they get rescued, too?"

She shook her head, her gaze still on the dock. "I don't know," she whispered.

Once again, Paul Reagan took over, both hands on his daughter's shoulders as he jostled her out of the way. "No further comment. That's all for now. Thank you for your—"

"But Miss Reagan." Pushy Milani Kekoa wouldn't take no for an answer. "Is there anything you want to say now that you're safe and sound? Isn't there anyone you'd like to thank for your survival?"

Shannon finally stared into the camera, her beautiful pale blue eyes stabbing Adam straight to his heart. "There's, umm, no one."

Adam turned away from the television, ready to explode. "Where the hell is Squeaks?"

Chapter Twenty-Three

"What do you want?" Shannon didn't ask so much as she shrieked. Her father's private jet hurtled eastward, and she was on it. Linda sat at the front of the plane with Jimmy. He'd gotten his first bath while a doctor treated her broken arm, then handed her a mechanical breast pump. Jimmy was her baby, but she couldn't hold him, much less bathe or nurse him. Enough was enough!

"Sit," her father demanded, his eyes dark and angry. "If you're done throwing temper tantrums, I'll tell you."

She glanced at the top of Linda's head, the only part of the blonde shrew she could see above the seatback. That woman had turned the swivel chair forward. Right now, she had Jimmy, and Shannon was losing her mind. She sat, her throat dry and her heart pounding.

This man in front of her was no longer her father. Paul Reagan had grown darker since she'd boarded his Gulfstream to accompany the drones to Hawaii, and not because he'd been worried about her. He seemed frail, as if he'd aged in the last week. The event he'd staged with the press had taken its toll. By the time he'd ducked into his limo, he'd been sweating and his hands shaking.

"Why are you doing this to me?" she asked for the umpteenth time.

"Because you *will* represent Reagan Industries from now on. You *will* act professional when you do. Your public demeanor *will* be above reproach every day, and you *will* do as you're told."

"When haven't I?"

He frowned, his lips puckered, his bushy brows pinched into a tight *V*. All he needed was the pencil-thin moustache to twirl between his fingertips, and he'd look like the dastardly villain he was, older but just as mean. "It's a dog-eat-dog world, daughter. You'll see. You won't have time for anything but the business for a long time." There was something odd about the way he mouthed *daughter*, like it tasted bad on his tongue. He licked his lips all the time, his tongue constantly on the move as if saliva had become a scarce commodity.

"I'll do whatever you ask, but I'm that baby's mother, not your buddy Linda." She jumped back to her feet. "The only way I'll entertain taking over your company is when you give my son back."

Paul Reagan struggled to his feet, clutching the armrests until he stood face to face with her. She didn't see it coming. The blinding slap knocked her against the nearest passenger seat.

You... You hit me.

The shock of being struck for the first time in her life robbed the compartment of air. She fell to her hands and knees. Her eyes watered, but she glared up at him. He leaned into her face, his lips curled back, and his yellowed teeth bared. Foul breath wafted into her nose. "You think you can give me ultimatums? Me? I'll have you know I'm the king of ultimatums!"

Shannon lowered her head from his hysterical rant, her palm to her tender cheekbone. No one spoke a word in her defense. No one scrambled to intervene. Not Linda, the butched-up nursemaid. Not the Bobbsey Twins. No one.

"Do you think I've built this empire so you can squander it away like some two-bit whore?" he bellowed.

She blinked at the venom spewing over her. If he'd been willing to hit her, what would he do to Jimmy if she offered further resistance?

"It's time you grew up and took your place in the world. You're not like the rest of your silly girlfriends. You're a Reagan. It's time you acted like one."

Shannon licked her swollen lip, tasting blood and salty tears. She wiped her eyes. She had no girlfriends, but her father wouldn't know that. How could he? He knew nothing about her. The time to cry had passed. No more tears. No more foolish, loving daughter, either.

He stuck a bony finger into the soft hollow under her chin and forced her head up. "Look at me when I'm talking to you, will you?"

Summoning the nerve, she rose shakily to her feet and faced what Paul Reagan had become. Wispy strands of silvery hair had replaced the dark. No longer trimmed or tidy, it hung over the protruding forehead of a skeletal face. His tongue flicked in and out of his mouth over thin lips, his skin peeling and cracked. Spidery black veins bulged through the transparent skin his forearms. He was sick. Very sick.

There was a time she would've cared. Not any more.

He stared down his imperious nose at her. "This is the way it will work from now on, *little girl*. You will return to live at Reagan Manor. Linda will provide childcare to that thing you gave birth to, while you take over my business and make a profit. No profit, no mommy time, understood? You *won't* squander my life's work. Do I make myself clear?"

Your life's work. That's what this is all about. You. Just you.

She couldn't answer. Her nostrils flared with defiance. He seemed to think he'd won, and maybe he had, but only for the time being. She'd experienced genuine and very tender love during her island time. There was more in the world than outrageous wealth and power.

Her father rambled on. "You and I will hold a press conference and announce the change in two days. You'll move into my office so I can better train you in the propriety and intricacies of my trade. Got it? Eventually, we'll sanitize the flimsy cover story we just sold to the press to better explain the crash you survived and the whereabouts of the drones." He dropped his hand and swayed but only to hold onto the seat to catch his balance.

With her mask of indifference in place, she planned. *I will get Jimmy back somehow, and we'll run away. I'll call Adam. He'll come for me. I know he will. I have means. I'm not helpless. I have my own place, my own company, and my own money. I can write for a living. I don't need you or your pathetic excuse for a dynasty. Just Jimmy. Just Adam.*

Her father sat heavily in the seat across from her, sighing as he mopped a hand over his brow. It seemed he didn't expect her to answer. He'd had his say. His eyes fluttered closed. Rapid, short breaths told Shannon that exhaustion from hitting her—and telling all those lies—had worn him out.

"You'll see," he said tiredly, his eyes still closed. "Reagan Industries is a hard beast to tame, but like it or not, you're all I've got. You may not be much, and you may not want the successful business I've spent a lifetime building, but you will do it. Just wait."

No, Father. Just you *wait.*

"Adam!" Ember ran straight to him the minute he stepped off the elevator, hugging him to her ample bosom in a sisterly embrace that never ceased to amaze him. How this voluptuous woman could come across so innocent with all of her well-endowed and luscious feminine attributes was sometimes the office joke, but that was Ember—a free spirit and one of the few people Adam allowed to hug him. Mostly because he had no choice. Ember overflowed with spontaneity. She never asked. Never judged. Just hugged.

"You've got to see this." She bubbled over with her usual effervescent warmth, her hand clamped onto his wrist while she dragged him to her desk. "Me and Mother have been working nonstop since Shannon disappeared. See here?" She forced him to sit at her computer screen.

He had no choice at that, either. It had been precisely two dreadful days since he'd left Hawaii. Instantly, Mother slid her chair alongside him. "I've been worried about you," she said quietly. "Let me show you what we've found."

Also known as Sasha Kennedy, the techno-geek who controlled information flows, internal and external for The TEAM, Mother was extremely capable and hands down the best on the East Coast at her job. She could be a dynamo when it came to obtaining intelligence most others couldn't or didn't know how to locate, whether from federal or private servers. He suspected she dabbled in hacking; she was that good. Unfortunately, with that whiz-kid personality came a propensity to gossip. She was harmless, lovable—and nosey.

He turned to the screen, thankful he didn't have to lie and say he was fine. She had a copy of the latest edition of the local newspaper on her desk, along with an interview with the Navy protocol officer. He'd already read it, and Mother was no doubt up to her ears in a dozen double-checks on any hint of intel in that article that she didn't already know. Yeah. That good.

Short and succinct, the article included a stock picture of a navy utility boat, similar to the one that had swept Shannon and Squeaks out of his life. No mention was made of any members of The TEAM being on that island, however, or in the crash with Shannon. Adam understood why the standoff with the Koreans went unexplained. The government might have covered that up for the sake of domestic security, but that seven other people had gone down in the crash deserved mention.

The article detailed how the National Transportation Safety Board was conducting their usual round of investigations. More information would be forthcoming. Stay tuned. Enquiring minds needed to know.

Adam knew better. When and if the NTSB located the black box to that downed Gulfstream, and if the DoD didn't squash some of the details of the story, Paul Reagan would. At the very least, they'd both apply enough whitewash until the truth was no longer recognizable, and the Korean espionage was palatable enough for public consumption. Reagan would invent some cover-up. The Feds would go along with it. Adam knew how it worked. He'd been in the Navy. He'd seen bullshit in action before.

Mark Houston came to stand behind him, his strong grip on Adam's shoulders like a brother. "Good to have you back. Briefing in five. Alex wants you to meet someone."

Adam only nodded, the kindness of his fellow agents hard to deal with when he had a hole in his heart the size of Texas. All the niceties and quick comebacks of a normal day in the office failed him. He was the walking dead, and the dead didn't speak.

Mark didn't linger. He'd said all he needed. Adam blew out a slow breath, still trying to steady his nerves.

"Okay, so we'll be quick." Ember pushed her chair alongside Adam's and pointed to the middle of a black-and-white satellite reconnaissance shot on her screen. "See this? Bring it in closer, Mother. It's still too hard to see it."

"How's this?" The picture zeroed into focus so quickly that Adam blinked, then blinked again to see it better. It wasn't just a photo. It was live-streaming video. Of Shannon.

"It's her," he whispered. Someone else's heavy hand landed on his shoulder, but he disregarded it because there on the front walk of Reagan Manor stood the woman he adored, with two black shadows at her heels. At least, that was who he thought he was looking at. "How'd you get this? Is this live? Is that really her?"

"You bet it's Shannon Reagan and it's live," Ember said, "but that's not all. Show him the other picture."

Mother's false nails clattered her keyboard magic. "Give me a sec. Okay, here you go."

The live image of Shannon de-pixilated as a static image appeared. Adam leaned closer. The overhead view depicted a woman beside a long, black limo. It could've been anyone. "What am I looking at?"

"You'll see. Zoom it in," Ember requested, but Mother was already zooming. She worked adeptly, her manicured fingertips tapping sure and steady as the grainy image evolved into crystal clarity.

"We got this just after Miss Reagan returned to the manor," Mother explained.

"But that's not Shannon," Adam declared. This woman was bigger. Boxier. Downright ugly. "Who is she?"

"You know, I don't really care." Ember leaned into his left, pointing to the thing in the woman's arms. "Don't look at her. Look at this little guy. This is what you need to see. Right there. See him now?"

There, at the tip of her finger, was a light spot in the picture. Adam squinted. Still nothing. Just enough pixels for hope to jump-start his heart. Could it be? *God, please.*

"Wait," Mother muttered. "Let me clean the picture up." Whatever she did, it worked. The pixels morphed into a discernable and very tiny face.

Adam choked. The puckered, sleeping face of Jimmy Malone was so clear he could make out the tiny boy's hands, clutching his chin like he was deep in thought. "It's him. Thank God. It's Squeaks. He's safe."

Ember leaned into Adam's shoulder while he clenched his jaw and tried like hell not to fall apart. Just knowing that baby boy was okay helped as much as it hurt. He wanted to hold that man-child again, maybe sing another lullaby. Tears filled his eyes that he'd never let fall. He wanted to hold Shannon too, but at least they were alive. That much was good enough. For now.

Adam bit his lip and stifled his emotions. It would've worked, too, if Ember hadn't had her hands on his arm, comforting him with all her gentle ways. Mother made it worse when she handed him a tissue. Damned if that firm grip on his shoulder didn't belong to his boss. "They're safe. Now ladies, if you don't mind, Adam and I have work to do."

"Aw," Ember protested, her hand still pressing Adam to the chair. "But we just got him back. We need him."

Alex didn't respond, which wasn't unexpected. He was the hard driver in the office, the man who said, "Jump," while everyone else asked, "How high?"

Adam needed to get away from these two motherly women before he made a fool of himself. His heart might be breaking, but SEALs never cracked. They sucked it up. They packed it away. Never let their weakness show.

"Coming, Boss." He pushed his chair from the computer and stood, but before he left, he leaned into his genius lady friends. "Thanks," he whispered hoarsely. He meant to say more, but his emotions got the best of him. He swallowed hard, and damned if Mother didn't grab onto his wrist before he made his getaway.

There, in front of God and everyone, she did what he'd never seen coming. She got to her feet and smothered him in a hug, her lips pressed to his ear as she pulled him down to her level. "We're going to get her back, Adam," she declared in a stern whisper. "That little boy of yours, too. Whatever's going on inside Reagan Industries, we're going to bust it wide open, and we won't stop until we do. Do you understand?"

He couldn't speak, so he closed his eyes and absorbed the kindness she offered him, breathed in her over-abundance of powdery-smelling cologne, and nodded. It didn't solve the problem, but it sure helped knowing he had the TEAM on his side.

Mother released him and grabbed another tissue out of her desk drawer for herself. "You tell Alex I'll be right there. I just need a minute. Go on. Get."

He turned toward the Sit Room. Hell. At this rate, it would be a really long day.

The conference room was full of sympathetic, friendly faces when he took his seat. Everyone not on assignment was there. Senior agents Mark and Harley sat with junior agents Maverick Carson, Taylor Armstrong, and Eric Reynolds on one side of the oblong table. Mother and Ember came in and quickly took the two empty seats on the opposite.

Connor and Izza sat together, looking happy and well-rested for a change. Adam had no doubt they'd spent their first night home loving their children and each other. He couldn't look them in the eye, sure his would display a bright red neon *Broken Heart* sign. Ember's husband, Junior Agent Rory Dennison, filled the other seat.

Alex sat at the head of the table with a man Adam didn't recognize. Middle-aged. Military-styled haircut. Icy black eyes that glittered from the only unfriendly face in the room. The overhead screen lowered and the room darkened as Alex made introductions. "Team, this is Agent Atchison from the Special Activities division."

That raised Adam's eyebrows. Special Activities division? Of the Central Intelligence Agency? That was one federal entity Alex hadn't tangled with before. Why now?

Agent Atchison rose to his feet and took over the meeting while Alex watched over steepled fingers. "As you all know, Mr. Brit Paxton was apprehended and killed by one of your agents. Unfortunately, that action was taken without consent and approval of the Agency."

"So?" Adam snapped, instantly on the defensive. "I killed him, and I'd do it again. It was self-defense. He would've kill Shannon Reagan if I hadn't gotten him first."

Atchison glared at Adam. "As I said, once again you interfered with an active investigation."

"Wait a minute." Harley spoke up. "What's this *once again* business?"

"You guys knew what happened in South Dakota?" Adam connected the dots fast and furiously. "Were you there that night?"

"Of course we were there. Gangjeon was our double agent."

"That North Korean spy worked for you? Was Paxton there, too?" Atchison didn't have to answer for Adam to know damned well Paxton was the ass who'd shot him. He rubbed the still healing divot beneath his collarbone.

Atchison's eyes raked over Adam. "You may have known her as Tia Mia, but she was one of our best and deep inside North Korean naval intelligence for years."

"I didn't know her at all, I just buried her," Adam said bluntly, his hackles up. Even angry, he respected Gangjeon. She'd gotten damned deep into North Korea. That woman had balls of steel and it was a damned shame she'd been murdered.

"Who killed her?" Atchison demanded.

"Ask Paul Reagan. We thought his security guard Ramsey was behind everything until your operator washed ashore, and he turned up dead."

Atchison upper lip twitched. "You still have her satellite communicator."

True story. Adam hadn't handed anything he'd brought back from the island over to the CIA. Not Ramsey's knife or Paxton's Glock, but especially not the communicator. Not until Mother spilled its guts and decoded every last piece of intel hidden inside of it.

"I'll give it to you when you start answering my questions. Now tell me. Were you in South Dakota when I damned near died? Was killing me part of your *active* investigation?"

Atchison sniffed. Adam took that for an affirmative. He stood, every muscle tensed to knock this arrogant spook on his ass. The bloody crawl to his gear bag had nearly done Adam in that night, and through it all, this guy did nothing but watch when he could've provided aid or at least called for help. Some brother-in-arms he was. "You bastards knew I'd been shot, and you left me to die?"

The CIA agent blew out a small breath. "The Agency doesn't compromise the integrity of an undercover operation just because—"

"Integrity?" Now Alex was on his feet, both fists clenched. "Screw your Agency bullshit! You call attempted murder and leaving an injured man behind integrity?"

"I call national security a helluva lot more important than any one single man or woman!" Atchison roared over Alex. He stabbed his index finger to the tabletop. "So does every last one of you sitting around this table. Don't give me your fucking *'never leave a man behind'* bullshit. You're here to serve and protect, just like me, and you get paid goddamned good for it. You're the guys and dolls who stepped up for the job. None of you were drafted and sure as hell, no one came looking for you to do this thankless job. Shit, you're not even G.I." He spat the last word at Adam. "Now sit your ass down and give me that damned communicator!"

It wasn't every day Alex got blasted and took it. When he sat, so did Adam. On the edge of his seat. His boss didn't need trouble with the CIA, so he pulled the device in question from his pants pocket. With one thrust, he sailed it along the smooth tabletop to the arrogant agent at the other end.

Red-faced and sweating, Atchison secured it inside his suit pocket without taking his eyes off Adam. "Did you open any of Agent Gangjeon's digital files?"

"I scanned her Facebook page and some of her e-mails, but you already know that. What do you really want?"

Atchison didn't answer. Apparently, sharing time was over. He pointed the remote in his hand toward the overhead projector. A black-and-white picture flickered to life. It depicted CIA double-agent Gangjeon and Paxton, in close proximity—as in real close, under-the-sheets, proximity.

Another shot flashed on-screen, this one also an intimate and extremely personal shot of Paxton leaning over Tia Mia, nose to nose and obviously hard at work. Both lovers seemed oblivious of the camera. Yet a third photo revealed them walking across a green lawn, their hands entwined, the look on their faces carefree. She didn't look the part of an undercover agent, and Paxton didn't look the part of a no-good, cheating scoundrel, but Adam knew different. These were the assassins he'd encountered on the grassy plains of the Sioux nation. It was Tia Mia and Paxton who'd stolen the first Hummingbird drone and Paxton who'd shot him. They were behind this whole ugly mess. Not Paul Reagan.

The fourth and final image flashed on-screen. In it, Shannon stood with her hand on Agent Gangjeon's shoulder, her head tilted sideways, obviously whispering something into the Korean operatives' ear. The slideshow flicked off and the lights came back on.

Adam waited. Whatever Atchison said next, he wouldn't like it.

Chapter Twenty-Four

"Miss Reagan is a traitor," Atchison stated. "She's complicit in the illegal sale of highly classified intelligence to a known enemy of the United States."

"Who'd she sell it to?" Adam shot back at the arrogant G-man.

"Do I have to spell it out? She attempted to transact with someone she mistakenly believed was a DPRK agent, when in fact, Gangjeon worked for us."

Adam pushed away, his fists planted, knuckles down to the tabletop. "She did not."

"We have evidence."

"You've got nothing. Shannon Reagan is as decent as they come. She's not a traitor. Paxton sold those drones to the North Koreans, and you know it. Your double agent should've given you all the proof. For hell's sake, look at your own damned pictures."

"It was her computer access codes that were used to—"

"She never had computer access! Only basic I.D. to get into Reagan Industries, and Paxton stole that," Adam bellowed. Everything out of this obnoxious man's mouth pissed him off. "She asked for higher level access, but her father wouldn't give it to her. Don't you guys have a wiretap on his phone or something inside Reagan Industries to verify that? Hell, what's the good of grooming a double agent for seven years if you still jump to conclusions? How stupid are you?"

Atchison stared him down, but Adam caught the shadow in the man's deadly gaze. Yeah. The CIA had Reagan Industries wiretapped, videoed, and under close scrutiny. For a clandestine federal agency only authorized to operate outside the confines of the United States, they sure were busy in hometown Rosslyn, Virginia.

"She's been under constant surveillance," Atchison ground out.

Adam squared off even as he took his seat. "Check with Paul Reagan. He can verify everything I just told you. His daughter's no spy."

"Now you're defending him?" Atchison's brow spiked. "Interesting, not that it matters. Keep away from her."

"Did you ever think maybe Miss Reagan had a gutful of her husband sleeping around? That maybe all you've got is a shot of her telling your sleazy double agent to back off before she gouged her eyeballs out of her head? Jesus Christ, don't you guys have fraternization rules about sleeping with the enemy?"

Atchison never batted an eye. "You won't get another warning, Torrey. Stay clear of the Reagans."

That was it. Adam kicked his chair to the floor behind him. Connor and Izza were on their feet right alongside him this time. The tension in the room expanded, reverberated, and thundered in Adam's head. This was nothing more than a pissing contest that this measly Fed had no chance of winning.

"I'll visit Shannon Reagan any damned time I choose." Adam caught a glance at Alex out of the corner of his eye. The guy was unusually quiet, considering the uproar he was usually in the middle of. "I'll tell you what, Atchison. You bring me damning and irrefutable evidence that Shannon did what you're accusing, and then I'll back off. Until that day, you and your spooks stay the hell out of my way."

He caught the twinge of lip muscle as Atchison tried to look intimidating. The man was perturbed. He'd come there expecting to be obeyed, not threatened. *Well, guess what, asshole? No one bullies me. Not in my house. Not at my job, and sure as hell not in the middle of my team.*

Apparently Alex agreed. He made no attempt to pacify or protect Atchison from Adam, and neither did he patronize his way-off-the-reservation, pissed-off junior agent. Atchison turned to Alex, though, no doubt expecting the CEO of The TEAM to run some kind of gentlemanly interference. Guess again. That boat had sailed.

Alex nodded once toward the Sit Room doors, his icy blues as cold and as deadly as Adam's. He'd just offered Atchison his silent *'don't let the door hit you on the ass'* nod. Adam settled down. Alex in his corner meant the war was already over. Atchison just didn't know it yet.

The CIA agent breathed in a deep breath and took his time expelling it. He leaned over, his fingertips splayed to the tabletop and his face down. When he lifted his head, his gaze arrowed to Adam. "Let me make myself perfectly clear. This operation is officially out of your jurisdiction, and you, Junior Agent Torrey, are out of your league. Any further interference or attempt to contact Miss Reagan will be construed as complicity. Don't think I won't bring the full weight of the law down on your hard head and anyone else who aids and abets. Do I make myself clear?" He scanned the circle of agents ending at Alex.

Adam didn't answer. Neither did Alex, or anyone else—not until an angry and very unsatisfied CIA agent let himself out of the Sit Room and slammed the door behind him.

The TEAM went wild.

"Who does he think he is?" Izza turned and shot multiple derogatory hand signals at the closed door. "He's got a lot of nerve. This isn't a third-world country he can steamroll over on his highway to hell. He's got no business threatening American citizens like he just did."

"Sit down, Izza," Alex said. She sat, but her outburst lingered.

Adam still stood, every muscle primed to fight. He gritted his teeth and studied his boss. Now was the moment. He'd always respected Alex on principle. The man worked hard, had a stellar reputation in the intense world of spec ops, and he wasn't a half-bad businessman. But this was rubber-to-the-road time. If Alex meant to back away from doing what was right because some jerk-off out of the CIA told him to, Adam was through with The TEAM. He could go it alone. He'd done it before.

"He does have a point," Alex said quietly. "This is out of our jurisdiction."

"I'm outta here," Adam said, pissed to his gills and flat out not going to swallow any more bullshit. "That'll take care of your jurisdictional problems. I'll clear my desk and—"

"You'll shut up and sit down." Alex leveled a bemused smirk along with his curt order. "And no, you won't quit. You do, and that bastard will have exactly what he wanted. He's blowing smoke up your ass, and you're sucking it in. He came here to see what you knew. That's all."

Adam cast a glance around the table. Everyone seemed to be waiting on him. Harley leaned back in his seat, relaxed and watching with the same twinkle in his eye that Alex had. Mark, too. Even Connor and Izza seemed to know something Adam didn't.

"What?" he finally asked.

"Sit." Alex nodded him down, his fingers interlocked on the table in front of him.

Reluctantly, Adam righted his chair and took his seat.

Alex continued. "The CIA seems to think you know something about the disappearance of the drones."

"Wait." Adam stopped him with a palm to his face. "Disappearance? I thought the Navy had them. Didn't they retrieve them when they extracted us?"

"They did, but somehow, all four drones went missing from the Navy lab in Anacostia last night."

"No shit?" Adam had no idea. That was why the cheesy grins and nods from everyone else. "Don't they have surveillance video in their lab? Can't they tell who did it?"

"It was disabled."

"Sounds like someone's running a black op on the Navy to me," Izza murmured.

"Someone's sure been busy," Harley said.

"Damned busy," Connor agreed.

"What would I have to do with their disappearance?" Adam asked, his hackles still on edge. "Just because of what happened in South Dakota? Does the CIA think I stole that drone, too? Man, that's a stretch."

Alex nodded, his chin resting on his thumb, his index finger stretched alongside his jaw in intense concentration. Adam waited. He thought he knew everything, that Paxton had killed Ramsey after he'd killed Paxton's love interest, the North Korean operative. Then Paxton had to kill Donavan because the kid saw him kill Ramsey. And for sure, it was Ramsey who'd killed the flight crew. Everything that had gone down so far had everything to do with the drones. Didn't it? So how did Shannon's disappearance figure in? And why was Ramsey on the Gulfstream in the first place? Was he there to protect the drones from Paxton or was he in on it with the traitor? That actually made sense, but Paul Reagan had to be involved. Adam just didn't know why or how.

"What aren't you telling me, Boss? What do you think is going on?"

Alex shook his head in denial. "I'm not certain I know yet. Think about South Dakota for a minute. Who do you believe shot you?"

"At first I thought it was Ramsey, but it was more likely Paxton now that I've seen him and the CIA's double agent together. That explains the woman who stole the first drone. She had to be the Korean operative. She and Paxton did it. Atchison all but confirmed that much."

"Possibly." Alex seemed to be looking through him. "How did they know you were going to be there?"

Adam shrugged. "I was beta-testing Reagan's experimental GPS. The second it flicked on, he knew exactly where I was."

"Or Paxton and the Korean had someone inside Reagan Industries," Harley said quietly.

"Then they..." Adam glanced around the table at his friends. Could one of these people be a double agent, too?

"Ah-ah. Oh, no you don't. Don't you go looking at me like that, Junior Agent Torrey," Mother snapped. "If anyone's the spy in here, it's you. You're the new kid on the block. Besides, David sweeps for bugs every morning. He'd find a listening device the second one showed up inside TEAM HQ, damn it. Sheeesh!" She poked a long, scolding finger at him. "I know what you're thinking. Knock it off."

"I didn't mean you guys. I was just..." Adam back-pedaled. That was exactly what he'd thought. Mother was right. There was no way a leak could come from inside The TEAM. Heat flamed his cheeks. He was as big an ass as Atchison.

"We've got a bug-detection system in the lobby and elevator, too." Harley spoke up. "We'd know if someone was carrying long before they made it inside."

"Then maybe our server got hacked," Adam offered, searching for a logical explanation.

Wrong again.

"Say what?" Mother's head turned so fast, Adam leaned back in his chair to escape her laser eyes. "You're really starting to piss me off."

"But it's poss—"

"No, it isn't!" Again that fancy, manicured fingernail stabbed at his direction. "You'd better watch the next word that comes out of your mouth, or you're never getting my help again. I can set you up with a damn piece of papyrus and an abacus faster than you can say Jackie Robinson."

"Okay, okay." Adam bowed to the force of his genius computer gal. He'd caught the gleam in Ember's eyes the second he'd put his big foot in his mouth. Once wasn't enough, but no, he'd screwed up twice. He bit his lip and swallowed his pride. "Who then?"

"Who do you think?" Mother huffed. "Someone who is not us, that's who. And here I've been helping you find your girlfriend. Humph."

"I'm sorry." Adam offered instant contrition. "You're right. I don't know why I said that, except—"

"It's someone inside Reagan Industries," Alex interrupted the sparring match before Adam had a third chance to piss Mother off. His gaze pierced Adam, seeing right through him, and nailing him to the wall at the same time. "Someone who has a vested interest in making sure those drones are not available to the Defense Department."

"Why not? They work," Izza said. "We saw them in action."

"Yeah," Connor agreed. "They buzzed us the day you guys showed up. Shannon dropped them when she gave the kill code."

Alex's brow lifted at that detail. "She had the kill code?"

This was so not going the way Adam had hoped. Now Alex sounded suspicious. "Yes. She contacted a friend of hers, a Reagan Industries engineer, Terrence Moore, the night before the flight, after her father refused her access to proprietary files. This Terrence dude sounds like a straight-up guy, though. He thought someone besides him and Reagan should know how to shut down the drones, so he gave the kill codes to her. It's not a big deal."

"Yeah. It was cool," Connor said. "Three drones buzzed in. She stared them down, punched one of them bad boys in the nose, and all she said was, 'God bless America,' and they dropped."

"Just like that." Izza snapped her fingers, a proud tilt to her head. "It was right out of *Star Wars*. You should've seen her."

"She was the bravest out there," Adam whispered.

"That she was," Connor agreed. "She helped all of us, and some of us needed a lot of help."

Alex still stared. Adam's throat went dry. How could he still suspect Shannon?

"Did you see the drones fire their lasers?" Alex asked. "Lift off their landing docks? Recharge? Anything?"

"No," Adam replied. "They talked to us. That's pretty much all they did. Fly and chat. One knew Shannon."

Mother sniffed. "Hmmpf. That ain't nothing. I can make your electric stapler talk if I want it to."

Adam hadn't taken his eyes off Alex. Mother was right. All they'd seen was a flying, talking robot. There were kid's drones on the market that could do what they'd done. Hell, the commercial drone industry had exploded in the last couple years. The Hummingbirds hadn't done anything out of the ordinary, not that Adam needed them to use that laser they supposedly had.

"What's your plan, son?" Alex asked quietly.

Adam stuttered, not expecting that direct question. Yeah, he had a plan all right, but sharing it with the whole team wasn't on his agenda. Alex eyed him intently. Damn. Now the devil really was in the detail.

"I'm going to Reagan Manor to talk with Shannon. She's not answering her phone. I have to see her."

"May I suggest you not—?"

"I said I'm going." Adam stood again, sick and tired of being manipulated and told to back off. "You don't have to like it, Boss. I'm still going."

Alex motioned for him to take his seat again. "Not as one of my agents, you're not. The CIA will be laying for you. Don't be stupid. Let's not give them what they want so quickly."

"I'll go," Izza offered.

"Me too." Connor pushed his chair back, a cocky smile on his face. "I owe Shannon my wife's life, and mine, too. We were both in bad shape. She did a lot of crazy things out there, but every one of them was to help."

Adam heard other chairs scrape. It sounded like everyone was going with him, except Alex. He'd turned to Mother. "I have a better idea. Let's send someone they'll least expect. Sasha?"

"Yes, Boss?" Mother beamed. Silver-haired with premature gray, sharp eyes, as blue as Alex's, and always dying to do something clandestine if he would only let her, she couldn't have looked happier. "What would you like me to do?"

"Accompany Adam to Reagan Manor. Talk your way inside. You ought to be able to do that."

"I am a good talker, huh?"

What an understatement.

Alex rolled his eyes. "You're not going in to chat. Leave as many tattletales as you can. It's time we had eyes and ears inside Reagan Manor, too."

"I can do that." Mother's head bobbed effusively.

"Shannon owns a small publishing company," Adam remembered. "Mother could pose as an aspiring author. That might get her inside."

"Ooooh." Her eyes widened. "I've already written a book, you know. It's my autobiography. Maybe I'll see if she wants to publish it."

Alex pushed back from his chair. "Then it's settled. Leave now. The CIA won't be expecting anything so soon. Take Ember with you. Two women will look less suspicious."

Adam nodded. Hell, he'd take the Girl Scouts if they got him inside Reagan Manor.

Chapter Twenty-Five

"Miss Reagan, you have visitors," stuffy Hubbard, her father's male butler, announced in his stiff, formal tone.

"Who are they?" Shannon turned from the back-door window, her thoughts a couple of thousand miles away on an island in the Pacific. *I should've been happy there. I had it all. Jimmy. Adam. Me. The* real *me.*

"Two women. They say they're writers, ma'am." Never one to break protocol, he dressed in the uniform of all Reagan employees, only his was pressed and starched stiff as a board. She hoped her father paid him enough. Hubbard played the part of an uppity butler well, right down to his polished wingtips, and his lying eyes. If ever there were a murder in Reagan Manor, it would definitely be the butler *who done it*. That was how much she trusted him. Or anyone.

"Shall I show them in?"

"Yes. I'll be right there." The moment he left the spacious gourmet kitchen with all its polished copper pots, gray slate floor and black appliances, she tried the back door again. The alarm armed, its green light blinking like the rat it was. Damn it.

Biting back her despair, she knew she'd never leave, even if all the doors and windows were left wide open, not with Jimmy Malone locked away upstairs and under the same strangling scrutiny she was. They were prisoners in her father's house, and he held all the keys. The knowledge suffocated her every thought.

She turned from the locked exit, needing to breathe. To run. Wishing she could fly. This regal edifice had always creeped her out, more so since she'd been forced to return to it. Maybe it was Hubbard. Maybe it was the echo in the too-big and too-empty rooms. Or the creepy basement the manor rested on. Even as a little girl, she'd hated going down there. There weren't enough lights. Or something.

But now? The stuffy mansion had become her prison.

Calming her fluttering nerves, she entered the hallway that led to her father's front entry. Each doorway along the narrow route sported elaborate moldings, cornices, and the crystal doorknobs of old-fashioned times. The floor itself was imported Italian marble, as cold as the man who'd ordered the construction of the imposing mansion.

Thick, black velvet drapes covered the windows, themselves patterned with diamond-paned glass, leaden jail bars filled with crystal lies that distorted even the sun's pure light. Shannon forced her gaze from the single slice of light falling between the shrouds of dark. She might see freedom if she looked outside, and she knew better than to long for it. Dreams were over with her heart trapped inside the Reagan dungeon.

Paul Reagan had made that clear. Her upstairs bedroom was three rooms down the hall from Jimmy's nursery, but the baby's door was always locked. Only Linda held the key. The Bobbsey Twins were only two of an army of clones, all sober-faced, silent, and watching every move she made. Accompanied, escorted, guarded—whatever. She no longer set foot outside the manor without them, so she went nowhere except back and forth to Reagan Industries. Besides, Jimmy was there.

Hubbard stood at attention, his hand on the open doorknob, tapping his foot and waiting. Just inside the imposing entrance, two women waited, their eyes taking in the grand accommodation. Shannon's heart leapt in her breast. Ember Dennison!

Shannon extended her hand in formal greeting, her voice restrained, hoping Ember took the hint and didn't give anything away to Hubbard. "How may I help you?"

Ember accepted the handshake, and smiled that sweet, quirky smile. She wasn't dressed in a flowing halter-top dress today. Instead, she'd worn a very reasonable schoolmarm skirt with a simple white cotton blouse, an oversized gray cardigan sweater draped over her shoulders nearly to her knees. The outrageous tennis shoes were replaced with black-and-white saddle shoes with bright neon green laces that matched her socks. She curtsied.

Shannon couldn't help but smile. Ember's presence helped her believe. There was still hope.

"Miss Reagan." Ember curtsied again. "My name is Lucille Ventura, and my friend here is Sasha..." She glanced at her accomplice, a silver-haired woman with bright blue eyes.

"Dickens," Sasha spoke right up. "Sasha Dickens, just like the old English gent." She dropped her satchel with an undignified thump and offered her hand. While she gave Shannon's a good hard shake, Sasha cast her attention up into the high cathedral ceiling. "Nice place you've got here."

"Thank you." Shannon smiled graciously, still keeping her emotions under tight control.

Sasha turned a full circle, taking in the view of the gold stars sprinkled on the indigo ceiling overhead. "I'm what you might call a prolific author. I was hoping you would look at my first manuscript, and maybe, you know, tell me what you think."

"I don't usually accept manuscripts at my home," Shannon said, hoping she sounded businesslike. It was hard not to throw all of her questions at Ember at once, to beg her to tell her how Adam was doing, but Hubbard would notice. He seemed to be waiting for further instructions. "But since you're here, let me take a look." She turned to the butler. "Thank you, Hubbard. That will be all."

"Shall I serve refreshments, Miss Reagan?" he asked, his nose in the air, as always.

"Yes, that would be nice." Shannon gestured toward the sitting room, steering her clients in the opposite direction of Hubbard.

"Yes, ma'am." He twitched a small nod and turned toward the kitchen. Not that *he* would prepare the refreshments. Oh no. He did know which maid or housekeeper to summon, though.

Shannon showed her guests into the sitting room and closed the door behind her. But even then, she cautioned Ember with a finger to her lips, motioning for them to sit on the couch. "How can I help?" she asked stiffly.

"Well, Miss Reagan." Sasha pulled a three-inch thick manuscript from her satchel. She was dressed much the same as Ember, but the piercing intelligence in her eyes took Shannon's breath away. This woman was analyzing, calculating, and recording all she saw. "It's like this. I've been writing the story of my life for a few years now, and it's much better literature than a lot of books on the *New York Times* best-seller's list. Honest. I'd like you to publish it for me. See what you think." She leafed through the first couple of pages of the heavy, three-inch document before she turned it around and plopped it, title up, onto Shannon's lap. "Like this part right there. Why don't you read it, then tell me if it isn't the most romantic way of telling a love story that you've ever seen. Go on. Tell me. I'm a writer. I've had plenty of rejection. I can take it."

Shannon drew her index finger down the page to the lines Sasha had indicated. There between the black lines of print was a handwritten message in red ink.

I miss you and I love you ~ Adam

A hiccup squeaked out of her. Unbidden tears betrayed her depth of feelings. Lowering her head, she feigned disinterest while her heart thumped a loud *Hallelujah!* from Handel's Messiah. Her soul soared, fell to earth, then soared again. Hubbard would be back shortly. Eyes and ears were everywhere. Her father had the entire place wired. She couldn't be seen or heard having an emotional meltdown, but—*he loves me.*

"Perhaps we can do business," she said softly, squeezing her fingers tight to still the tremors. Just to touch those written words offered strength she hadn't felt in days. She gulped, needing Adam's arms around her. His confidence.

Ember reached one hand across from the couch to Shannon's arm. That steadying touch radiated nothing but friendly warmth, the first in days. "If you could, ma'am, there's another real good part on page three hundred and eighteen. You might like to read it, too."

Shannon hurriedly thumbed the pages. Again, bright red masculine penmanship buoyed her spirits. *I won't stop until you and Squeaks are in my arms again. I don't know what's really going on. All I know is that we belong together. You. Me. Squeaks. I trust you. Be strong. I'm coming.*

God, I love him. She looked up into Hubbard's sharp eyes. He stood at the now opened door, a tray of refreshments in his hand and a piercing scowl on his snooty face.

"Oh, my goodness, Hubbard. You've returned just in time." She offered the weighty manuscript for the butler's perusal, hoping she'd disguised her feelings. "You really must read this paragraph. I think I might just have found the next greatest love story. It's making me cry. Here. Please. Come sit with me and tell me what you think."

"No, ma'am." He sniffed, depositing the tray of finger foods and ice water on the coffee table between them. "I don't read romance."

No, of course you don't. You're too busy spying on me.

She tried again, knowing darned well he wouldn't. "May I read it to you then? It has the perfect angst, and all the tenderness of the greats."

"Shall I pour, or will that be all, ma'am?" he asked, instead of answering. "If so, I have more important things to do."

Shannon relented, feigning disappointment. "I'll pour when we're ready, but you'll have to read it when it's finally in print then." She caught Ember's cute wink as Hubbard shut the door on his way out.

Sasha blew out a soft sigh. "So you think there's a chance?" she asked slyly.

"I do. This manuscript has given me hope for a new generation. Maybe a series." Shannon breathed a full breath, gulping the hope of it into her soul. The weight of the world slipped a bit off her shoulders.

Ember smiled. "We knew if we could meet you face to face, you'd like it."

"You have no idea," Shannon said.

"So, what should we do next?" Sasha leaned her elbows to her knees. "I mean, what's the next step? Do I need to hire an editor, or will you do that for me? What about cover art?"

Shannon smiled, happy that Sasha stayed in character. Whoever she was, she was good at this undercover business. "I'll take care of the editor, the cover art, and the copyright. You just start writing your next book. We'll need to build your fan base, and that's the best way to start. It would be a good marketing strategy to release the second as soon as possible after the first."

"I can do that." Sasha grinned like a Cheshire cat.

"Well, that was easy," Ember said slyly. "What with all the bars you've got all over the windows, it seems to me you're locked up tighter than the gold in Fort Knox. We didn't think we'd get to meet you."

"We are very secure," Shannon, directed her gaze to Ember. "I'm sure you understand the need for state-of-the-art security in this day and age." She tried not to over-emphasize *'state of the art,'* but hoped she conveyed her precarious circumstances.

Ember nodded to confirm she got the message. "Important people need to be extra careful. There are a lot of crazies out there, huh?"

"Yes." Shannon glanced upwards, indicating the upper level. "Some of us must be extra careful."

Ember smiled, winked again, and extended her hand as she rose from the couch. "Come on, Sasha. You got what you came for. You're going to be an author. How cool is that?"

"Wait." Shannon hurried to the desk. "My card." She scribbled a quick note on the back. "If you need anything, don't hesitate to call. I'll speak with one of my editors later today. She'll call to let you know when she can fit your book into her schedule."

Sasha took the business card and promptly stashed it inside her bra. "It's been a pleasure meeting you, Miss Reagan."

"You too." Shannon escorted her new best friends to the front door. "I look forward to working with you."

"I get the feeling that maybe you and me should go shopping for shoes or something." Ember's eyes twinkled before she grabbed Shannon in a big hug. Once she had hold, Ember whispered in her ear. "He's outside in our car. He's listening to every word. Come with me."

Shannon pulled back. Her heart stopped. Temptation called, but motherhood had already made her choice. Every feminine instinct screamed 'Run to him!' but she couldn't. Not without Jimmy.

"I can't," she whispered back. "Not today."

Ember released her slowly, a glimmer of hurt in her eyes. "I understand," she said quietly. "Find a way. Maybe next time."

"No," Shannon shook her head, speaking low. "There can't be a next time. It's too risky. He needs to forget me."

That must have been the last straw for the man listening to the discreet conversation. The front door burst open, and there he was, all six-feet-three of a fierce, angry male.

"Shannon," Adam barked, still scanning the entrance for her. The hard angles of his face softened as soon as he made eye contact. All that fierceness faded away. "Shannon," he breathed her name with so much reverence and love, his hand extended. "I'm here."

"Adam," she cried, her heart thrown wide open and her caution to the wind.

One moment she stood there, dumbfounded and paralyzed. The next, she was in his arms, trying to melt into him so they'd never be parted again. He'd come for her, just as she knew he would. Every neutron, cell, and particle in her body tuned to him, her heart beating in time to the thunder in his chest.

"I love you," he growled, his words branding her heart with red-hot tendrils of forever.

"And I you," she murmured, needing to feel his lips on hers again. Clutching his face in her hands, she felt his tears. Somewhere out there, Ember and Sasha stood watching, but Shannon only saw Adam, only felt the heat of his love coursing through her body, only wanted more. As soft as the island breeze, he pressed his lips to hers, asking for a chaste kiss.

"You're coming with me," he said hotly into her mouth. "Get Squeaks. You're—"

"No!" Perish the thought. Reality slapped her down. She jerked out of his arms at the truth he must never know. "I can't. You have to go. Leave. Leave now."

"No, Shannon. Not this time." He reached for her again, but she shifted farther away.

"No!" Danger signs exploded in her head. All her father's sinister oaths came back in triplicate. She'd just given herself away and betrayed her son by this impossible foolishness. Her father now had evidence of her treason on video. "Get out! All of you! Get out!"

"But Shannon..." Adam froze. His face blanched white. Her words were killing him, but she couldn't stop. Everything came down to this point in time. Her future. Her happiness. Adam or Jimmy. There was no choice. Jimmy won.

"Leave. Do it now, or I'll call the police," she barked, pointing sternly to the open door.

"Miss Reagan." Hubbard had arrived, his voice calculating and very nearly concerned. "I have called security and the police. They'll be here shortly."

"Thank you, Hubbard. Please make these people leave."

Ember and Sasha stood with Adam at the door, the same bewildered expressions on their faces. Shannon turned away from the hurt in his eyes, her own squeezed tight against the pain clawing up her throat. Desolation stabbed at her. There was no way out of this. He couldn't save her. Not any more.

His last words cut the deepest. "I'll always love you."

Chapter Twenty-Six

Three long months. Two days. No breaks. No sign of Shannon. Squeaks either.

Adam watched with the rest of the world as the vivacious, charming billionaire's daughter turned into a recluse. Her father publicly proclaimed her nerves were shot after her near fatal accident at sea, and that she suffered more than she would tell.

The TEAM discovered that Shannon closed her small publishing company, and sent her editors packing. Book signings were cancelled. Promotions ceased. Sightings of her baby boy were even more rare than before, and mention of Jimmy Malone only appeared in tabloids where rumor and conspiracy theories prevailed. Some postulated that there never was a baby. That Jimmy Malone was nothing more than the wild imagination of a distraught woman well on her way to coming undone. Or a cleverly crafted publicity stunt to soften public opinion of the eccentric man behind Reagan Industries.

The Tattle Tales that mother had secreted inside the manor never transmitted one iota of intel. No doubt the Reagan security system squelched any and all bugs. Paul Reagan was smart like that.

Alex expended thousands of dollars and hundreds of his team's man-hours attempting to break Paul Reagan's hold on his daughter, but to no avail. Agent after agent had watched the manor for days on end. Still no sign.

Adam waited. And waited. But the hope of ever seeing Shannon again grew dim.

Finally, she made her business debut on the cover of a prestigious New York business magazine, where her father publicly proclaimed her to be his successor to the throne. He planned to relinquish the reins of his vast industrial kingdom within the year. It was odd that the reporter who relayed the story used only older photos of Shannon, instead of taking a current shot of her with her son. *That* would've been newsworthy.

Instead, the article was factual and short, devoid of the human-interest side of the future megalomaniac of the century. It was about Paul Reagan and his business. *His* plans. The interview was devoid of any mention of her future, only as it pertained to the company. There wasn't a single quote from her lips. No charming anecdote about her son, Paul Reagan's heir, either.

The debacle at the Reagan Manor hadn't gone unnoticed by the CIA, but they didn't press charges as Agent Atchison threatened. Instead of retribution, there was stony silence, which was just as well. Adam was ready to fight the world. Arrogant Atchison's smug face would make a good target. Anyone would. So Alex sent Adam out of the country on one remote op after another. Too busy to fight, but never too busy to forget, Adam waited for some news to break. Just one word.

He kept his nose to the grindstone only to return home to his overgrown Irish Setter pup and an empty house that, although she'd never been in, spoke of Shannon and her son at every turn. It whispered to Adam in the dead of night of soft blue eyes and warm caresses, the light on her face when she'd given birth to a soul so tiny that Jimmy Malone shouldn't have lived. But Jimmy did. He was tough. Like her.

The emptiness reminded Adam of the day when his arms were full of a beautiful mother and child, the day he'd poured his love into them both with his silly songs. He'd never sung to anyone like that before, not even after he'd had a few too many. He waited for the day he'd have them both. The day she'd want him back. The day he could sing again.

It was the night after he'd come home from South America that he saw her.

Ember called, waking him from much-needed sleep at the ungodly hour of three a.m. "Adam. Turn on CNN. Hurry!"

Was she out of her mind? Why was she awake in the middle of the night? Ember sounded buzzed, but Adam did as he was told. He fumbled for the remote, his mind numb from lack of sleep, the stress of a successful but exhausting covert mission, and the eternal jetlag of too many back-to-back ops. The flight home had been long and bumpy. Air Force cargo planes didn't offer first class. Only grunt class.

The debrief with Alex that immediately followed touchdown proved nearly as excruciating as the flight home. The man's attention to detail knew no bounds, but he'd also brought good news. It seemed the South American dictator whom Adam had just *visited* was overturned shortly after Adam left the country. The illicit, drug-funded government he'd hidden behind was reduced to shambles by the good work of one undercover agent who knew how to drop in unannounced, turn trusted compadres against each other, and bug out before the going got tough and bullets started flying.

Alex was proud. The State Department was pleased. They all wanted to chat Adam up with their praise, but he was running on empty. He'd been that way since Hawaii. After retrieving his best bud, Seamus, from the Mortimers on his way home, he snagged a couple cheeseburgers for the two of them at a local burger joint, and collapsed on top of his bed to get some shut-eye, grubby clothes and all. Until Ember called, he had planned to catch a few ZZZs.

The flat-screen sizzled to life, blinding his weary eyes with brilliant LED technology. He squinted to see what all the fuss was about, then bolted upright, startling Seamus. The dog groaned a tired yawn, pawed at Adam, and closed his eyes again.

There she was, Miss Shannon Reagan, only—there she wasn't. This woman on TV couldn't be her. There had to be some kind of mistake. The resemblance was nearly unmistakable, but... Shannon? Really?

"It's a replay of her interview this afternoon. She looks bad, huh?" Ember asked quietly in his ear.

"Damn," he mumbled, his hand to his mouth in shock at what he was seeing. "What'd she do to her hair?"

Shannon stood at a waist-high podium, her shorter-than-short hair slicked back in the fashion of anorexic European models who looked more like teenage boys than mature women. Dressed in a black dress-suit that did nothing for her figure, she gripped the edges of the flimsy stand. The curves he'd noticed that first day in the Sit Room were gone. Gaunt from her once lovely face to her feet, the skeletal person now addressing the world was someone else entirely. He peered closer to make sure it really was her.

"Yes," she snapped, her once melodious voice now harsh, cold, and commanding. Her soft lips were thin, her brows arched with power. She held her chin too high. God, she almost resembled Paul Reagan. "As we all know, the Hummingbird Hawk technology was lost at sea three months ago. It won't be duplicated. Instead, Reagan Industries has decided to pursue legal action against Mr. Alexander Stewart, the owner and Chief Executive Officer of the covert surveillance company, The TEAM, for malfeasance in the performance of his contract."

She drew in a breath, but before she could continue, a reporter piped up. It seemed the press wasn't interested in Reagan Industries' legal issues. "How's your son, Miss Reagan? We haven't seen him since you arrived home. Is he well?"

Adam leaned into the screen. He very much wanted to know how Jimmy Malone was. Seamus yawned beside him, stretched, and went back to sleep.

"Will there be anything else?" Shannon dodged the question, but Adam saw the shadow that crossed her face. She'd hesitated before she'd declined to answer, scoping out that reporter as if deciding whom to trust.

"How's Squeaks?" Adam whispered to the woman he loved. "Have you changed so much you don't care about him, either?"

It seemed so.

"Hey. Are you still there?" Ember shouted into the phone, which by now had dropped to the bed.

He lifted the receiver back to his ear. "Yeah. Still here."

"Wow, huh?" Ember was too full of excitement for this hour. "I wondered when we'd see her again. It's been a long time."

"Three months," he muttered, his eyes still glued to the screen. "This is my fault. I blew it. I forced her to shut me out. I never should've trapped her the way I did that day."

With his remote control, he backed the interview up to replay and record. Once again he watched the glint of pain cross Shannon's face at the mention of her son, and once again, the sight of her hurting stabbed his heart. This wasn't the Shannon he knew. This wasn't her at all.

"Any sightings of Squeaks lately?" he asked Ember. "Anywhere?"

"No, but we haven't missed a day of surveillance. They must have a doctor come to the house for his well-baby check-ups, because that little boy doesn't leave the..."

Adam lost track of Ember as the on-screen interview continued.

"What about your publishing company, Miss Reagan? Will you ever write another book or publish again?" another reporter piped up. "You've had several best-sellers. How could you let such an enterprising business fall to the wayside? What about what you want? Where does your dream figure into your father's plans for you?"

Shannon blinked, and for a split second, Adam saw her again. Whoever that reporter was, he'd sucker-punched her where it hurt.

With a groan and a bounce forward on the bed, Adam's feet were to the floor and his hands on her face, tracing the harsh angles that had once glowed with passion instead of television wonder. Seamus groaned at the disturbance, but Adam's attention was on the flat-screen.

My poor Shannon.

His arms ached to hold her. There she was again, trying to be someone she wasn't, trying to please her father while all her shattered dreams were laid bare for dissection by the nosey media. She wasn't tough enough to stand up to the barrage of questions from this shark tank. Anyone could see that. Her grip on the edge of the wooden podium betrayed her. She held it too tightly. She was scared to death. He read it in her eyes. Hell, anyone who loved her could see that.

"What's he done to you, Shannon baby? Where have you gone?"

"I've put all that foolishness behind me." She faced the camera head-on, answering the reporter and Adam at the same time. "In two months, I'll be taking over Reagan Industries. Life goes on. It's time to get back to work. Thank you for coming. That will be all."

"Hey! Adam!" Ember yelled again.

Adam moved the phone back to his ear, his heart still on that pretty lady he used to know. He smoothed his fingertip over her stern mouth. He'd kissed those lips, only they weren't so thin and taut then. They'd been lush and honey-sweet. Warm, not cold. And she used to smile.

His finger travelled down the screen to her neck, then down to the barely noticeable swell of her breast. The plump pillows were wasted away. The cords in her neck tight. He could almost feel her trembling beneath him. Were the rumors correct? Had she suffered a nervous breakdown?

His instincts told him not Shannon. No way would she fall apart, not the way she'd manned up every step of the way out there in the Pacific. If anything, she'd proven herself to be as tough as the black operators cast away on that desert island with her. The real Shannon was still in there. She had to be.

"Whatcha gonna do?" Ember's bubbling enthusiasm drained what energy the sight of Shannon hadn't already taken from Adam.

"There's nothing I can do," he whispered. "You heard her. She doesn't want me in her life. You were there. You saw her."

"Yeah, but—"

"Shush, Ember. I want to hear this."

One reporter had gotten progressively insistent. His television station's microphone boom nearly bumped Shannon's head when she attempted to leave. "What about the others who were stuck in the Pacific Ocean with you when your plane went down, Miss Reagan? We have information that a three-man crew and three more passengers were on the same flight. Surely some of those six people survived. Do you ever wonder where they are and how they're doing? Do you keep in touch with any of them? Do you even care?"

Damn. That reporter knew how to hurt a gal.

Shannon turned and faced her viewing audience. Adam's heart stopped. Again, it seemed she looked straight at him. So many emotions poured out of those sad eyes. Flashing anger mixed with—pain? Grief? Determination? His breath hitched.

It seemed the whole world waited along with him to hear her answer.

She tossed her head in insolence at the question, her upper lip curled in disgust. "I don't think of them at all."

She turned and walked away, not knowing the solid kick to his heart she'd delivered. It literally knocked Adam flat to his back. He groaned, the message loud and clear and finally received after all these months of wondering. Shannon Reagan had moved on.

Despite the foolish hope in his heart, it was obvious. The fact that she hadn't reached out once to him or Ember cinched the deal. She'd written a quick *I love you* on the back of her business card that fateful day that Ember and Mother got in to see her, but logic told him it was time to let her go, to get over her. She didn't need some redneck like him in her life. Hell no.

Judging by that ritzy outfit and the cluster of gold chains draped around her neck, she was still Gucci and caviar, while he'd never be more than beer and pretzels. She was that damn sleek Gulfstream; he was a nothing more than a bumpy ride on a military cargo transport. She was the universe. He was a HALO jumper in the night, and on his way down at that. Hell, she was Reagan's daughter. She had nowhere to go but up.

But even as he groaned in bleak despair, the truth roared out of him. *She's my everything.*

"Adam. Adam. Are you still there?" Ember could be so damned annoying. "Do you hear me?"

He lifted the receiver to his ear one last time. "Sign me out. I'm not coming in tomorrow. I'm taking a personal day."

"Why? Are you sick?"

"No," he ground out through clenched teeth. *Hell, yeah, I'm sick. I'm damn sick and tired, and I want to be left alone.*

"Adam." Her voice softened.

"What?" He wished she'd take the hint and signoff. The wish had no more than bubbled up when he noticed silence at the other end. He checked his screen and sure enough. Call ended. He'd accidentally, maybe purposefully, hung up on her.

He tossed his cell to the bed and stared at the ceiling, forcing the pain back down into the cellar of his heart. Men like him were made to see too much and maybe do too much, to suffer so others wouldn't have to, and to keep on moving no matter what. Wounded, dying, or mad at the world—it didn't matter. They had a distasteful job to do, and it was all they knew. A man like him kept fighting until the last soldier and sailor died or the final mission was complete. Only this wasn't a mission. This was hell, and he had to keep moving if only to save what was left of his sanity. Shannon certainly had.

Seamus rearranged his long legs and flopped his hard head onto Adam's stomach. Running his fingers through the sappy dog's long silky hair brought the pain back. Adam stifled the anguish climbing up his throat. His silly dog whined, like he knew his master was hurting. That simple kindness from the big dog broke the damn.

"I love her," Adam said softly. He should've been stronger. Meaner. Tougher. But truth be known, even a hard man craved that one sweet spot where he could rest his head from the ways of the weary world. Maybe find the comfort of a good woman who loved him more than he loved himself. More than he deserved.

Seamus snuggled closer. One heavy paw flopped onto Adam's chest. The dog was moving in to stay. He must've needed that sweet spot, too.

Adam flung an arm over his furry friend. "She didn't look happy, did she, boy?"

Seamus didn't reply, because well, dogs can't talk. But he groaned, and Adam took that for conversation.

"I think you're right." He scrubbed his hand over his face, wiping his weakness away. "I wish I could see her. Hell, I wish I could get her out of that house. Squeaks too. I bet that's all she needs—to get away from that twisted old man she calls a father."

Seamus groaned again, barely keeping his end of the conversation alive, but Adam's analytical brain had already kicked into gear. He glanced outside. He was a Navy SEAL, goddamnit, and SEALs don't quit. They thrive when everyone else thinks all is lost. They fall out of the damned sky and they hit their mark every son-of-a-bitchin' time. They hump all day to make things right, and they can find and save anyone on the planet. Jet lag could wait. Enough talk. Time for action. Name the place. Name the time.

"Sorry, buddy." Adam pushed Seamus off and onto his side where the hound just groaned again. He had one personal day to make his plan work, and he meant for Shannon and Squeaks to be back where they belonged by the end of it. "Thanks for listening."

Seamus glanced over his shoulder, his eyes still bleary with sleep, and Adam went to work. Flipping the light switch on extracted another canine groan, but Adam was wide-awake, focused as hell, and one hundred percent back on target.

He poured himself a whiskey, pulled his gear bag off the floor, and settled down on the bed beside his dog, a rescue plan formulating in his square, red-necked, and extremely hard, military head. He might not be in Shannon's social network, but damn it, she wasn't herself right now. Anyone could see it. Somehow, he would get inside Reagan Manor. He'd prove Paul Reagan was a snake once and for all.

He set his face-paint, his shaving kit, and his mess kit aside, then lifted a week-old and very soiled shirt to his nose. Phew. It smelled to high heaven. He'd taken every last camouflaged shirt and pants he'd owned with him to South America. He had no choice. He had to do a quick load of laundry first.

Seamus snored softly, oblivious to his master's plan. The silly dog wasn't coming on this mission anyway. Adam let him sleep.

He was on his second glass of whiskey and deep in thought in his laundry room when a light tap sounded at his door. *Who the hell?* He tossed a fabric softener sheet into his dryer and set it on a normal cycle before he peered out the peephole. There stood a gorgeous blonde with her hair pulled up in a ponytail on the top of her head.

Ember?

He opened his door and got the surprise of his life. Rory stood there too, his arm draped across her shoulder, his dark eyes piercing Adam to his core. The man had a way of seeing right through people. Adam was speechless. There was no lie or excuse he could come up with that Rory would fall for. Yet another covert agent stood to behind Rory.

Oh, shit. Alex.

Adam waved them in, his mouth clamped shut and his heart sinking. He was dead before he'd gotten started. Ember grinned. Adam stepped aside as Seamus bounded out of his apartment to perform the usual puppy meet-and-greet for some of his best friends before they could come in out of the hall.

"Hi Seamus!" Ember knelt to fondle the wriggling Setter like he was an overgrown kid, slapping his side while the rambunctious, four-legged youngster all but bowled her over. Alex hadn't said a word, which didn't bode well for Adam's day off.

Rory stood watching his wife schmooze with the dog, while Adam held his breath. He was made. Damn it. Ember had ratted him out.

"Kennel," Adam commanded once Seamus made a couple rounds. The dog gave one last '*I'm so happy to see you guys*' grin and headed for his crate just inside Adam's bedroom door. After a couple circles inside the big plastic den, he flopped noisily to his side, his smiling muzzle and one huge paw hanging out the crate.

"Why are you guys here?" Adam finally asked, sure this was going to be one of those come-to-Jesus meetings that Alex was known for, the kind where he chewed butt and spit nails and stupid guys got fired.

"We figured you'd still be up," Rory offered nonchalantly in his quiet way. What he really meant was—*what are you thinking?* He was here to talk common sense. Adam was past that point.

"I called Alex," Ember confessed, like Adam didn't already know that.

"Why'd you do that?" he asked her pointedly. She got the message. She was a rat and she knew it, but she shrugged in that cute little-girl way that she used when she knew damned well she was in trouble. It didn't work this time. He wasn't happy with her. This was yet another feminine trick most dumb jocks fell for. A pretty gal batted her eyes, and the rules suddenly didn't apply anymore. Well, guess again.

"Lay off. She's just worried about you." Rory stabbed a finger in Adam's chest. "We all are."

"And we're here to help," Alex spoke up. "What's the plan?"

"The plan?" Now it was Adam's turn to act innocent. "I don't have a plan. I just got back from a long op. I've had a drink, and I'm—"

"Stop the bullshit. Spill." Alex didn't fall for it, not for a second. Damn. Adam sized up the odds. Three highly trained covert operators against one, a no-win situation for sure. He licked his lower lip, certain Alex had Mother drawing up his severance check.

Might as well get it out in the open. "I'm going into Reagan Manor. Tonight. Alone," he qualified.

"To do what?" Alex asked, point blank.

"To get Shannon and Squeaks out of there."

"With face paint and what? Your cloak of invisibility?"

Adam caught the sarcasm Alex had leveled at him. "Fire me if you want, but I'm going to see her."

"And then what? She calls the police again? Or better yet, Paul Reagan shoots you for B and E? He'd be within his rights, you know."

"He won't catch me breaking and entering." Adam stood his ground. "Look. I didn't ask you guys to be here. If you don't like it—"

"You're no ghost," Alex snapped. "Your expertise is HALO. Not urban warfare. You're a flying squirrel, damn it."

Yeah? So? Adam ground his teeth in exasperation, wiping his hand over his head. The problem with taking his boss on was that the man fought dirty. He went straight for the throat. He could be mean and nasty—*and right.*

Each agent had their own special talents, and yes, Adam was the number one flying squirrel in The TEAM. Connor, Izza, Rory, and Zack were hands down the most accurate long-distance sharpshooters. Harley was the TEAM's canine handler, and without a doubt, Ember and Mother were geniuses at anything computer related. *So what?*

"I don't care, Boss. You saw the interview, didn't you? Shannon needs someone." *And that someone is me, not you.*

Another quiet tap at the door, and Adam couldn't believe his apartment was suddenly freaking TEAM central. There stood Connor and Izza, already decked out in the perfect face paint and cammies needed for a covert insertion.

"Hey," Connor said calmly, as he smacked Adam's shoulder on his way inside. "Who called this meeting?"

Izza flashed her pearly whites and ducked in with her husband. "Good to see you again, brother. When are we leaving?"

"Don't any of you guys sleep?" Adam asked in bewilderment.

"Sleep can wait. We have a better plan," Ember declared, her green eyes lit with her usual excitement.

"This job will take expert coordination." Rory stepped forward to stand with his wife. "I'm going with you."

"And you need a real ghost." Alex dared him to ask, but Adam couldn't stop his big mouth. "You? You're coming with me?"

Alex shot him a disgusted look. "Hell, no. You guys are coming with me."

Chapter Twenty-Seven

"Can I see him? Please? Just once before I have to leave?"

Shannon hated the pleading in her voice, but she'd learned just how low a desperate woman could sink. It seemed there was nothing she wouldn't do—grovel, beg, or cry if it bought her a chance of seeing her son.

It galled that she had to ask, but since Adam had breached Reagan Manor and her initial reaction to him was caught on video, her father had exacted cruel and punitive measures. Linda was in charge of all things Jimmy Malone related. Shannon had a business to run. The two decrees never seemed to meet in the middle where a mother and her baby boy were allowed to spend sufficient time together, to actually get to know each other.

It was early morning. Shannon had an early afternoon flight to catch, but she desperately needed one glimpse of her son to endure the week ahead.

Linda Perkins, the butched-up bitch from hell, stared Shannon down from the nursery door, blocking any view of Jimmy like some squared-off prison matron with a burr up her butt. Her crooked nose twitched, no doubt bent out of shape that she'd been disturbed by someone as pitiful as Jimmy's real mother.

"Please, Linda. I'll do whatever you want. I have to go out of town for a week. I'm going to Dallas. I won't be able to see him the whole time, and I just thought... I hoped..." Shannon stammered, her frustration adding wordy explanations, like Linda needed or cared.

Jimmy's warden sniffed her puffy nose in that self-righteous way of hers. "He's sleeping now. You know the rules. You can see him when you get back."

Shannon's heart sank. Another week without seeing Jimmy would kill her, and pumping breast milk was no substitute for the feel of her sweet babe in her arms. His breath. His touch. God, how she craved that little boy. She shouldn't have to ask to see him.

Shannon clenched her teeth, holding back the tears along with the overwhelming need to punch that baby-stealing bitch square in the middle of her ugly face. Just once. "Linda. Please. This is wrong. You know it is. He's my son. You have no right—"

"Is there a problem?"

Great. Her father decided to weigh in. Shannon's hopes of spending any time with Jimmy seeped out of her open-toed heels and sank into the intricate weave of the expensive Turkish rug at her feet. She could've cried.

"No, Mr. Reagan," Linda answered brightly, her one-thousand-watt smile replacing her previous condescension. "Miss Reagan was just leaving, weren't you, missy?"

"I want to see Jimmy." Shannon whirled on her father. "You can't keep doing this to me."

"Shannon," he soothed in that sickeningly sweet tone of voice, the cane he now used tapping against the baseboard.

The sicker he got, the more he pulled the doting father routine. "I trusted you once, remember?"

"Bullshit!" she snapped, surprising herself with the venom in her tone. But then, life was one hell of a surprise, wasn't it? "If you ever trusted me, you would've been honest, but no. I've lost track of your lies, and now you've got me lying for you."

"Tsk, tsk, tsk." He shook his head, muttering as he approached. He used a cane now, though he'd still not admitted to her what his health issues were. Something was seriously wrong. He'd never pushed her to understand how Reagan Industries worked like he did now, but neither did he completely confide in her, either. Why would he? Everything about him had always been about mystery and misdirection, his way of controlling the world. And her. "It's hard being the richest woman on the East Coast, isn't it? It takes a great depth of dedication and stamina, which you're only now beginning to realize, aren't you?"

"It takes treachery and deceit," she hurled back at him. "You've never spent any time with Jimmy. Not once. He's your grandson. Your only heir."

"And that is why we do what we must do, my dear," he purred, still so very much in charge and out of touch. "We take care of business now so your descendants won't have to dirty their hands or knees later."

"Like I do?" she snapped. "It's been months, Father. Three long months. Enough is enough. How much money do you need? How much power? Isn't owning the world enough?"

He studied her silently for a moment, his crafty eyes sliding over her face like he was still searching for something he would never find. She didn't share any part of his dream. Couldn't. Wouldn't! Not if he waited until the end of time.

For a moment, the rheumy depths of his gray eyes reminded her of her dead ex-husband, Brit Paxton. Emotionless. Cold. Desperate. Filled with disgust. "It isn't about the money or the power, little girl. Surely you've realized that by now."

Stop calling me little girl!

"What then?" Her head hurt. She was tired of the mind games. Life wasn't the calculated chess game of strategy and destroying one's enemies that he made it out to be. There was more to it than power and success. Adam had showed her just how much more at what should've been the worst time in her life, but now stood as the best.

Shannon caught the sob that sprang forth from her mouth at the thought of being in Adam Torrey's strong arms again. She forced it back down into her gut where all her other regrets lay curdled and sour. Adam was lost to her, and if she wasn't careful, Jimmy would be, too. The very real fear that her father would hurt her child or send him far away lingered like a malevolent threat between them. He'd implied, but had never actually spoken the words, but Shannon didn't doubt for one second that he would.

She stifled her anger and faced the father she'd grown to hate. "I want to see him before I leave. That's all. Just for an hour. Linda can stay and watch me while I'm with him if that will make you happy. Please."

Her stomach churned as she stood waiting, her heart wrung out with the total despair and misery of her plight. The longer he made her stand there, the darker she felt. All hope was gone. Each day was one grinding repeat of the last. Her only bright spot in this whole universe was that three-month-old boy who finally resembled a normal birth-weight baby. Jimmy had filled out; his cheeks plump considering all he'd been through in his short life. At least he still recognized her. He smiled when he saw her. That was what kept her groveling like a simpering fool for one more day...

Shannon swallowed another sob. *Please, God. I can't live without my baby. Please let me see him. I promise I'll go to church. I'll do anything you ask. I'll...*

She stopped cold. How could she promise the God in heaven she'd be better tomorrow when she knew wouldn't? When she knew she'd willingly spread every last one of her father's lies if it bought her an extra minute with Jimmy? That she was on her way even now, to swear on a stack of bibles that Alex Stewart and his men had intentionally defaulted on their contract, that they'd lost the Hummingbird Hawks out of sheer negligence? How could she beg blessings she didn't deserve when her very next words and actions would slander decent and honorable men? Had she become so twisted that she really believed she could lie to God, too? That He could be manipulated?

She bit her lip at the bitter truth. The simple answer was—yes. She'd become more like her father every day. Too soon, the old Shannon Reagan would disappear. She'd finally be the daughter he'd always wanted. She'd be—*him.*

He sighed as if he'd read her mind and appreciated the comparison.

Then read this. I hate you, she mentally threw back at him, in case he really could. It was possible. He'd read her like a book from the moment he'd forced her to move back into the manor again.

"Ten minutes." He relented, nodding toward Linda. "Let her in, but watch her closely. Make sure she doesn't have the chance to make any outside calls while she's in there."

Linda nodded. "Yes, sir. I'll be sure."

Shannon breathed a small, sad sigh at her miniscule victory. Ten minutes with Jimmy was nothing. It would pass so quickly. The tears came unbidden, drenching her face before she set foot inside Jimmy's powder blue prison. Goodbye was already in her heart. Ten minutes? That was all?

Her weary mind did the math. Six hundred seconds and not a single more. Linda would make sure of that. How could Shannon see the sunshine of his sweet smile for such a brief moment only to be torn from him again? Yet in she went, her eyes hungry for the sight of his smiling eyes, her fingers and hands greedy for the touch of his petal-soft baby skin.

"Jimmy," she whispered to her little guy. "Mama's here."

He lay asleep on his side, but she eased her fingers beneath him and picked him up from his bassinet. The warmth of his cuddly body filled her heart, instant sunshine to the dismal organ it had become. Jimmy wiggled, sighed, and nuzzled his mother's neck, as if she'd never left his side.

Ah! She wanted more time to nurse Jimmy again, to feel his lips tugging life from her breast, but it had been so long since she'd been allowed the privilege. She pumped so that witch Linda could hold him while he relished a rubber nipple instead of his loving mother. All the joys that Shannon had lost visited her now. Tears baptized her baby as she held onto this dear, dear life.

She knew it now. All those babies mingled with baby animals in Grandpa Denver's dream were her purest, unrealized dreams. She was already pregnant then. Those dreams must have been the subconscious quest of her lonely soul for the family she would never had. For love. For Adam.

She shuddered as that truth exploded in the darkness of her despair, bringing the tiniest spark of flickering hope to life. Just as quickly, the memory of his reckless anger when he'd breached the manor sliced at her heart. He'd filled the doorway, his shoulders flexed and squared, his eyes ablaze as he'd searched for her, as if he'd meant to fight all odds to rescue her. The moment tumbled back upon her. The look of pure love in his eyes when she'd run to him. The way he'd caught her up and crushed her in his arms like he'd never let her go. The manly smell of his neck when she'd burrowed into him, needing him so badly that she'd lost her mind for that one hopeful moment. That she'd almost lost Jimmy. That she'd utterly betrayed Adam.

But now…

Linda's stalwart body blocked the exit like a bouncer, her arms crossed over her squared-off bosom, both sets of jowls locked against her muscular neck in grim determination, and an evil glint of one-upmanship in her eyes. The bitch had won another round, and she knew it.

Shannon turned away, shielding her slumbering babe from the awful truth. Escape was never on her mind. She had accepted her fate because of Jimmy. She flattened her nose against his downy head and closed her eyes, willing them both back to a tropical island where the kindest man on earth sang her child's first lullaby. Where he'd gently reminded her that, *'It's okay to be scared. Us boys are kinda scared, too.'*

To Adam.

His name poured into the cracks and crevasses of her broken heart, a cooling balm that couldn't heal or mend her ever again. Not any more. The damage was done and she was the one who had done it. Where once he'd sheltered her against the hard wall of his body, now his name only brought regret for blessings lost. She cupped Jimmy's tender head against her lips and cried. She trembled with the coming doom of empty arms. The minutes fled. So few. So fast.

Shannon buried her face in the crook of his neck, absorbing the sweet scent of this tiny man-child, afraid Jimmy might grow up to be a replica of his only role model, his selfish, conniving grandfather. Somehow this child had to know she'd been there; that she'd held him and loved him from the deepest depths of her mother's soul. That there were better men to follow. Her soul screamed for that someone in her life, someone noble and fierce and—Adam.

"I'll always love you," she whispered tearfully to both the loves in her life. "Please know that. No matter what I say, no matter what I have to do for the rest of my life, please know I do love you."

Jimmy squirmed in drowsy slumber, his tiny lips puckered in an adorable pout. Shannon sang the only song her tender heart could bear, the song that bound her to both the babe in her arms and the gentle warrior she'd betrayed.

"You are my... sunshine..."

Raul Ortega stood in his bathrobe at the door of his condo, a coffee cup in one hand and a totally struck-dumb look of surprise on his olive face.

"May I come in?" Adam finally asked. At seven in the morning, he knew he had a lot of nerve showing up. Just not a lot of time.

"Umm, sure." Raul backed up a step and nodded Adam inside.

"You do know who I am, don't you?"

"Sure, you're that guy who got kicked out of Reagan Manor after you tried to get into see Miss Shannon."

"Who's there, honey?" a woman's voice called from the other room, possibly a bedroom. Adam wasn't sure. He'd hoped Raul lived alone. He didn't need another witness.

Raul studied him for a second before he answered. "Go back to sleep. It's just one of the guys I work with."

Adam relaxed. Raul was a good man. He could tell.

"Can I get you a cup of coffee?"

"Yes, sir. That would be nice."

Raul nodded toward the kitchen, and Adam followed. "You take sugar or cream?" he asked as he poured a cup.

"No, sir." Adam took the hot black drink in his hands, not needing the caffeine as much as the camaraderie of one of Shannon's trusted friends. He counted on this gentleman to be that guy.

Raul opened the sliding glass patio door off the kitchen. "It's a nice morning. Let's talk outside."

Adam followed him to a pleasant patio lined with redwood planters full of yellow flowers. Raul nudged a small trike out of his path to a picnic table. "Sorry. The grandkids were here. This is about Miss Shannon, isn't it?"

Adam settled at the other side of the patio table, not sure how much he should divulge. The plan he and Alex had refined under the cover of early morning darkness hinged on too many variables in the light of day. Raul was one of those unknowns. Adam had to proceed with caution. "I saw her on the television last night. She seemed..." The only word that came to his mind was— "lost."

Raul reached across the table, his hand stretched forward, palm down. It wasn't exactly a gesture of acceptance, but it helped. "I saw the newsfeed, too. She's not the happy woman I used to know. She's not my Shannon."

"Why not?" Adam asked, his heart bleeding for all he suspected was going on inside Reagan Manor.

Raul shrugged, his eyes on his cup. It seemed he had to be careful, too.

"You don't have to tell me anything if you don't want to," Adam assured him. "I just want to help her if she needs it."

Raul's dark brown eyes stabbed him then. "Do you really?"

"Yes," Adam said, "but I don't know if she wants me to."

"She doesn't know what she wants right now." Raul took a long, slow drink. "You're right. She's lost. She used to tell me everything, but now..." He looked across the shared common area behind his home. A dozen other condos faced Raul's patio, but no other neighbors were out yet. "Whenever I drive her, she just sits in the back seat and stares out the window. I ask her stupid questions about the weather, but she never answers. It's like she turned into one of those zombie people in the movies, like she's dead inside and nobody can reach her. At first, she cried, but now? She barely says good morning."

Adam's gut clenched. Raul had just confirmed his fears.

"Me and Margareta have talked many times. We don't know how to help Miss Shannon."

"There is a way," Adam began, "if you're willing to help."

"You have a plan? Will it be dangerous?"

Adam shook his head and pushed a small card across the table. "All you need to do is drive Shannon to this address. There's no risk to you. None at all."

"Today?" Raul fingered the card, reading the address.

"Yes," Adam said softly. "It has to be today. She's leaving for Texas on flight thirty-three-eleven out of Dulles at one p.m. She'll be gone for a week."

"How do you know all that?" Raul asked, but then he waved his hand at Adam. "Never mind. I don't want to know."

"All you have to do is come up with a reason to make an unexpected stop on the way to the airport," Adam whispered. "Can you do this?"

"Oh, yes, señor," Raul beamed. "I would do anything to make my Miss Shannon smile again."

Good. So would I.

Chapter Twenty-Eight

I hate my son-of-a-bitchin' life. Every hour of it. Every day. All of it.

Shannon gritted her teeth, angry at what she had devolved into. Some critics and know-it-alls in the literary world decried authors who utilized profanity in their writing. Whether for emphasis or reality, they condemned vulgarity as taking the low road. What was the self-righteous spiel? If you can't say something nice, don't say anything at all?

What the hell do they know?

She understood now why people drank and why they did drugs. Why they stepped in front of trains and jumped from bridges. Why they cracked from the stress and pressure of barren, empty lives, their hope and innate goodness suctioned away day after pitiful day. Why they were driven to kill. She'd thought of all the possible remedies for her pain each bleak night she'd lain alone on her bed, her teary eyes fixed to her dark ceiling, and her heart on that sleeping infant down the hall.

There seemed no hope of ever raising her son, not as tightly as Paul Reagan controlled every minute of her daily schedule. Linda would get Jimmy's first words and his first steps. She'd be the one he ran to when he fell and bumped his head that first time. She'd be the one to hear his first word, the first time he said, "Mommy."

Shannon balled her hands into fists at the abhorrent thought that Jimmy might actually view Linda as his real mother. That he might love her like a son, while Shannon was consigned to the bleakest shadows, forever skulking at the edge of his life like a distant relative, but never truly part of it.

Ahh! She understood too well the need for opiates and murder, for suicide, because she needed relief from the nightmare she was caught up in, the lies she couldn't escape.

Her once stellar vocabulary had disintegrated along with her heart. She saved the little that was left of her gentleness for her son and him only. Everyone else could fuck off.

Forcing a deep breath, she lifted her fingernails from the crescent shaped depressions in her palm and uncurled her fingers. The last thing she needed was the piping-hot coffee that nosey Hubbard had left on her dresser, but she wrapped her fingers around it and drank it anyway. Black. Bitter. Scalding. *Just like me…*

The pain it offered jolted her system with all the push and shove she wanted for the nasty week ahead. She meant the stimulant to mask the misery in her heart, and in a way, it did. Caffeine pumped her up. It turned her into an overly energetic and demanding whirlwind of focused destruction. One day she'd have to ease off the beverage, but today she needed every last ounce of it to rule the world like she was expected to—with blind devotion to her father's plan, quick obedience to his miserly decrees, and the carrot of a stolen moment with Jimmy for a reward.

She gulped another foul mouthful, wincing as the slow burn trickled past her heart and down into her churning stomach. The acid in her gut ate at her, but who the hell cared? She'd already pumped for Jimmy's sake. Until she returned from Texas—

Shannon slugged down the last of her bitter dregs. With her mask and ulcers in place, she steeled herself for another day in Dante's fiery furnace, otherwise known as Reagan Industries.

Her father's treachery had worked it's damnedest. From morning to midnight, she ached from the bitter crush of his control. There was no relief. Either she complied or…

She honestly didn't know how low he would sink to keep her in line, but he'd scared the hell out of her enough that she walked on eggshells most days. Most night, too.

The irony was that some people wanted to be her. They wanted to be rich and famous, have servants at their beck and call, and a limo driver whose only job was to run her bitchy ass back and forth to the office every day. *Fools. Every last one of them.*

Shannon stuffed the portfolio with the legal action suit against Alex Stewart into the deepest folds of her fine Italian leather briefcase. Even it was stylish, decadently expensive, and an enormous waste of money, just like everything else stamped, etched, or carved with the Reagan name. The briefcase looked good. Others coveted it. But today it held the instrument of a slow, painful death for a man she might have respected in another place and time.

She flicked a stray thread off the sleeve of her over-priced pinstriped suit in disdain. Today she would become Armageddon for the finest covert surveillance company on the East Coast. Like it or not, she would destroy them. She'd read Alex Stewart's backstory. She knew how The TEAM came to be, how he'd struggled when he'd left the Marine Corps and eventually figured out that he was more than a scout sniper, that he had excellent business sense.

Not many entrepreneurs truly did. Most wanted power or wealth. Alex seemed to want neither, yet he'd achieved both. Established in quaint Alexandria, Virginia, The TEAM thrived under his tough brand of leadership, a difficult thing to manage in these bleak economic times. She knew he'd recently built a modest home near the Shenandoah Valley, and that he employed a helicopter to fly himself and some of his employees to work every day. It seemed he doted on his employees as much as his wife, Kelsey.

He donated millions to various charities, including the one his wife personally oversaw for kids living on the streets of D.C. *Raymond's Kids*. What a stupid name. No doubt there was a bleeding-heart story behind that one, too.

Shannon grunted to herself. She already knew what kind of a man Alex Stewart was. She'd shaken his hand and couldn't help feeling that it was she who'd failed him. If he didn't believe that now, he surely would by the time she was through with him.

By the week's end, The TEAM would be burned to the ground, if not literally, then by default of its lost reputation. Honesty had nothing to do with the five days ahead of her. Paul Reagan had set the bar high, but she intended to jump it, maybe fly over it if she had to. He'd better not be lying this time. She needed that one full day with her son when this godawful task was done.

Alex Stewart had to go down, and with him—Adam.

The pieces were falling into place.

Adam marched up the elegantly designed brick walkway to the home of one Terrence Moore. He hit the doorbell, stepped back a respectable distance and waited. The old colonial was well kept, its window trim painted hunter green and the walk swept clean and tidy. A spinning whirligig of a hummingbird floated back and forth in the gentle breeze by the concrete stairs.

Adam found himself wondering how much it would cost to buy a home like this, a place that spoke of nothing but peace on a calm summer morning, a neighborhood where a little boy could grow up safe and sound. Where a man could carry his wife across the threshold and start a new life.

The thought pleased him as much as it worried. Even if today went as planned, would a wealthy woman Like Shannon want to live here in hometown America when she was used to posh and elegant Reagan Manor? Who was he kidding? Shannon had more money in her coffers than any state on the eastern seaboard, maybe all of them.

But there he was, already committed and damned sure going to see where this day ended. If nothing else, he meant to get Shannon and Squeaks out of her father's clutches.

When no answer came from within, Adam knocked loudly on the matching hunter green door. Ember had been right in calling Alex. An army always made better headway in a battle than a single warrior, not matter how righteous the cause. Raul was every bit the friend he'd expected. One down. One to go.

When no one answered the door, Adam checked his cell phone time, sure he'd heard Ember right. She'd done her homework. Terrence Moore would leave for work in half an hour. It was early enough. He should be home.

Adam peered around the evergreen shrubs surrounding the porch and into the plate-glass window of an old-fashioned living room. It looked like his granddaddy's place, right down to the doilies pinned to the back of the easy-boy recliner and the copy of *Field and Stream* on the coffee table. Something was off. The place looked deserted. Only a light in one of the back rooms was turned on.

Time to dig a little deeper. Adam headed around the side of the house. A silver Lincoln parked in the two-car garage, easy enough to see through the paned window of the side door. Again, the backyard was as peaceful as the front, but damn. If the old guy wasn't home, the battle to save Shannon and Squeaks was lost for the day.

Just as Adam lifted his knuckles to the back door, he froze. *Shit!* He'd found Terrence Moore, prostrate on his kitchen floor, his face down and his right arm extended. From the four-paned window, Adam could see the blood pooled beneath Moore's head. He pushed the unlocked rear door open.

"Mr. Moore," he called gently, on his knees and his fingers to Moore's neck feeling for a pulse. Once he'd located a steady beat, he dialed for emergency assistance.

Moore groaned, his eyelids fluttering.

"Lie still," Adam urged. "The paramedics are coming. Can you tell me where you're hurt?" He scrambled to his feet and doused the towel hanging off the kitchen counter with cold water to make a quick compress.

Mr. Moore was alive, a little roughed up, but coming around. He clutched the towel to the back of his head and wrinkled his nose. Between that and his messy head of pure white hair, he could've passed for a human version of a garden gnome. "Who are you?" he asked groggily. "Why are you in my house, young man?"

"I came here to talk to you about Shannon Reagan and found you unconscious. Take it easy."

The poor guy struggled to rise, but Adam made him take it slow, only allowing him to sit up and lean against the nearest cabinet. Mr. Moore rubbed the back of his head. "Dag nab it. Some scallywag used my noggin for baseball practice. You see who did it?"

"No, sir, I'm sorry. Like I said, I just got here." Adam grinned. This spry gentleman was his granddaddy all over again.

"I don't remember seeing you around before. Are you one of my new neighbors?"

"No, sir. I'm Adam Torrey. I'm—"

"Oh. You're that fellow who lost the prototype."

Adam pursed his lips and nodded, chagrined his reputation consisted of that single blunder. "Yes, Mr. Moore. That would be me. Junior Agent Adam Torrey at your service."

"Humph," Terrence snorted. "You seem like a nice kid. Are you my friend or not?"

"Sure," Adam answered quickly, not certain where that question was headed.

"Then stop calling me Mister. It's Terrence."

"Yes, sir."

"And none of this 'sir' business, neither. It's Terrence, darn it. Just Terrence. Do you understand?"

Adam allowed a small smile. "I do now. Good to meet you, Terrence. Shannon thinks a lot of you."

"Where is she?" The old man scrambled onto his knees, pulling himself to the edge of the kitchen counter. Terrence wasn't out of his head by any means, and he knew stuff. Important stuff. Piercing gray eyes beneath craggy white brows studied Adam, analyzing as only the older generation could do.

"She's flying to Dallas Fort Worth early this afternoon for a week-long business meeting. Are you sure you're okay?

Terrence swayed, but grasped Adam's forearm with surprising strength. "Jiminy crickets, I'm not dead. Now, move your keester. I can't stand around all day. What do you think I am, a spring chicken?"

Adam guided him to one of the wooden kitchen chairs, easing him slowly to the seat before he let go. "You're almost there. Okay, now sit."

"Will you be quick about it and just set me down? Dag nab it. I said I'm fine," Terrence grumbled as he plopped down with a big sigh. "Whew. Maybe I am a might dizzy. Thanks."

"It's okay." Adam took the chair next to him. "I'll wait with you until the paramedics get here. They'll need to check you over."

"Adam Torrey, huh? You part of the Torreys up in New Hampshire?"

"No, sir. My family's from South Carolina. They've been there since the Revolution."

Terrence nodded. "Palmetto State, huh? Never been there."

"You ought to come visit when you're feeling better. I think you'd like my granddaddy."

"Is he much like you?" There were those gray eyes again, still sizing Adam up and seeing right through him while they did.

"No, sir. If anything, I'm like him, and darned proud of it."

"Huh," Terrence snorted, but Adam caught the sparkle in his eye. "South Carolina was the first state to secede from the Union during the Civil War. You know that, don't you?"

"Yes, sir, it was and we're still a bunch of rebels today." Adam would have preferred getting down to business, but he needed Terrence to get his bearings first. This old guy was one surprise after another.

"Ain't nothing wrong with being a rebel. What's wrong is not standing up for something you believe in. That's what people forget. Now, you were going to tell me why in the blue blazes you're in my house." Again with the bushy brow over the evil eye routine. This older gent's cantankerous mannerisms were growing on Adam. "Oh, wait. You already did, didn't you?"

"Yes, sir, I did. I came here to ask you about Shannon."

"What's she to you?"

Adam sighed, not willing to reveal all that Shannon meant to him. Not yet. Not until he knew more about this man she called friend.

"Have you seen her lately?" Terrence didn't wait for an answer. "Because I sure haven't. I've been over to that dungeon Paul calls a home more times than I care to remember. Either she's been one sick little gal since she got home, or he's pulling something again. The last time..." Terrence stopped short, his mouth clapped tight like he'd almost said too much. He blinked hard, but his eyes watered.

"Exactly what did he pull before?"

Terrence looked down the hall instead of meeting Adam's gaze. The evil eye was gone, replaced by a shadow of—guilt? Now it was Adam who scrutinized Terrence. "You don't have to tell me anything, sir, but did you happen to see Shannon on television yesterday?"

Terrence scratched his hand through his hair. "No, son. Guess I might have gone to bed a tad early. You know how it is when you get to be my age. A fellow needs his beauty sleep."

Adam wrangled his cell phone back out of his pocket and pulled up the YouTube video currently making the rounds.

"That can't be my little Shannon," Terrence said, squinting to view the small screen. "Get me my glasses. They're over there." He glanced around the floor. "By the refrigerator, dag nab it."

Adam retrieved the spectacles. The old man's amazement at what he saw on You Tube mirrored Adam's. "Oh, my. What's going on? She looks just like..." He clamped his mouth shut, glancing at Adam only to avert his eyes just as quickly.

"Have you seen something like this before? What's Paul Reagan doing to her?"

Terrence handed the cell phone back to Adam, his lips tight, but those appraising grays were still meat forks stabbing for a tender spot.

"Listen," Adam started again. If this guy wanted a weak spot before he'd ante up, Adam intended to give him one. "This is not the woman I knew when we were stuck on that island. We went through hell together. I helped her deliver Squeaks. Shannon is the purest, sweetest woman on earth. If her father's up to something, if there's any chance that he's hurting her, you've got to tell me. She's in trouble. I can feel it in my gut."

"Squeaks? What in tarnation is a Squeaks?" Terrence muttered.

Adam took a big breath. Was it possible this fellow didn't know Shannon had a son?

"Squeaks is her baby boy, but she calls him James Malone. Jimmy Malone. You didn't know she had a baby, did you, sir?"

The old guy shook his head. "She told me she had a bun in the oven before she left, but I didn't know she had him. Dag nab it. That means that little guy of hers is three months old already. I haven't seen him. Not even once."

Adam caught the regret in Terrence's words. "I know you gave her the kill code to deactivate those drones. Thank you for trusting her. Seems to me she feels closer to you than she does her own father."

Terrence licked his lips, a nervous glitter in his eye. "Can you get me a drink of water, son? I'm a might thirsty."

"Sure." Adam retrieved a glass from the cabinet to the right of the sink, exactly where his mother kept her glasses in her kitchen cupboard back home. He let the water run cold, then filled the glass. When he turned around, the old man was gone. Darn. Terrence was as fast as Granddaddy, too.

"I'm in here," he called from one of the other rooms. "There's something I want to show you."

Adam peered around the corner, hoping Terrence didn't intend to treat this like a home invasion after all, and show him the business end of a double-barrel shotgun.

The old guy stood in his living room, one hand on the fireplace mantle. "Get over here."

Adam obeyed. "Here's your water. Can I help you sit down?"

"That'd be nice." Terrence breathed out a trembling sigh and sat with a huff in the nearest easy chair. After he took a long swallow, he pointed to the mantel. "See that picture? Bring it here."

Adam did as he was told. The woman in the portrait was Shannon all over again. He settled onto the couch to listen, fully aware the YouTube video had struck a nerve in Terrence and that Terrence might know what was going on in Reagan Manor.

"This is Olivia Reagan, Shannon's mother." Terrence's voice softened as he fingered the woman's cheek. "Paul doesn't know I've got this picture, but then, he hasn't been to my house in years. Shannon was just a little girl when her mother died. What a hard day that was. Look at her, would you?"

Adam took the frame in his hands, noticing the gilded roses carved into the walnut that surrounded the lovely photograph. The portrait depicted a smiling Olivia Reagan with little Shannon in her lap. She faced her mother, both hands on her shoulders while Olivia smiled upwards at whoever the photographer was. She was maybe thirty, give or take a year. Shannon looked to be around two. Whoever'd taken the shot had captured the glow in Olivia's eyes. It matched the light he'd seen in Shannon's eyes when she'd finally asked to hold her newborn son.

"I took that picture," Terrence said quietly. "Before I say another word, I want to know your intentions towards my... towards Shannon. Why are you asking questions about her? Why do you care?"

Adam returned the honest appraisal. His dad had taught him there was only one way to make a friend out of a potential enemy, and that was to look the man in the eye, and be the kind of friend a man would want to have.

"Honestly, I love her." Sharing those sweet sentiments proved his undoing. Tears he would not let fall misted his vision. "That's all my intentions are, but you saw the video. She's hurting. Whatever's going on inside Reagan Manor is destroying her. I can't stand idly by. I have to get them out of there. That's why I'm here. I need your help, and I need it today."

Terrence leaned into his hands, covering his face with trembling fingers.

Adam hadn't meant to hurt his feelings. "I'm sorry. I didn't mean—"

He waved Adam's apology off, struggling to regain his composure. "No, son. It's me who's sorry. Here I'm bragging about being a rebel and standing up for what I believe in, only I should've done it twenty-two years ago."

Chapter Twenty-Nine

"How old are you?" Adam had to know.

Terrence lowered his eyes. "I'm sixty-two."

Adam did the math. If Shannon was twenty-five...

"Oh, stop trying to figure it out in your head," Terrence snapped. "Look at her. Does that perfect little girl look anything like Paul Reagan?"

Oh, hell. I'm right. Terrence Moore is Shannon's father.

"What happened to Olivia?" he asked quietly. "Do you know?"

The elderly man sucked in a deep breath as his grief filled the tidy sitting room. "As God is my witness, I never knew. One day she was happy, like you see her in that picture there, but the next day she wouldn't talk to me. She threw me out of that awful dungeon he calls a home when I went to visit; said she never wanted to see me again. I couldn't get in to see her after that, not even once. He kept her locked up tighter than a parakeet in a cheap, dime-store cage."

That scenario sounded familiar. "But why?"

"He's a damned genius, that's why." Terrence dashed the tears off his cheek. "He's always dreaming up fantastic inventions, and then finding a way to make 'em work. He's the one who single-handedly built the Purity Power Pak, you know? The one NASA uses to keep their optical mirrors on their long-range satellites in perfect focus."

"I didn't know that," Adam admitted. Until now, he hadn't cared what Paul Reagan invented. He didn't care about Paul Reagan at all. Genius or not, the man seemed to do more harm than good.

"But I really think he'd suspected all along that we cared for each other. That we'd been seeing each other," Terrence whispered, his eyes gazing out the window. "She was younger than him. Hell, she was younger than me, too. Olivia was a beautiful woman, but so lonely. He was a smart man alright, but not smart enough to know that a woman like her needed companionship more than she needed platinum and diamonds. He always had something more important to do, and he spent too much time in his lab. He wasn't cheating on her, but in a way, he was. It might not have been with another woman, but he loved his work more than his wife. Anyway, he asked me to take her to a dance one night. Said she was nagging him, and—" Terrence choked. "My Emma Sue had passed. Olivia and I were like two birds with broken wings. We needed each other."

"And then she got pregnant."

Terrence nodded. "He never confronted me, but I'm sure he knew right off the bat that Shannon wasn't his. He seemed happy about her birth. We all were. But one day, it changed. Just like that. It was like he turned a switch off. He grew more secretive and sneaky. He shut me out first, then Olivia did, too. Little by little, she wasted away."

Adam bit his tongue. He hated to ask, but he needed to know. "How did she die?"

Terrence stared at nothing, his eyes vacant. The moment stretched until he snapped out of it. "He said she hit her head in the bathtub, that she drowned. It was an unattended death, so an autopsy had to be performed. The medical examiner found water in her lungs. He ruled it accidental. It fit Paul's version. There was no way to prove anything else."

"But you suspected murder?" Adam's heart pounded.

"I honestly don't know what I suspected. That's why I couldn't quit Reagan Industries. I had to stay close to hear any news about Shannon."

Adam stood, glancing at the clock on the mantle. He needed to go. Shannon was in more trouble that he'd suspected. "I need to get her out of there today. Will you be okay to wait for the paramedics by yourself?"

"No!" Terrence barked. "You said you needed my help. Now what in tarnation do you want me to do?"

Adam hesitated. Mr. Moore was still shaky, and all this true confession business hadn't helped get his strength back.

"Dag nab it," he growled. "I'm not dead yet. Let me help. I owe Olivia that much."

"Can you get access to the Hummingbird Hawk drones?"

"You mean the ones that got *lost at sea*?" The old gent's brow spiked again, this time with a healthy dose of sarcasm. "Them the ones you're talking about? The ones the Navy let slip out of their hands?"

Adam held his breath. Either Terrence stepped up to the plate and helped save his daughter, right then and there, or he failed her again. "Yes, sir. Those drones."

"Just where do you think they are?"

"I think we both know where they are, don't we?"

Terrence shook his head. "Damn him if they are, but yes. If Paul stole them from the Navy, they'd be stashed in his lab. They might already be stripped down and on their way to the incinerator. What do you want me to do once I find 'em?"

Adam knelt at the side of Terrence's chair and explained what he needed. By the time he was through, Terrence was on his feet and as spry as that spring chicken he claimed he wasn't.

"Are you sure you're up to this?" Adam asked, holding the man's elbow for support and still not willing to risk his life.

Terrence straightened to his full six-foot height and gave his chest a hearty smack. "Never felt better."

He proved it when someone knocked at the front door, and he all but raced Adam to answer it. The paramedics had arrived, better late than never. "Don't you young fellows have anything better to do?"

"Umm, we got a call someone was injured?" A surprised young man's voice wavered. "Does anyone here need medical attention?"

"Nope. Just headed to work. You boys go save someone who needs saving. It ain't me." Terrence waved them off his porch as he told Adam, "I'll be seeing you later."

"Yes, you will." Adam pressed his chin into the two-way radio at his shoulder while Terrence sauntered out the door. "Can I get someone to ensure Terrence Moore makes it safely to Reagan Industries? Driving a silver 1980s Lincoln. He's just leaving his residence on Hawthorne, but he had a suspicious visitor before I arrived. Someone roughed him up. He's still unsteady."

"On my way." Harley's voice came through loud and clear. "Are you sure he's fit to be driving?"

"He is at the moment. Watch over him for me?"

Harley chuckled. "You know I will. Be safe."

"Copy that." By the time Adam hit the sidewalk, the paramedics had sped off, and Terrence's silver Lincoln idled alongside his SUV at the curb. "You got a foolproof plan to save my daughter?"

"Yes, sir, I do." Adam nodded as he sank into his driver's seat. "The next time we meet, I'll be introducing you to your grandson."

The old guy's face lit up. "Dag nab it, I'm a granddaddy. Quit your lolly-gagging. You've got work to do."

Adam hit the ignition button. Terrence drove one way; he drove the other.

Two down, and God willing—one to go.

"Your limo is ready, Miss Reagan." Hubbard stood outside her bedroom door like the obedient manservant he was not.

Shannon didn't acknowledge him on her way to the winding staircase. Hubbard was her father's butler, not hers. She didn't owe him courtesy, much less trust or casual conversation. He could bring the bag inside her door or not; it didn't matter. Someone would. Someone always did.

At the top of the staircase, she paused to evaluate her reflection in the floor-to-ceiling mirror. She pushed a stubborn strand of long hair off her forehead. The damned thing wouldn't stay put.

That was the day she'd rebelled—the day she'd hacked her hair off to spite her father. It was nothing more than adolescent acting out, and of course, Paul Reagan had been less than pleased. She just hadn't expected to end up on the floor again.

"Who do you think you are?" he had bellowed after he'd slapped her, the veins on his forehead dark and throbbing.

Picking herself up, she didn't answer. She knew exactly who she was. How could she have missed it all these years? He hadn't hit his daughter. No. He'd hit a marketable commodity. A winning slogan. That was all, just the bright new face of Reagan Industries, only with a bright red handprint marked it.

Her passive act of aggression was still aggression, and he'd met it head on. Her defiance forced him to repackage her, so to speak. With a snap of his fingers, a top-notch stylist was flown in to transform her shorn hair into the latest high fashion do, fresh from Paris and all the rage. The carefully crafted television commercials were redone. The photo shoot of her at her desk in Reagan Towers, too. The pithy, witty slogans.

In less than forty-eight hours, Reagan Industries was transformed into an upbeat, win-all, take-all, twenty-first century business to watch out for. The only things he couldn't alter was the lie of how she'd always wanted to follow in his proud footsteps. The lie of how she'd chosen to get Jimmy Malone baptized just to rename him Paul Maximillian Reagan the Third. The lie of how pleased Paul Reagan the Second was to finally have the grandson he'd *always* wanted.

And last, but certainly not the least, the lie of how she was driven to please her father after her near fatal crash at sea.

Yes. All those fucking lies.

She tugged at the stubborn hair still flopping over her brow until frustration exploded through her fingertips. With one final yank, it fell to the floor. *I hate you!* She clutched another handful. *And you!*

More oily strands littered the ornate carpet. With one final tug, she let the last handful fall, glaring at her now disheveled reflection. The fire in her eyes. The sneer on her lips. The flush of pure self-hatred on her cheeks. *There. That's better. Let Daddy's fancy French stylist fix that.* She stabbed a pointed fingernail at the mirror. *And you're next, Alex Stewart.*

Aggravated with her increasing lack of self-control, Shannon clicked her overpriced six-inch heels on her way down the marble staircase, enjoying the quick, sharp staccato of pure insolence against marble. The world thought that expensive substance was hard as stone? Ha. They hadn't seen anything yet.

The change to her once kind spirit amazed her. She used to look to the sunshine, but now she inclined more toward shadows. Darkness hid the light of day and all she used to be. A woman can only cry buckets of tears for so long before they turn to shards of ice.

Her father wanted her mean enough to subdue his enemies? She'd show him mean, then cruel and heartless. She'd show everyone who got in her way.

You want it, Father? By hell, you've got it.

Right on cue, Hubbard opened the heavy wooden door that kept the real world out and living hell inside. She passed through the ornately carved entrance without a word to the pathetic tool he was. He'd probably report her breach in etiquette back to her father, along with her temper tantrum over her hair.

Well, good. Hurry back to dear old Dad, you lying two-faced dog. Tell him everything I did and everything I didn't do. While you're at it, pick up after me. Take out the trash. And go to hell.

As always, Raul stood patiently waiting for her at the open limo door, smiling like he actually cared. He was another she used to trust. No more. Never. Ever. Again. Trust was a commodity for weaklings, and she, Shannon Reagan, the face of Reagan Industries, was anything but.

"Miss Shannon." He tipped his chauffeur's cap when he saw her, his eyes lit with the gentle glow she remembered. She dropped her gaze, not answering him as she ducked to enter the rear seat of the limo, directly behind the driver's seat. This was her spot, one of the few sanctuaries left to her in the world. Raul needed to shut up and drive. That was what he got paid for.

"Dulles Airport again, Miss Shannon?"

He knew damned well where she was going, so she stared out the smoked-glass side window instead of replying. He wanted to chat. She had nothing to say. Let him figure it out.

"It's a beautiful day to be flying." He offered another interesting tidbit of nothing.

Let it rain. Let it hail. Let it snow, for all she cared. Today was the end of the world for Alex Stewart.

She sunk her chin to her palm, her elbow on her knee and stared at the depressing, sunny day. The order of the universe was all wrong. The weather ought to reflect the pain and misery of the world. If she ruled the universe, it would. She'd change the forecast to match her moods, her tantrums, and her decrees.

You and you and you shall die. Let it rain.

And you, sir, shall go hungry for a thousand days. Let it pour.

And all liars shall go to hell. Let it burn!

She bit her lip—hard. Her pitiful life was the ultimate game of survival and she *would* win. Those fools competing for measly millions on reality television had nothing on her. The trick to her power was in using the reputation of her father's killer instincts. Everyone was already scared to death of him. She only had to glare, stare and be just as rude as Paul Reagan. Hell, it wasn't even difficult to do anymore. She was his daughter, wasn't she? Wasn't that what Reagans did? Didn't they destroy everything and everyone they touched?

Shannon clenched her stomach at that lie. The only reason she'd changed was that sweet boy locked away in an upstairs prison, doors away from hers. The cruel creature she'd become ate her alive from the inside out. The truth settled in of its own accord. Her father was killing her, and she let him because she didn't know how to stop him. Paul Reagan was capable of murder—hers.

A single tear eked out of the corner of her kohl-black, mascara-lined eye. She used to be a good person. That was what Adam had seen, the woman he thought he loved. Who had she become? Even the trembling mouth he'd kissed now betrayed her descent into the deepest depths of Hell with its edgy vulgarity. God, she wanted out of the mess she was in, just not bad enough to desert Jimmy.

The miles flew by. Raul ceased small talk. Just as well. He used to be her confidant, but he worked for her father. Who knew whose confidant he really was? She didn't. Her world had become two-way mirrors and betrayers all around.

I want my baby back!

She stifled the ever-present scream in her heart before it had the chance to burst forth from her lying lips. Today would be the end of Alex Stewart. Tomorrow it would be someone else, and every day forth she would prove how low she could stoop, how evil she could be if only because it was the only way. Jimmy would survive, even if everyone else had to die...

Her hand rose automatically to her mouth, her knuckles to the bite of her teeth as she visited more pain onto the bitter beast she'd become. Reduced to a trapped animal willing to chew its leg off to escape, she allowed another tear. Only there was no escape. Chewing her knuckles would only invite more questions, and worse, it might limit her visitation rights. It might give her father more ammunition. He might think her on the verge of a mental breakdown, which she very well might be. She certainly felt like she stood on the brink of insanity often enough these past three months. But how would she save Jimmy from the padded cell of some expensive asylum?

She clasped her hands in her lap, twisting the bleeding knuckle, smearing the blood into her palm, so no one would see the real Shannon. So no one would know that only her love for the tiniest man in her life kept her from the edge.

Raul's sad eyes met hers in the rearview mirror. "What do you want?" she snarled. *Had he seen? Will he tell? Shit, is he going to cry? He looks like he's scared of me.*

He should be.

"I'm sorry, Miss Shannon," he said softly, almost timidly. "I need to stop for fuel. The tank is nearly—"

"Do it then." She knew better. He didn't care about her. Even if he'd seen that she'd hurt herself, he wouldn't admit it. Not anymore. As it was, he probably got a monthly bonus for spying on her. He was like all the others—blind, indifferent, and more worried about a steady paycheck. "Make it quick."

He bobbed his stupid head like a chicken pecking for food. "Thank you, ma'am. I will."

I wonder what he'd do if I slapped his cap off. Probably nothing. He'd make allowances for me because of my wealth, just like everyone else does. Hell, he'd probably pick his cap up, put it back on, and ask me to do it again.

Raul made a sharp right turn into the nearest gas station. Several other customers were at the pumps, but Shannon's mind was a thousand miles away, rehearsing the exquisitely detailed lies she'd memorized to make the world believe the negligence of Alex and—*Adam.*

For a fraction of a heartbeat, the darkness lifted. Her heart stuttered to life. Her blood warmed. Shannon closed her eyes against the ugly task ahead and let his name spill back into her soul. The smell of surf and sea and sweat, his gentle hand cupping her breast, and the red flush of his embarrassment tantalized her senses once more. *Ah, that man.*

She leaned back into the upholstered leather seat, remembering everything. He'd called her brave. He'd thought her strong. He'd sung to Squeaks, and he'd told her that he loved her. And that storm they'd braved together…

What she wouldn't give to go back to that beach, to be warm and safe in the circle of his hard arms. To know the power of the universe had met its match, and to believe that, with him, she could withstand any storm. There for a moment, she'd actually believed…

Ha! She bolted upright, her spine stiff, not needing the tender touch of fine leather any more than she needed another man in her life. She snorted her disgust at Adam's stupid assessment of her, and forced her hardened heart to the evil task at hand. Adam knew nothing. He was nothing.

One of her father's prickish bodyguards would meet her at the airport. He'd be with her every step of the way for the next five days, and no doubt, he'd stand outside her hotel room during the night, too. These guys were amazing robots. It seemed they lived for her father's cold-hearted decrees.

Raul had the audacity to open the opposite passenger door, something he didn't usually do. What now? Was he offering someone a ride? What did he think this was, a cab? *Damn him*. He'd just waved a stranger into the limo.

How dare he?

Chapter Thirty

"Who the hell are you?" she barked, before the guy had a chance to sit his unwelcome ass on the seat. The wind of autumn blew in with him. She couldn't see more than his scruffy hair, a glimpse of an unshaven face, and broad shoulders. *The nerve of some people. This is the last straw.*

"Get out," she ordered. "Right this minute. Get out of my limo and catch the bus."

When he turned to face her, the gentlest, darkest blues bathed her in tenderness once more. Her heart jumped high in her throat, blocking breath and the mean words on the tip of her tongue.

Adam?

He pulled the door shut, but he seemed stiff. Unsure. Bright red and green buttons blinked from the handheld device he'd set on the floor between his boots. "I just scanned your limo for bugs. Your father isn't listening, and we need to talk."

She couldn't believe her eyes. *Adam. He came for me. He's here. He's really here.*

Every nerve in her body sung at the sight of him. Love raised its weary head as that gentle melody resonated all the way to her sad, pitiful soul. A thousand broken dreams screeched up from her heart and—

Ahh! The pain of remorse! Her sins assaulted her in Technicolor. She'd screamed at him that day, told him to leave, and made it worse when Hubbard called the police to report a break-in. She'd betrayed and hurt Adam, and yet—

He's here.

He offered his hand, the glow in his eyes warm and pure with the light she craved. She couldn't move. Didn't dare touch him for fear he'd evaporate. The fingers now stretched toward her were strong, his open palm calloused with the hard work of an honest man who worked for another honest man who—

Whose character I'm going to assassinate.

Guilt slithered its icy stranglehold across her shoulders and around her neck, squeezing the hope back out of her. She still had a dirty job to do to that other honest man. To this one, too. Only then could she see Jimmy. Alex had to die. Adam had to leave. And she had to return to Hell.

"I love you," he whispered softly—and with a stifled cry, Shannon fell.

In one desperate leap, she flung herself across the distance between them and into his arms. Just as she knew he would always do, Adam caught her. A desperate groan ripped free from her heart, while the fears she'd dealt with for weeks burst out of her. "He's got Jimmy! He's got my baby! I have to go. I have to kill Alex! You can't be here! I have to—"

"Shush," he commanded with love, and instantly, she stilled, listening to him suck in the same great breaths that she was. Loud and steady, his honorable heart throbbed beneath her ear. This man was all about strength, and she needed him desperately now.

"What do you mean, kill Alex?"

"I'm on my way to Texas to ruin him financially and his reputation and… I'm scared," she whined, all her fears unstoppable with the dam broken. She swallowed hard. "He's got my baby."

"I know," Adam breathed into her hair, stroking her shoulders and down her arm. Gentling her. She shivered under the warmth of his touch, not realizing how cold she'd become. "You're safe now."

"No, I'm not. Neither is Jimmy." Shannon tried to push him away, but he held her tight, and then she felt them. His tears trickled down onto her face. Adam was crying.

"I'm sorry. I never meant to hurt you," she choked. "Oh, Adam. Oh, God, I had no choice."

"I know that, Shannon." He brushed a quick hand over his cheek. "You've only done what you had to do, but answer me one thing. Where's Jimmy? Right now?"

"The nursery on the second floor, in the northwest corner of the house. You'll never get in. That's where Linda rules. No one can get past her. And guards are everywhere. And Hubbard. And—"

"Shannon. Look at me." Adam shook her slightly until she lifted her head and met his eyes. The deep blue ocean had never looked truer. She wanted nothing more than to wrap herself in his love and run away with him and Jimmy. "You're that little boy's mother and you're his sole legal custodian, right?"

She nodded.

"Do I have your permission to remove your son from Reagan Manor?"

He wasn't talking sense. Hadn't she just told him that getting into Jimmy's room was impossible? Adam persisted. His index finger tipped her chin up. "Do I?" he asked again.

"Yes." She bit her already tender lip. Legality hadn't mattered with her father. Why should it matter to her now?

Adam relaxed his hold and wiped his face with another swipe. Shannon eased back enough to see him better. The tears he'd missed still glistened on his lashes, and the love that this brave man had for her and a boy who wasn't his flesh and blood touched her heart.

"I'm so sorry," she cried again, cupping his cheek. The second she touched him, he squeezed his eyes shut, and her heart melted. This kind, gentle bear of a guy was there to rescue her despite her betrayal.

He turned his mouth into a radio at his shoulder and muttered hoarsely, "Northwest corner. Second level."

"Copy that," a disembodied, tough chick voice answered.

Shannon's heart leapt. "Is that Izza?"

He nodded, but cautioned, "Don't ask anything else, okay?"

"But... my father has Jimmy." What could he or Izza possibly do to change that?

"Talk to me, Shannon. Tell me what's going on. Please?"

Hysteria bubbled out of her, blocking her weak hold on self-control. "I have to go. You don't understand. He'll hurt my baby, and… No! I just can't do this. Get out!" She pushed with all her might, but this time Adam held her tighter.

"He's using Jimmy to control you, isn't he?"

She nodded. "He's sick. I have to take over the business, or I'll never get to see my son again. Let me go! I have a plane to catch!" Her escalating panic pitched her into a full-blown need for Adam to Get. Out!

She raised her hand to strike, but he caught it in midair. "No!" he roared. "No more!"

And she stopped struggling.

Adam pressed that mean hand to his lips, blinking at the sight of her bleeding knuckles. Tenderly, he kissed each self-inflicted wound, pouring love back into her with the soft caress of his lips. He didn't take his eyes off her. She couldn't take hers off of him. His next words pierced straight to her motherly soul. "No more running, Shannon. Today, we fight. Today, you stand up to your father, and you never look back. You hear me?"

"You don't know him. He'll hurt Jimmy. I have to—"

"No, Shannon. There is no choice. He'll hurt you and Jimmy if you stay. Today, you take your son back, and you leave home. With me."

She shivered as those strong words filled her soul. "Say it again," she whispered, daring to believe.

Adam bowed his forehead to hers. "Come with me. I love you, and I love that little boy of yours. You're the best HALO jump I've ever fallen into. Please let me help you. Let's go get your son. What do you say?"

"I want to." She nodded, swallowing hard as bravery glimmered for the first time in months. The words were no more out of her mouth than fear clutched her heart and the roller coaster ride of terror began again. Bile rose in the back of her throat. She changed her mind. "No. I can't. I'm scared. It's too dangerous. I have to go. Goddamn you! Let me go!"

This time, he didn't yell to get her attention. Instead, Adam traced his index finger around her ear, pushing her ugly short hair back. "It's okay to be scared," he crooned. "I'm scared too, but mostly I'm mad. Aren't you mad?"

What a stupid question! Why the hell did he think she was screaming?

"At your father, Shannon," Adam clarified. "Aren't you angry at him?"

Oh, God, yes. She nodded, still fighting the urge to run to do Paul Regan's bidding. "He's got a woman named Linda Perkins guarding Jimmy, and she's mean, and his men are everywhere and they're—"

"His men work for Alliance Security," Adam cut her hysteria short. "I've worked with a couple of them overseas. They're SEALs, and they're damned good, but my guys are better. And I don't give a shit how tough that nanny thinks she is."

Shannon held her breath, weighing the risks to the daring plan Adam proposed. She stood to lose everything. What did he have on the line? "I don't know," she said, her heart pounding in her ears.

"Then let's start with what you do know."

She gulped. *What do I know? Fear. Retribution. Betrayal. Stress. Anorexia. Bulimia. The list was endless.*

"Do you know how much I love you?" Adam asked, the hurt in his eyes shining again. "Do you know you don't have to fight your father alone? Come on, Shannon baby, Izza and Connor are pulling for you. Think."

Rational thought was nearly impossible. "You… you called me Shannon baby. I remember. My mother used to call me that." Somehow that tender endearment from long ago carried tremendous power at that precise moment. Shannon could almost believe the universe was on her side. That her mother was somehow looking over her and Jimmy.

Adam traced the line of her jaw, the curve of her quavering chin, his eyes searching hers. "You must have been everything to her, too."

Shannon calmed, trying with all her heart to do as he'd asked. *Adam loves me. I don't know why, and I don't deserve it, but he does. Maybe, just maybe, I can do this. With him.*

"The first time I saw you in the Sit Room, my heart fell to the floor at your feet. Didn't you see it?" he whispered huskily. "Honestly. I thought I made a fool of myself in front of you—heck, in front of everyone."

She shook her head. She'd been too much out of her element that day. Too bullied.

"You were scared then, too, but you surprised the hell out of me."

"I threw up," she reminded him, her words a reality check in the very quiet limo.

"Yes, but you also made a promise, and you stuck to it, which is more than your father ever did."

"But I was different. I'm not that person any—"

"Yes, you are. You're still you." He put a stop to her belittling rant. "Come on, Mama. Let's go get Squeaks out of prison once and for all. Let's save your baby."

"Okay," she said softly, her heart calm for the moment and her hands tucked inside Adam's. He made standing up for herself seem possible. "But this is going to make my father very mad."

"Good," Adam declared with a growl. He planted a kiss in the middle of her forehead. "I intend to make him damned mad today. Maybe every day from now on."

He rapped on the window, signaling Raul to get behind the driver's wheel again.

"Is everything better now?" Raul asked as he climbed inside. One look at Shannon, and he passed a box of tissues over the car seat.

Shannon looked up from the warm embrace of Adam's arms, accepted a tissue and wiped her nose. The day of repentance had come. Raul had only ever treated her with kindness. Reaching for his hand, she offered the first of many apologies she intended to make. "Can you forgive me, Raul? I've been so cruel to you."

He lifted her hand to his lips for an undeserved kiss. "Remember who you talk to? It's me. Your driver, but first, your friend. There is nothing I wouldn't do for you. You're my only boss and the only Reagan I love. Only you."

Tears blurred her vision. Adam offered no help. "You hear that, Mama? You're my boss, too. Only you."

Chapter Thirty-One

I can breathe.

Even with his heart pumping like the Clemson U brass band at the homecoming game, the mere act of holding Shannon again calmed Adam to his boots. She trembled like a leaf under his chin, but that would cease the instant she had Squeaks back in her arms.

She'd lost weight, her once nicely rounded bottom now so boney that it dug into his thighs. He didn't care. That could be remedied just as easily with a thick cut of prime rib, lobster, maybe a glass or two of red wine, and whatever else her heart desired. Heck, the moon and the stars seemed reachable with her in his arms—if she wanted them.

They sat in silence, absorbing each other while Raul pulled the limo into traffic.

"He'll know something's wrong when I don't show at the airport," she worried.

"Already thought of that," Adam replied. "Raul? You're on, buddy."

With a cheesy smile, Raul winked in the rearview mirror and dialed Reagan Manor on the limo's smart phone. "Let me talk with Hubbard, please."

"Where are you?" Hubbard growled over the speaker.

"At the moment, I have a flat tire, so I'm—"

"I doubt that. You wouldn't be moving with a flat tire now, would you?"

"How do you know I'm still moving?" Raul's brow crinkled in the rearview.

"I know everything," Hubbard purred.

"Well, if you're so smart, then you know traffic's too thick to pull over right now," Raul snapped. "Wait." He pulled over to the shoulder. "There. I stopped. Are you happy now?

Hubbard never missed a beat. "Do you require roadside assistance, Mr. Ortega?"

"Don't you know that, too?" Raul retorted. "Never mind. Some guy just stopped. It looks like he'll help me. I'll be back on the road in five minutes. Will that suit you?"

"She mustn't be late. This meeting means everything to Mr. Reagan."

"Don't worry." Raul's wink caught the rearview mirror. "Miss Shannon is the only reason I do this thankless job."

"That can always change."

Raul hung up on Hubbard's sarcastic threat. "I didn't know he was tracking the limo, did you?"

"I'm not surprised," she murmured, her voice suddenly far away.

"Does he track everything and everyone he owns?" Adam asked, still keeping her snuggled on his lap and his arms around her. She'd calmed, but she sounded lost and apprehensive again.

"I think so. My father has hidden cameras in the house and spies everywhere. Hubbard is one of them."

"Then plan B it is." Adam leaned into his two-way again. "You guys back there?"

"Following your every move," Rory answered.

"Who else is helping you?" Shannon looked so dang cute peering out the back window to catch a glimpse of whoever was running interference.

Adam winked as he responded. "It looks like Reagan's got a GPS transmitter in the limo. We need a ride."

"Coming right up." Rory had no sooner finished speaking than a hunter green SUV pulled in front of the limo and parked, its turn signals flashing.

"Will you be okay?" Adam asked Raul.

He beamed at Shannon. "Don't worry about me. I was looking for a job when I found this one. It's been an honor, Miss Shannon. I will never forget you, *mi amor*."

She pulled out of Adam's arms to give him a hug. "He can still hurt both of us, Raul. Please stay safe."

"I'll be in touch, buddy," Adam told the chauffeur. "Don't you go taking off to the Bahamas or anything crazy like that, you hear?'

"Never." Raul smiled and released Shannon as he waved them out the door. "Now go. Get your precious son, my sweet fairy princess. Be happy again."

Adam pulled her out of the limo to her feet, for a moment thrilled to be there with her. Early morning Crystal City traffic whizzed by. It would've been the perfect moment, but Shannon fell apart. "I have a breast pump!" she spat at him.

What the hell is a breast pump? Adam didn't have a clue. Was it one of those painful beauty treatments women did to enhance their figures? It didn't matter, not to a guy who could fix anything that needed fixing, by hell. If she hated it, he hated it, too.

Shannon raked stiff fingers through her disheveled greasy hair, yanking at it. She used to look so elegant.

"Stop hurting yourself." He reached for those mean hands.

"You don't understand," she cried. "I can't even nurse my own baby. I'm just a… a cow!"

Oh, that kind of a pump…

"Shh." Adam pulled her against him, smoothing a hand over her poor head to gentle her. "You'll be holding Squeaks before you know it, and you can nurse him day and night if you want. Just wait and see."

She calmed instantly. "Squeaks? I haven't heard him called that in a long time."

"What does he call Jimmy?"

"He doesn't," she groaned. "He hasn't visit much, just enough to change Jimmy's name to Paul Maximillian the Third."

"Blah." Adam stuck out his whole tongue at that awful, pompous name, hoping to at least make her smile. "Names can be changed. Which would you like, Jimmy Malone or Squeaks, because we can—"

Shannon whirled into him, clutching his face in her hands as she crushed her mouth to his. She seemed to be pouring desperation into a frantic kiss that ravaged, bruised, and bit. She climbed up his body, her anguish suddenly out of control—fierce, raw, and feral.

Adam obliged. This poor woman was that tiny glass Christmas ornament held fast in a wicked vise for too long.

Too delicate for the enormous pressure that had been forced on her shoulders, she was coming apart in his hands, shattering all over him. Breaking now that she'd been tossed a lifeline. She just didn't know which way to fall.

"I'm here, Shannon baby," he promised for time and all eternity. "You're not alone any more. I'm here."

She sobbed and he hefted her off her feet, one hand at the back of her head, the other on her backside, molding her to him. Anchoring her. Whatever she needed to get through this next showdown with her old man, he meant to give it to her. Right there on that busy Crystal City highway.

Smoothing her hands feverishly over his head, she gripped him tight, her nails digging into his scalp, holding him in place while she ravaged his mouth. It was hard to breathe in the midst of this surprise attack, but he was a guy. He managed.

"Save my baby, Adam," she gasped raggedly into his mouth. "God, oh, God, please save Jimmy."

"That's why I'm here," he murmured around her ravenous lips and tongue. "I've got the whole team working to get Squeaks. It's going to be okay. Trust me."

"I do," she said fervently, licking his lips and breathing too fast and too hard. "I really do, I just... I just... God, he's more evil than you know."

Adam eased his fingers into her hair until he had a thin handful. Tugging her away from his face, he bumped his forehead to hers, needing her to listen up. "Believe me, Mama, I do know how bad Paul Reagan is, but we get Jimmy back first, then we deal with your old man. Plan on it. Know it down to those strappy heels you're wearing. Today is Jimmy Malone day. After that, it's happily-ever-after, got it?"

She pressed her cheek against his nose, her hands still clinging to his head. "I love you so much," she whispered as she straightened her skirt. "You're right. I can do this. Let's get our baby back."

Zing. Goosebumps shivered up his neck. That single word shot straight into the deepest caverns of his soul. *Our.* Did she have any idea what she'd just said? What it meant to him?

"Will you two lay off the smooching and get your butts over here?" Ember ordered from where she stood at the SUV, all wide-eyed and watching. "Stop with the mushy stuff. We've got us a baby boy to rescue, and I can't wait to meet him in person."

Shannon looked to Ember, then back to Adam. "Yes," he said softly, pressing her knuckles to his lips. "Let's get *our* baby back."

The minute the women were within distance, Ember squealed and grabbed Shannon in a sisterly hug. "You poor thing."

"Come on, ladies. You can do that later, too," Rory called from inside the vehicle. "Get your butts in here. We're losing daylight."

Adam guided Shannon into the back seat, then eased in beside her.

"This is Rory," Ember introduced her husband as everyone fastened their seatbelts. "Rory, my very best friend, Shannon Reagan. We're going shopping for shoes one of these days. Baby boy shoes, too."

"Hey, Shannon. It's sure good to see you again," Rory said brightly, pulling away from the limo, his focus on the traffic. "Today's the day, huh?"

She nodded. "What's going to happen now? How will you guys get past Reagan security?"

"We're not." Rory's dark blue eyes sparkled with mischief in the rearview mirror.

Adam hurried to explain. "We've already got people inside."

"You do? Who?"

"Only the best ghost in the business. You've met the ghost before. You know who I'm talking about."

"I do?"

"Sure you do!" He leaned into her hair and whispered one word. "Alex."

"Your boss? He's helping me? But... oh no, not him!" She buried her face in her hands, crying so hard that she hiccupped. Then she cried harder. The poor girl was wearing herself out with all these emotional breakdowns.

"It's okay," he crooned, trying to undo whatever he did that made her so miserable.

"It's just that *he's* helping me," she ground that out, like it was a bad thing. "*Me!*"

"So what? Alex thinks a lot of you. Of course he's helping. Hell, who do you think's paying my salary?"

"You don't understand!" She tipped her head back, her eyes squeezed tight, and wailed.

Adam was smitten all over again. He'd never seen anything cuter in his life. Not that he understood her, but that puckered lip was just plain adorable.

"B-but I'm supposed to be on my way to Texas to—to..."

"To what, darling?" Rory asked gently. "Take your time and spit it out."

Adam caught the exasperated look from Rory in the rearview mirror that plainly said *'women!'* "It's no big deal, Rory. Shannon was just on orders to destroy Alex and his business today. That's all."

"That's all? That's all!" Shannon cried, but she didn't get the time to elaborate. The regal stone archway over the wide circular driveway beckoned at the end of the street. Black iron pillars joined with the stone fence to offer an intimidating invitation to enter. Or not.

"We're there," Rory prompted. "Let's keep it together, folks. We've got work to do and people to meet."

"Oh no. What do we do next?" Shannon asked breathlessly.

Adam studied the logistics, immediately planning an alternate escape route for the agents they had inside the manor. Or a rescue. "We wait. Our man inside will contact us. When he does—"

"You mean Alex?"

"Yes. When Alex gives us the signal—"

"What's the signal?"

With a finger to her overactive lips, he explained before she could interrupt again. "The signal could be a phone call or a—"

"Is that a baby blanket?" Rory pointed to the front of the house where a white piece of cloth now draped from an opened window.

Ember giggled. "Leave it to the boss."

Adam turned Shannon to face him. "What would you say to your father if Jimmy wasn't stuck inside Reagan Manor?"

Shannon swallowed hard. He read disbelief with every wide-eyed blink. "I'd, umm, tell him I was leaving, and I wouldn't even pack. I'd just walk out the front door, and I'd run as fast as I could, and I'd never look back and... why?" Her breath caught. "Do I have to talk to him? Is that why we're here?"

"No, Mama. You don't have to talk to him ever again." He nodded toward a man walking away from her father's house with quick, long strides. Like an arrow, he didn't deviate from his target destination by one step. "Open your door, Shannon. This guy's with us."

Adam kept his hand in the middle of her back. The poor woman was shaking so hard, she couldn't get the door open. It didn't matter. The moment he reached them, Alex pulled the door open and slid in next to Shannon. He made that leather bomber jacket he was wearing look damned good. A little snug maybe, but good.

By now Rory and Ember were both hanging over the back of the front seat. All eyes were on Shannon and Alex."

"I see you've got your package," Alex said, amusement crinkling the corners of his eyes. The cocky guy wasn't even winded.

Adam circled one arm around Shannon's back and shoulder. "You bet. Had a little trouble at Terrence Moore's, but he's en route to fulfill his part of the mission." Adam checked his watch. "He ought to be there by now. Harley's got his six. How about you? Any trouble inside?"

Alex glanced back at the supposedly unbreachable Reagan Manor. "Not yet. I had a little talk with your friends from Alliance Security. They won't be working for Reagan Industries any more. Connor took the butler out easy, but Izza had to suppress the nanny. Damn woman was strong as an ox. She went down fighting until Izza tasered her. Damn. I have got to give that agent another raise."

"Will they need a ride?" Rory asked.

"No. They'll meet us back at Mortimers'." Alex turned to Shannon on the seat beside him. "I have something for you."

Adam placed his hand at the base of her neck to steady her. Still, she trembled. The poor girl was holding her breath, and he honestly didn't understand why. Alex would never hurt a woman, least of all Shannon. If she only knew how much he'd offered up in time and money to get to this day, she'd be hugging him instead of berating herself.

A tiny voice murmured from within the leather hideaway. Shannon choked, and covered her mouth with one hand. Very gently, Alex pulled the zipper of his jacket down to reveal the chubby little boy of her heart.

"Ahh!" Shannon cried, and Jimmy Malone tumbled into her waiting arms, his fist stuffed in his mouth and his two bright eyes taking in his new world.

Tears blurred Adam's vision when she gathered her baby to her chest as if she'd just found her reason to live again. He knew the feeling. He didn't care who saw. He pulled his little family onto his lap while he and Shannon cried over Squeaks together.

By the sounds of the sniffling coming from the front seat, they weren't the only ones. In short order, the SUV pulled away from the curb. The happiest mother on the planet had her precious baby back, but Adam knew damned well.

The war had just begun.

Chapter Thirty-Two

Joy hurt so good. In the twinkling of an eye, she had her life back. Shannon leaned into Adam, her seatbelt forgotten as Rory drove them to where she didn't care. As long as her guys were with her, any place would be home.

She sucked in another deep breath, willing the essence of her sweet son back into her soul. It was minutes before she lifted her eyes to see where Rory was headed, but then she couldn't tell where they were. Jimmy had fallen asleep, and the darkness was gone. Even the Virginia sun seemed brighter, more golden, and full of promise than it had earlier.

Ember still hung over the front seat, the biggest smile on her face as she smoothed a hand over Jimmy's round, little head.

"This is my son, Jimmy Malone," Shannon introduced him through her tears. "My baby."

"Aww," Ember murmured. "He's beautiful. He looks like you."

Alex sat half-turned beside Shannon, his eyes a little misty, too. "This little guy never made a peep."

"Thank you," she whispered, sorry for all she'd intended to do to him.

"It was my pleasure." He looked as casual as they come, even after the tremendously dangerous feat he'd just accomplished. Sneaking into her father's manor undetected couldn't have been easy, and yet, he did it—for her.

Confession was supposed to be good for the soul. Shannon gulped past the lump of regret still stuck in her chest. Her soul needed to feel good again.

"I've been cruel to you," she whispered. "I can never pay you back for this. I owe you my son's life." She had to be looking like Alice Cooper by then, crying through all that black mascara she'd applied earlier when she needed to look hard and tough. "I was going to Texas today to begin a smear campaign against you. I was going to—"

"Oh, that." Alex dismissed her apology with his index finger to her lips. "Trust me. I've been slandered before. I wasn't worried. But answer me this. Are you happy now?"

She nodded, blinking hard. Happy was such a little word. Regret so big. "But I was going to destroy you," she said past his finger on her mouth.

Clear blue eyes twinkled. "No, you weren't, Shannon. Your father was going to *try* to destroy me." Alex traced a line down her chin, where he left a gentle pinch. "You're a good person, Shannon. I never doubted you so don't doubt yourself now. You're not Paul Reagan. You never could be."

"But I—but he—"

"But you would have done everything you could to save your son. I would have done the same if I were in your shoes. I'll make you a deal. Why don't you take care of that cute little guy and let me take care of your father? Good enough?"

She shivered. Could it be that easy? She couldn't see Alex any more. All she could do was bless the top of Jimmy's sleeping head with more of her tears as she promised, "Yes."

"Are we there yet?" Adam teased, one arm still wrapped around her shoulder.

"You sound like Tyler. Hold your pants on," Rory said, referring to his son as he turned off the highway and onto a gravel road. "And yes. We're there."

Tall oak trees way to a rustic cedar home beneath a lush canopy of pine and oak. The circular drive deposited them at an old-fashioned porch complete with wide stairs and cedar rockers, two outdoor-style sofas, and a wooden porch swing. Two little boys burst through the elegantly carved wooden front door before the vehicle rolled to a stop. A red-haired woman followed, a big smile on her pretty face.

"Are they here?" Judy asked, ducking to see past Rory.

"Yep."

"Unca Wowy!" one little boy squealed. He'd already climbed halfway into the driver's window. "You is here! Andy Emma!"

Rory climbed out, fending off the boys as they tumbled up his legs. He caught both in one armful, swinging them over his head with a big growl. By the time he was done, they were upside-down by their ankles, their uncut hair brushing over the gravel, and squealing, "Swing us! Swing us! We wanna ride!"

Shannon took it all in. Adam had told her about Harley's wild boys. Or maybe Harley had. She couldn't recall. One little guy was red-haired, the other light brown. Rory swung them back and forth a few times before he laid them carefully onto the grassy lawn and told them to settle down so they didn't wake their new cousin.

"Come on, guys," Adam said. "Let's meet Harley's wife, Judy, and the terrible two."

Alex and Ember waited with Rory and Judy, but Shannon had no desire to leave the security of the SUV. Then she'd be visible. A target. Paul Reagan wouldn't let the destruction of his legacy go unpunished.

She pressed Jimmy to her chest and reluctantly climbed out of the SUV to join Adam. Her heart kicked into high gear the moment she stepped into the open. She needed more time, and a safe place to process all that had happened. And to hide. She glanced back at the driveway they'd just travelled. Her father was coming for her. She could feel it in her bones.

"Aww, there he is. Look, boys," Judy called her rowdy youngsters to her side. "There's baby Jimmy."

The brown-haired youngster charged Alex instead. "Unca Alex!" He, in turn, grabbed the boy by his armpits and swung him up to sit on his shoulders. "Settle down, Georgie. You need to be quiet for a minute. There's a baby here. He might be sleeping."

"Shh-h-h-h." Two pudgy fingers covered Georgie's lips as he stage-whispered to his twin brother. "It's a baby boy. Yike us. He's sweepin'. See?"

"Aww." Redheaded Little Alex nodded adamantly from his perch on Rory's shoulder. "He so cute!"

"Harley's told me so much about you, Shannon," Judy said. "We're delighted that you'll be staying with us for a while."

Shannon cringed, frustrated that others were making decisions for her. "I am?"

Adam smoothed his hands over her shoulders. "Sorry. I should've asked you earlier, but honestly, it's been a crazy morning. I forgot. This is Harley's wife, Judy Mortimer, and those rug rats are Sponge Bob and The Beast. I told you about them, remember? Anyway, Judy and Harley offered safe refuge for as long as you need it."

"I not a beast, he is!" Little Alex giggled, pointing at his brother.

Judy chuckled. "Actually, Harley blabbed the minute he knew there was a plan. He's been dying to get you here where he can look out for you. We'd really love it if you stayed with us, Shannon, unless you'd feel safer somewhere else. We'd understand."

"No, I..." Shannon glanced over her shoulder again, unsure where that *safer somewhere else* might be found. So much depended on this one chance at freedom. Reagan Industries had the resources to not only squash this plan, but to annihilate everyone involved with it. How could she risk the lives of Harley's lovely family to save hers? "I'm just... It's just that... I don't want to put you and your family in danger."

Adam's arm snaked around her as he burrowed his face into her neck. "Hey, Mama. We had a deal, remember? You take care of my man, Squeaks. Let me and my guys take care of your old man."

"Come in while you decide." Judy led the way up the porch steps and into her home.

Instead of accepting the invitation, Shannon turned into Adam. "Are you leaving me?"

"No, ma'am, I am not," he whispered as he turned her to the porch. "I might have to tear myself away from you and Squeaks to do my job one of these days, but I'm never leaving you. You got away from me once. It won't happen again."

"But my father..." Try as she might, Shannon couldn't shake the feeling that Paul Reagan was on his way.

"Trust me. He doesn't know where you or Squeaks are. I promise." Adam stopped her at the doorway. "Besides, do you see that barn over there?"

Shannon followed the direction he pointed. A rustic red barn stood opposite the house on the other side of a wide, grassy yard. "Yes. I see it."

"There are about ten well-trained attack dogs in that barn and a couple litters of German Shepherd puppies. Harley raises canines for the local police departments. You can't see them because the dog runs are on the other side of the barn, but trust me. Harley keeps a couple of those dogs on the premises at all times. You'll see them playing with the boys, but make no mistake. Harley's dogs don't take kindly to strangers sneaking into their pack unannounced. Besides..."

He turned her into his arms. "You've got me, Alex, Rory, and Ember on your six, not to mention Connor and Izza will be here soon. Judy's got a mean left hook. Sponge Bob and The Beast think they can take all comers. You're not in this alone."

Shannon let out a tentative sigh. Being safe again would take some getting used to.

"Come on. Let's join the hubbub." Adam led her inside. Judy waited near the entry, but everyone else was already seat in the expansive great room to the left. Floor-to-ceiling windows poured light into the house. Rory wrestled on the floor with Little Alex, while Georgie dangled upside-down off the couch, giggling. He waved when he spotted them. "Hi, Unca Ad."

"Hey, Beast."

Judy reached for Jimmy. "Aw, may I hold him?"

"Fuck, no!" Shannon shrieked, shielding her baby from this stranger. No one and no place was safe from Paul Reagan. Couldn't these people get it?

The room quieted. Ember blinked, and it seemed everyone held their breath.

"Oooo," Georgie whispered in Alex's ear. "She said a naughty word, Unca Awex."

Adam never faltered, just eased Shannon into his side, one palm warm and gentle on her shoulder. "It's okay. It's all good, folks. Jimmy needs a nap. Same room as last time, Judy?"

"You bet." She grasped Shannon's wrist instead of her son. "Let me know if you need anything. We're here for you, honey."

"I'm... I'm sorry," Shannon murmured, ashamed, and her eyes brimmed at her despicable behavior. *God, I'm exactly like my father.* "It's just that I'm—"

"It's just that you need to snuggle that baby of yours for a long, long time. I would if I were you, and it's me who's sorry. I should've known better. Come here, honey." Judy put her arms around Shannon and wrapped her and Jimmy inside one of those all-encompassing, motherly hugs Shannon hadn't realized she needed until then. She squeezed her teary eyes at the raw emotions surging back to life, while the woman she'd just cursed held her tight and patted her back. The real Shannon Reagan was reawakening, and she was a pathetic mess.

"I'm making tacos tonight," Judy whispered, swaying gently from side to side. "You go take a long nap with Jimmy.

I'll send one of the boys up when dinner's ready. Are you going to be okay here?"

Shannon bit her lip. "I don't know," she admitted quietly. "My father's coming. He'll hurt anyone in his way and he'll take Jimmy back."

"I'd like to see him try," Judy growled, and somehow that strong conviction helped.

"I'm sorry I, umm, over-reacted."

"That's what us mothers do, Shannon," Judy murmured confidentially. "We over-react and we're damned mean when we do it. Harley says I turn into the biggest, baddest bitch on the planet when anyone messes with my boys. It's that mother bear instinct in us. It doesn't ask, it just shows up and watch out when it does."

Shannon almost smiled. "But I'm the biggest and baddest bitch," she whispered so the boys couldn't hear her this time.

"Break it up, ladies," Adam cajoled. "You're both certifiable, ahem, mothers of the year." He tugged her out of Judy's embrace and steered her toward the winding stone staircase along the far wall. "We'll be down in a while."

"I wanna go, too," whined Georgie, bucking against Alex to be let loose.

"Not unless you want to take a nap," Alex said.

Shannon didn't hear Georgie's reply as she hurried up the stairs with Jimmy tucked in tight against her. She all but ran over the luxurious Persian rugs on the hardwood floor. Past the rustic wall hangings of hunting dogs and ducks. Everywhere she looked, the Mortimer home imbued calm, but the nagging sensation remained.

He can find me anywhere.

Adam ushered her into a spacious room at the far end of the wide hall. A lovely deck beckoned beyond the patio windows. Dense green trees engulfed the house, providing a cover that no one could see through. No one except—*him.*

"Shut the drapes."

Adam glanced over his shoulder, as calm as she was stressed. "Are you sure? It's a beautiful day out there."

She nodded, her nerves strung so tight that a fiddler could've plucked "The Devil Went Down to Georgia" on them in ten seconds flat.

Adam did as she'd asked. He didn't make eye contact, probably waiting for her to take more than one step inside the room, but she couldn't. Paul Reagan had to be flaming mad.

"Will you look at this?" Adam had wandered to the baby bed tucked in the corner near the expansive, king-sized bed. Both constructed of gleaming logs, only it swung on a cradle. A red-and-black checkered bumper-pad lined the inside. A huge black teddy bear with a red ribbon with white polka dots sat next to it. The crazy bear looked as if it was smiling, its fluffy paws folded over its potbelly. A basket of diapers and other baby supplies stood on the changing table beside the cradle. Everything looked too good to be true. Because it was.

He is coming.

"You'd never know to look at him, but Harley's the biggest sap when it comes to kids. I'll bet he picked out this goofy bear."

"Uh-huh," Shannon replied absentmindedly on purpose, as she eyed the rough-hewn beams overhead. A rustic, antler chandelier graced the cathedral ceiling. It was a nice room, but if she was safe, why was she hyperventilating? Why was this last step so hard to take?

Poor Jimmy squirmed, arching his back. Shannon loosened her grip on him. By the sounds of it, Connor and Izza had arrived. All those tough male voices coming from downstairs should've made her feel protected. Izza's, too. Shannon had plenty of capable covert agents under this roof, but—were there enough?

Adam wandered into the en suite bathroom. Out of sight. She gulped, trying to swallow the terror that separation created. There had to be a way to settle down and relax. She opted for trite conversation to keep Adam talking. His steady and calm baritone was the only thing keeping her from running. "W-why'd you stay here?" She honestly couldn't remember.

"You know. I'd just broken up with my ex." He turned the shower on. "Will you be okay out there while I clean up?"

She wasn't inclined to answer. He'd stepped out of her line of sight, but she heard his boots thump to the floor, followed by the *zip* of his pants. He closed the bathroom door, but left it cracked. "I won't be long. Make yourself at home. There's food and stuff to drink in the kitchenette. Judy stocks a mean fridge."

There's a kitchenette?

Her nose twitched at the fragrance of eucalyptus drifting from the steamy bathroom. Her ears perked up. Adam was just beyond her line of vision, scrubbing himself clean and humming like it was no big deal. One of Judy's little boys squealed downstairs. A dog barked. And Jimmy touched her chin with his fingertips. He smiled up at his real mother through still drowsy eyes, and Shannon's sun came out, bright and warm and glorious.

"Oh, I've missed you, baby of mine," she breathed into his downy hair. The soft sweet baritone of the man in the shower belted out some song about country roads, West Virginia, and Blue Ridge Mountains, and Shannon took that all important first step into her brand new life. Then another. She closed the door behind her, and left Paul Reagan behind.

Motherhood took over. "Let's get you fed," she whispered to her hungry baby.

Judy had thought of everything, including a hickory rocking chair by the deck door. Shannon kicked off her heels and nestled into the rocker. She unbuttoned her business suit and unsnapped the front of her push-up bra. Jimmy was going to nurse from his real mother this time, not from some latex nipple while some baby-stealing woman beamed down on him like he was hers.

Shannon stilled the storm in her heart and summoned what few relaxation techniques she had left. It had been so long. Lifting Jimmy to her breast, she forced herself to breathe deeply, exhale slowly. A nursing mother needed to be calm. Izza had taught her that.

It didn't work. Jimmy nuzzled back and forth, growing frantic. His sweet little face scrunched into worry lines as he searched for what he was used to.

"It's okay," she crooned, despite her growing doubt. What if she'd lost the chance to bond with him? Her heart dropped. What if he wanted—Linda?

He growled a tiny growl of frustration.

"Come on," she urged, panic rising. "You can do it."

Jimmy stiffened, tipped his head back, and let out a squawk. And Shannon remembered that day on the beach. Those sweet lullabies and the man who sang them. She let the words roll off her lips. *"What child is this who laid to rest on Mary's lap is sleeping..."*

The time out worked. Her son latched onto his mama. The wrinkles dissolved from his face, and Squeaks closed his eyes in pure, infantile bliss. By the time the carol to her new life ended, the love of that good man singing in the shower had righted her floundering boat. The storm was past. Burrowing into her cocoon, she gave her son what he needed most.

Herself.

"Shannon?"

She didn't answer.

"Shannon? Are you out there?"

Still no answer.

Adam wrapped the towel around his waist and peeked his head out the bathroom door. He couldn't help the smile that cracked his face. There she was, asleep in the rocking chair, her head bowed to Jimmy's. The poor thing had to be worn out from her daily endurance tests with Paul Reagan. Adam had a cure for that. He turned the flannel comforter back on the bed—the sheet, too. As smoothly as possible, he scooped her into his arms.

"What are you doing?"

"Shh, don't wake Jimmy. I'm putting you kids to bed. That's all."

She didn't protest much more, so he snuggled her into the pillows. Without asking, he eased her out of her skirt, removed her silk stockings, and pulled the blanket up. Two sleepy faces smiled dreamily at him.

"Don't go," she murmured.

"I'm not." To prove it, he eased his slightly damp body, towel and all, alongside hers. "Go to sleep. I'll be here when you wake up."

"Adam?" Her eyes were closed again. This girl was fading fast. "I love you," she muttered. "I really love you."

"I know." He kissed her cheek, fighting the depth of his feelings for her. "Believe me, Shannon baby. I know."

Chapter Thirty-Three

"Want milk, Mama!"

Shannon lay still with her sleeping babe at her side, listening to the sounds of a happy home emanating up from the ground level. Judy's soft response was harder to make out, but the other little boy who lived in the house came in loud and clear. "Me, too. Me, too!"

Adam lay behind her, his chest to her back and a heavy palm on her hip. Slow, steady breaths told her he was sound asleep. She snuggled into the shelter of his strong, hard body. Where had he just been? South America? The man had to be tired, but he was also honorable. A thick bath towel definitely lay between their semi-naked bodies.

Why wasn't he like everyone else, intimidated by her father's wealth and power, and content to back off when she'd screamed at him? Why had he dared to intercept her at the gas station? Of all the unlikely cohorts, her nightmare had ended because of the unexpected charity of a company of snipers. How bizarre was that? Snipers who cared? It seemed an unreal situation, and yet, out of the blue, Adam and his team had ridden in on their white horses and saved her.

She closed her eyes, breathing deeply of the comfort of a brave man. On top of being fearless and to-die-for handsome, Adam smelled good. Really good. She inhaled deeply, detecting some masculine body-wash mixed with the heady scent of his damp hair, minty toothpaste, and deodorant.

Still snoring softly, he dipped his nose into her neck, filling that sensitive hollow with the moist heat of a relaxed male in slumber. Delicious delight sparked deep in her core. She shivered, stretching against him to take in more of the sensation she craved. The brush of his freshly shaved chin against her ticklish neck. The feel of his lips barely brushing her skin. Ah, this handsome, wonderful man was difficult to resist, especially sound asleep and vulnerable like he was. How much better if he were awake?

Her fingers curled, wanting very much to manhandle him. Heat, flamed up the insides of her thighs. Uniquely feminine muscles that hadn't clenched in over three months, to be exact, contracted, relaxed, then tightened again as if they knew precisely what she needed. Did they? Oh, yes. She wanted that handsome body awake and responsive, the sooner the better.

Her bedroom door cracked open, interrupting her deliciously wicked plan. A little boy's face peeked around two grubby hands that gripped the knob. She couldn't tell which twin this was because, well, she hadn't really looked at Harley's boys until now. This little guy looked exactly like his brother except for his unruly, sandy colored hair. He pushed the door open a little wider, curiosity peaking his brows. "Kin I come in?"

"Sure. Do you want to see the baby?" Of course he did. Didn't everyone?

"Uh-huh!" No sooner said than done. But just as the twin scurried to the end of the bed, Adam stiffened and stretched, nudging her backside with his hips. The hand that had been on her hip snaked beneath the covers, then under her blouse to rest on her ribcage, and Harley's little boy had better make this visit sweet and short. *Real short.*

Adam muttered thickly in her ear, those nice warm fingers encouraging her love-starved body as they smoothed upward. "Sleep well?"

"Yes." She arched her neck to look at him. A hitch caught in her throat. They'd been sleeping together. Kind of. For once, she wanted more than just close encounters.

"Let me take care of this nosy little guy first." He kissed her forehead as he disengaged his wandering hand. "Then I'll take care of you."

She focused on breathing. *Yes, please.*

"Hey, Sponge Bob," Adam said quietly. "If you want to see the baby, take your shoes off."

"Which one's Sponge Bob?" she asked.

"Georgie."

Noted. Now if she could just remember.

The twin climbed onboard and plunked down at the end of the bed and proceeded to grunt and groan one of his miniature logger-style boots off. At least, he tried. For all of three seconds. "Unca Ad?" He stuck the boot at Adam. "Kin you help?"

"You bet. Come here, little buddy." Adam leaned onto one elbow.

Sponge Bob wiggled his butt along the comforter, three-legged crab-walking and sticking his foot forward. When he was finally close enough, Adam grabbed his ankle and pulled him up and over Shannon's legs. The little guy squealed, "Again! Do it again!"

"Shhh, Jimmy's still sleeping." Adam whispered as he released the twin, both boots finally off.

"No, he isn't." Shannon eased herself and Jimmy higher on the pillows so Georgie could see the baby.

"Aww, baby's so cute," he whispered. That in itself tugged at Shannon's heart. This little Harley look-alike had finally caught on how to be quiet. Too late maybe, but he seemed to be so earnestly trying, his hands clasped under his chin and his hazel eyes bright.

"Guess where he was born?" Adam asked.

"In the barn?"

"No." Adam chuckled as he reached over Shannon and grabbed the boy. "Jimmy isn't a puppy. He was born on a desert island way out in the middle of the Pacific Ocean."

"Whoa," Sponge Bob breathed in amazement as if he knew where or what the Pacific was. "I got borned in Mama's tummy."

"You did, huh?" Adam ruffled his fingers through the boy's hair. "Now, run along. Tell your mama Jimmy's awake. We'll be down in a bit."

"Okay!" Georgie bounced off the bed and ran for the door. "Bye, bye!"

"Don't forget your boots." Adam tossed one boot off the bed.

"Okay!" Sponge Bob raced back, grabbed his boot, and started for the door again.

"Don't forget your other boot." Adam tossed the other boot.

"Oh. Yeah." Sponge Bob raced back with a big smile, snagged his lost sock, and headed out again.

Shannon giggled when the door finally closed behind him. "He left one of his boots."

Adam sighed. "That kid. I was always finding their stuff in my room, in the bed, in the bathroom. You name it. Tonka trucks, baseballs, shoes, sometimes socks, sometimes other things, too. Found a sippy cup full of potato bugs one time."

She traced a finger along the edge of his jaw. *How on earth did I get so lucky? He's handsome, brave, and strong. He loves kids and dogs—and me.* "You like it here, don't you?" she asked.

Adam snagged her roving finger between his teeth. "Yeah, I do. It's quiet. Away from the world…" he mumbled. "I like the space between neighbors and the fact that there are no streetlights. It gets so dark out here you can see the stars. Even the gravel roads are cool. Guess they remind me of home. But enough about them." He released her finger as his lips caressed hers, brushing fire over them. Tasting. Asking.

Her lungs demanded air, and along with that deep breath came the masculine scent of the aroused male at her side. Her worries melted with that bow to carnal temptation. Unfortunately, Jimmy chose that moment to remind them he was still there.

Adam leaned back, breaking the sizzling arc between their mouths. His gaze dropped from her chin to her exposed chest, her blouse having come open, and the tops of her breasts on display. He clearly coveted her, his eyes hooded, his breathing heavy.

Shannon groaned with the physical needs of her sex-famished body. *Oh, please, not now, baby of mine. Go back to sleep.*

But Jimmy persisted with a high-pitched demand for attention.

Shannon drew in a deep breath and exhaled slowly. Jimmy came first. The tumble under the sheets had to wait. Before she could answer her son's call, Adam snagged him up from the covers and lifted him overhead. The baby blinked big, dark eyes, his heavy head drooping down while he grinned. Shannon had to give Linda that one tiny credit. She had kept Jimmy healthy and happy.

"You, Squeaks, need to be changed," Adam declared, wrinkling his nose. "You stink."

Shannon rolled to her side intending to change Jimmy's diaper. She'd caught the rank odor the moment Adam lifted the blankets. "I'll do that."

"No, I can handle this little guy." Adam pushed off the bed, the towel still wrapped around his waist, and the baby in his hands. "Don't go anywhere. We'll be right back."

Shannon dug her heels into the mattress to push herself up to the headboard. It gave her a bird's eye view of the room, which really was the perfect guest room. But she had better things to look at.

Goose bumps prickled her bare arms and shoulders at the sight of her man with her son. She remembered that scrumptious, all-male physique now. Slabs of muscle called pecs hung below broad, rippling shoulders. Who was the Greek god who had shouldered the world in ancient mythology? Hercules? Shannon couldn't rightly recall, not with her brainpower befuddled and her body, umm, hungry. Only it wasn't her stomach growling. Uh-uh.

Instinctively, she ran one hand beneath the blanket to her breasts, now full and aching for that man's attention. His touch. His mouth. Just the thought of his hand palming her breast and maybe pinching it arched her back, and she, Shannon Reagan, flamed into wanton need. Her most secret places flooded with slick anticipation. It had been a really long time since she'd been romanced, much less felt this needy. How odd that the sight of this man's careful handling of her little boy-child was hands down the most romantic thing she'd ever seen. How strange that it stirred her soul to believe. That it created an overwhelming desire to give him every last piece of herself.

The round scar left from the South Dakota bullet punctuated his left collarbone. Another scar that she didn't yet know the story behind, glanced his left ribs with a small, circular hook. Maybe a knife? Yet there he stood, a half-naked, dangerous man who knew the darker sides of life, taking care of a baby as small and innocent as Jimmy. It warmed every last speck of her heart.

He tugged on what had to be a messy diaper. "What have we got here?" There it was again, that gentle beast side of him, playful and tender.

Shannon wrapped her arms around her knees to control her burgeoning sexual need and settled in to enjoy the view. Adam had shaved. He looked cleaner. Less dangerous. Incredibly hot.

When he lifted Jimmy's skinny legs up, a diaper wipe in the other hand, Adam's nose crinkled all the way up his forehead. He turned his face to the side, one eye open, one closed, and muttered, "On second thought, this one's for you, Mama. Get your butt over here and take care of your son."

"Oh, now he's my son?" The easy banter between them surprised her. Everything seemed familiar and carefree with Adam.

Lifting the flannel comforter, a cool breeze wafted over her bare skin. Except for her blouse, she was mostly undressed. She shrugged both shoulders, teasing back. "Sorry. You'll have to figure it out. I'm naked."

He shot her a crooked smile, wiggling his brows. "Don't give me that line. You'd have to lose all your clothes to be naked. Now move it."

She shivered despite the heat blossoming up her neck and over her face. Watching him try his darnedest to avoid changing a messy diaper was so much the routine a husband and father would employ. Okay, so maybe it wasn't the most romantic sight, but her heart thought it was. It kept doing crazy flip-flops.

"Judy bought the robe at the foot of the bed for you," he tried another ruse. "I'd sure like to see you in it."

"You'd sure like to watch me reach for it, too, huh?" She knew better. This man wanted an eye full, and she didn't know if she was brave enough. "Can you reach it for me?" Dumb question. Of course he couldn't. He had his hands full of baby.

Adam shook his head, the biggest, salacious grin on his face. He intended to look, and when he did, he'd whistle and wink those sexy brows and make certain he saw. Everything.

It wasn't as if he hadn't seen most of her already. Shannon dropped the flannel and headed for the plush. Only when she was once more concealed, did she meet his eyes. He hadn't whistled, but he stood there with the sappiest look on his rugged face.

"What?" she asked, her cheeks flaming and the robe pulled tight.

"You're beautiful," he whispered.

"No, I'm not." She turned aside. It had been a long time since anyone had complimented her. Of course, then he spoiled it. "Now come get this stinky little boy of yours."

Shannon took over the diaper-changing duty while Adam wrapped his arms around her, making it a little difficult to get the job done. "I like this," he muttered into her hair, his hands running up and down her arms, her padded back to his bare-naked chest.

She wiggled against him.

"Be careful, or Jimmy's going to get a lesson in biology," Adam whispered huskily. "Especially after that strip show you just put on."

"It wasn't a strip show. It was a mad dash for cover." Playing and flirting with this man felt good.

"I liked it," he growled as he traced his tongue along the edge of her ear. When tiny nibbles pinched her neck, she tilted her head to the side, craving Adam's touch down to her soul. He'd become not only her savior, but her resurrection, too. She was born again. Tenderness had reawakened, and along with it, came a new awareness. A sensitivity. She couldn't speak. Just feel. Just crave. Each of her five senses were heightened and in bright, sharp focus. She knew precisely what she wanted. And who.

Shannon wrapped the soiled diaper into a tight bundle and tossed it into the covered waste receptacle beside the changing table.

"Is he hungry?" Adam asked hoarsely, his nose in her hair, his hands roaming to the curve of her hips.

"No, but I am," she breathed.

He tilted her face up, and she closed her eyes, her hands still fastening Jimmy securely to the table. Very gently, Adam kissed her. The tip of his tongue slid over the seam of her lips. When she opened for him, he growled into her mouth, "I want you."

Need blazed, a wildfire that instantly consumed every nerve and muscle, arcing over her scalp in a sizzling current that burned all the way to her toes. When she pushed into Adam, he molded his magnificent body around hers, his steel aligned perfectly with the cleft in her backside. His fingers splayed across her stomach, pressing her into him.

But Jimmy…

"I have to put him to bed," she murmured.

"Then do it," Adam growled. He scraped his fingertips over her prickled nipples, playing with fire.

"Baby of mine," she whispered fervently, planting a kiss to the top of Jimmy's head as she lifted his charming self into her arms. "You're going to play in bed for a little while. There's a big teddy bear already in there with your name on it. He'll keep you company."

She laid her smiling son on his back at one end of the baby bed, while Adam nestled the stuffed bear at the other end. "It will give him something to look at," he said, positioning the bear's smiling face toward Jimmy. "How's that, little man? Me and your mama aren't going too far. Holler if you need us, okay?"

Shannon beamed. Adam talked to her son like Jimmy might answer. The normalcy of the moment hit her hard. Not once had her father spent any time with this cute little guy. By the time Adam turned to her, she'd clouded up again. He smiled, his palm to her jaw while he thumbed her tender sentiments away. "What am I going to do with you?"

She couldn't answer. Didn't need to. With one slight bend of his knees, she was on her way back to bed. The comfy bathrobe didn't last long. Neither did his extra-large towel or her underwear. She lay there on the edge of the king-sized mattress, breathless, on her back, and her battered self completely exposed to his pleasure. Adam knelt over her ankles, his eyes black and dangerous as he descended with the sheets billowed over his broad shoulders.

Her breath caught. As often as they'd lain together on the island, he'd never stalked her like he did now. Adam cocooned them in privacy. "You never know..." he said as he leaned into her neck with a heated breath.

No more talking. Shannon reached behind Adam's head and pulled him into her face, sealing his mouth to hers in a desperate need to satisfy. She let her fingers do the talking, pushing one hand between them and down his abdomen to parts below. He groaned deliciously in her ears when her fingers made first contact. This was what she'd wanted on that speck of sand and beach in the Pacific. This man. This velvet shaft of steel. She worked him with long, smooth strokes, relishing every last inch of him.

"I want you," she murmured, sure she had him right where she wanted him—on the edge of that same precipice with her, that place in time where life had stranded them with one disaster after another. She wanted at last to fall, to take that final step into happily-ever-after, and she wanted him to come with her.

"Not this way," he muttered thickly, untangling his legs and other body parts from her reach. He tumbled her up and over as he leaned backward until she straddled him, her knees tucked against his hips and the rest of her right where she wanted to be. He throbbed hot and dangerous beneath her as he rearranged the blankets to shield her from the possibility of her three-month-old son's view.

"I want to look at you while we do this," he murmured, his hands warm and sure on her breasts, fondling and strumming the hard nubs her nipples had blossomed into. Too soon, his palms moved to her hips. Then her butt. With a gentle squeeze of her ass, a quiet grunt and a lift, he impaled her. Painfully. Wonderfully. Slowly.

She dropped her palms to his magnificent chest and let this gentle man fill her. It took a moment, his girth and length more than her body could accommodate. The contradictions of their physical bodies enticed waves of shivers. All of that velvet steel was hers for the taking. For this brief instant, she was anchored to the heart and soul of him. The man who'd breathed life into her premature baby now filled her. Her body expanded to let him in. She arched her back and looked upward, wanting every last centimeter. Giving her all. Taking his all. Needing more.

As the warm blankets slid off her shoulders, rippling fire coursed up the inside of her thighs to clench him. Adam was caught as much as she. Gloriously snared with love.

Shannon lowered her head and opened her eyes. The most glorious male lay beneath her, tucked in tight. Darkest indigo beset with turquoise embers held her fast, while Adam filled her to the hilt in an erotic rhythm of give and take.

Bump and grind. She whimpered. The rippling blaze turned into a firestorm, licking her body with tongues of flames, pushing her into the stars. She hadn't left the bed, but she flew. Higher. Highest. The most pleasant scorching blaze consumed her, pushing her until one whispered shriek escaped her lips, "Adam."

"I'm. Right. Here," he growled and offered one final thrust, then—he flew with her.

Quivering fireworks burst through her as she shattered. Euphoria sluiced down her spine to that intimate joining of their two bodies. And Shannon fell to earth and to Adam, a newborn star finally come home. He was very smart to hold her so tight. She knew the truth now. She was no different than him. She really could fly.

Pressed to his thundering heart, contentment filled her from the crown of her head down to her very happy toes. Relaxation beckoned as the luxury of those big, manly hands smoothed her shoulder blades, warming while they secured her safely to earth. The sensation of this mating was entirely new. Thoroughly delightful. A woman could get used to it. To him.

He kissed the top of her head. "Do you hear that? He's talking to the bear."

Sure enough, Jimmy Malone cooed and giggled softly from his bed.

Shannon crawled carefully up Adam's handsome body to pause at his still wet lips. "Adam?"

"Yes, my love," he said, his hands in her hair and the most reverent light on his face.

"I love you," she told him, as if he couldn't already tell.

She fell again the moment he smiled.

Chapter Thirty-Four

The morning turned to afternoon before Shannon stirred. Adam expected a startle reflex when she woke to find herself in a strange room. Instead, her hand wandered to his stomach and downward.

"You're awake?" Soft blue eyes asked a different question than her lips.

He snagged her hand, lifting her tempting fingers to his mouth. "My hell, are you still hungry?"

"Yes," she answered quickly, and he nearly laughed. Jimmy was quiet, so Adam rolled Shannon onto her back, his elbows at the sides of her head and the happiest glow on her face. Tracing a line that began at the end of her chin and extended up to her soft, sweet lips, he satisfied a fraction of her appetite with a long kiss. Or so he thought.

The fingers roaming up his back and over his shoulder blades turned insistent, and he was a captured warrior with no hope of quarter being granted. Not that he wanted relief from the sinfully wicked charms of this beautiful temptress. Adam succumbed. The sheets stood no chance of keeping them covered while they entwined and played again.

Shannon was very hungry, but so was he. Finally sated once more, he wrapped her up toga-style in the linen sheet, and restored his bath towel to his hips. They stood watching the sleeping baby.

"When should he eat again?"

"I don't know," she admitted, a shadow creasing her brow. "I've never done this before."

"Don't worry. He'll tell you when he's hungry. Join me?" Adam tugged her away from the crib, intent on distracting her from the simple detail every mother should know about her child. Ushering Shannon into the bathroom, he closed the door. "Let's shower."

She demurred, her reticence reminding him how foreign romance and honest male attention must seem to her. He turned the shower spray on and unwrapped his fair lady. The angel of his dreams stepped out of the sheet and into his arms. It would've been perfect if she hadn't caught a glimpse of herself in the full-length mirror.

"Fuck! Look at me. I *do* look like Alice Cooper!" She leaned over the vanity, total disgust on her face as she scrubbed at her eyes.

Truth was, he couldn't stop looking at her. He saw no flaws, just the other half to his soul and all of his heart. But that ugly word caught him short. It just wasn't her. Okay, so her black eyeliner was a little smudged. She did have extra gray tearstains all the way to her jaw. Now that he looked at her, that short hair-do was standing on end, too. Still, she was beautiful to him.

"No wonder Judy looked at me like I was crazy. Fuck, you should've told me," she demanded. "How could you let me look like this?"

He called the game. "Shannon. Stop with the language. You're better than that, and honestly, that little boy out there doesn't need to hear his mama swearing like a sailor. Stop berating yourself, too."

The minute she turned on him, he took hold of her wrists and pulled her gorgeous naked body into his, his heart beating loud and furious. *How could he let her look like that?* Apparently, he didn't see the same thing she did. All he saw was perfection. He wouldn't change a thing.

"I'm sorry. I used to be nice, but I look like—"

Enough!

He covered her still flapping lips with his and crushed the temper right out of her, claiming that tender, swollen mouth until she breathed all that angry fire into him. Never separating, he lifted her into the shower stall with him and let the warm water cascade over her angry, bewildered face.

Hunger roared out of her. Shannon all but climbed up his body again, anchoring her slender arms around his neck while she wrapped her legs at his waist. The angle provided a waterfall over them both and the perfect position for deeper access to her.

He pushed himself into her tender folds, acutely aware that she needed this physical connection desperately. The tongue that had only seconds before been angry and mean, now lapped circles around his mouth. Over his lips. Down his chin to his neck. The sweetest heat filled his senses.

The marble tiles were cold when he pressed her back to them, but the intensity of her hunger vanquished the chill. That same feral creature that had assaulted him on the Crystal City highway, returned with fingernails that scratched and teeth that bit. She drew no blood, just seemed to need to force her love onto him. To afflict him with it. He let her play. Let her win. Let her take all she needed, for as long as she needed, while the room filled with steam and sex.

He had all the time in the world for her. Shannon was his one and only, and he meant her to know it. At last she ceased grinding her core against him, still impaled but breathing hard, her race won. He fastened her to the wall and set an easy rhythm without the angst. Only love.

All he needed in life, he now held at his fingertips. Adam took less than a heartbeat before his heavy breathing joined hers. He cradled her tender, quaking body against his while aftershocks clenched through her. Good hell, this woman was strong. And demanding. He liked that she'd taken control.

With their heads bowed together, Shannon lowered her feet to the shower floor, but then she turned away from him, her hands flat to the wall. Taking her silence for a momentary pause in the action, he grabbed the shower gel and slathered it over her shoulders and down her back to the delightful pink cheeks of her butt. The individual vertebrae along her backbone stuck out rigid against his palm, the same as her shoulder blades. "You need to eat," he murmured, slanting the shower spray to rinse.

"I don't know why I did that," she said quietly.

"Did what?" He feigned innocence, pulling her back to his chest as he cupped those soft, plump breasts. Of her entire scrawny body, only her breasts had maintained the fullness he remembered, most likely because of that breast pump thing. He wondered if it hurt when she'd used it.

She sighed, her right hand hooked around his neck while he let his thumbs strum a silent melody of love over the tips of her nipples. They pebbled instantly as he watched the reaction over her shoulder. His body sprang to attention, ready to dance again.

Shannon turned to face him, cupping his jaw. "Did I hurt you?"

There she was, a little woman of maybe five-five asking a big, tough guy like him if she'd hurt him with a little rough sex? Hell, they hadn't even broken anything.

He grinned. "If I said no, would you do it again?"

Adam should've known better. She leaned into his lips, and then he could tell she was crying. He let the shower gel slip to the floor and gathered her up like the lost soul she was. "The only way you could hurt me is the day you leave. You're not telling me goodbye, are you?"

She shook her head vigorously, and that cinched it. He dropped to one knee, bare-ass naked with his heart in his throat, right there in the Mortimer's guest-room shower. Adam clamped onto her hand. "Shannon. You and Squeaks. Stay with me forever. Marry me."

She blinked, her lovely lashes glistening with droplets of water and tears. Damn it, he'd made a fool of himself. He should've waited. He should've known better. At least he should've dressed for the occasion. Women liked flowers and romance. Diamonds. All she was getting was some crazy, naked guy who—

"Yes," she hiccupped.

He could barely hear her answer over the shower and the pounding in his heart. "Did you say—?"

"Yes. I said yes, Adam. I would love to marry you." The most gorgeous smile filled up her very pretty face, big black raccoon eyes and all.

Judy's taco dinner turned into her usual lavish affair with bowls of homemade salsa, mounds of grated cheddar cheese, and a tray filled to overflowing with sliced melon, wedges of pineapple, and fresh pears. Izza supplied a piping hot platter of homemade tortillas while Ember and Rory teamed up to fry enough sopapillas to feed an army. Connor missed dinner. He'd driven to Adam's apartment to rescue Seamus from his crate. But the best happened when Shannon lingered in the kitchen with the ladies after dinner.

Adam would've stayed with her, but soon as the women started discussing childbirth, he learned more about breast pumps than any guy needed to know. He quickly excused himself and joined the manly conversations out on the Mortimer front porch, where Alex and the guys had congregated.

A friendly face beamed up from the steps beside Alex. Adam reached for Mr. Moore's hand. "Terrence. You made it. How's the head?"

"Ah, that tweren't nothing." Terrence waved it off. "But if I ever catch the guy who did it, he'll be wishing he was fishing."

"Do you remember what happened yet?"

"Nope. One minute I'm filling my coffee maker with water. The next, I'm seeing stars."

"Whoever it was took something though," Harley added. "Tell them."

One of Terrence's eyes squinted nearly shut, his brow arched over the other. "That joker stole my Reagan Industries I.D. right out of my wallet. When I got to the gate this morning, the guards wouldn't let me in."

Adam frowned. That set the plan back. Now what?

"Don't worry none. I've got old age and treachery on my side, son." Terrence held up another I.D. card with a sly smile. "Knew I'd need this rascal one of these days."

"So you were able to check the serial numbers? Was I right? Do they match the ones from the island?"

"Not only were you right, but I found all five drones. Not four."

"Five?" Adam hadn't seen that one coming.

Terrence nodded. "Yessirree, Bob. All five prototypes are sitting in their cradles in the lab. They're scheduled for destruction first thing tomorrow."

"He's working with the Koreans," Adam hissed. "He's been behind this whole thing from the start."

"The bastard called while you were asleep," Alex added grimly.

That raised Adam's brows. Alex hadn't let on during dinner that he'd heard from Reagan. "What's he want?"

"To talk to his daughter, like I believe a damned thing that comes out of his mouth."

"No," Adam snapped. "He had his chance. All he did was hurt her. No more."

"He said he was sorry." Alex dropped another piece-of-shit Reagan lie before he climbed down the steps and faced the parking lot that had once been the Mortimer lawn. Now it looked like a parking lot for trucks, Jeeps, and Izza's Hummer.

Adam joined him. "You're not seriously thinking of talking to Reagan, are you?"

Alex shrugged. "It won't hurt to listen."

"When? Where?"

"Tonight. His place."

"Reagan Manor?" Adam rubbed the creepy shiver off the back of his neck at the mention of that hellhole. He'd only been inside the one time, but the memory lingered, and none of it was good. Even before he'd seen Shannon that morning, he'd felt the darkness hovering over the place.

"I've already notified the CIA, but Atchison needs evidence. We'll wear wires."

"So now he wants our help?" Adam let out a deep breath of who gives a shit. Atchison could go to hell for what he'd said about Shannon.

Alex twisted his neck from side to side with an audible pop. "He's a fed. What do you think?"

"The answer is no. Shannon isn't going anywhere near her father."

"He won't let us in without her. Don't you think you and I can keep her safe?"

Adam raked a hand over his head. "It's not that. It's him. I don't trust the son-of-a-bitch, and neither do you. He's up to something."

"And so are we," Alex replied evenly. "Listen. We can let the CIA run with it, and you can bet your ass they'll screw the pooch on putting this bastard in prison, or we can go in prepared and nail him to the wall. Reagan's no dummy. He stole those UAVs back from the Navy for a good reason, and we need to know what that reason is. Tonight. Shit, Adam, maybe the Korean's weren't the only ones involved, did you ever think of that? What if ISIS in on board with Reagan's treason? Or China? What if he sold the damned things to two different buyers?"

"No," Adam said firmly, his mind made up. "Find another way. Shannon isn't going. Don't even ask her."

"Don't ask me what?"

Adam pivoted smartly, and damn it. There she was, at the top of the porch stairs. He swallowed hard at the determination in her eye, not sure how much she'd heard. "Where's Squeaks?" he asked, stalling for a way out. "How's he doing tonight?"

"He's fine. Judy's playing with him. What's going on, Adam? What don't you want me to do?"

Alex picked a good time to keep his big mouth zipped, damn him. Still Adam stalled. Shannon was nearly herself again, her eyes bright with her old zest for life. She'd relaxed to the point of sharing Jimmy with people she trusted, because she could, damn it. How could he risk all of that again?

"Your father wants to see you," he admitted honestly, "but you don't owe him or anyone else a damned thing, Shannon. Go back in the house and stay there."

A small but genuine smile fluttered over her face. One brow lifted. "Did you just tell me what to do?" she asked almost coyly.

He blew out a long-suffering sigh at that loaded question. He hadn't meant to boss her, but then again, maybe he did. She was his bride-to-be, his woman, but mostly, he couldn't risk losing her the same day he'd finally got her back. He'd never survive. "I just don't want you anywhere near your old man. Let the CIA take him down. He's their problem now."

"But you need my help to do that?" she asked Alex pointedly.

"Yes," Alex answered in that brusque, no nonsense way of his that was really pissing Adam off. "But Adam's right. You've been through enough. We'll find another way."

She rubbed her palms up her arms. "No, Mr. Stewart. I'll go, but only because I want to tell him to his face to go to hell."

Adam bowed his head, his body once more clenched for war with that rat bastard Paul Reagan, only this time Shannon was square in the middle of the firefight. Worse, she'd had time to think. She wanted to be there. She wanted that one last word with the man who'd nearly destroyed her, and damn it to hell. Reagan had it coming, but nothing about him was as it seemed. The man was a slick, snake-oil salesman, his promises full of poison. A liar through and through.

Connor chose that moment to pull up in the driveway, and in seconds, a flurry of red hair and long legs bounded out of his SUV. Seamus was officially in the house, or at least on the porch and mugging everyone in sight. Ordinarily, that would've made Adam smile. Not tonight.

"Is dinner ready?" Connor asked innocently.

Adam growled, pissed at the world all over again. "Not yet. Get your gear. You're coming with me"

Shannon cringed, and every time she did, her shoulder and neck muscles tightened up. Her heart pounded too hard, but she had to do this. She had to face her father one last time.

They were in Connor's SUV and headed back to Reagan Manor. Alex rode shotgun. She and Adam sat in the rear, while Rory and Harley followed in another TEAM vehicle. The only good part of this hazardous road trip was that Jimmy was safe with Judy. It didn't hurt that Harley had loosed every last one of his adult dogs to roam the Mortimer premises before The TEAM hit the road.

When Alex mustered his troops, he'd called a veritable army. Not only did Sasha show up within seconds of his call to arms, so did Mark Houston and David Tao, as well as a few other TEAM hunks she hadn't met before. Better yet, they'd arrived in tactical gear, only to be attacked by two little boys who called them all 'Unca!' at the top of their lungs. There was Unca Gabe and Unca Maverick, not to mention Unca Taylor, Unca Zack, and Unca Lee, plus a few other *uncles* whose names she hadn't caught.

The Mortimers' great room had quickly transformed into *GI Joe* Central. She'd never seen so many well-built, massive men in one place. Despite their rugged physiques and obvious alert statures, Zack snagged Jimmy and settled into the nearest rocking chair, while Maverick and Gabe dropped to their hands and knees on the floor to play with Georgie and Little Alex. Mark came in from the front porch talking football with a couple more guys.

"Are all these guys coming with us?"

"Hell, no. They're staying here. Judy made tacos." Adam was angry with her, but he'd still made her laugh.

"You're kidding. They came for dinner? Dressed like that?"

"Sure. They're men. What'd you expect?" He'd pulled her into his arms and buried his face in her hair. "Only you, me, and Alex will meet with your father. Connor, Rory, and Harley will stick close for backup, but these guys will make damned sure nothing happens while we're gone."

"I have to do this," she'd said quietly, her back to Adam's front and his arms around her. "He has to know."

"Yeah. I get it. I know." Adam wasn't happy. He wanted her safe, and honestly, Shannon understood, but if she didn't face her father tonight, he'd think he'd won. After what he'd put her through these past months, that galled her the most. Paul Reagan had to understand he could never use Jimmy against her again. That she'd had enough.

But she also wanted to know why he'd badgered her to take over the company to the point of extortion in the first place. Why he seemed intent on grinding her into the ground at all cost. What was so important that he felt the need to treat his only daughter so shabbily? Was it because he sensed he didn't have much time left to live, that he was dying? For that matter, was he? She didn't know if she cared.

Adam and Alex were accompanying her as bodyguards. Adam had fixed her up with a wire to relay all conversation with her father back to Connor, Rory, and Harley who would be standing by on the premises. CIA Agent Atchison had secured court-ordered authority for the wiretap. If things turned hostile, Adam's guys could be inside Reagan Manor as quickly as CIA backup. It sounded scary, but foolproof, and

Shannon felt good for a change. This was one confrontation with Paul Reagan she intended to win.

Because of Adam's faith in her, she'd turned a corner. Her life was back on track. She could breathe full, deep breaths without hyperventilating, and she wasn't afraid. Her father was nothing more than a bump in the glorious road to her future, because she, Shannon Reagan, was on her way to the altar with the real love of her life.

Adam's warm hand slid over her kneecap, squeezing firmly. "I can still call this off," he offered quietly.

Shannon jerked out of her reverie to face him. Smiling, she covered his hand with hers, interlocking their fingers. Adam's grip tightened, curling her fingers into his. He lifted her knuckles to his mouth, his gaze soft and heated. "Just say the word."

"We're here," Connor advised, and the chance to turn tail was gone.

"I can do this," Shannon said calmly.

Adam's lips thinned, but he nodded. "Just don't say a word about the drones. Let Alex bring them up once you've had your say. If their whereabouts comes out while you're resigning, fine. If not, let it go. I know you're angry, and you have a right to be, but don't egg him on too much. You really don't know what he's capable of."

"Do you?" She had to ask. A shadow had darkened Adam's brave features. "What aren't you telling me?"

He placed a kiss to her first knuckle. "Do you know how your mother died, Shannon? Do you know anything about her death at all?"

Shannon released her seat belt and moved into Adam's side. "I know that she drowned in the bathtub. She'd been depressed and she slipped on the tile and hit her head. My father said she didn't suffer. She just slipped away. Why are you asking me this now? Did he…?" Her mouth went dry. *God, no.* "Did he kill my mother?"

Adam shook his head slowly. "I honestly don't know, but be damned careful in there. Don't let him talk you into staying. Don't get too close." His lips skimmed another knuckle, the moist heat of his mouth lifting goosebumps up from her skin. "Come back to me, Shannon."

She lunged at him, her arms around his head and that handsome face to her breasts. "I can't come back, because I haven't left you, and I never will."

"Gear up," Alex said quietly from the front seat. "Stay sharp."

Ducking into Adam's face, she planted a quick, wet kiss on his mouth. "I'll be careful, I promise. Trust me."

The deep breath of a worried male warmed her heart. "It's not you I'm worried about."

Shannon climbed out of the safety of Connor's SUV and into the night. Adam came quickly around the vehicle to her side. Ambient lighting illuminated the way forward. How long Connor would stay there or if the other guys would join him, she didn't know. She hadn't been part of that short but terse conversation between Adam and his guys before they'd rolled out.

The manor's high-tech security cameras swiveled as she approached with her vanguard, Adam at her right, Alex at her left. She drew in a deep breath and rolled the tension off her shoulders. In an hour, maybe less, Paul Reagan would be history.

But when she reached for the doorknob, the entry swung open. Hubbard blocked her way, stiff, formal, and as condescending as ever. "Is Mr. Reagan expecting you?" he asked haughtily. How he could look down at her and still keep that snooty nose in the air used to amaze her. Not tonight.

The nastiness she'd washed down the shower drain bubbled to the surface with a vengeance. Like it or not, she was Paul Reagan's only living heir, and unless he'd changed his will in the last few hours, she was a force to be reckoned with. She honestly didn't mind if he had changed his will. The Reagan inheritance came with too many chains and strings. Who needed an anchor?

"You're still here after you let Jimmy get kidnapped?" she asked, infusing her tone with as much bitchiness as she could. "My father wants to see me, so move out of the way, Hubbard. I can still fire your ass." Pushing past him, Shannon glanced over her shoulder at Adam. "He's usually in his study. This way."

"Miss Reagan, stop!" Hubbard scurried to head her off. "He's not to be disturbed. He's in a meeting."

"When isn't he?" Shannon kept on going. "He's always in a meeting. Who with this time, his lawyer? Is he already changing the will? Good."

"Take it easy," Adam muttered.

Defiantly, Shannon marched to the solid oak study door, her steps fast and sure.

Hubbard grasped the sleeve to her flannel shirt; the one she'd borrowed from Judy because she hadn't packed anything casual for her business trip to Texas. "Miss Reagan. Please! I must insist—"

She turned on him, ready to bite his head off if he said another word, her hand already turning the knob that secreted her father's deceit from the world. "Get out of my way. This is my house. Not yours."

She caught Adam's amused smirk. Hubbard stood shoulder to shoulder with him in the hall, but was obviously having a hard time maintaining his normal imperious stance. Adam kept edging over, taking more and more of his personal space. Every fraction Hubbard relinquished, Adam took. And more. He winked, and her confidence soared.

She pushed the door open. This might be fun after all.

"Shannon!" Paul Reagan looked up from his desk and smiled that sickly smile that twisted his mouth. *God, it had to hurt.* "How nice to see you. And you brought the men I wanted to talk with. My, my, and just in time, too. It's okay, Hubbard. I'll see her now. Carry on with what we discussed earlier."

This man would lie when the truth sounded better. He wasn't happy to see her, not the way his eyes shifted from her to his butler and back to her again.

"Father, she said curtly. "I'd say it was good to see you, but it isn't, is it?"

Shannon strode in with her back straight and her mind made up. This was the end.

He offered his gnarled hand like she was a stranger instead of family. He coughed and covered his nose and mouth with the handkerchief in his other hand. She took hold of his hand and found it cold and clammy. Was he really that sick? Gray snake eyes slithered over her face, giving her the urge to wipe the slimy feeling of his touch away.

Only when she released that treacherous hand did she spy the guy in the corner behind her. The guy hiding in the shadows of the leather wingback chair. The bastard covering his nose and mouth with a cloth just like Paul Reagan was doing. His lying eyes gave him away.

She had to look twice. "Brit? What are you…?"

The room tilted. Her vision blurred. The walls wavered beyond the wingback, then melted into pastel watercolors. She reached for the edge of her father's massive desk, but missed. Two loud thumps sounded somewhere behind her.

"I'm… falling," her mouth said while the floor pulled her down. Down. Down…

Chapter Thirty-Five

Drip. Drip. Drip.

"We're in a damned basement," Adam growled as the fog in his head lifted. "Where the hell is Shannon?"

Whatever gas clever Hubbard had sprayed into his face stung like a hive of angry hornets. Adam blinked, unable to wipe the crap out of his eyes with his hands tied behind his back. No wonder old man Reagan had his nose covered. He wasn't sick, just a sneaky bastard.

"Who was that with Reagan?" Alex asked hoarsely from nearby.

"Looked like Brit Paxton, her ex, but it can't be. I shot that son-of-a-bitch back on the island. I know damned well I did." His mouth was on overload, and he was mad as hell. Being tied to a heavy wooden chair in a cold, dank basement with a dripping faucet nearby didn't help. "He's got Shannon, damn him! He'll kill her just like he did her mother!"

"You think we're still at the manor?" Alex sounded eerily calm. Had to be the effects of the knockout gas or whatever Hubbard had doused them with.

"Hell, we could be in Paris for all I know, Boss." All Adam wanted was that hoity-toity butler's neck in his hands so he could hear the bastard's bones crunch when he choked the shit out of him. There was no stretch to these restraints.

Leaning hard from right to left, he meant to rock the chair until it broke or tipped over. No go. The heavy thing wouldn't budge. Not an inch. It had to be bolted to the floor. Rage rankled all the way to his gut. He wanted out. He had to get to Shannon. Now!

"Do you think they'll eat all the tacos before we get back?"

Adam stopped moving not sure he'd heard right. Tacos? Really? Alex was hungry at a time like this? For a smart man, he'd suddenly gotten dumber than shit. "You know what, Boss, stop talking." *You're pissing the hell out of me.*

"Just asking."

Adam jumped, startled when fingers brushed over his knee down to his ankles. "Damn. Is that you?"

It had to be Alex, but why hadn't he answered? Two snaps and Adam's feet were freed. Someone patted his shoulder before he freed Adam's wrists. "Why aren't you talking?"

"You told me to keep quiet," Alex answered, as calm as could be, the smart ass. "Didn't want to rock the boat."

Adam rubbed his sore wrists. "What do you have, a pocket knife?"

"Never leave home without one. Now let's get the hell out of here."

Adam stood and flexed, thankful to be free. He'd have been a lot more thankful if his boots didn't land in a puddle of water. "Son-of-a-bitch. Where'd that come from?" He noticed something else. The temperature in the pitch-black room had changed. The dripping sound turned to a trickle. Then a roar.

A deluge hit him in the face.

"Wake her up. I want her to see this," a man muttered from out of the murky fog.

Shannon could barely lift her head. She breathed heavily. One moment she was awake, the next groggy. Dopey. Drugged.

"Snap out of it," another person ordered, just before he stuck his thumb in her eye socket and peeled one eyelid open. The walls spun as the light poured in. She seemed to be stuck on an evil merry-go-round. At least she wouldn't fall off of this wild ride. The rope biting at her arms made sure of that.

Some guy stuck his face into hers, but too close. His nose looked bigger than his eyes. He looked familiar in a nauseous way. *Looks like Brit, but he's dead. Isn't he?*

Words about drones and Koreans and an offshore account filled her ears, buzzing like little bees that didn't make sense. Dillon's smiling face flashed into her head. Why not? Everything else had. Connor's surfer-blue eyes. Harley kept falling out of the sky. A big red dog swirled around with her in the cyclone of powder-blue baby pelicans she was caught up in. Nothing. Made. Sense.

"We don't have all night. Wake her up."

That voice she knew. Definitely dear old Dad. A hand appeared out of nowhere. The darn thing slapped her face to the left. *Ouch!* Then to the right. "Stop hitting me!"

"Then wake up, my stupid little ex-wife."

It was—Brit?

"What… what are you doing here?" she asked, still trying really hard to figure things out. "You're dead. Adam shot you. I saw him do it. You're brains were everywhere."

"Well, thanks for being so blunt. Now I know how my brother died."

Paul Reagan sat beside her in a wheelchair. His unknown condition must've deteriorated since he'd lost control of his precious legacy. At her other side? Yes. Brit Paxton. Her undead ex-husband. His perfectly tweezed eyebrows lifted. "You never saw the big picture, did you?"

She grimaced as two of him multiplied into four, then became just one again. "The what?"

"The big picture, Shannon. Come on. Wake your dumbass up." Brit leaned in, his face too close and his head cocked, like he was trying to unravel a riddle. He pushed the heel of his hand against her forehead. For an instant, he morphed into her father, the same I-can't-figure-you-out disgust in his eyes. "That guy on the island killed Bart, you simpleton. Bart. My twin brother. Not me."

Brit. Bart. Bart. Brit. The drug whirled the names around her pounding head like an olive at the bottom of an endless and very dirty martini. *Shit. Shart. Brit. Bart. All the same to me...*

He slapped her again. "Will you wake the hell up?"

"I'm awake!" she mumbled as loudly as she could. Damn his ass. He kept hurting her! A second of clarity burst through the dizziness, though. She just needed a few more seconds to be back to normal, and she could figure this puzzle out. Twins? Really? The fog lifted a little more. Oh, yeah. This guy had facial hair, a goatee like the guy Adam killed. Brit didn't. *But doesn't that make this guy—Bart?*

"It's running, Mr. Reagan. The chamber will be filled to capacity in six minutes."

Oh, great. Hubbard is here, too. Figures. Wait. What chamber? What's running?

"Are the new guards standing by for transport?"

She nearly chuckled, but only because she knew what happened to the old guards. Alex scared them off, and he'd scare these off just as fast. *Ha.*

"Yes, Mr. Reagan. They've been informed to go as far out to sea as possible. Just like last time."

"Then let's get this over with."

"Wait." Shannon stiffened in her chair, arching away from Brit or Bart or whoever he was, and fighting to come to her senses. A soft rope bound her hands, but her feet and legs weren't restrained. She planted both feet and pushed up straighter in the chair. "What's going on?"

"Put her over here," her father ordered. "Damn it. I don't have all night."

"Who are you?" she asked as someone shoved her chair to a big-screen television. Too close. The programming had more snow and fuzz than the inside of her doped-up head. Her bleary eyes could barely make out the dark waterfall on the screen. It could've been sewer pipes. Looked like it. Maybe an irrigation ditch? *Who cared?* Not her. She let her heavy head drop to her shoulder for a few more ZZZs.

"Who am I?" The Brit look alike jerked her head up. "Why, I'm the man who's been taking care of your sorry rich ass, and how do you repay me? You become a writer. A publisher. A nothing. Bart and I should've dispensed with you years ago."

Anger dispatched what was left of her confusion. She eyed this imposter through hooded brows. "You're Bart?"

"No. I'm Brit. Get it straight. Your boyfriend killed Bart. He was the one on the island with that cheap little Korean trick, Tia Mia, remember her? You can't have forgotten how she seduced who you thought was your husband. You're not that dumb, are you?"

I might be. Brit never had facial hair, but you do. Doesn't that make you—Bart? Why do you keep telling me you're Brit? He's dead.

He crouched directly in front of her chair and thumped her forehead with the heel of his hand again. "Look at me. I'll explain it one more time."

She squinted, not sure why facial hair made a difference. Any guy could grow a goatee as flimsy as the peach fuzz on his chin.

"Shit, it's not rocket science. Bart and I were identical twins, look-alikes, right down to our johnsons."

"Why?" She had to know. "What could you possibly get out of lying to me? By pretending you loved me? By marrying me?"

"Closer to your old man, for one thing. Closer to your inheritance for another." He peered into her face. "For a gal with your education, you've always been dumb as hell."

Shannon blinked. He was definitely Brit. He'd told her how dumb she was enough during their short marriage. "But my father never liked you."

"Not true. Your father never liked Bart, at least not until the whole drone fiasco. Then he came in rather handy, didn't he, Paul?"

"That's true, he finally served a higher purpose," her father muttered.

"Drone fiasco?" Shannon asked, still not getting the connection.

Brit nodded. "Haven't you figured that out, either? They don't work. The photovoltaic cells in the solar panels can't hold the charge we anticipated they'd be capable of. We oversold them. By the time Paul and I figured that out, Uncle Sam had us on the hook for a couple thousand. What the hell were we supposed to do? Go public with this kind of a miscalculation? I don't think so. We, shall we say, *encouraged* Bart to hook up with that Korean operative. He never knew he'd been set up, the dumb bastard. He was as trusting as you. He really thought he was some kind of a super spy."

"But I thought you worked at the DOJ?" she said weakly. This betrayal went so deep. All those years wasted.

Brit snickered. "Let me spell it out. Bart worked for the Department of Justice. Of the two of us, he was the dumb twin. I was the smart one. I worked on the drone project before I met you. I was the head electrical engineer. Anyway, one day your father called me to his office. Said he had a proposition. Said things weren't working out, that he needed a competent heir to leave his business to. Said there was one catch. That poor bastard would have to marry you."

Her father chuckled, if that phlegm-filled sound in his throat could have been mistaken for mirth. "I recognized a man after my own heart. You did good marrying him, *little girl.*"

"You…" Shannon took a deep breath to clear her head. "You knew Brit before he asked me to marry him?"

Paul Reagan coughed, his hand to his mouth. "I knew he'd make a better son than you ever would."

"So what'd you do? Flip coins to sleep with me?" she asked Brit.

"Only after Tia came into the picture. We both had our flings, but Bart got too serious with that chick. He wanted out. We fought. I lost, and baby…" he patted both hands to his chest, "you got me."

"That night. It was you…" Tears welled up as the humiliation of her night of spousal rape came back on her. He made it sound so cavalier, the jerk.

Brit shrugged. "Don't take it so hard. I'll take good care of Jimmy once you're gone. After Paul gets him out of that farmhouse you've got him stashed in, we'll bring him up to be a helluva lot smarter than you. He'll go places. Too bad you won't be around to watch."

That stung, but Shannon pushed her humiliation down as the mother bear inside of her lifted its deadly head. They could do what they wanted to her, but not Jimmy. "You used me," she bit out at her despicable father. "You set this whole thing up. You meant for that jet to crash on that specific island, too. You meant to kill me."

He scowled and shook his head, but it was Brit who filled in the rest of the details. "Oh no. That one's on you. You volunteered to accompany Stewart's TEAM. After all of these years living with your father, you should've known. Nice guys always finish last."

"Did you ever care about me?" she asked, not ready to accept that she'd been so thoroughly deceived.

Brit sniffed through that arrogant nose of his. "Not really. Look at it this way. In the end, you served a higher purpose, just like Bart did." His gaze skimmed down to her cleavage. "Man, you could use a good boob job. Too bad you never listened. I could've made you, well, more noticeable at least."

He might as well have slapped her in the face again. There was a day she'd very nearly succumbed to his nagging and done just that to make him happy. Him, the man who'd never loved her.

His words from her dream of months earlier revisited her. *We have to take a shower. We have better things to do than waste time on you!* Now it all made sense. Her brain had been trying to tell her something all along, that's why the dreams.

"Grandpa Denver," she blurted out, not knowing what she'd intended to ask.

"Oh, so you figured that one out, but not that you were getting screwed by two different men?" He shook his head, gave her knee a hard slap, and got to his feet. "Shannon, Shannon, Shannon. You're the dumbest bitch in the world."

"You killed him." Shannon shook the last of the drug out of her head. "Your mother's father. Why? How could you do that?"

Murdering someone kind enough to reach out to her in a dream seemed infinitely more diabolical than deceiving her through a traitorous marriage. Both were evil, but killing the man who'd raised you?

"Why not? We needed the old fart out of the way before you came into the picture. Didn't want him to catch onto what we were doing." Brit pantomimed being hung by a noose. "It was your old man's idea. Kill the old geezer. Sucker you into marrying me."

The idea galled her to her core, but it explained things, too. Like why Brit seemed cold one moment, warm the next; like how he seemed capable of working all the time. It made sense now. He never had boundless energy. He was just—two men. It also explained why her father liked him when she'd introduced them. Paul Reagan already knew Brit Paxton. Their plan was already in motion.

"But why, father? What did I ever do to—?"

"Because you're no better than your cheating mother," he hissed. "I needed a real heir. A *chosen* heir. Someone I could trust with my company, not some worthless bastard."

"What?" Again she had no idea what he was talking about.

Paul pulled the wheels of his wheelchair close enough that he grabbed the collar of her flannel shirt and jerked her into his face. "Didn't you know? Your slut of a mother cheated on me with every man she ever met. I only kept you because I hoped you'd turn out different once she was out of the picture. My mistake. I never chose you. You're a bastard."

"I'm... I'm not your daughter?" His words cut her down as much as they lifted her up. Not being of Paul Reagan's flesh and bone actually brought a surge of hope. "You did kill her, didn't you?"

Brit grunted. "Yeah, definitely not genius material, Paul. Damn, you sure know how to pick 'em. It's a good thing you came up with plan B."

"Why not just sell your business to Brit? Wouldn't that have been easier?"

Paul coughed up a wad of something into the tissue in his hand. "And what? Tell the world that my marriage was a failure? Admit that my wife cheated on me. Me! The richest, smartest man in the world? Let her sniveling bastard traipse the world for everyone to fawn over? How would that make me look?"

"So you killed all those people because you didn't want to look bad?" Shannon rolled her eyes in disgust. This time Paul Reagan's hand snaked out and slapped her face. She turned from him and stopped asking questions. Maybe she was the dumbest bitch in the world. Paul Reagan wasn't just sick. He and Brit were—psychotic.

The picture on the screen diverted her attention from the bizarre kangaroo court taking place in the Reagan study. Something moved within all that murky, splashing water. She could see it now. Something big with—arms? Hands? Boots?

Oh, my God. Faces. Adam! Alex!

"You're killing them! Stop it!"

Brit scrubbed his hand over her head, mussing her hair. "She's got it now."

Paul turned to watch the screen with her, the skin at his neck crepe-like as he stretched his chin forward. "Trust me, it won't take long. The three of you needed to disappear. After tonight, I'll wait a day or two until the authorities—"

"You can't do this," she screamed at his calm prattle. "Let me go. Stop it!"

Brit grasped her head and forced her to watch as the water filled the small room in the basement, that windowless room that had always creeped her out. The one with the open-ended pipes in the wall, filled with spider webs and funny whispers. A dim yellow light flickered on revealing Adam's and Alex's final moment, their faces tilted upward to the last pocket of air. She watched in horror as that air bubble shrank then disappeared. Bowing her face to her knees, she pleaded, "Please! Stop this! I'll do anything you want. Anything!"

Paul leaned in confidentially, his elbow on the arm of her chair. "It's too late, *little girl*. All you need to do tonight is die just like them. Just like your mother."

"Don't you want to watch?" Brit changed the subject, his face alongside her cheek, his mouth nearly on hers as the screen displayed nothing but shadows and bubbling, swirling water. The cold barrel of a gun slid along the hollow of her throat. "Or would you rather go first? It'll be easier than watching these suckers drown."

Shannon tilted away from him. There had to be a way to save Adam and Alex. And Jimmy! She couldn't just sit here and watch. She wouldn't! Something snapped deep inside. The feral darkness Paul Reagan had fostered leapt forth, tearing its way out of her with claws, teeth, and—the cunning wisdom of a desperate mother's rage.

"You can't do this," she whimpered, like the weakling they thought she was—just before Brit leaned in close with another line of bullshit. Just before she bashed her forehead into the long, straight, elegant nose.

Crack!

"Shit! You bitch!" He dropped his pistol and jumped to his feet, his hand to his face. Blood spurted from his nostrils. Bright red rivulets of red ran through his fingers and over his perfect white teeth and that stupid goatee.

Jerking sideways, she lifted both feet and punched them into the middle of Paul's chest. He was an easier target.

Brittle. Old. Slower than dirt. He fell out of the chair to the carpet. Kicking his empty wheelchair out of her way, she turned her body into a twisting, flailing, battering machine. She needed out of those ties before either of these madmen could get to her!

In seconds, the ties unraveled. Free of the wingback, she charged Brit. She needed that gun! Shannon flew at him, slapping and punching, scratching and kicking. Brit countered, swinging a fist, but he never connected. She didn't know how to fight. Not really. She only knew what he treasured most. Cocking her knee, she nailed those really tender balls of his with as hard a kick as she could muster. Down he went, clutching his privates and whining.

She got to his gun before he could recover and hefted it like she'd seen Adam do on the island. Shooting was another thing she didn't know how to do, but tonight? Scared little Shannon Reagan was gone.

The new wicked had arrived.

Chapter Thirty-Six

Thank God for good buddies. After Connor, Rory, and Harley stormed Regan Manor, they'd come to the rescue. Not a second to soon. Adam was on the edge of eternal darkness by the time they broke open the basement door, shadows inside his head and taunting him with the thought of never seeing Shannon or Squeaks again.

He took the winding stairs out of the basement two at a time, his heart stuck up high in his throat and his lungs on fire. He couldn't get back to the study fast enough, not with Shannon in there with that murdering bastard, Paul Reagan and his sidekick, Paxton.

Alex followed closely somewhere behind. The rest of they guys, too, but hell! How could Paxton be alive? How was he here in Rosslyn when Adam knew damned well he'd left him dead on that island in the Pacific? It made no sense, but Adam didn't really care. He didn't have time to think. He could kill the son-of-a-bitch as many times as he needed killing.

Swiping a quick hand over the sodden holster at his hip, he loosed his weapon. That he still had his nine mil either proved how inept Reagan's new security staff was, or how over confident. They hadn't disarmed him or his boss, probably because they didn't understand the first thing about how tough black ops guys really were. Well, guess again. A decent handgun withstood a helluva lot more than water.

Adam cleared the cellar door with one blast of his palm, surprising that weasel who'd tried to bully Shannon earlier. *Hubbard, is it?*

"Where is she?" Adam barked before he hauled off and punched that snotty face with the full force of his fist. Hubbard collapsed like the pantywaist he was, and Adam kept going.

"Study," Alex growled, as if Adam didn't know.

They hurried, but the damned study door wouldn't open. He paused just long enough to detect Shannon's voice raised in anger inside. "No!"

"It's too late." Paul glanced back at the television screen. Her eyes followed, listening for that rat bastard Hubbard, and keeping an eye on her whimpering ex, too. Bad move on her part. In that split second, Paul jerked a gun up from beneath the lap blanket that had fallen to the floor with him. Fatal mistake—for him.

"You think I won't kill you?" she yelled, gripping the pistol like she knew what to do with it. It almost felt natural in her palm, but this was the first time she'd held a weapon. Surely Brit had turned the safety off. No way she could miss at this range, right? "Where are they? Tell me. Now!"

His lips curled back, his weapon shaky but trained on her. Yeah. He'd do it. He'd kill her in a heartbeat. Like she didn't already know that?

"I said tell me where Adam is!" She fired a warning shot past his head.

Enlightenment flickered in Paul's aged eyes. The gun in his hand wavered, then righted. "You'll never get to them in time. They're already dead and on the dock. Or under it."

"Where?" she shrieked. "Which dock?" If not her, someone could still get to Adam and Alex and save them. Maybe the authorities. There was time.

"Now you listen, little girl—"

She straightened her right arm, peering down the length of blue steel, meaning every word. "You listen! If you value your life, you'll tell me—"

He fired! He actually bared his teeth and fired! The shot burned her upper arm, but even after all of his crimes, it surprised the hell out of her. *What am I thinking? That he's still my father? That he cares? Hell, no!*

Down she went to her knees, not because she was wounded, but because someone had pushed the door open behind her. It had to be Hubbard, the snake. He'd always wanted a piece of her. She shoved the door shut with a backward kick. Hubbard could wait his turn.

Shannon centered the reticle of her weapon on Paul's chest.

He squinted down the barrel of his gun, his hand shaking.

She aimed, her heart pounding in her throat.

Death was about to come to Reagan Manor only this time, Paul Reagan would die.

Damn it to hell! Adam only got one quick glimpse before the door slammed in his face, but it was Brit Paxton in there, alright. The blood covered son-of-a-bitch lay on his side, a pocket pistol in his hands and pointing it behind the door. That was why Adam couldn't get in. Shannon must have taken refuge behind the wingback, now overturned and blocking his entry. Paxton meant to kill her!

Not going to happen. Adam lowered his shoulder and plowed into that solid oak door. The chair *would* move, by hell, and this time, Paxton would stay dead.

"Damn you, Hubbard! Stay out!" He'd effectively shoved her out of Paul's line of fire and into Brit's. The cheater had a smaller pistol in his hand, and where it came from, she had no idea. She ducked behind the wingback and kicked at the open door.

It didn't shut. Instead, it bounced off the well-muscled arm that had just stretched into view. Small-arms fire in close quarters exploded. One crack of death. Two! She flattened her belly to the floor, needing to take stock of her desperate situation. The odds were bad, three against one. What the hell was going on? Did Hubbard have a gun? Who was he shooting at?

Paul Reagan glared at her from the other side of the wheelchair, seemingly unafraid of the gunfire, his teeth still bared like fangs. He meant to kill her.

The time had come. There was no other way. He wouldn't tell her where Adam and Alex were. Worse, if she died, they would, too. This evil man had to die, so she could at least call for help. That accurate assessment had no more registered in her brain when it instantly transmitted to the tip of her index finger and—*BOOM!*

Every sliver of muscle and bone from that fingertip to her shoulder blade reverberated with the powerful discharge. A different kind of enlightenment blossomed over Paul's countenance. His lips curled back in surprise as dark red blood spurted out of his kneecap. He stared straight at her, his pistol still on target. "No!" he hissed.

She couldn't stop. Thunder cracked from her hand again. The second shot shoved him backward into the front of his desk. His body went limp. The pistol in his hand sank to the floor, but Shannon had a head full of adrenaline and two men to save. She pushed to her knees ready to take on Brit and Hubbard too if need be.

The open study door still blocked her view. It couldn't be Hubbard. Someone must've called the police. *Get out of my way! There's still time. I can save him!*

She jerked the door aside and ran into the solid wall of— *Adam?*

Her eyes lied. How could he be there? He'd drowned.

But it was him, and Alex too. They were both dripping wet and looking like hell, but breathing hard.

"You're alive!"

Adam nodded, his jaw clenched tight. Hard. Her gentle warrior stood too somber. He should be happy to see her, but no tender smile welcomed her. No sweet words graced his lips. Instead, he looked incredibly—sad? His gaze flickered to the weapon in her hand. Easing it out of her clutch, he tucked it into his belt and locked onto her elbow instead of hugging and kissing her like he should have.

A scuffle sounded beyond the room as a crowd of men in black pushed their way through. Adam tugged her under his arm and stepped into the hall, letting them pass. "We have to move," he whispered. "Now."

Wordlessly, Alex led the way into the grand marbled entry. Men garbed in FBI SWAT gear streamed through the open doors. Connor, Rory, and Harley stood with Hubbard, his hands cuffed behind his back, his nose still upturned.

"Did you get it all?" Alex asked.

Harley nodded. "Every last word."

Shannon broke free from Adam to confront the traitorous butler. "You knew that Paul Reagan killed my mother all this time," she hissed. "You knew he meant to kill me, but not once did you lift a finger to help me."

Hubbard stared her down. "You weren't even blood."

"And you are?" she shrieked. Man, did everyone know she wasn't Paul Reagan's flesh and blood but her? Her hand snaked out of its own volition and struck that smug face. "I was my mother's blood! And until tonight, I thought I was Paul Reagan's! Did you help him kill her? Huh, did you? Did you help him drown her, you sick excuse for a human being? You know what? You're fired!"

She curled her fingers and punched him again square in that pompous, upturned nose before Adam could restrain her. Hubbard deserved so much more! Her inner devil had yet to relinquish hold, and she felt powerful. *I am the only Reagan heir. I am Reagan Industries, Goddamnit. No one can touch me. They wouldn't dare.*

She sucked in a deep breath that should've cleansed the monster from her heart. It didn't. "Let's get out of here," she snapped at Adam.

Instead of complying and following at her heels like the lap dog he wasn't, Adam pulled her out of her intended path and pressed her gently against his chest. "Shannon, look at me."

The tone in his voice caught her unprepared. "What's wrong?" she asked, suddenly seeing him for the first time. His eyes were filled with blood where the white osclera should've been. The deep ocean blue was more black than blue. A large black bruise with a nasty cut colored his left cheekbone. Another cut bled over his right eye, dripping a thin line of red along his orbital bone. His clothes were drenched, still dripping on the marble floor. The poor man had nearly drowned. He was hurt. He needed help. She turned to order a medic to his side.

"Shannon," Adam whispered hoarsely. "Do you know what you've done?"

"Of course I know what I've done. You're both alive, aren't you?" she bit out. It seemed so obvious. *I'm not apologizing. Paul Reagan's wrong. I'm right, and because of it, he's dead. You're alive. Problem solved.*

"You're hurt." Adam fingered her arm tenderly.

Glancing down, she finally noticed the bright red stain soaking through Judy's flannel shirtsleeve. Huh. She'd been grazed. Paul Reagan did that. He had meant to kill her. Funny. She hadn't felt it until then, but it stung. "I guess he got me."

Piercing blues stabbed her with the saddest remorse. Had she changed so much Adam no longer loved her? Was she looking at the first step away and goodbye? Irritation rankled at the back of her neck. She didn't have time for this. She had a business to run. *What the hell's wrong with you, Adam?*

"Look at me, Shannon baby. Talk to me. Do you know what just went down? Do you really understand?" He pulled her close until her breasts flattened against his chest, still looking deeply into her eyes, for what, she didn't know.

"Of course I understand," she snapped, not sure what the hell he was talking about. "I don't need you to—"

A gurney rolled by, pushed by a somber member of the FBI forensic team now on sight. It passed beneath the elegant chandelier hung high above the Reagan family crest to the side of the entry doors. Until a moment ago, it had been her family crest.

Shannon blinked. *Who is in that bag? Was it Brit? Had he died, too? Or was it Paul?*

Half of her cared. Half did not. But with every squeak, awareness seeped through the adrenaline. The chaos in her soul stilled and her rage melted into shadow. She blinked again, unable to take her eyes from the body bag. It concealed a tall man. Two pointed bumps beneath the black vinyl betrayed where two feet laid.

Death rolled out the grand doors of Reagan Manor, leering, reminding, and stabbing a long pointed finger back at her.

Denial fled, and along with it, her magnificent power. Her knees buckled. If not for Adam's strong arms, she would've stumbled. Still she watched, riveted to the passing of the evil she'd wrought within the house where a lonely, little girl had once lived with her nanny. She whispered the truth at last. "I killed him."

Another gurney came forth from the dark hallway. It had eight shiny wheels with black rubber tires, and it squeaked a rhythmic 'screech, squeak, screech' as it rolled along. Not loud. Just soft sounds, like the little girl crying within her now. The men who pulled and pushed it along the grand marble entry didn't smile. No one did.

"I killed my father," she whined, "the man I thought was my dad. What have I done?"

Adam pulled her tight, his hand strong at the back of her head as remorse hit fast and hard. His strength anchored her, smothering her to that broad chest that could pass for body armor all by itself. If only she could crawl inside of him to save herself now. Somewhere on his body he still harbored the evil thing she had used to take a life. How could he love her now that he knew? *I'm a murderer.*

"It will cut you low the first time," he muttered into her hair, "but always remember. He gave you no choice. You did what you had to do."

She tipped her face up to his, needing desperately to explain, but needing absolution more. "And he was killing you."

Loving eyes gazed down at her. "He tried," Adam said quietly.

Shannon reached for Alex, needing his forgiveness, too. "I love you," she stated. There was no other way to put it. He might as well know. She loved all her heroes. Did they still love her?

"I know." He lifted her knuckles to his lips and kissed them, his eyes full of the same sadness as Adam's. "Real families are like that. We hang with you when no one else will."

"I had to do it," she explained again, a hint of hysteria climbing up the back of her throat. "He was killing you. I… I had no choice."

Alex shot Adam a curt, dark glance. "Get her the hell out of here."

He complied instantly, ushering her swiftly through the front doors and out into the chilly evening. The need to defend her actions persisted.

"I had to do it," she told him again, hating the edge to her voice, that falling-off point she might never be able to return from. She'd come so close to losing herself until this very morning when Adam had turned her life around. Could he do it again? Better question, could she?

He guided her to Connor's SUV. The door was no more than shut when the awful thing she'd done exploded in her mind. Long vicious tentacles of horror squeezed the false pride out of her. "I had to do it," she cried. Hysteria crept closer.

"Look at me," Adam commanded, his palms to the sides of her head, pulling her into his view.

The blackest panic filled the vehicle. She couldn't meet his gaze. Not yet. "I had to do it," she repeated, unable to stop the relentless chant in her head.

"Shannon, damn it. Look at me."

She did, afraid of the condemnation she'd see in those gorgeous eyes that used to light up with so much love. Before tonight. Before she'd taken a life. Her internal thesaurus provided the ugly word and the shame of—*patricide.*

"Let it go. You did what you did to save me," Adam said softly. "Get it straight in your head right damned now. Know it in your gut. You aren't a murderer, and you aren't a sinner. You put down the dog who most likely killed your mother."

She nodded vigorously as the words tumbled out. "He did. He said he did. He drowned her, and he would've killed you and Alex."

"And you," he added softly. "Paul Reagan would've killed you if you hadn't got him first."

"It was Brit's twin brother on the island who you killed. It was Bart. You killed Bart, not Brit."

"And I'd do it again," he hissed.

"What... what happened to Brit?"

"Don't worry about him, he's—"

"You did it, didn't you? You killed him? He... they... they killed their own grandfather."

Adam accepted that bit of unsubstantiated information, too. A single tear glinted at the corner of his eye. "What else, Shannon baby? What else do you know now?"

"He never loved me." She choked. "I was blind. Brit was Bart *and* Brit. They were twins and they... they tricked me. Paul Reagan tricked me. He... he never loved me and he killed my mother. All these years... I wish I'd had the chance to meet her. Just once. I don't want to live here, Adam. I don't want the manor, and I don't want any part of Reagan Industries. I don't want to be his heir!" She spat the venom out of her mouth and out of her soul.

"Do you know how much I love you?" Adam ran a warm palm down the side of her face. "Do you have any idea how thankful I am for the tough choices you made tonight?" The single tear fell free from his eye, rolling down her arm like a crystal diamond before it remembered it was only water and lost its shape.

"I killed him," she said simply, her angst diminished and her strength gone. "I did it because he would've killed us."

"That's right." Adam rubbed a gentle circle over her cheekbone with his thumb. "He was the evil one. Never you."

Shannon took a deep, cleansing breath. Black fog faded as the weight of too much deceit and too many lies lifted from her soul. "I'm going to marry you," she reminded Adam quietly.

He breathed his answer into her hair. "You'd better believe it."

Chapter Thirty-Seven

The minute they'd hit the Mortimer's, Shannon got to see that mother bear side of Judy Mortimer in action. "Damn you, Harley," she cussed when she met them on the front porch, her green eyes throwing sparks. "Get her inside. You guys were supposed to keep her safe. You know where to take her, Adam."

"I did keep her safe," Harley muttered. "She's here, isn't she?"

Adam knew better than to argue. A registered nurse by profession, Judy tended to take over when injuries struck too close to home. Because of the nature of their business, she'd patched up a few tough guys and gals over the years. The only downside was they usually got an earful while she did it. He steered Shannon into the kids-off-limits room aside the kitchen, otherwise known as Judy's office.

"I told you to take her to the emergency room," she snapped at her husband even as she opened drawers and set up a sterile work area. She nodded at the wooden stool next to the counter. "Shannon, take a seat. Adam, help her out of that bloody shirt and into the clean scrub hanging behind the door. Wash your hands, Harley. A gunshot wound should be reported. You know better than this. You too, Adam. Your eyes are bloodshot. You're soaking wet. What happened to you? Where's Alex?"

Adam filled in the details, how Alex, Connor and Rory were still talking with the FBI and police, but specially the part where Harley busted in Reagan's basement door and saved his life. All Harley got for being the hero of the night was an eye roll. In between Judy's magnificently sharp-tongued opinion of his faith in her medical skills, they were treated to more headshakes and icy glares, but best of all? She made Shannon smile the way she bossed the men.

"Honestly. These guys think they're invincible," Judy muttered as she flushed the bullet crease, making Shannon flinch. "Thank God this is a superficial wound. I need a size five suture, Harley. Steri wound closure strips, too. Four of them. Adam, don't just stand there. Get out of those wet clothes before you get sick."

"I will when we're done here," he said evenly. He wasn't about to leave Shannon's side, not even or an angry mother bear.

"I mean it," Judy grumbled. "You're dripping on my floor."

"And I'm not going anywhere. I'll mop later."

Judy huffed, but relented. Adam hovered as close as he dared without getting in the way. Harley assisted while Judy stitched Shannon's upper arm, her sharp eyes not missing a beat. "You guys are going to be the death of me yet. Damn you both, you could have lost her. Am I hurting you, honey?"

"No, but Harley did save Adam, Judy, and then Adam saved me," Shannon said quietly. "We'd all be dead if it wasn't for your husband. Thank you Harley. I owe you my life."

Damned if he didn't turn shy and shrug it off with a cute blush "It was my pleasure, darlin'."

Judy shook her head. "You should've stayed here and let the guys take care of that bastard. That's what they do."

"No, Judy." Shannon earned a spiked brow for that one. "He killed my mother. He had to pay."

"I know that, honey. It's just too bad you're the one who had to do it." Judy glared up at Adam. "You'd better take good care of this girl."

He winked at Shannon, so damned proud of her. "Only for the rest of my life."

The second round of tacos was just as good as the first, but the pretty lady at Adam's side was a million times better. Man, even with taco breath, Shannon tasted good. He'd sampled her lips enough since they'd gotten back to the Mortimers'. He would know.

She hadn't gone far from his side after Judy doctored her, only to shower and change clothes while he did the same. For now, Adam and Shannon occupied one of the many leather loveseats in the great room, crowded together like two teenagers who couldn't bear to be apart. Judy was right. He'd almost lost Shannon and he knew it.

Shannon had more family than she'd realized. God bless him, Raul Ortega showed up with his wife, Margareta, and God bless her, too. She brought enough flan to feed a small army. Little man Squeaks was happily lost somewhere in the crowd, and Shannon seemed okay with it. If Judy, Ember, or Izza didn't have him tucked away, one of the guys or their wives did. Adam had even seen Alex and his wife, Kelsey, along with their daughter, Lexie Rose, cozied up in the kitchen with the little tyke.

Adam was proud of Shannon. She wasn't the innocent little ball of fluff he'd once thought, and tonight proved it. This kitten snuggled under his arm with her hand on his chest had some deadly claws, sheathed for the moment. What she'd faced in the Reagan study was damned tough, but once again, she'd met the challenge head-on.

So what if she got a little too pumped with adrenaline and the self-righteousness that often followed a fiercely fought battle. Most guys did—until they had time to think about what went down in combat. That's where Adam came in. He had a plan to keep her from thinking too hard. He just needed everyone to go home.

Of all things, CIA Agent Atchison had the nerve to show up like he'd been invited. Judy pre-empted a TEAM versus CIA confrontation by inviting him in, then stuck a platter of delicious food under his nose like he deserved it. Adam wasn't sure if she knew that Atchison had labeled Shannon a traitor months earlier, but she had a funny way of showing her TEAM spirit by asking the wolf in.

The one-big-family mood in the great room cooled. Harley made it worse when he handed Atchison a frosty root beer, then offered up a round of introductions instead of tossing him out on his ear.

Holding his tongue was no longer an option. "You were late," Adam growled when the introductions got around to him.

"No, I wasn't. I was there all along," he answered with his mouth full of taco.

"What? Watching? Like you did in South Dakota?"

"We're always watching." Atchison's brow arched when he spied Shannon. "Miss Reagan, I'd like to talk to you about your father's residence and business when you're up to it. I'm sorry about what happened with your father." He almost sounded contrite.

"I'm not," she declared boldly. She shifted, her body aligned with Adam's but her shoulders squared. "What do you want to know? Ask."

"Not now," Atchison said gently. "Any day next week will be soon enough. Mr. Stewart already turned over the taped conversation. I think we've got what we need for the moment. Call my office when you're ready to discuss your way forward."

"My way forward? You mean if I intend to continue the drone research? Is that what you're asking?" She stiffened, and Adam smoothed his hand down her bicep, letting her know he was there.

Atchison nodded, his eyes narrowed and steady on Shannon. "That among other things."

"So, Shannon darlin'," Harley drawled from his comfy chair near the fireplace. "You're now one of the richest women on the eastern seaboard, and I for one am damned glad to know ya. I've got an idea for a canine drone I'd like to talk to you about. It fetches beer and it even barks."

Leave it to Harley to add a touch of levity to what had become a serious discussion.

"Kin I have a drone, Mama?" Little Alex asked from his man-cave under the coffee table.

"No, son. Get ready for bed," Harley teased.

"Aww, Daddy."

"I'm not keeping Reagan Industries or the manor," Shannon declared stiffly, her body tensed. "I'm selling it all. Maybe Jed McCormack's engineers can take over the drone project. Maybe Jed can do something good and decent with the company for a change. He's got the clout."

The more she talked, the more she trembled, and the more Adam tightened his grip on her shoulders. Not once since she'd left the manor had she made the mistake of calling Paul Reagan father. That betrayal had cut deep.

"I'm a simple person, Agent Atchison," she told him in no uncertain terms, her chin tilted in defiance. "If I meet with anyone next week, it will be with my attorneys to begin divestiture of all Reagan holdings, personal and otherwise. As of tonight, there is no Paul Reagan and there is no Reagan Industries." She turned to Alex. "Can you help me with that?"

His answer came without one second of hesitation. "Anytime, anywhere, Shannon."

Adam nodded at her rock solid assessment of her future. This woman meant to put her nightmare of a father in the past where he belonged. *Good on her.*

"It won't be that easy. You have stockholders to consider," Atchison said quietly.

"Maybe not. Shannon was Mr. Reagan's only heir," Mother piped up from the corner where she sat chatting with

Terrence. "According to his will, Shannon now holds the majority of stocks in the company. She's a billionaire. I think she can do whatever she wants with her assets."

Adam slanted a frosty bottle of the real stuff in a silent salute to Mother, thanking her for her support. She winked back. So did Terrence.

"So you're Sasha Kennedy," Atchison asked, his gaze zeroed on Mother. "I'd like to talk with you later, too."

She had the good sense to smile and keep her mouth shut for a change, smart strategy for the master hacker Adam suspected she was.

"Miss Reagan," Atchison leveled a piercing eye back at Shannon. "You might as well know. The Agency's had an ongoing investigation into Reagan Industries for years. There were too many unexplained deaths among his competitors, too many disappearances, and too many coincidences. I'd be glad to give you a full report when you're ready."

"I'll let you know when I'm ready," she retorted, and Adam could have kissed her for the smart way she handled the CIA agent.

"One thing you need to know now," Atchison kept on going. "The elevated cistern behind the manor is how Reagan flooded the basement compartment. He's done this before. We'll be dismantling it and checking for DNA evidence. You understand."

"Take it," she said evenly. "Sell it to Korea for all I care. You're the guys with all the foreign contacts."

Ouch. Atchison actually flinched at that insinuation. After all, it was the CIA's double agent who'd cheated with the man Shannon believed was her husband at the time. Shannon was in rare form, not taking a single step back. Adam eased her against his body. She had leaned forward during the discussion, but the last thing she needed was to go after this guy like Adam knew damned well she was capable of doing. Atchison needed to back off and give her some space, too. Shannon had learned from the worst to take no prisoners.

"Did he honestly think the North Koreans wouldn't notice his drones didn't work?" Alex asked. He'd been uncharacteristically quiet since he'd returned from the manor, but then, he did have his sleeping daughter on his lap and his pretty wife snuggled into his side. Adam envied him his ability to know when to stand back and let others take the fight.

"No, Mr. Stewart. I'm guessing Reagan simply banked on the inherent distrust between our country and the Democratic People's Republic of Korea. Why would we believe their accusation of Reagan fraud, when we can't believe a word they say?"

"I thought I took your Agent Gangjeon out in South Dakota," Adam muttered quietly. "Was I wrong? Was she injured?"

Atchison grunted. "You got her alright. You hit her left shoulder, but that moron Paxton stashed her in a local motel. By the time we got a decent report from her, Reagan already had the missing drone."

"It would have been helpful if I'd known about your double-agent before I sent my men and Miss Reagan into harm's way," Alex growled. "You ever hear of professional courtesy?"

Atchison never blinked. "Maybe next time, Stewart. Maybe next time."

Another growl rumbled across the room from Lexie's dad. "There won't be a son-of-a-bitchin' next time."

Shannon twisted to look Adam in the eye. "Did you know Brit had a twin brother?"

He knew what she was really asking. *Did you keep secrets from me, too?* "Heck, no. I didn't see that one coming. It didn't dawn on me the drones were fake, either, not until early this morning when I couldn't sleep. It was the only thing that made sense. I just needed Terrence's help to prove it."

"There's something I need to tell you, young lady," Terrence said brightly to Shannon. "Where's that son of yours?"

She scanned the room, looking for Jimmy. "I think he's…"

"Here." Zack Lennox raised a hand high from the huddle where he was surrounded by his daughters. LiLi, Song, and MiKi were perched on the armrests of his La-Z-Boy, hovering like little mothers in training over the sleeping baby boy in their daddy's arm. "The girls are trying to convince me we need a brother. They might be right. This little guy's a charmer. I'm starting to believe I need another man in the house."

"Get your own," Adam muttered teasingly. "That one's mine."

"Aww," LiLi grumbled in her bossy, oldest sister way. "But Uncle Adam, he's so cute, and I'd take real good care of him. You know I would. Let me keep him."

"And he's just my size." Song's bright brown eyes sparkled in the fire's glow. "Kin we keep him? Please?"

Adam had to smile. Those three little sisters just might get their wish. He'd caught the light in Zack's eye and the covert glance at his wife, Mei, but he'd also caught the light in Shannon's eyes. "You're going to adopt Jimmy," she stated. Not asked.

"Yes, ma'am. The minute we're married, I'm making it official." She bowed her forehead to his lips, and he knew she was close to falling apart. "I told you I love you, woman," he muttered huskily. "Don't you get it? You and Squeaks are mine, and you always will be."

"Whoa!" Izza squealed. She'd been hunkered down with Connor on the couch by the window. "Did I hear the M word? Are you kids getting married?"

That got all the women's attention. By the time they settled down, Ember was in charge of a ladies luncheon to make wedding plans, Kelsey knew the perfect place to buy Shannon's wedding gown, and Maverick's wife, China, had volunteered their farm for an outdoor wedding with all the trimmings. In the midst of the happy turmoil, Terrence climbed to his feet and crouched to one knee at Shannon's side, his eyes bright with unshed tears.

Adam stilled. This was it, one of those once-in-a-lifetime moments that Shannon's day had already overflowed with. He flattened his palm to the middle of her back to steady her once again.

"You might as well, know, Shannon. I loved your mother. I did." Terrence began slowly, his lower lip quivering. "You don't remember her, but I do, and I loved her with every beat of this old ticker. I wasn't always this old, you know." A big tear fell out of his eye when he nodded toward Zack and

Jimmy and the Lennox girls. "And I love my grandson over there, too. You should be proud of him."

"You're not old, Terrence." Shannon reached for her friend, cupping his cheek gently. "I wish I could remember my mom. Everyone said she was the kindest person they'd—" She froze. "*Your* grandson?"

For once, all the children stilled, even Georgie and Little Alex. No one in the Mortimer household so much as crunched a nacho chip. The cat was out of the bag.

"Didn't you ever wonder why you're so special to me?" Terrence asked softly, his eyes brimming. "It's true. You're my daughter. You belonged to Olivia and me. You're really our child."

Shannon fell into her real father's arms, crying, "Why didn't you tell me?"

"Ah, Shannon baby," he murmured, his nose pressed into her hair and his eyes overflowing. "I'm sorry. I should've been brave like your young man here, but I was afraid Paul would've hurt you if he'd known for sure. I'd already lost Olivia. I couldn't bear to lose you, too."

"But all these years…" She choked, the anguish in her tone incredibly raw and sad. "He killed my mom."

Poor Terrence cried, "I know. I know, but I could never prove it, baby girl. Believe me, if there was any way I could've gotten you out of there and away from him, I would have."

Damn him, even Agent Atchison teared up at the happy reunion.

At last, Shannon tipped back on her knees and smoothed her fingertips along her real father's damp cheek. "Tell me about her, Terrence. I want to know everything."

The tender revelation couldn't have gone better. Terrence looked like the saddest, happiest man alive cradling his daughter. Shannon's new life was just beginning. Adam's too.

"I gotta poop, Daddy," Georgie stage-whispered.

Harley chuckled at that untimely childhood revelation spoken so eloquently.

Izza snorted, just a little.

Rory outright laughed. Heck. Everyone did.

Kids. You've got to love them.

Chapter Thirty-Eight

"Goodnight," Adam announced to all. "I'm taking some personal time, Boss. Maybe a week."

It had been a long twenty-four hours. He was beat. So was Shannon. Terrence had already gone home, Agent Atchison and most of the gang, too. Little Alex and Georgie were in bed, and the Mortimer house had settled with the quiet night. Only Alex and Kelsey remained with a slumbering Lexie Rose cuddled on their laps.

"Take two," Alex said. "You've earned it."

Adam had learned early in his time with The TEAM not to argue with his boss. He collected his sleeping son in one arm and his bride-to-be in the other.

She circled her arms around his waist and tucked her fingers inside his belt at the side of the crib. "Brit planned to raise our son after he killed me," she said quietly. "Jimmy would have grown up to be just like him."

"Bullshit," Adam hissed softly. "Jimmy's got more of you in him than of that sperm-donor creep. This little guy would've given Paxton a run for his money."

She chuckled. "I hope so."

"Count on it. Jimmy's already beat the odds for preemies born on desert islands. Then he outwitted Linda What's-her-name and escaped Reagan Manor. Now he's smart enough to know he's ready for bed. Look at him. He's your son through and through."

"It's embarrassing," she said quietly, her eyes on the sleeping child. "Why didn't I know my husband was really two different men? How dumb am I?"

Adam turned around to face her. "Knock it off, Shannon. You're not dumb by any means. Paxton and his brother were psychotic bullies who tricked you. How could anyone have seen that coming?"

"But I slept with them. Both of them. And that's not all. Everyone I ever loved has lied to me."

"And whose fault is that? Yours? For not being a snake in the grass like they were? Not hardly. Your only fault is seeing the good in people."

"But still…" She disengaged from his arms and sat on the edge of the bed, tracing a pattern on the comforter with her fingertip, then erasing it with a brush of her palm, all while not looking at him. "Why did Brit and Bart do that to me? What'd they get out of playing that sick game? There wasn't anything in it for either of them."

"That's where you're wrong. By cheating you, they always had an alibi. They could swear they were with you. Don't kid yourself. Both Paxton's had a lot to gain by using you like they did."

"I honestly never thought of that." The weariness of the day had gotten the best of her.

"Of course not. Your thought process doesn't work like Paxton's or Reagan's. You're honest. The real question is how did you turn out to be so innocent? How'd you avoid growing up like your old man all these years?"

She shrugged. "It was easy. He never had much time for me, and it's not like Brit did either. I used to feel sorry for myself because other girls had daddy/daughter dates. They went on fun things like family picnics. They celebrated anniversaries and birthdays. Christmas." She seemed especially intent on tracing a heart on the comforter, only to smooth it out with one swipe. "But maybe I was the lucky one. Paul Reagan didn't see me most of these past twenty years, only hen he had to. All that loneliness might have been a blessing in disguise."

Adam hadn't thought of all little girl Shannon had missed in her childhood, but he saw it now. She'd lived a fairly sterile life. A sad life. No happy mother to greet her in the kitchen after school with a hug and fresh baked chocolate chip cookies. No wise father to teach her how to throw a fastball—or whatever it was that fathers taught little girls. He couldn't imagine it, not with his big family.

"That's why you love books," he said simply. "They give you what you couldn't find at home. You've been escaping Reagan Manor all of your life, haven't you?"

She nodded, her gaze steadfast on her fingers. "I'm going to ask the police to test the water system in my old home and at the manor. If there's something there, if anyone put some kind of a hallucinogen or drugs in the water, they should be able to find it, don't you think? Agent Atchison mentioned coincidences, and I think he's right."

"Alex can take care of that for you. You're talking about those crazy dreams you had, aren't you? You think Brit drugged you?"

She nodded, still not meeting his eyes. "It's one possibility. Either that or I'm crazy. I might as well have married an ax murderer, Adam. I've certainly lived with plenty of them."

"You're not crazy, damn it." He crowded into her, shifting his legs between her knees to get her attention. "And now you're marrying a sniper who falls out of the sky for a living. Are you up for it?"

At last she lifted her chin and looked at him. She smiled and had the good grace to blush, but damned if she didn't run a fingernail up the seam of his zipper and back down again. "Are *you* up for it?"

Instantly, his body hardened at the touch of this capricious woman. He'd held onto her all night long on the loveseat, but it hadn't felt as seductive as that one little tease. The fire in his blood raged hot and fierce, and he was amazed how he craved her luscious body, hell, how he craved everything about her. The taste of her lips. The soft touch of her fingers on his belly and sinking lower. How the sound of her breathy sigh vibrated every last vertebrae in his spine and straight to his groin. When her fingers dipped below his belt, he automatically sucked in a deep breath to give her room to reach what she was after. The night was young after all.

Adam kicked off his boots and dispensed with his jeans. Shannon had a good hold of him by then, running the show. Or so she thought. At this rate, she'd never get into that silk nightie.

He eased her back onto the mattress. She might have been duped by a mentally deranged father and an idiot husband, but that day was done. He'd seen the real Shannon in action, first on the beach, then with Paul Reagan and Atchison. The world had another thing coming if they thought she would stand down and let anyone run over her again. Like now. If she didn't slow down, he couldn't promise how much longer he could last. A tingle sizzled up his spine. He might just have a tigress by the tail.

"Answer me this, Shannon," he egged her on, needing her to focus on him and not the sins of the past. For now she lay between his splayed hands, his arms stiff and supporting him while she stroked and played. "Have I ever lied to you?"

A lovely smile blossomed over her face. "Which is why I'm here," she whispered, her blue eyes dark and hazy. She ran her tongue over her bottom lip, biting it while she continued stroking and petting. "You stuck with me when you should've run the other way. You and Raul and Terrence."

"And Alex and Connor and Izza and... and..." Deftly, he sank to one elbow and maneuvered her out of her clothes, taking in the delectable view while trying to remember everyone who'd come to her aid, but damn. His brain wasn't working so well any more, not with her bare body spread out like a feast, his for the taking and his blood already running hot. That red thong barely covered anything. He smoothed one palm down her hips to her backside, his fingers sliding between the cheeks of her ass to grab a handful. "Do you always wear sexy underwear to a gun fight?"

She demurred. "Kelsey brought some clothes for me when she same over. Apparently she's got a fun-loving, trouble-making side. Do you like?"

Hell, yeah, he liked. His heart lurched up his throat. This woman wanted him and he wanted her. Better yet, she loved him. She trusted him and he wouldn't let her down. He lowered his body to hers and licked her bottom lip, then bit it gently, tugging and teasing it just to hear her moan. That scrap of red silk hit the floor, and they were tangled beneath the sheets.

He let her have her way. Let her play. This woman knew what she wanted. By the time she was through, every last inch of him ached to be inside of her, cocooned in her silky body. He'd never felt so aroused. She had a way of woman-handling him, and he liked it. Every scrape of her fingernails. Every moan and feminine grunt. Every sultry, satisfied lick and sigh.

He gave back as good as he got until, at last, she relinquished control and he took over. Just in time. He shackled her prowling hands over her head and blanketed her with his larger body. "I love you, Shannon," he declared gruffly at the point of entry, right where her needy whimpers signaled he'd driven her crazy with desire. Right where there was no turning back, no stopping the freight train of passion they'd set rolling.

By then, all she could do was writhe against him and beg, "Adam. Please. I need this. I need you."

Enough said. He pitched his body forward into the woman he craved with all of his heart and soul. She matched his pace, her body writhing beneath his, driving him higher as she climbed with him. And higher.

The first time they'd made love was pure, wanton need at last released. The second, frenzy in the shower. But this? Absolute branding, their bodies melted together in the flames of love. Eternally claiming each other's souls. He meant her to know she was his, that he would stand by her until the day he died. That he would die for her.

It didn't take long for her to shatter. He plunged into her delicious, wet warmth for another sigh. Another needy 'ah.' Another whining 'oh.' One last muffled 'Adam!' screamed into her knuckles so she wouldn't wake the baby. With one last grinding thrust, she dug her fingernails into his back and came apart in his hands and Adam emptied his all into her.

She raked her fingers through his hair, breathing hard, her slender body still clenching his, quaking with after shocks. "That was… that was…" Shannon couldn't catch her breath, "oh, my God, that was something else. I saw stars, Adam. Really. I did."

He growled out a deep rumble of utter male pride, thrilled that he'd pleased her. They'd both worked up a sweat. Rolling to her side, he rested his ear to her pounding heart while he caught his breath. She'd pleased the hell out of him too.

Shannon was his past, his present, and his future, his tropical sunrise and his nighttime sky. She was fire and ice with a splash of tequila, the perfect mix of intoxication and determination. Give and take. Love and lust. Her taking the initiative like she just did meant she intended to be his partner. His equal. His mate. Forever. Maybe longer.

"I love you so much," she whispered into the top of his head, her fingertips seductively light on his chest and edging lower.

A grin cracked his cheeks at this audacious and obviously sex-starved woman, but hey. A man's got to do what a man's got to do. Adam pulled her onto his hips, his fingers clutching her ass, and there she was, straddling him, her sensual body lifted above him, and her eyes wide open. His entire universe. His world. His true Polaris. He traced her pretty jaw with the back of his fingers, and instantly, she rubbed her cheek into his palm like a cat. Maybe that tiger.

"I only saw one star," he murmured, his baritone more growl than voice, his heart in his throat and so damned full of love for this fierce woman he could cry. "I only saw you."

He knew it then. From that day forth, another constellation would glitter in the night sky—the Adam Torrey family of stars. Another beacon would guide him home. He'd found his one sweet spot, and her name was… Shannon baby.

THE END

Sneak Preview of LEE

Book 12
In the Company of Snipers

Get me the hell out of here!

Tess Culver exploded through the door and ran, her boots hitting the flat surface of the roof like her life depended on it. Truth was—it did. Either Clint was where he was supposed to be or she was going to die. The jerk better be there.

"There he goes!" Angry voices bellowed behind her. "Hurry! Catch him!"

Ha! The fools on her tail still thought she was a guy. Well, good. Let them think that. Next, there'd be shooting, and all those tough guys could kiss her—

Zip! Ping!

She ducked. Right on schedule, two shots whizzed past her and splattered against the low brick wall that edged the roof. Adrenaline ramped up higher, like she needed more. Fire burned in her lungs. That familiar out of breath taste of copper, sulphur, and bile rose at the back of her throat. A sharp right turn ahead, and glory hallelujah, she'd be home free—if Clint did as he was told, damn his lazy ass.

She skidded around the corner, dug her toes in and headed north to the circular front of the bombed-out palace, the best point for her most daring getaway yet. With her heart pounding incredibly loud in her chest, her feet slapped the surface of the roof louder. And faster. Too quickly the edge approached.

Closer.

Faster.

No more roof to run. Nowhere else to go. She vaulted up onto the curved wall where all could see. Back when Darul Aman Palace was still an actual palace instead of a bombed out relic of bygone days, this might have been a primo place to take in a romantic view. Not tonight.

Zip! Ping!

Whew. That one was close. Clint had better be waiting for me.

Glancing down to the rubble forty feet below, there was no brother waiting for her and no truck. Damn! She whirled to face her pursuers, the prize still snug in her left hand and a sneer blossoming on her face despite her precarious position. These fools would never see her hesitate. Tess Culver didn't have it in her to admit defeat even in the face of it. One way or the other, these bumbling security guards would remember this day.

For months she'd been on the prowl. Listening. Watching. Connecting dots to explain exactly what was happening to the ancient Afghan treasures suddenly missing from the National Museum in Kabul, the prestigious building just north of where she stood now. One artifact had eventually surfaced in Kuwait, a lovely golden necklace of inestimable value, now lost to the world because it was in the private collection of Saudi Prince Kalim Abdul Hazzan. Then another piece hit the news, a simple carved knife handle of ivory inlaid with lapis lazuli and emeralds, turned up at an auction in, of all places, Sotheby's in Paris. Like the common people of Afghanistan could just drop in there to view it.

Tess decided right then and there. The plundering and pillaging of Afghanistan's treasures and artifacts had to stop. That was the day the cat burglar within Tess arrived like a witch summoned from another world. She hadn't realized she had a knack for thievery until the Sotheby's story broke, but the exquisite treasures and relics had to be saved. She knew so many of them by name and loved them all. The gold coins from the Yuezhi Chieftan. Hellenistic tritons. Scythian golden artifacts. And more. All now bartered on the black market because of a few greedy men, buyers and sellers, all of them hypocrites and liars who proclaimed national loyalty to the country they claimed they loved while they sacked it.

She spat. Yeah, right. Like liars the world over, they loved themselves more.

All six of the museum guards behind her screeched to a halt, bumping into each other, they'd stopped so quickly. Uniformed and sweaty after chasing her up four flights of stairs from the basement, they looked like the pigs they were. Dumb. Bumbling. Stupid if they thought the edge of the roof would stop her. That they were there participating in the demise of this country by protecting the true thief at large made them accomplices worthy of the same disgust. She had enough to go around.

The one with a thick, black Manchu approached cautiously, his fingers beckoning toward the bag in her hand, but his eyes glued to her. "Give it back."

"What? This?" she growled hoarsely, her throat ragged from the run. The bag dangled off her index finger like it meant nothing to her. The best part of this heist was these guys didn't know if she was still armed or not. She wasn't. She'd accidentally dropped her gun when the final door hadn't opened as easily as she'd expected. Fortunately, the roof was dark. Not knowing whether she was armed or not, combined with shadows kept them nervous. Wary. Off balance. It also gave her a few more seconds to catch her breath. She cocked an ear to listen for the familiar sound of her lazy brother's truck. *Where is he?*

Mr. Manchu seemed the bravest of the six since he was the only one who approached. He scowled in that patronizing way of Afghani law enforcement officers when they thought they had the upper hand, or when they assumed their quarry was just a dumb, hungry kid.

"You must return what you have stolen, boy." He nodded knowingly while he spoke, like she would agree just because he told her to.

Guess again, tough guy.

"Come." He waggled all four grubby fingers, urging her to repent and give up. "You are young. The chief will go easy on you. I will make certain."

"Chief? You mean Sherazi?" she taunted. Assistant Museum Curator, Mr. Abdul Sherazi, the lowest of the low, had yet to make his appearance on the roof, not like she'd expected him to climb all those stairs. A chubby thief like him had to keep a low profile, almost as low as a thief like her. Only their motives differed. He was selling the treasures of his country to the highest bidder, for greed and greed alone.

But she was stealing them to save them from men like him, for honor, for time and for Afghanistan's posterity. She had a contact who could and would give this particular national treasure safe passage to a museum in Paris. It might not be available to the common Afghani citizen, but it would be protected until the future day that Afghanistan was safe again.

A thinner guard stepped forward, his gun clasped in both hands and aimed at her head. "You'll never get away. There are six of us and only one of you."

Yeah, but you're all fat and stupid.

She panted for more air, analyzing alternatives. Six armed men on a roof? Her back to the edge? These idiots still believed she was a boy? A girl couldn't get any luckier. Still... She glanced to the barren yard below and the wall beyond. *Clint better damned well better get his dumb ass in gear! I'm running out of time.*

Time for a little one-upmanship. She needed to stall. Hoping these guys were all lousy shots, Tess shook the knitted cap off her head and let her other accomplice, the wind, catch the length of her hair. It was important these guys know they'd been beaten by the best, and her name was—

"He is a woman! An American woman!" Mr. Manchu hissed. Another guard spit in disgust. Yeah. She got that a lot from the macho guys in this country who thought women were created to serve. Not her. Not Tess Culver.

At last, an engine rumbled below. Clint *was* there. About time!

Relief washed through her. She scanned the wall's edge, searching for her mark. The letter X she'd scratched on the wall during her one and only dry run meant life tonight. Any deviance spelled splat in bright red. Three grand stories down was a helluva drop. She slid her boot heel over the X and offered a charming smile to the men who would never be as smart as she.

"You will die in prison for this crime!" Mr. Manchu growled. "I will make sure of that now! A thousand lashes with a good, stiff cane are not enough for an infidel like you!"

"No. I will kill her here and now." Skinny Guy couched to a firing position, one knee on the ground and licking his lips like he couldn't wait to end her. She got that a lot, too.

Another guard stepped forward, his lip curled in a sneer. Then another. Suddenly, every guard turned brave, like they all wanted a piece of her. How strange in this culture that a thieving boy got more respect than a thieving woman. "No, wait. We must rush her. Catch her. Then she will be ours to do with as we please."

"Sorry guys. That ain't never gonna happen," she taunted as she verified her landing zone. Clint. Truck. Good to go.

Ping.

Damn. Which one of these guys shot me? That was way too close.

"No. No. No." Still holding the bag where they could all see it, she waggled her finger at the guard crouched to his knee, scolding. "If you shoot me, this little baby will be gone for good. I'll drop it. You don't want that, do you? What will your boss say when you fail to return it to him so he can sell another piece of Afghani history to line his pockets?"

He squinted down the barrel of his pistol. Closing one eye, he scrunched his face, and lined her up again.

She blew out a breath of satisfaction. *Men. They never listen. Oh, well. Time to go.* Tess blew him a kiss over her fingertips and calmly said, "Bye boys." Spreading her arms wide, she tipped backwards, and dropped. It was a short trip, but one she'd planned thoroughly for.

The crush of the air bags on the flat bed beneath her whooshed a very welcome 'gotcha' when she landed. *I love you, Clint!*

Tess rolled a backward somersault onto her feet, and danced off the inflatable bag to the wooden rail of the bed. While Clint maneuvered the truck along the Palace grounds, gears shuddering and headed to Char-Qala Road, she swung feet first over the railing and angled her svelte body through the open passenger window and into the cab, her hair still fluttering in the breeze. The treasure in her hand felt sweet. The safety of the passenger seat cushion on her backside didn't feel half bad either. She'd done it. Again! One more treasure saved! One more crook cheated of his payoff!

Raking a hand through her hair, she pushed the tangled mass over her shoulder where it belonged. No need for that windblown look now. Sex appeal had served its purpose tonight. Those idiot guards were probably staring over the edge of the palace roof at this very moment and wondering how a mere woman could have outsmarted them. *Ha! Men are so dumb.*

"You were late enough. You need a better watch, Clint. One that tells time." she muttered, stashing the prize beneath the seat but not making eye contact with her brother. Not yet. He wouldn't like it when she did.

Stunts like this only worked with precision planning and timing. Besides, another theft from the Taliban would not go unnoticed. She'd actually been surprised there were only six guards after her tonight. She'd expected more considering the value of the item in her bag. Glancing out her side window, she watched for trouble. So far, so good. No one followed, and she heard no sirens, but what if Clint had arrived even one minute later? This could've gone really bad. What the hell was he thinking? Of saving his lazy ass?

He hadn't answered. She didn't really care. Her brother was like that. Weren't most men? Sullen. Moody. Easily irritated by women smarter than them, or always too tired, too hungry, forever complaining, and whining because they couldn't get laid. Whatever. Let him sit there and want. As long as he drove fast and got this big rig under cover like they'd planned, she didn't really care what her brother thought.

Still it irked her. Clint should be happy at her success. He should be proud. She'd just pulled off the heist of the century and risked her life to do it, not his. In fact, now that she'd thought more about it, he should be damned happy.

"It wouldn't hurt you to show a little enthusiasm," she snapped at him.

"Oh, baby. I'm damned enthused," a sexy baritone rumbled.

Her heart leapt to her throat, and whoa. Her nipples peaked to life at the sexy male with simmering green eyes glowering back at her. "Who the hell are you? Where's Clint?"

Junior Agent Lee Hart grabbed her wrist at the same time Tess latched onto the door handle and simultaneously, reached beneath her seat for her ill-gotten booty. He'd expected she'd run, but there was no way this little gal was getting away from him.

"Back off," she snarled, shoving her door open with one booted foot and ready to jump.

"Not going to happen." He yanked her back into the cab and against him. The door slammed like he meant it to when he executed a hard right off the palace grounds. Tess Culver was every bit as determined. She hadn't let go of the door handle or the prize, not like that bag in her hand was his first priority. Still, if he lost it, Alex would have his head.

"I said let me go!" She turned on him with all of her one hundred twenty pounds of feminine fury He endured the ensuing clawing, scratching, and pummeling. It made driving in a straight line a little tough, but not bad enough he'd let go of the steering wheel or her wrist.

Tires screeched around another corner, a difficult maneuver for a big rig going as fast as it was. Letting his foot off the gas, he let the truck right itself, while he continued onto the designated pick-up location. Not necessarily the one she'd intended, but safe and quiet nonetheless.

"Let me go," the spitfire behind that whirl of hair and nails demanded. She'd released the handle to beat on him more efficiently, while holding the bag with her ill-gotten booty far away from him. Not a problem. Being assaulted with one female hand and two booted feet was not that lethal. He'd been in tighter spots and been hit with plenty more.

"Give it up, Princess. You're caught." He kept his voice calm and just a little condescending, but his shackle on her wrist stayed extra secure. This little gal knew a lot of tricks; he had to give it to her. Sideways in her seat now, she twisted, kicked and spit, a real wildcat in her endeavors to break free. He didn't care what she tried until she aimed one boot heel at his head.

"Come on. Don't do that," he asked nicely. "It's just going to hurt." *You not me.*

A split second before she followed through with that smart aleck kick, he exerted pressure on her wrist, which radiated up her slender arm to her shoulder. Snap. Crackle. Pop. Dislocated. Just like that.

"Ouch! Damn it!" she shrieked, sagging back into her seat, her tongue licking over lipstick red lips, her tangled hair hanging in spirals over her angry, sweaty face. She clutched her injured arm with the hand that held the bag. "You bastard," she ground out, blowing her hair out of her eyes with a big breath. "You broke my arm."

"Told you it was going to hurt. It's not broken though. I wouldn't do that to you." He spared a quick glance, not sure why he felt the need to explain. Damn, even mad like she was, she was pretty, all the more dangerous in Lee Hart's book. He always was a sucker for sassy brunettes.

Thank you for reading Adam!

Be sure to check out the rest of the guys and gals of Irish Winters' series: *In the Company of Snipers*

Other Irish Winters' books:

King of Hearts, Deuces Wild Series, *#1*

Joker Joker, Deuces Wild Series, *#2*

Smoke, Hearts and Ashes Series, *#1*

Ash, Hearts and Ashes Series, *#2*

Coming soon!

Seth, In the Company of Snipers, *#17*

One-Eyed Jack, Deuces Wild Series, *#3*

YOU are the key to this book's success!

Please tell other readers why you liked Adam and Shannon's story by leaving an honest review at the retail site where you purchased it. Recommend it to your friends. Lend it. Most of all, enjoy it!

The best way to keep up with my new releases, giveaways, and actionable intel is to sign up for my spam-free newsletter at IrishWinters.com.

About the Author

Irish Winters is an award winning, Amazon best-selling author who, when she isn't writing, dabbles in poetry, grandchildren, and rarely (as in extremely rarely) the kitchen. More prone to be outdoors than in, she grew up the quintessential tomboy on a dairy farm in rural Wisconsin, spent her teenage years in the Pacific Northwest, but calls the Wasatch Mountains of Northern Utah home. For now.

She believes in making every day count for something, and follows the wise admonition of her mother to, "Look out the window and see something!"

Connect with Irish!
On Facebook: https://www.facebook.com/author.irishwinters
On Twitter: https://twitter.com/irishwinters1
Or at www. IrishWinters.com